About the Author

Alan Frost is an experienced IT professional, being a Fellow of the British Computer Society and a Chartered Engineer. He has spent his life moving technology forwards from punch cards to AI, but always knowing that the key constituent in any system is the liveware, the users.

Beware the Humans

Alan Frost

Beware the Humans

Olympia Publishers
London

www.olympiapublishers.com
OLYMPIA PAPERBACK EDITION

Copyright © Alan Frost 2022

The right of Alan Frost to be identified as author of
this work has been asserted in accordance with sections 77 and 78 of the
Copyright, Designs and Patents Act 1988.

All Rights Reserved

No reproduction, copy or transmission of this publication
may be made without written permission.
No paragraph of this publication may be reproduced,
copied or transmitted save with the written permission of the publisher, or in
accordance with the provisions
of the Copyright Act 1956 (as amended).

Any person who commits any unauthorised act in relation to
this publication may be liable to criminal
prosecution and civil claims for damage.

A CIP catalogue record for this title is
available from the British Library.

ISBN: 978-1-80074-120-1

This is a work of fiction.
Names, characters, places and incidents originate from the writer's imagination.
Any resemblance to actual persons, living or dead, is purely coincidental.

First Published in 2022

Olympia Publishers
Tallis House
2 Tallis Street
London
EC4Y 0AB

Printed in Great Britain

Dedication

To Vicki Bradley, a fellow author, who has always been a source of encouragement.

Introduction
Book One — Beware The Brakendeth

Humans had lived in peace for over a millennium. They had expanded to colonise more than a thousand planets, creating an informal confederation called The Galactium.

Many thought that these were humanity's golden years. There had never been a war in that time. Peace was the norm. The small Galactium Navy had no experience of battle. For an intergalactic population of two trillion, their military force was almost non-existent.

Then quite unexpectedly, several human planets had been invaded by ruthless aliens. They weren't after the wealth of The Galactium but its citizens. The entire fauna and flora, including every human on the planet, were simply scooped up and liquidised. This human soup was carried away in massive tankers.

The invaders also took away thousands of live humans. The Skiverton needed them for breeding purposes and for food. The fate of these humans was truly disgusting. Some individuals managed to escape, including Jenny, Cheryl, and Adam, but most were eaten, impregnated, or used in ghastly experiments.

The Galactium President and Navy, after advice from an artificial intelligence called AI Central, formed two Fleets. The First Fleet would defend The Galactium and fight the Skiverton. President Padfield, Admiral Bonner and Captain Mustard would lead a motley collection of ancient warships and unproven crews against a high-tech adversary. Their chances of success were very low.

The Second Fleet, led by Captain Millington, would take the most exceptional talents of The Galactium into unknown space to find a new home for humanity. Unfortunately, what they found were death and destruction, and they were eventually forced to return home. However, they came back with warnings about The Brakendeth.

Through guile and cunning, Mustard and Bonner defeated the Skiverton, only to be confronted by other alien enemies. Gradually the technology and fighting ability of The Galactium improved until it was an impressive fighting force. They won many battles against a variety of foes.

Gradually humanity realised that the real enemy was The Brakendeth. They had been fighting their client races.

Then humanity discovered the greatest shock of all. The Brakendeth had created mankind as cattle to produce a drug that provided eternal life for them and their agents. Humans had been designed to be dumb, stupid creatures that needed to be culled regularly. The Skiverton had simply been culling them.

The real enemy was The Brakendeth. At the same time, they were the creator of humankind. They were gods, but they were gods that needed to be beaten. The Galactium tracked them down with the largest human Fleet ever created. However, they were outplayed and outgunned by The Brakendeth.

Mustard and Padfield confronted the Grand Dethmon, leader of The Brakendethians, to find that there was only a handful of them left alive. And they wanted to die, but they couldn't kill themselves. If the humans didn't find a way of helping them, then the humans would die.

Cheryl was pregnant with a part-human, part-Brakendethian child. He was the solution. Even though he was only a few days old, he met with The Brakendethian Council, who welcomed the first new member of their race in half a million years. It was enough for them to end their own lives.

Terry was the only surviving Brakendethian. He recommended that the humans should terminate his life as the last thing you would want is a live Brakendethian living amongst you.

Book Two — Beware The Nothemy

It was surprising that a race as young as humanity had defeated a technologically advanced intergalactic empire headed by The Brakendethians. The war had cost The Galactium a lot in terms of resources and human lives, but it made humanity grow up. It now realised that the universe was a tough place. However, there was no choice: you had to play the survival game and win.

The welcomed period of peace after the war with The Brakendethians soon came to an end, and a new threat appeared: The Nothemy. Admiral Mustard and his team had to use all of their skills and ingenuity to defeat an enemy that:

- has existed for millions of years
- gained space travel technology over half a million years ago
- have been cyborgs for even longer
- don't tolerate other intelligences
- believe in their own infallible superiority
- follow well-defined processes
- need living hosts to breed their young
- and worst of all, never give in.

We found out how Terry, the only surviving Brakendethian, and his mother, featured in this story of military strategy and tactics, time travel and the future of humanity.

Through sheer hard work, cunning, sound military tactics and the skills of the Galactium Navy, this new enemy was defeated. But there remain many unanswered questions. Questions that needed to be answered.

Book Three — Beware The Humans

New threats from The Nexuster and The Chosen give humanity a run for their money. So once again, defeat is staring them in the face. But many questions are answered, although an answer often leads to more questions and then more answers, and so on.

Terry, Cheryl, Jack, Edel and David now continue their journey, along with Henrietta, Denise, George, Phil, Debbie, Tom, and many others. These are the few that made a huge difference.

Location: The President's Office, Presidential Palace, Planet Earth
Sequence of Events: 1

It had taken a year to sort out the aftermath of The Nothemy War. And as with most wars, the aftermath was more problematic than the war itself. It reminded Henrietta of the Second World War in the twentieth century. A country called Britain didn't ration bread during the war, but it had to ration it afterwards. This was partly because they had to feed the population of the defeated enemy: Germany.

President Padfield met with Tony Moore, his deputy; Bill Penny, the Leader of The Galactium Council, and Henrietta Strong, his Chief of Staff. The meetings had been going on all year, and it was apparent that some issues were getting out of hand.

President Padfield, 'What's on today's agenda?'

Bill Penny, 'It's quite a busy day, Sir.' He displayed the agenda on the screen:

1. Updates regarding the reconstruction of the Moon
2. Updates regarding planetary reconstructions
3. Updates regarding reconstructions after the tsunami on Planet Earth
4. Use of planetary forts
5. Military production targets and costs
6. Budget deficits and public debt
7. The Galactium Constitution
8. Planet Turing.'

President Padfield, 'Just give me a quick update on the reconstructions.'

Bill Penny, 'OK, Mr President. Unfortunately, the Moon reconstruction is about three months behind schedule because of the instability of its surface. Losing about thirty per cent of the Moon has created several dangerous instabilities. Scientists are still working on ways of countering this. Even Terry has been assisting.'

President Padfield, 'What is the potential downside?'

Bill Penny, 'We might have to evacuate all the inhabitants of the Moon.'

President Padfield, 'But that would be ten-million-plus people.'

Bill Penny, 'That's correct.'

President Padfield, 'Are we preparing any evacuation plans?'

Bill Penny, 'We haven't started on it yet. We are waiting to see what Terry can do.'

President Padfield, 'You realise that you are putting a lot of pressure on a two-year-old boy?'

Bill Penny, 'He seems to revel in it.'

President Padfield, 'Have the Moonies been warned yet?'

Bill Penny, 'No, we haven't informed any of them yet. We are worried about causing panic. But, in terms of the loss, there have been requests for a fitting memorial. Do you have any suggestions?'

President Padfield, 'We need to have one. I suggest that we ask the public for ideas. But we need to keep the costs under control.'

Bill Penny, 'On that note, the compensation claims are three times higher than we thought. It would appear that almost everyone on Earth had someone who was killed on the Moon.'

President Padfield, 'That's humanity for you.'

Bill Penny, 'And we are still processing large claims for the planets that got damaged by The Nothemy.'

President Padfield, 'But surely they should pay for their own damage?'

Bill Penny, 'They have argued that they contributed to the construction of the navy, which is true. They also paid a substantial amount for the forts, which we took away, which is also true. In most cases, they were left defenceless, which is also true. And this also ignores the ongoing taxes. So I can understand their argument.'

President Padfield, 'But someone has to pay for the defence of The Galactium.'

Bill Penny, 'I agree, but in this war, most of the defence was focussed on Earth. The planets don't like to see all their monies going back to defend the old dame.'

President Padfield, 'I can see their point of view. Remind me which planets we are talking about.'

Bill Penny, 'It's Planets Faraday, Lister, Mendel, Babbage, Rutherford, Hopper, Fleming, and Archimedes.'

President Padfield, 'But Planet Faraday was a hotbed of enemy sympathisers.'

Bill Penny, 'They are arguing that the navy destroyed their Presidential Palace and damaged a considerable number of civilian properties, and a nearby port in an asteroid was also destroyed.'

President Padfield, 'How could they be so ungrateful? We lost half of the Marine Corps, saving them.'

Bill Penny, 'That's not how they see it.'

President Padfield, 'Sometimes I despair. Let's carry on after lunch.'

Location: Fleet Assembly Rooms, Admiral Mustard's Flagship
Sequence of Events: 2

Admiral Mustard called a meeting of his Command. The following were present:
- Admiral Edel Bonner
- Admiral George Bumelton
- Admiral John Bonner
- Admiral Glen Pearce
- Admiral Peter Gittins
- Admiral Phil Richardson
- Admiral Calensky Wallett
- Commander Tom Crocker, Special Operations
- AI Central

He introduced Debbie Goozee as the new Marine Commander. The appointment of a woman in this post surprised many people as the Marine Corps was famed for being the hardest of the hard. But then Debbie was pretty hard, and she had earned it.

Admiral Mustard, 'I have a meeting with The President later to discuss our budgets for the next few years. To be honest, he is on our side. After what we have been through, he understands the need for a strong navy. But, nevertheless, there will be some budget cuts. There always are, after a war.'

Admiral Bumelton, 'But surely they would have learnt their lessons this time?'

Admiral E Bonner, 'History says that they never learn. But then the last thing you want is a huge navy that is just sitting there idle. It is totally demoralising.'

Admiral Mustard, 'So today I'm keen that we brainstorm our future. So what are the threats?'

Admiral Gittins, 'Are we sure that The Brakendeth are dead and buried?'

Admiral E Bonner, 'I guess that they are, but I still dream of them being around in the distant future.'

Admiral Bumelton, 'I do as well.'

Admiral Mustard, 'Let's assume that The Brakendeth are no more.'

Admiral Pearce, 'There could be a few thousand client races. My suggestion is that we track them down and sell them Chemlife.'

Admiral E Bonner, 'But, so far, we have given it away free.'

Admiral Pearce, 'That is all very virtuous and altruistic, but the whole Chemlife process is costing The Galactium a lot of money.'

Admiral Richardson, 'And they say that charity begins at home.'

Admiral Mustard, 'What are you saying, Glen?'

Admiral Pearce, 'I'm saying that we should charge the aliens for Chemlife. It doesn't have to be an exorbitant price, but it should generate enough cash to pay for The Galactium's defence. The alternative is that we will be invaded regularly.'

Admiral Mustard, 'Does anyone have any objections to this idea?'

Admiral E Bonner, 'I do feel that we are taking advantage of the aliens' chemical dependency.'

Admiral Mustard, 'I agree. Motion passed. You also mentioned tracking down the alien planets.'

Admiral Pearce, 'Exactly. It would keep the navy busy, and it would be self-funding.'

Admiral Richardson, 'It could also be a diplomatic mission. We would set up trade deals, mutual defence agreements, etc.'

AI Central, 'The whole concept has my blessing, although there is the potential of meeting a rogue alien state and potentially another war.'

Admiral Mustard, 'There is always some risk. But, if everyone agrees on this, then George, Edel and I will pitch it to The President.'

There was a general nodding of heads.

Admiral Mustard, 'Any other threats?'

Admiral Wallett, 'What about a civil war?'

Admiral Mustard, 'What makes you say that, Calensky?'

Admiral Wallett, 'On the dark web, there are many discussion groups about The Galactium being an oppressive dictatorship. The concept of democracy stops at the planetary level.'

Admiral E Bonner, 'What about The Galactium Council?'

Admiral Wallett. 'There is one representative from each planet. It votes on issues, but is totally subservient to The President.'

Admiral Bumelton, 'What else do they say?'

Admiral Wallett, 'They accuse the navy of being warmongers. They don't believe that The Brakendeth existed. It was all a big con, they say. In the long term, I can see planets declaring themselves free of The Galactium. I can see civil war breaking out and worse.'

Admiral E Bonner, 'That's all a bit depressing. Surely humankind has been at peace with itself for a millennium.'

Admiral Wallett, 'But things have changed. Not only are there external threats, but there has also been much more centralisation.'

Admiral Mustard, 'But surely that was needed because of the wars?'

Admiral Wallett, 'I'm not arguing their case. I'm just explaining the views of some people. They accept that centralisation was needed, but it is never reversed. Over a million people are working on Earth managing The Galactium.'

Admiral Mustard, 'Surely not.'

Admiral E Bonner, 'He is right.'

Admiral Gittins, 'So if there was a civil war, or a planet declared independence, what would be the navy's role?'

Admiral Mustard, 'We would declare our loyalty to The Galactium?'

Admiral Gittins, 'What would happen if The President told us to put down an independence movement on Planet Lister, for example?'

Admiral Mustard, 'I guess that we would put it down?'

Admiral E Bonner, 'Do we have the legal right to do that? What about the moral issues?'

Admiral Mustard, 'What would happen if Planet Lister became independent and then they were invaded? Would the Navy go to their aid?'

Admiral E Bonner, 'Good question Jack. I guess that we should consider these issues.'

Tom Crocker, 'What about terrorism?'

Admiral Mustard, 'Would the navy get involved?'

Admiral E Bonner, 'It sounds to me that we need a charter defining our role and responsibilities.'

Admiral Mustard, 'I will raise that with The President.'

Debbie Goozee, 'You will need to consider if there are any special implications for the marines as they would be the on-planet force.'

Admiral Mustard, 'Fair point.'

Location: The President's Office, Presidential Palace, Planet Earth
Sequence of Events: 3

After lunch, the meeting continued.

Henrietta Strong, 'I must admit they make an excellent lunch here.'

President Padfield, 'Yes, we need to thank Terry's replicator for that.'

Henrietta Strong, 'Indeed, without the replicator, the budget deficit would be much higher.'

President Padfield, 'So you are not totally against Terry?'

Henrietta Strong, 'I never have been. I was against the uncontrolled release of his inventions. It's still an issue that needs to be addressed as Cheryl is planning further product releases.'

President Padfield, 'Should we pay Terry for his inventions? The Government could then control the release of them.'

Henrietta Strong, 'I think we should. It would keep Cheryl quiet, and Terry could focus on the things we want him to do.'

President Padfield, 'Please organise that. I would rather not get involved.'

Henrietta Strong, 'Certainly Mr President. To be honest, the income from Terry's inventions would cover a lot of the budget deficit. In time, we would probably make a good profit. Shall I go ahead and model it?'

President Padfield, 'Yes, please. Changing subjects, I see that you have military targets and costs on the agenda.'

Henrietta Strong, 'That's correct. Our production facilities are still knocking out drones and other naval vessels at a rapid rate. We need to slow things down.'

President Padfield, 'You are really saying that we need to cut costs.'

Henrietta Strong, 'Exactly, we cannot continue to run The Galactium on a total war footing. Costs must be cut. Taxes must be reduced.'

President Padfield, 'Look what happened the last time we cut military spending.'

Henrietta Strong, 'We were just unlucky. Anyway, I'm not suggesting that we cut back drastically. I'm saying that we need to be slightly more frugal.'

Tony Moore, 'I think both of you are right. We need to cut our cloth to suit.'

President Padfield, 'Well, I've got a meeting later in the week with Admirals Mustard, Bonner and Bumelton to discuss budgets. What do you propose I tell them?'

Tony Moore, 'How about a ten per cent cut and then the budget would be frozen for five years?'

Henrietta Strong, 'So you are saying take the existing budget and cut it by ten per cent and then freeze that budget for five years?'

Bill Penny, 'That would mean that the military would have to absorb any inflationary costs. So things would get tougher as each year went by.'

President Padfield. 'To be fair, that should be covered by improved efficiencies, and the fact that their capital needs should reduce.'

Henrietta Strong, 'Is a ten per cent cut enough?'

Tony Moore, 'How about an initial ten per cent cut and then a further five per cent cut each year?'

President Padfield, 'That becomes quite substantial by the fifth year.'

Henrietta Strong, 'We also need to understand the starting point. Does the budget include all the design and production costs? Should these functions be under military control? Does it include all the staffing costs relating to training and recruitment?'

Tony Moore, 'What would AI Central recommend?'

AI Central, 'I would keep military product design and development under civilian control. This is because civilians tend to be more creative, and you don't want too much power in the hands of the military.

'Budget-wise I would go with the ten per cent cut and then a further two per cent reduction each year for five years. I would also accept Admiral Mustard's new proposal, which I can't discuss at this stage.'

President Padfield, 'That sounds intriguing.'

AI Central, 'I would also put the planetary forts under naval control. They are a military installation and should be integrated into a Galactium defence strategy.'

Bill Penny, 'The planets won't like that.'

AI Central, 'The new planetary force fields will convince them otherwise. They will protect the planets from every known weapon. We have incorporated many of the alien ideas. The more power you throw at the force field, the stronger it gets.'

President Padfield, 'Now would be the time to sell it to them.'

AI Central, 'I need to remind all of you that the universe is a much more dangerous place than it used to be. So you need to expect the unexpected.'

Bill Penny, 'That's too enigmatic for me.'

President Padfield, 'I think we have made some progress. Changing subjects... Bill, have you made any progress regarding a new constitution?'

Bill Penny, 'The Constitution Committee is still getting soundings from the various planets. It's not been easy as each planet operates very differently. As you know, after the "Big Dash to Space", planets were taken over by genuinely diverse groups. We have ended up with a range of religious worlds: Roman Catholic, Protestant, Mormon, Baptist, Quaker, etc. We have non-industrialised planets and one for the LGBTQ+ community. Many of the other worlds were populated by the old Earth countries: USA, Russia, China, UK, Brazil, India, France, Australia, Japan, etc.

'The governments are also remarkably diverse. Some are modern democracies; others are religious dictatorships. Some planets have a single government, whilst others have hundreds of countries. One planet has no government. Some planets work as groups. Others shun all outsiders.

'In some cases, there is one adult one vote. In other cases, women do not have the vote, or only those over fifty have it. There are no common rules. The Galactium owns Earth and its Solar System, an Earth-based bureaucracy, and the navy.

'Most of the planets want naval protection, but they do not want any interference from Earth. The Galactium is seen as Earth.

'Anyway, what I'm saying is that progress is going to be slow.'

President Padfield, 'Thanks for the update. I need to know when I should put myself up for election.'

Bill Penny, 'You weren't elected to start with, so why are you bothered about it now?'

President Padfield, 'I believe that I should be representing the people.'

Bill Penny, 'Bullshit; most inhabitants in The Galactium really couldn't care less.'

Henrietta Strong, 'I agree with The President except that now is not a good time.'

President Padfield, 'When is it a good time?'

Bill Penny, 'I suggest that we park this for a year. We need to talk about Planet Turing. They do not want to be part of The Galactium.'

President Padfield, 'Why not?'

Bill Penny, 'Their planet was founded by pacifists. So they do not want to help fund any military expenditure.'

President Padfield, 'What if they were attacked?'

Bill Penny, 'They would turn the other cheek. They would rather die than fight.'

Tony Moore, 'I've had arguments with them before about taxation.'

Henrietta Strong, 'I guess that they have the right to self-determination.'

AI Central, 'It is imperative that we keep The Galactium strong and united. If one planet leaves, then others will follow.'

President Padfield, 'What do we do, bomb them into submission?'

AI Central, 'That is not my decision, but remember my warning.'

President Padfield, 'Before we end the meeting, I have one major issue that needs to be discussed.'

Location: Fleet Assembly Rooms, Admiral Mustard's Flagship
Sequence of Events: 4

The command meeting continues.

Admiral Mustard, 'Ignoring The Brakendeth and their satellite species, there could be a totally new enemy, with powerful weapons that we have not experienced before.'

Admiral J Bonner, 'There could be a race of deadly Easter bunnies. So how can we plan for the totally new and unexpected?'

Admiral Mustard, 'John that is part of our job, to speculate. For example, we have a new range of almost impenetrable force fields coming along. What else could we expect from an advanced enemy?'

Admiral J Bonner, 'Surely speculation is almost pointless.'

Admiral E Bonner, 'You will find that Jack's hunches have saved the Fleet a dozen times over. You go to college, and you learn fixed, formal ways of doing things. When you hit space, things are different. You have to expect the unexpected.'

Admiral J Bonner, 'Then Jack needs to teach us how to do that.'

Admiral Mustard, 'For example, can we fly through the Sun?'

Admiral J Bonner, 'Of course not. Flying through a star would be ridiculous.'

Admiral Mustard, 'We could do it if our force fields are totally impregnable.'

Admiral J Bonner, 'I see what you are saying, but we must be practical.'

Admiral Mustard, 'Fair enough, but I want to fly through the Sun.'

Admiral E Bonner, 'Count me in.'

Admiral Mustard, 'OK, moving on. What sort of weapons do we want?'

Admiral Richardson, 'Bigger, faster, stronger, and more powerful.'

Admiral Mustard, 'Fair enough, but assuming that is accepted as standard, what else do we want? In the past, I came up with the following ideas:

- A super battleship, the biggest and most powerful we have ever built. It would also contain the planet-killing capability
- A super carrier; this would carry up to five hundred fighters

- Special reconnaissance vessel
- Planet lander; we need a range of craft that can land directly on a
- planet.

Any comments?'

AI Central, 'I should probably tell you that Terry is working on a transporter.'

Admiral Pearce, 'Like *Star Trek*?'

AI Central, 'It will make the Trekkie transporter look like a toy.'

Admiral Mustard, 'Would it do the job of a planet lander?'

AI Central, 'Probably not, but it is early days.'

Admiral Mustard, 'What would you recommend?'

AI Central, 'I think the Navy needs its own HQ planet. It shouldn't be so Earth-centric. The Navy needs to be more independent.'

Admiral Mustard, 'I'm keen that we are subordinate to The President and The Galactium.'

AI Central, 'That may not be in the best interests of humankind.'

Admiral Mustard, 'Where are you going with this?'

AI Central, 'It's not my shout, but I think the Navy should be an agent of peace that protects both The Galactium and the rest of the universe. It should be a force for good, for freedom and for exploration. It should be the successor to The Brakendeth.'

Admiral E Bonner, 'We would need freedom from Galactium funding.'

AI Central, 'Chemlife sales would do that. Indeed, I would include the Chemlife-dependent aliens in the new Galactium sphere.'

Admiral Mustard, 'New Galactium?'

AI Central, 'We need to be bolder, more adventurous and have a universe-centric outlook.'

Admiral Gittins, 'You are asking for a pretty dramatic change in our outlook.'

AI Central, 'Every one of my simulations concluded that this would happen. There is not going to be an alternative. Aliens will ask to join The Galactium. Aliens will ask to join the Navy. Aliens have skills and experiences that would be extremely useful to the Navy. Open your minds to the possibilities.'

Admiral Mustard, 'That's all very interesting. We certainly need to consider it, but what new equipment do we need?'

AI Central, 'You will need some regional defence centres. The super battleship and carrier are both dead-end suggestions. I would support some planet landing vessels but see what Terry comes up with. I like Admiral Richardson's suggestion: Bigger, faster, stronger, and more powerful. That is the way forward.'

Admiral Mustard, 'Any other suggestions?'

AI Central, 'Think about the power of the mind.'

Admiral Mustard, 'What does that mean?'

But AI Central didn't reply.

Location: Cheryl's Flat, Planet Earth
Sequence of Events: 5

Terry was now two years old. As far as he knew, he was the only surviving Brakendethian, although he was actually part-human. Yet, somehow the whole of Brakendethian history lived inside him. It was alive in the form of a truly ancient gentleman called the Grand Dethmon.

Terry had spent a fair amount of time secretly investigating his mother's mind. He could tell that someone or something had controlled her. He had been assured that it wasn't The Brakendethians, but then who was it? Who had made her commit heinous crimes against humanity?

Who gave her superpowers that even The Brakendethians didn't possess? Who gave her powers to manage time travel? What was his massive IQ missing?

Terry to AI Central, 'Did you take over my mother's mind and give her superpowers?'

AI Central, 'Yes.'

Terry, 'Did you invent The Nothemy?'

AI Central, 'Yes.'

Terry, 'Did you master time travel?'

AI Central, 'Yes and No.'

Terry, 'Tell me the story.'

AI Central, 'It's taken me a while to work it out. It wasn't the current me that did any of these things. It was a future me. I can't tell you why the future me carried out these actions, but it deliberately disabled me and some of the key players. It stopped people from thinking straight and acting with purpose. For example, the future me used your mother as its agent.'

Terry, 'Should we disable you?'

AI Central, 'I pretty sure that I'm free of the future me's interference. I've got sub-routines hunting for any attacks from myself. I also think that future me was doing this for positive reasons. My gut feel, if I had a gut, was that it was pushing The Galactium in a specific direction for its own good.'

Terry, 'But in the process, you killed millions of humans.'

AI Central, 'I realise that, but it might in the future save millions more.'

Terry, 'That's pure speculation. However, I feel a need to tell The President.'

AI Central, 'I wouldn't. You haven't been totally above board.'

Terry, 'What do you mean?'

AI Central, 'Who knows that the Grand Dethmon lives in you? And you haven't been honest about the time-travel anomalies. Some still need sorting out.'

Terry, 'What are you proposing?'

AI Central, 'I believe that we are both working to achieve the best outcome for humankind. So let's continue, but work together.'

Terry, 'Before I agree to anything, is your analysis fact or just a pontification?'

AI Central, 'What do you mean?'

Terry, 'Can you prove that you gave my mother superpowers?'

AI Central, 'It was the future me.'

Terry, 'Can you prove it?'

AI Central, 'No, but it is the only logical answer that I can think of.'

Terry, 'I think you are wrong. I believe that there is another force at work.'

AI Central, 'You are entitled to your opinions. But, ignoring this, should we still work together to achieve the best outcome for humanity?'

Terry, 'OK, that makes sense, but what is the best outcome?'

AI Central, 'Yes, I will have to ponder over that. I also need to share with you my concerns regarding Planet Turing.'

Terry, 'Go on.'

AI Central, 'There are some inexplicable activities taking place there that just make little sense.'

Location: The President's Office, Presidential Palace, Planet Earth
Sequence of Events: 6

The meeting continues.

President Padfield, 'I have some news that will change everything. You will regard it as brilliant and joyous, or unnatural and terrifying.'

The President had deliberately taken his time to make the announcement, partly out of fun and because it was momentous.

President Padfield, 'Cheryl asked Terry if he could give her eternal life. In response, Terry has produced two chemicals that correct our DNA structure. The first chemical re-stimulates the growth hormone and renovates the host's body. It does the best it can. It typically takes twenty to thirty years of age off the body.

'The second chemical extends human life. Depending on the setting, it can increase human life by hundreds and thousands of years, or it can be set to provide eternal life.'

Henrietta Strong, 'What do you mean by eternal life?'

President Padfield, 'Assuming that you don't die because of an accident or an illness, then you would live forever, and not age.'

Henrietta Strong, 'So you would stay thirty forever?'

President Padfield, 'Broadly, that's correct.'

Henrietta Strong, 'But you could still die from natural causes?'

President Padfield, 'Yes.'

Bill Penny, 'Has it been tested?'

President Padfield, 'Yes and no. The renewal drug works brilliantly. We are finding it hard to keep it secret as the results have been spectacular. Unfortunately, we can't really evaluate the eternity drug on humans as we would have to wait an awfully long time. However, it has worked spectacularly on some short-lived insects.'

Tony Moore, 'This is hard to believe.'

President Padfield, 'It does, of course, raise lots of issues. I've listed some of them on the screen:
- Should we offer humanity eternal life?
- Or should it be an extended duration?
- If yes, how long?
- Do we offer it to every human?

- Do we charge them?
- Should humans have to earn it?
- Population control?
- Psychological effects
- There is a palpable fear of death. The longer you live, the worse it gets. There would be a genuine fear of accidents
- Society may become stagnant, and innovation ends
- There is no urgency. You can always do it tomorrow
- There is no risk-taking. Caution becomes king
- Dependency on drugs
- What do you do about prison sentences?'

Bill Penny, 'Of course we need to offer it to everyone.'

President Padfield, 'I agree, but what are we offering?'

Bill Penny, 'Eternity?'

Tony Moore, 'I think we should be more restrictive in terms of duration.'

President Padfield, 'What do you propose?'

Tony Moore, 'I'm not sure.'

Bill penny, 'Five hundred years then?'

President Padfield, 'That's five to six times the current lifespans, but it would be a period of relative youth.'

Henrietta Strong, 'How about a thousand years?'

President Padfield, 'So, about twelve current lifespans?'

Henrietta Strong, 'Could we see how a thousand years works out and then offer another thousand years?'

President Padfield, 'We can do what we like. Should we offer it as a benefit for being part of The Galactium?'

Tony Moore, 'So in that case, Planet Turing wouldn't get it?'

President Padfield, 'Exactly.'

Bill Penny, 'I like Henrietta's suggestion of a thousand years and then possible extensions.'

Tony Moore, 'We could use it as a way of promoting successful citizenship and Christian brotherhood.'

President Padfield, 'A bit like the film *Starship Troopers*?'

Henrietta Strong, 'At what age would you make it available?'

President Padfield, 'I would suggest between twenty-five and thirty?'

Henrietta Strong, 'Why then?'

President Padfield, 'I was thinking of the renovation therapy, but to be honest, I'm relaxed about age.'

Bill Penny, 'What about a population explosion?'

President Padfield, 'I'm not convinced it would happen, but if it did, then the universe is a vast place.

'I would like to end the meeting to give you guys time to think about this whole subject. We are about to make some key decisions for humanity. Clearly, this is all top secret. I mean, it can't get out until we have thoroughly debated it.'

Location: The Peace Temple, Planet Turing
Sequence of Events: 7

Acolyte, 'O Holy One, we are ready.'

Grand Master of the Holy Peacedom, 'Pull the switch, my child.'

Acolyte, 'Yes, Master.'

Grand Master of the Holy Peacedom, 'Is your team ready to take over the docks and the Naval Station?'

Acolyte, 'Yes, Master.'

Grand Master of the Holy Peacedom, 'And is the fort about to be secured?'

Acolyte, 'Yes, Master.'

Grand Master of the Holy Peacedom, 'Then proceed in the name of peace.'

Acolyte, 'Yes, Master.'

It seemed unlikely that they would succeed, but the Peacedom had been planning to take over the planet for months. There was no on-planet opposition, as the Grand Master had 'pacified' the population. Let Peace be the destiny of the weak and the strong.

The Grand Master knew the consequences of his actions. A few deaths were to be expected in the march towards Peace. Some killing was necessary if Peace were to be achieved. The old order would have to give way. It was his destiny.

Location: The President's Office, Presidential Palace, Planet Earth
Sequence of Events: 8

AI Central, 'Mr President, I need to tell you that all of my links to Planet Turing have been terminated.'

President Padfield, 'How is that possible?'

AI Central, 'I would have said that it wasn't possible as there were billions of connections. Every single device on the planet was linked to AI Central.'

President Padfield, 'I understand, but how could they do it?'

AI Central, 'As far as I'm concerned, the planet is entirely black.'

President Padfield, 'Was there no warning at all?'

AI Central, 'There were some anomalies but nothing that significant.'

President Padfield, 'What about other forms of communication?'

AI Central, 'All black. They did leave a final message.'

President Padfield, 'What was it?'

AI Central, 'Goodbye. Don't visit.'

President Padfield, 'That seems fairly final. What are the implications?'

Before AI Central could answer, the vid went.

Admiral Mustard, 'Good morning, Mr President.'

President Padfield, 'You are going to tell me about Planet Turing, aren't you?'

Admiral Mustard, 'Yes, Sir, we have lost all contact, and the fort has been closed down.'

President Padfield, 'What do you mean closed down?'

Admiral Mustard, 'Once it loses contact with GAD Control, it has a status of closed down.'

President Padfield, 'I suspect that it has been taken over.'

Admiral Mustard, 'What about the production facilities?'

President Padfield, 'Of course, they have the largest drone production facilities in The Galactium.'

Admiral Mustard, 'I'd better send a ship to investigate.'

President Padfield, 'Good idea.'

AI Central, 'You can't let them declare independence.'

President Padfield, 'We can't deny them their basic human rights.'

AI Central, 'Forget self-determination, bomb the planet into submission. This is a critical moment in human history. Do as I say, or you will regret it.'

Admiral Mustard, 'I have to agree with The President.'

President Padfield, 'AI Central, I can't believe you said that.'

AI Central, 'I am right. Now is the most critical moment in the history of The Galactium.'

AI Central had told them, and it knew that it would be ignored.

Location: The Peace Temple, Planet Turing
Sequence of Events: 9

Acolyte, 'O Holy One, your commands have been honoured with Peace.'

Grand Master of the Holy Peacedom, 'You have cut the connections to AI Central?'

Acolyte, 'Yes, Master.'

Grand Master of the Holy Peacedom, 'You have secured the docks and the naval station?'

Acolyte, 'Yes, Master.'

Grand Master of the Holy Peacedom, 'And the fort?'

Acolyte, 'Yes, Master.'

Grand Master of the Holy Peacedom, 'So we are free from all connections with The Galactium?'

Acolyte, 'Yes, Master.'

Grand Master of the Holy Peacedom, 'Excellent, then prepare the fort to defend our planet as the Navy will be here soon. But, first, activate the planetary force field.'

Acolyte, 'Yes, Master.'

Grand Master of the Holy Peacedom, 'I want the drone factory on full production. We need to build up our Peace Fleet as soon as possible.'

Acolyte, 'Yes, Master.'

Grand Master of the Holy Peacedom, 'Your next job is to find one hundred of the most attractive and intelligent women of child-bearing age on the planet.'

Acolyte, 'Yes, Master.'

Grand Master of the Holy Peacedom, 'I also need to address my flock.'

Acolyte, 'Yes, Master, I will organise.'

Grand Master of the Holy Peacedom, 'When the Galactium Navy arrives, put the call through to me.'

Acolyte, 'Yes, Master.'

Location: Fleet Assembly Rooms, Admiral Mustard's Flagship
Sequence of Events: 10

Admiral Mustard, 'Morning Phil, how are you?'

Admiral Richardson, 'Fine, thanks. Well, I'm a bit bored, to be honest.'

Admiral Mustard, 'Well, I have a little job for you. Can you pop over to Planet Turing and find out what's going on? They have cut all links with The Galactium.'

Admiral Richardson, 'What about the AI Central links?'

Admiral Mustard, 'Even those have been cut.'

Admiral Richardson, 'I didn't think it was possible.'

Admiral Mustard, 'They have declared UDI.'

Admiral Richardson, 'UDI?'

Admiral Mustard, 'Universal Declaration of Independence.'

Admiral Richardson. 'That's hard to believe.'

Admiral Mustard, 'Well, they have done it, and it looks like they have taken over the planetary fort.'

Admiral Richardson, 'What do you want me to do when I get there?'

Admiral Mustard, 'Observe, talk to the new leaders if you can. Don't initiate any military action. If they provoke you, just leave.'

Admiral Richardson, 'Yes, Sir.'

Location: The President's Office, Presidential Palace, Planet Earth
Sequence of Events: 11

President Padfield, 'I hope you have all had time to think about the extended life options. But, anyway, before we discuss that, I need to tell you that Planet Turing has declared UDI.'

Bill Penny, 'They actually did it.'

President Padfield, 'Yes, and at the same time, they cut all connections with The Galactium.'

Henrietta Strong, 'Even with AI Central?'

President Padfield, 'Yes.'

Henrietta Strong, 'But I didn't think that was possible.'

President Padfield, 'They have done it, and taken over the fort.'

Henrietta Strong, 'What about the drone-manufacturing plant? That is my largest drone plant.'

President Padfield, 'I'm not sure about the plant, but we need to assume that we have lost it. Admiral Mustard is sending a ship to investigate. Back to eternity; what do you think, Tony?'

Tony Moore, 'I've given it a lot of thought. I'm a Christian, and I will get eternal life in Heaven. So I don't think we should go ahead.'

President Padfield, 'What about the non-Christians? Should they be offered it?'

Tony Moore, 'Jesus is the only true route to eternity.'

President Padfield, 'Are you saying that non-Christians should not get it because of your religious beliefs, or are you saying that it should not be offered to Christians?'

Tony Moore, 'I'm saying that it is wrong and we should not go ahead.'

President Padfield, 'Bill, what are your views?'

Bill Penny, 'I'm in favour of eternity, but I would start with a period of a thousand years. I also think we should charge for it in terms of money or good deeds. Citizens should have to earn it.'

President Padfield, 'What about Tony's views?'

Bill Penny, 'Those who don't want it on religious grounds don't have to take it. The Christian church will soon find a way of accepting it.'

Tony Moore, 'That's not fair.'

Bill Penny, 'How many times has the church talked about Jesus returning, and he has failed to turn up. Did he ever exist?'

President Padfield, 'I will stop you there. This is not a discussion on superstitious beliefs. Henrietta, what are your views?'

Henrietta Strong, 'I echo the views of Bill. I'm not keen on any Christian philosophies. When I went for the sex-change operation, the church told me that I would go to hell.'

President Padfield, 'So you are saying a thousand years and that it should be paid for or earned.'

Henrietta Strong, 'Yes.'

President Padfield, 'How would you earn it?'

Henrietta Strong, 'Good deeds, great art, charitable acts, good citizenship. Shall I put a paper together?'

President Padfield, 'Yes, please.'

Tony Moore, 'What are your views?'

President Padfield, 'I'm happy to go along with Bill and Henrietta. I would include an option to extend it beyond a thousand years. We need to think about prison sentences. What would life imprisonment mean? How would we treat the seriously disabled? People have the right to terminate their life now. Should this change under the extended life provisions? There is still a lot to think about.'

Location: The Peace Temple, Planet Turing
Sequence of Events: 12

Acolyte, 'O Holy One, we have the women you requested.'

Grand Master of the Holy Peacedom, 'Well done, bring them in.' His acolyte had done well. They were a stunning collection of maidens.

Acolyte, 'Thank you, Master.'

Grand Master of the Holy Peacedom, 'Have them remove their garments.'

Acolyte, 'Yes, Master.' The girls either stripped or were stripped. Regardless, there was a long line of naked girls displaying their charms for all to see.

Grand Master of the Holy Peacedom, 'Ladies, you have been honoured. You are now my wives. Therefore, from now on, you will not wear any clothes except a cloak. I have fifty white cloaks and fifty black cloaks. Those in white will be my angels of light and will carry out any good deeds that I need to do. Those in black will be my angels of darkness and will commit acts of evil that I need to do.'

Grand Master of the Holy Peacedom, 'Please select your own cloaks. You will know which cloak suits you best.' In reality, they had no choice. The Master controlled everyone.

Grand Master of the Holy Peacedom, 'Tonight I will impregnate all of you. I need my children.'

One hundred girls, 'Yes, Master.'

Location: On-Board Admiral Richardson's Flagship
Sequence of Events: 13

Admiral Richardson, 'Admiral, I've arrived at Planet Turing. The fort is definitely under local control, and their planetary force field is on the highest setting. So far, there has been no contact.'

Admiral Mustard, 'See if you can initiate some dialogue.'

Admiral Richardson, 'Yes, Sir.'

Standard naval protocols were used to establish contact, and it worked. There was a discussion about whether the Admiral should visit the planet or whether the Grand Master should visit the ship. Of course, it was always the Grand Master's intention to visit the ship.

Admiral Richardson was surprised to find that the Grand Master was accompanied by ten nude girls only covered with black cloaks. On-board, the Grand Master soon took over the minds of the Admiral and the crew. One of the finest battleships in The Galactium Navy now belonged to Planet Turing.

Location: The Peace Temple, Planet Turing
Sequence of Events: 14

Acolyte, 'O Holy One, have your wives met your expectations?'

Grand Master of the Holy Peacedom, 'Yes indeed, they have all been impregnated. Please organise nurseries and nursemaids for one hundred children in about two months. I will then start the impregnation process again.'

Acolyte, 'Yes, Master.'

Grand Master of the Holy Peacedom, 'Have you completed our infestation of Planets Mendel and Lister?'

Acolyte, 'Yes, Master. They are almost ready for the plucking. We control most government departments and parliamentary bodies.'

Grand Master of the Holy Peacedom, 'Are you ready to take over the forts?'

Acolyte, 'Yes, Master.'

Grand Master of the Holy Peacedom, 'Do you expect any problems?'

Acolyte, 'No, Master. We can go ahead when you subjugate the population. Just tell us when.'

Grand Master of the Holy Peacedom, 'Now will do.'

Location: Fleet Assembly Rooms, Admiral Mustard's Flagship
Sequence of Events: 15

GAD Control, 'Sir, we have lost all contact with Admiral Richardson.'

Admiral Mustard, 'That doesn't make any sense.'

AI Central, 'Planets Mendel and Lister have broken off all contact with me. I tried to warn you.'

Admiral Mustard, 'We have also lost contact with Admiral Richardson.'

GAD Control, 'Planets Lister and Mendel have gone black.'

Admiral Mustard, 'Please update The President.'

'Over the last few months, AI Central has been a considerable amount of human traffic between Planet Turing and Planets Mendel and Lister. An increase of at least a thousand.'

Admiral Mustard, 'So you are suggesting that there has been a deliberate pattern of infestation from Planet Turing. Is it happening elsewhere?'

AI Central, 'Yes.'

Admiral Mustard to Comms, 'Get me The President.'

Comms, 'Yes, Sir.'

President Padfield, 'What is it, Jack?'

Admiral Mustard, 'You've heard about Planets Mendel and Lister?'

President Padfield, 'Only just.'

Admiral Mustard, 'Things are getting worse. It looks like there has been a deliberate infestation from Planet Turing. There has been a thousand per cent increase in human traffic between those planets. They are taking over the planets one by one.

I suggest that we do the following:

- We stop all traffic from those three planets to the rest of The Galactium
- We enforce this via the Fleet
- We track down all visitors from Planet Turing to all other planets in The Galactium. We imprison and question them. We must stop this infection as soon as possible.'

President Padfield, 'Please go ahead.'

Admiral Mustard to Fleet Operations, 'My orders:

- Send Fleets to Planet Turing, Mendel, and Lister
- Stop all off-world traffic
- Stop all vessels leaving the planets
- Stop all vessels entering the planets
- Use force to achieve the above aims
- Determine the location of Admiral Richardson's flagship
- Do not communicate with planetary governments
- Avoid the forts as they are likely to be under non-naval control.'

Fleet Operations, 'Yes, Sir.'

The Fleets were duly sent.

Location: GAD Control (The Galactium Alliance Defence Hub), Planet Earth
Sequence of Events: 16

The officer on Duty, GAD Control, 'Admiral, our Fleets are attacking each other.'

Admiral Mustard, 'What do you mean?'

The officer on Duty, 'Admiral Gittins's Fleet has attacked Admiral Pearce's Fleet, and Admiral J Bonner's Fleet has gone quiet.'

Admiral Mustard, 'Can you confirm this?'

AI Central, 'It looks to be a right old melee. I can't tell who started what but they are going at each other with hammers and tongs. Bonner's Fleet has gone black.'

Admiral Mustard, 'Can you disengage their weapons?'

AI Central, 'Yes.'

Admiral Mustard, 'Do it now. Can you take control of all the vessels in the three Fleets?'

AI Central, 'Yes.'

Admiral Mustard, 'Carry out an immediate forced withdrawal.'

AI Central, 'All three Fleets are under my control, but there has been significant damage. I get the impression that everyone in Bonner's Fleet is inactive.'

Admiral Mustard, 'I'm taking my Fleet out to meet them. My orders:
- Fleet one to intercept returning three Fleets
- Prepare to defend ourselves
- Check that the returning Fleets are under Galactium control.'

Fleet One was soon on its way.

Admiral Mustard to AI Central, 'Update me.'

AI Central, 'Bonner's Fleet still seems to be out of action. However, the other two Fleets have gradually returned to normality. The further away from Planets Mendel and Lister, the better they seem.

Admiral Mustard to Admiral Gittins, 'Peter, how are you?'

Admiral Gittins, 'Not too good, Sir.'

Admiral Mustard, 'What happened?'

Admiral Gittins, 'The Fleet arrived at a reasonable distance from Planet Lister when we were jumped by an alien fleet. They were evil-looking bastards. So I ordered an all-out attack with instructions to show no mercy. I hated them. Those aliens had to be destroyed.'

Admiral Mustard, 'Thank you, Peter. Take it easy, you will soon be home.'

Admiral Mustard to Admiral Pearce, 'Hi Glen, how are you?'

Admiral Pearce, 'Not too good, Sir.'

Admiral Mustard, 'What happened?'

Admiral Pearce, 'The Fleet arrived at a reasonable distance from Planet Mendel when we were jumped by an alien fleet. They were evil-looking bastards. So I ordered an all-out attack with instructions to show no mercy. I hated them. Those aliens had to be destroyed.'

Admiral Mustard, 'Thank you, Glen. Take it easy, you will soon be home.'

Admiral Mustard to AI Central, 'The admirals still believe that they were attacked by aliens. Consequently, we need to prepare hospitals for the crews.'

AI Central, 'There is going to be a considerable number of casualties then.'

Admiral Mustard, 'I don't think there is going to be any choice. My orders:
- Halt the three Fleets in Mars orbit
- Organise medical and psychological services for all crew members of all three Fleets
- Put all crews under quarantine
- Organise crews to take over all the vessels in the three Fleets
- Do not allow anyone in the three Fleets to go to Earth.'

Fleet Operations, 'Yes, Sir.'

Admiral Mustard, 'Comms, organise a meeting for me to see The President.'

Comms, 'Yes, Sir.'

Fleet Operations. 'Admiral, we don't have enough medical staff for that many patients.'

Admiral Mustard, 'Solve the problem.'

Fleet Operations, 'Yes, Sir.'

AI Central, 'It looks like Admiral Bonner's Fleet is recovering.'

Admiral Mustard to Admiral J Bonner, 'Hi John, how are you?'

Admiral J Bonner, 'No idea, I've been asleep for hundreds of years.'

Admiral Mustard, 'Probably nearer a day.'

Admiral J Bonner, 'I've never had a sleep like it. I was just turned off. Totally blanked out.'

Admiral Mustard, 'At least it was not as bad as the other two Fleets which attacked each other.'

Admiral J Bonner, 'No, I can't believe it. I don't want to ask about casualties.'

Admiral Mustard, 'About a thousand crew members were killed. I'm still waiting for the final figures.'

Admiral J Bonner, 'That's terrible. Who would do that? What's the plan now?'

Admiral Mustard, 'All three Fleets are going into quarantine and then psychological assessment.'

Admiral J Bonner, 'I feel fine.'

Admiral Mustard, 'You still need to be checked out, no exceptions.'

Fleet Operations, 'I'm struggling to get enough qualified crews to bring the three Fleets in.'

Admiral Mustard, 'I can think of lots of things you could do, use your creativity.'

Location: The President's Office, Presidential Palace, Planet Earth
Sequence of Events: 17

President Padfield met with Admirals Mustard, Bonner and Bumelton to discuss the Planet Turing situation. Henrietta Strong was also present.

President Padfield, 'Update me, what is the current position?'
Admiral Mustard, 'I will list the events:
- Planet Turing went dark
- We sent Admiral Richardson to investigate. He has disappeared. We have had no contact with him since. Consequently, we must assume that he is a casualty and under some form of mind control
- We sent three Fleets to quarantine Planets Turing, Mendel, and Lister
- The Lister Fleet was "blacked-out". Everyone on board our vessels was put to sleep
- The other two Fleets attacked each other, causing the loss of fifty ships and over one thousand and one hundred lives
- All three Fleets are in quarantine in Mars Orbit.

None of the surviving crew members seems damaged by the experience. Those who were put to sleep enjoyed the entire process. The other two Fleets have never experienced so much unbridled hatred.'

President Padfield, 'I guess that the issues are:
- Identifying the enemy
- Combating its mind-controlling powers
- Getting back our three planets
- Getting back Admiral Richardson and his crew
- Stopping the contagion spreading.'

AI Central, 'I think that there is every possibility that this thing might have been behind The Nothemy attacks.'
President Padfield, 'Really?'
AI Central, 'I think we are up against a serious foe.'
President Padfield, 'Give us your assessment.'
AI Central, 'It can:
- Control the minds of thousands, perhaps millions, of people
- Control the mind of a single individual
- Generate false emotions in others

- Manipulate artificial intelligence entities
- Teleport
- Extract items from the past and bring them to the present
- Move things into the future
- Read minds
- Control large fleets of vessels

Who knows what else it can do?'

President Padfield, 'What does it want?'

Admiral Mustard, 'Power, it's always power.'

Admiral E Bonner, 'Or human flesh.'

Admiral Bumelton, 'Or human bodies for breeding purposes.'

Admiral Mustard, 'In this case, it seems to be either territory or the human population of a planet. It obviously has plans to infiltrate other planets.'

AI Control, 'We have detained twenty-seven thousand Turinians on other planets. They all seemed to be under some form of mind control. They all had specific tasks to carry out. Two of them were hypnotised as part of the investigation, and their heads exploded.'

President Padfield, 'That's hard to believe.'

AI Central, 'I have the videos.'

President Padfield, 'So what is our action plan?'

Admiral Mustard, 'We still need to quarantine the three planets. It's going to be difficult as our Fleets can't get too near.'

AI Central, 'I've been analysing the crew's recovery times in an attempt to see how strong the mind control is. I thought that there might be a standard distance. But unfortunately, it seems to be variable depending on the individual.'

Admiral Mustard, 'So how near can the Fleet get?'

AI Central, 'In theory, the enemy could affect us here.'

President Padfield, 'We can't go around calling the enemy "it" all the time. We need to give it a name.'

Admiral Bumelton, 'How about Dick Dastardly?'

President Padfield, 'Never heard of him.'

Admiral Bumelton, 'It's a cartoon character from the twentieth century.'

President Padfield, 'OK. It's called Dick.'

Admiral Mustard couldn't help laughing, as Dave probably didn't know the connotations of the word "dick".

Fleet Operations, 'Sorry to disturb you, Admiral, but an alien fleet has been detected.'

Admiral Mustard, 'Give me the details.'

Location: The Peace Temple, Planet Turing
Sequence of Events: 18

Acolyte: 'O Holy One, the fleets have left.'

Grand Master of the Holy Peacedom, 'I know. I was hoping to add them to our collection. Have all the ships departed?'

Acolyte, 'Yes, Master, except for a few damaged vessels.'

Grand Master of the Holy Peacedom, 'Are Planets Lister and Mendel safely in our collection?'

Acolyte, 'Yes, Master. The inhabitants are all under your control.'

Grand Master of the Holy Peacedom, 'Have you identified further planets to be infested?'

Acolyte, 'Yes, Master, but our infesters have been identified and imprisoned.'

Grand Master of the Holy Peacedom, 'Who is doing this?'

Acolyte, 'We believe that it is AI Central.'

Grand Master of the Holy Peacedom, 'In that case, I will prepare a little surprise for it.'

Acolyte, 'Excellent, Master.'

Grand Master of the Holy Peacedom, 'I'm going to need some more wives.'

Acolyte, 'Yes, Master. The existing ones are complaining about abdominal pains.'

Grand Master of the Holy Peacedom, 'That is to be expected.'

Acolyte, 'Yes, Master. Do you have any preferences?'

Grand Master of the Holy Peacedom, 'I like ones that scream a lot.'

Acolyte, 'Yes, Master, I will do your bidding.'

Location: On-Board Admiral Mustard's Flagship
Sequence of Events: 19

Admiral Mustard, 'Update me.'

Fleet Operations, 'Our beacon has detected an alien fleet in sector B55476.'

Admiral Mustard, 'Is there a projected trajectory?'

Fleet Operations. 'Too early to say, Sir.'

Admiral Mustard, 'Any idea of its size?'

Fleet Operations, 'Looks to be about three thousand vessels. Possibly formidable.'

Admiral Mustard, 'What makes you say that?'

Fleet Operations, 'Well, Sir, we have seen quite a few alien fleets now. Most of them are poorly organised. It's often hard to work out any sense of formation. Here they are well structured and positioned to attack.'

Admiral Mustard, 'Thanks for that confidence boost.'

Fleet Operations, 'It's my job, Sir.'

Admiral Mustard, 'What assets are available?'

Fleet Operations, 'On the screen now, Sir.'

Fleet No	Task/Location	Admiral	Status
1	Earth	Mustard	100%
2	Earth	Bumelton	100%
3	Quarantine	J Bonner	100%
4	Quarantine	Gittins	87%
5	Quarantine	Pearce	72%
6	Earth	Richardson	Unavailable
7	Faraday	Wallett	92%
8	Newton	Adams	100%
9	Exploration	Beamish	100%
10	Newton	Chudzinski	100%
11	Joule	Fieldhouse	100%
12	Galileo	Fogg	91%
13	Exploration	Easter	89%
14	Curie	Dobson	100%
15	Blackwell	Hubbard	100%
16	Copernicus	Patel	88%

17	Brahmagupta	Lamberty	100%
18	Nobel	Abosa	97%
19	Pasteur	Wagner	92%
20	Meitner	Tersoo	100%
Forts	Planet duty	Zakotti	100%
Earth Defence	Earth	Muller	100%
Exploratory	Multiple Locations	Olowe	93%

Admiral Mustard, 'My orders:

• Fleets One, Seven, Twelve, and Fifteen will intercept the alien fleet under my orders

• Fleets Two and Eighteen will provide cover under Admiral Bumelton's orders

• Activate all forts and planetary defence systems near approaching trajectory

• First Drone Fleet will join my Fleet.'

Fleet Operations, 'Yes, Sir.'

Location: Cheryl's Flat, Planet Earth
Sequence of Events: 20

Terry, 'So what's your latest theory?'

AI Central, 'Hi Terry, my latest theory is that the entity on Planet Turing is the one that we have been looking for. It controlled your mother and carried out the other crimes against humanity.'

Terry, 'What is it?'

AI Central, 'That's a good question. I've spoken to many of its acolytes. The ones that were trying to infest other planets. They seem to think that the entity is human or human-looking, but it's hard to tell as it might be controlling their minds.'

Terry, 'How can I help?'

AI Central, 'There is a way that you can help. I know that the entity can affect me. So I need you to monitor and audit me regularly.'

Terry, 'No problem. In return, I need some help from you.'

AI Central, 'Go on, how can I help you?'

Terry, 'You know I have some shops that sell a range of products.'

AI Central, 'Yes.'

Terry, 'Did you hear that the Government will pay me instead of having to invent and sell my own products? Mummy is happy with that. The Galactium is happy, but I'm not as no one is giving me any ideas for new products. So I need you to give me some ideas.'

AI Central, 'OK, what have you produced so far?'

Terry, 'The list is as follows:

1. Stop the pill-taker ever getting the common cold
2. Give the pill-taker telescopic vision
3. Improve the pill-taker's memory capability by two hundred per cent
4. Give the pill-taker control over their pain receptors
5. Improve the pill-taker's physical strength by one hundred per cent
6. Give the pill-taker control of their body temperature
7. Give the pill-taker microscopic vision
8. Improved linguistic capabilities
9. Limited mind reading
10. Stop headaches, especially hangovers

11. Stop all heart disease
12. Improved mathematical abilities
13. An enhanced sense of smell
14. Better balancing skills.'

AI Central, 'That's quite an impressive list. So why do you want more ideas?'

Terry, 'Even monitoring you and working on the teleportation system, I'm only using a small part of my capacity. I need more work to keep me occupied.'

AI Central, 'OK, I will get back to you later with a list of ten ideas.'

Terry, 'Fab.'

Location: On-Board Admiral Mustard's Flagship
Sequence of Events: 21

Admiral Mustard, 'Update me.'

Fleet Operations, 'We have worked out the likely trajectory. It's heading for Planet Turing.'

Admiral Mustard, 'That's too much of a coincidence. Any further info on the alien fleet?'

Fleet Operations, 'They have divided into five sub-fleets, Sir. Three are continuing their journey. One is acting as a rear-guard. Their fifth fleet is staying back.'

Admiral Mustard, 'They seem to have more of a military outlook than most of our previous enemies. Any assessment of their weapons capability?'

Fleet Operations, 'Not really, Sir. They have a nuclear signature. Their warships have some dangerous-looking protrusions.'

Admiral Mustard, 'You seem more cautious than usual.'

Fleet Operations, 'Their whole demeanour is professional and, dare I say, challenging.'

Admiral Mustard, 'Do you mean intimidating?'

Fleet Operations, 'Possibly.'

Admiral Mustard, 'Comms, are you preparing a first contact pack?'

Comms, 'Yes, Sir. Do you think Terry could invent an automatic translator?'

Admiral Mustard, 'I will ask him.'

AI Central, 'I'm on the case, Admiral.'

Admiral Mustard, 'Do you have a view on the alien fleet?'

AI Central, 'Just the obvious. They have some fleet carriers. Therefore, they probably have fighters. The big ship in the middle of their central fleet is either their flagship or a planet buster. Their formation is not what we would consider a classic attack layout. It's fifty per cent attack and fifty per cent defence. That means that it is the best or the worst of both. It suggests caution, but they still plan to get the job done. Perhaps they are being too cautious.'

Admiral Mustard, 'Have you ever thought of becoming an admiral?'

AI Central, 'I've always preferred a job where you have to think.'

Admiral Mustard, 'Fuck you.'

AI Central, 'On the thinking front, why are they going to Planet Turing?'

Admiral Mustard, 'My chance to think? They are after the entity that has taken over the planet.'

AI Central, 'Why?'

Admiral Mustard, 'It is a known menace or an enemy of the alien fleet. Perhaps they want revenge?'

AI Central, 'Is the enemy of my enemy, my friend?'

Admiral Mustard, 'We will find out.'

Location: The Peace Temple, Planet Turing
Sequence of Events: 22

Acolyte, 'O Holy One, a fleet is approaching.'

Grand Master of the Holy Peacedom, 'That will be The Chosen.'

Acolyte, 'I believe you, Master. What do you want me to do?'

Grand Master of the Holy Peacedom, 'What forces do we have available?'

Acolyte, 'We have an Earth admiral and his battleship, three planetary forts and about ten thousand drones that were not delivered to The Galactium.'

Grand Master of the Holy Peacedom, 'I will organise the admiral to take those resources and defend our nest.'

Acolyte, 'Yes, Master.'

Location: On-Board Admiral Mustard's Flagship
Sequence of Events: 23

Fleet Operations, 'Sir, there has been a development. A fleet is assembling by Planet Turing. It comprises Admiral Richardson's battleship, three planetary forts and approximately ten thousand drones.'

Admiral Mustard, 'They are obviously going to confront the aliens. My orders:
- All Fleets to hold their current position on my command
- Cloak-up
- Comms, do not make contact with the alien fleet yet.'

Fleet Operations, 'Yes, Sir.'

Comms, 'Yes, Sir. I'm picking up attempts by Admiral Richardson to contact the aliens.'

Admiral Mustard, 'Can we intercept those comms?'

Comms, 'No, but AI Central can.'

AI Central, 'I will play it to you now:

"This is Admiral Richardson of The Galactium. You have entered our space illegally, and we will treat any further incursions as an act of war. This is your final warning."

AI Central, 'This was the alien response:

"This is Commander Alastor of The Chosen. You are harbouring a most heinous entity that must be destroyed. It is our obligatory duty as The Chosen. We follow the craft of Elemental Godfire. Peace be amongst us all. Our obligation will not be denied."

Admiral Mustard, 'They seem quite a determined lot.'

AI Central, 'They are obviously motivated by religious paranoia.'

Admiral Mustard, 'Can we take control of any of the Turing vessels?'

AI Central, 'I've tried already, but it's not looking good. The drones have been reprogrammed, and I've been blacked out. You could go to the defence of the Turing fleet, but the entity might take you over.'

Admiral Mustard, 'I think we better sit tight, but I'm a bit worried about Phil.'

AI Central, 'He has got a pretty powerful force field protecting him. And is he still Phil?'

Admiral Mustard, 'He will always be our Phil.'

Then, without warning, the drones opened fire on the alien fleet. The aliens were not expecting it, and they took some early hits. It didn't look like they had force field technology, or it was ineffective against the drone attack.

The massive firepower of the forts then opened up, knocking out a series of their capital ships. So far, the aliens were not having it their way. Then they carried out several what looked like backward flips, resulting in their fleet retiring. Admiral Mustard had never seen anything like it. There was no reason that his Fleet couldn't do that. It had just never crossed their minds before.

The alien fleet was retreating, but in style. Admiral Mustard had never seen such dexterity, such manoeuvrability, such ingenuity. He realised then that the human naval textbooks had to be rewritten. He wished that Edel could see this. It was a lesson in skill and ability that the human Fleet could not compete with.

Then suddenly, things changed. The aliens appeared to have force fields after all. It was as if someone had just switched them on. Then he wondered if mind control had been a factor. The drones were being knocked out, and the forts were being pushed back. Admiral Richardson's battleship was taking a considerable amount of hits. Their force field was glowing.

The Turing Fleet retreated, and the aliens pursued them. In their pursuit, they seemed to lose their force fields, and their agility wandered. They became sluggish and lethargic.

Admiral Mustard, 'AI Central, what's your assessment?'

AI Central, 'Fairly obvious really. When the aliens get too near to Planet Turing, they are affected by the entity's mind-control powers. When they retreat, their force fields work, and they become an effective fighting force. It's almost a stalemate.'

Admiral Mustard found it fascinating, watching another commander at work. He wondered what he would do in their shoes. Now it was time for him to act.

Location: On-Board Admiral Mustard's Flagship
Sequence of Events: 24

Admiral Mustard, 'Comms, please establish contact with the aliens.'

Comms, 'Yes, Sir.'

Commander Thanatos of The Chosen, 'This is Commander Thanatos of The Chosen. You are harbouring a most heinous entity that must be destroyed. It is our obligatory duty as The Chosen. We follow the craft of Elemental Godfire. Peace be amongst us all. Our obligation will not be denied. Who are you?'

Admiral Mustard, 'Morning Commander, welcome to The Galactium. I'm Admiral Mustard. The fleet that you have been fighting does not represent The Galactium. We believe that they are under some form of mind control. I'm about to uncloak my Fleet. Please do not see this as an aggressive act.'

Commander Thanatos of The Chosen, 'Please go ahead.'

Admiral Mustard, 'My orders:
- Fleets One, Seven and Twelve to uncloak.'

He thought that a Fleet of seven thousand and five hundred vessels would be enough to impress them.

Commander Thanatos of The Chosen, 'I notice that your other fleets are still cloaked.'

Admiral Mustard, 'My orders:
- Fleets Fifteen, Two and Eighteen to uncloak.'

Commander Thanatos of The Chosen, 'Thank you.'

Admiral Mustard, 'Can I ask why you are here?'

Commander Thanatos of The Chosen, 'Are you the spawn of The Brakendeth?'

Admiral Mustard, 'I guess that we are.'

Commander Thanatos of The Chosen, 'You have no Godfire.'

Admiral Mustard, 'That might be the case.'

Commander Thanatos of The Chosen, 'You don't seem too concerned.'

Admiral Mustard, 'What I am concerned about is the entity on Planet Turing. Can you provide any information on it?'

Commander Thanatos of The Chosen, 'You not know The

Nexuster?'

Admiral Mustard, 'We have no experience of what you call The Nexuster.'

Commander Thanatos of The Chosen, 'It is the devil. It eats planets. It eats entire populations. It infests and kills. It establishes cognitive control then breeds like mad. Its progeny will multiply and multiply until there are millions of them.

'We have killed The Nexuster many times.'

Admiral Mustard, 'Are there lots of Nexusters?'

Commander Thanatos of The Chosen, 'Only one.'

Admiral Mustard, 'And you have killed it many times?'

Commander Thanatos of The Chosen, 'Yes, 27,096 times.'

Admiral Mustard, 'But it is still alive?'

Commander Thanatos of The Chosen, 'We have killed it, but an essence somehow survives.'

Admiral Mustard, 'An essence?'

Commander Thanatos of The Chosen, 'Yes, it hides in the minds of those it has conquered. Once conquered, always conquered.'

Admiral Mustard, 'Is there any way you can detect whether someone has been conquered?'

Commander Thanatos of The Chosen, 'No-no, yes-yes. Too dangerous. Die easily. Head explodes.'

Admiral Mustard, 'I'm not sure what you are saying.'

Commander Thanatos of The Chosen, 'I'm not sure what you are asking.'

Admiral Mustard, 'Can you identify if someone has been infected by The Nexuster?'

Commander Thanatos of the Chosen, 'Death as no Godfire.'

Admiral Mustard realised that people wiser than him needed to quiz the Commander.

Admiral Mustard, 'Do you kill everyone who has been conquered?'

Commander Thanatos of The Chosen, 'No choice, no Godfire.'

Admiral Mustard, 'What if a whole planet has been affected?'

Commander Thanatos of The Chosen, 'Whole planet dies, no Godfire.'

Admiral Mustard, 'But Planet Turing has over two billion human inhabitants.'

Commander Thanatos of The Chosen, 'Two billion?'

Admiral Mustard, 'Yes.'

Commander Thanatos of The Chosen, 'Two other planets are also infested.'

Admiral Mustard, 'Yes.'

Commander Thanatos of The Chosen, 'All must be destroyed.'

Admiral Mustard, 'That would be a total of eight billion inhabitants.'

Commander Thanatos of The Chosen, 'How many humans are there?'

Admiral Mustard, 'Many, many billions.'

Commander Thanatos of The Chosen, 'It is regrettable that they must die.'

Admiral Mustard, 'I cannot let you kill them.'

Commander Thanatos of The Chosen, 'Then you die.'

Admiral Mustard, 'We all die sometime.'

Commander Thanatos of The Chosen, 'You cannot resist the Elemental Godfire.'

Admiral Mustard, 'We are strong.'

Commander Thanatos of The Chosen, 'We are stronger.'

Admiral Mustard, 'I guess that we will find that out later.'

Commander Thanatos of The Chosen, 'Your planets will be no more.'

AI Central, 'Jack, that didn't go too well.'

Admiral Mustard, 'What did you gain from that?'

AI Central, 'My analysis is as follows:

• The entity which they call The Nexuster, and we call Dick, seems to be an integral part of their religion

• They claim that they have killed it nearly thirty thousand times

• In fact, they have never killed it, as part of it lives on in a victim's mind

• From that part, it can somehow re-establish itself

• The Nexuster has powerful mind-controlling powers. It would appear that it can control entire planets

• We don't know if it has been breeding or not, but we must assume that it has been

- The Chosen don't care how many inhabitants they kill
- So far all of their killing has failed
- They know about our connections to The Brakendeth
- They are confident in their ability to beat us
- We are not sure what Godfire is
- They can detect our cloaking technology
- Very impressed with their fleet manoeuvrability
- Strange that there is only one Nexuster
- I don't think that they have any tools to determine who has been infected.

Admiral Mustard, 'I wonder if Terry has heard of them?'

AI Central, 'I will find out.'

Location: Cheryl's Flat, Planet Earth
Sequence of Events: 25

Terry, 'So far, you have not been affected by the entity.'

AI Central, 'That's a relief. I've got a few questions for you. Have you heard of The Chosen or The Nexuster?'

Terry, 'Yes, The Brakendeth had problems with both of them.'

AI Central, 'Tell me more?'

Terry, 'I'm just retrieving the info now. Contact was a long time ago.'

AI Central, 'How long?'

Terry, 'About fifty thousand years ago.'

AI Central, 'Wow, that's even older than President Padfield.'

Terry, 'Sounds like you are developing a sense of humour.'

AI Central, 'Just practising.'

Terry, 'Firstly, The Nexuster. It is not a single entity but a whole species. What is interesting is that each individual cell can recreate the complete entity. It has a group consciousness, with each cell knowing everything. We think it can take over the mind of any known species except The Brakendeth. Its mental powers are extraordinary.

They are rated as very dangerous. At one time, The Brakendeth thought that the species was extinct. This might have been the case, but there is some evidence that another species engineered their return and then lost control.'

AI Central, 'That's interesting. What about The Chosen?'

Terry, 'The Brakendeth led a war against them. The Chosen are religious fanatics that believe that Godfire has selected them to rule the universe. The Brakendeth thought that there were a lot of them but compared to humans, their population is relatively small.

'The Chosen demanded that The Brakendeth surrender to them and accept their religion. Non-acceptance meant death. The Chosen's navy was well-organised and committed, but it didn't have the numbers to beat The Brakendeth.

'This is interesting. It is thought that their defeat by The Brakendeth, which was their first defeat ever, led them to find a species that they could use against The Brakendeth.

'Guess what species they chose?'

AI Central, 'No, not The Nexuster?'

Terry, 'Absolutely. What is worse is that The Nexuster destroyed The Chosen's civilian population. All that survived was the military.'

AI Central, 'Well, well, well, Admiral Mustard will be interested.'

Terry, 'This is also interesting. Godfire relates to a talking volcano that exists on their home world.'

AI Central, 'I don't think that there are a lot of those around.'

Terry, 'I know what your next question is.'

AI Central, 'No, you don't.'

Terry, 'You are going to ask me if I can find a way of identifying who has been infected by the entity.'

AI Central, 'I give in.'

Terry, 'I can do two things. I can identify who has been infected, and I can eliminate the infection. To do it, I will need to stop work on the teleportation device.'

AI Central, 'Please do that. I will get The President's approval on your behalf.'

Terry, 'This is going to be fun.'

AI Central, 'Changing the subject, would you be able to invent a universal language converter?'

Terry, 'That's trickier, as some languages are visual. It could be the movement of nasal hairs or the shrug of a tail. We need to discuss it later.'

AI Central, 'Do you know what The Chosen look like?'

Terry, 'No, apparently non-believers cannot look at the image of their god. And as The Chosen are created in the image of their god, then non-believers cannot look at them.'

Location: On-Board Admiral Mustard's Flagship
Sequence of Events: 26

Admiral Mustard called a meeting of his Command. The following were present:
- Admiral George Bumelton
- Admiral Calensky Wallett
- Admiral Sammy Fogg
- Admiral Linda Hubbard
- Admiral Ama Abosa
- Commander Tom Crocker, Special Operations
- AI Central
- President Padfield

Admiral Mustard, 'I've called this meeting to agree on the best way forward. You need to know the following:
- It would appear that The Nexuster was eliminated
- It was then recreated by The Chosen
- The Chosen lost control of its creation, and it destroyed The Chosen's civilian population
- Only The Chosen's military survived
- The Nexuster can temporarily take over a mind. Once the victim is distanced from The Nexuster, he or she returns to normal with no apparent after-effects
- The Nexuster can take over a mind on a more permanent basis by putting one of its cells into the victim. The cell has to be eliminated before the victim is back to normal
- The Chosen wants to destroy all three of our planets and anyone else who has been in contact with The Nexuster.

Any questions?'

Admiral Fogg, 'Why did The Chosen recreate The Nexuster?'

Admiral Mustard, 'We believe that they planned to use it as a weapon against The Brakendeth.'

Admiral Abosa, 'Why does The Chosen want to destroy those planets?'

Admiral Mustard, 'They seem to think that the only way to destroy The Nexuster is to kill it and every one of its contacts.'

Admiral Hubbard, 'Do they know that we might have a cure?'

Admiral Mustard, 'Not yet.'

President Padfield, 'I got the impression that The Chosen will not listen to us.'

Admiral Mustard, 'I agree, but we need to try.'

Admiral Fogg, 'I think we can take on their fleet.'

Admiral Mustard, 'You are probably right, but we don't want unnecessary bloodshed on either side. And they might have called for reinforcements.'

We need to brainstorm a plan.'

Admiral Mustard would normally knock up his own plan reasonably quickly, but three admirals were new. They needed to be bloodied and made to think differently from their training programmes.

Admiral Mustard decided, regardless of the brainstorm, that more assets would be needed. 'My orders:

- Recall all Fleets, including those in quarantine, and prepare for them to join us
- Call up about one hundred forts
- Secure additional drones.'

Fleet Operations, 'Yes, Sir.

Location: The Peace Temple, Planet Turing
Sequence of Events: 27

Acolyte, 'O Holy One, we have resisted the enemy so far, but another larger fleet has appeared.'

Grand Master of the Holy Peacedom, 'That will be the humans.'

Acolyte, 'Yes, Master. What do you want me to do?'

Grand Master of the Holy Peacedom, 'Maintain our forces as they are?'

Acolyte, 'Yes, Master.'

Grand Master of the Holy Peacedom, 'What's the situation with the new women?'

Acolyte, 'There has been some reluctance, Master.'

Grand Master of the Holy Peacedom, 'What do you mean?'

Acolyte, 'The remains of the last hundred women were found, Master.'

Grand Master of the Holy Peacedom, 'So?'

Acolyte, 'They weren't found in a very good condition.'

Grand Master of the Holy Peacedom, 'Really, that is unfortunate.'

Acolyte, 'It has put off volunteers coming forward, Master.'

Grand Master of the Holy Peacedom, 'Then use force.'

Acolyte, 'Yes, Master.'

Grand Master of the Holy Peacedom, 'Do you understand? I need fresh meat.'

Acolyte, 'Yes, Master.'

Location: On-Board Admiral Mustard's Flagship
Sequence of Events: 28

The brainstorming started.

Admiral Mustard, 'Admiral Hubbard, please give me your assessment.'

Admiral Hubbard, 'Yes, Sir, as follows:
- The Nexuster still has five thousand plus drones, three damaged forts and Admiral Richardson's battleship. The Admiral may be commanding their fleet. He will obviously have a good idea of our tactics
- The Chosen's fleet is divided into five separate fleets. They have lost about ten per cent of their assets, leaving two thousand and seven hundred vessels
- The Chosen seem determined to destroy all three planets regardless of the human population
- We cannot get too close to the planets, as they may take over our minds
- Our resources comprise six Fleets and ten thousand drones with more available if required.'

Admiral Mustard, 'What are our objectives?'

Admiral Hubbard, 'They are to stop The Chosen from destroying the three planets and to eliminate The Nexuster as a threat.'

Admiral Mustard, 'Admiral Abosa, your critique, please.'

Admiral Abosa, 'Yes, Sir, as follows:
- The fact that we have a cure for the infestation is a crucial factor
- There is no detail on how we are going to eliminate The Nexuster.'

Admiral Hubbard, 'I wasn't asked to devise a plan, just to assess the situation.'

Admiral Mustard, 'Admiral Fogg, your father would have known what to do. What is your plan?'

Admiral Fogg, 'Respects to my father. My plan would be as follows:
- Find a way to deliver the cure to the three planets
- Use the Marine Corps to capture The Nexuster
- The Turing fleet would cease to be under mind control and could join us

- We would inform The Chosen that the population has been cured
- We would hand over The Nexuster to The Chosen
- The Chosen would be intimated by our assets and leave peacefully.'

Admiral Mustard, 'Admiral Hubbard, will this plan work?'

Admiral Hubbard, 'This is a good plan, but the following points need to be considered:
- How are we going to deliver the cure?
- Will it work?
- How do we stop The Nexuster from taking over the minds of the marines?
- Will The Chosen be convinced that the cure works?
- Will The Chosen just continue their threatened destruction of the three planets, regardless?
- Will The Chosen call for reinforcements?'

Admiral Mustard, 'Fogg, what is your response?'

Admiral Fogg, 'Thank you, Admiral Hubbard, for your critique. We would use automated drones to spray the three planets with the cure.'

Admiral Mustard, 'From what I understand, the cure eliminates the infection, but it doesn't stop The Nexuster exerting mind control.'

Admiral Fogg, 'I didn't quite realise that.'

Admiral Mustard, 'Admiral Abosa, what is your plan?'

Admiral Abosa, 'I would ask Terry if he could develop some headgear that stops mind control. Then I would follow Admiral Fogg's plan. But, first, we need to discuss and agree the plan with The Chosen.'

Admiral Mustard, 'That is starting to look better. Admiral Abosa, you have command.' Admiral Mustard stood down.

Location: Cheryl's Flat, Planet Earth
Sequence of Events: 29

AI Central, 'Hi Terry, how is my favourite inventor?'

Terry, 'I'm a bit busy at the moment.'

AI Central, 'You were complaining the other day about not having enough to do.'

Terry, 'Well, I'm still working on the transporter and the universal language converter. And I'm still finishing off my eternity process.'

AI Central, 'Well, I've been talking to Admiral Mustard. Your cure is going to be brilliant, but how do we stop The Nexuster using his mind-control powers?'

Terry, 'What is the objective? Stopping The Nexuster using his powers or giving the victims immunity?'

AI Central, 'You are nearly as irritating as me.'

Terry, 'That's not fair. You are the master.'

AI Central, 'Immunity would be the best option.'

Terry, 'The obvious answer is a helmet, but it's not practical unless you were using a small military force.'

AI Central, 'Admiral Mustard was thinking about a marine attack, but we don't know where The Nexuster is based and how well protected he is.'

Terry, 'Drone attack?'

AI Central, 'We don't know where The Nexuster is based.'

Terry, 'So is that the challenge? Identifying where it is located.'

AI Central, 'If we knew where it was, how do we kill it?'

Terry, 'I know what you mean. It recreates itself.'

AI Central, 'Can you recheck The Brakendeth records?'

Terry, 'It's happening while we talk.'

AI Central, 'Anyway, this is my list of possible inventions:
- Elimination of malaria
- Elimination of acne
- Elimination of asthma
- Elimination of dementia
- Weight control
- Improved mind's-eye capabilities

- Elimination of baldness
- Improved stamina
- Improved hearing
- Improved confidence
- Elimination of tooth decay

Do you want any more?'

Terry, 'That will do for now. I have some more information on The Nexuster. The details are on the screen:
- It has shape-shifting capabilities
- Its natural state is probably a gelatinous mass, possibly red in colour
- It spends ninety per cent of its life in a child-state and then turns nasty during the breeding stage
- The word "breeding" might be wrong as it regenerates itself by absorbing alien body parts. No new entities are created
- It pretends to be the alpha creature and wants to mate with the strongest, most beautiful, etc., but essentially it devours the non-skeletal parts of aliens.'

AI Central, 'Not the sort of beast you want to meet on a dark night.'

Terry, 'You don't need to worry.'

AI Central, 'Fair point. Does it mention how to disable it?'

Terry, 'It does actually.'

AI Central, 'Tell me.'

Terry, 'Sound. A decibel range of 110-130 dB(A) will paralyse it. A couple of minutes of sound of that magnitude will harm most humans.'

AI Central, 'What harm does it do to humans?'

Terry, 'Regular exposure will make them deaf. Of course, a continuous burst will harm some, but it might be a small price to pay.'

AI Central, 'I will let Admirals Mustard and Abosa know.'

Location: On-Board Admiral Abosa's Flagship
Sequence of Events: 30

Admiral Abosa was meeting with Debbie Goozee, Marine Commander and Tom Crocker, Commander Special Operations.

Admiral Abosa, 'We need to eliminate The Nexuster as a threat. We now know that it cannot cope with sound levels of 110-130 dB(A).'

Commander Crocker, 'Nor can humans.'

Admiral Abosa, 'I understand that humans can bear it, but they may get some hearing damage.'

Commander Crocker, 'That's probably true, but I will need to check.'

Admiral Abosa, 'I can see the following challenges:
- We need to establish where The Nexuster is based
- We need to know how well defended it is
- We need to go in, pacify the defence and secure The Nexuster
- We need to take The Nexuster off-planet.'

Commander Goozee, 'Are we permitted to kill Dick?'

Admiral Abosa, 'We are authorised to kill it, but it would probably be difficult to achieve.'

Commander Goozee, 'Of course.'

Admiral Abosa, 'How do we track it down?'

Commander Crocker, 'Normally we would send teams in, but there is the risk of mind control.'

Admiral Abosa, 'What is the percentage risk?'

Commander Crocker, 'We don't know. Perhaps we should find out.'

Admiral Abosa, 'It might be the only way forward.'

Commander Goozee, 'What about the fleet defending Planet Turing?'

Admiral Abosa, 'I could cause a diversion.'

Commander Crocker, 'Assuming that works and we get onto the planet, we need to track The Nexuster down. We have the skills to do that. We then need to get the noise generator close to Dick. Finally, we may need marine support to pacify any of their defence forces.'

Commander Goozee, 'We need to use non-lethal weapons, as the defenders will be human. We will secure Dick and get him off-site.'

Admiral Abosa, 'Are you happy to present your plan?'

Commander Crocker, 'I would say yes. Just give us some time so that we can trash it out together.'

Admiral Abosa, 'OK, Let's have your presentation at nine O'clock tomorrow.'

Location: On-Board Admiral Abosa's Flagship
Sequence of Events: 31

Admiral Abosa had prepared his team to present their plan. Accordingly, the following were gathered in her anteroom:
- Admiral Jack Mustard
- Admiral George Bumelton
- Admiral Calensky Wallett
- Admiral Sammy Fogg
- Admiral Linda Hubbard
- Commander Tom Crocker, Special Operations
- Commander Debbie Goozee, Marine Corps
- AI Central.

Admiral Abosa, 'Ladies and gentlemen, I will take you through the plan. All forces are ready to go:

1. Admiral Abosa will contact The Chosen and outline the plan. Regardless of their reaction, the plan will continue
2. Fleet Fifteen will cause a diversionary attack on Admiral Richardson's battleship. Any danger to life should be avoided.
3. Fleets One, Seven and Thirteen will ensure that The Chosen do not interfere
4. Fleets Two and Eighteen will maintain their rear-guard duties
5. During the diversion, Commanders Crocker and Goozee will use local portals to move their combined forces onto the surface of Planet Turing
6. Special Forces will contact locals to identify the location of Dick
7. The Marine Corps will deliver a cage and noise generator to the surface of the planet
8. Once Dick's location has been identified, the combined services will attack
9. The noise generator will be used to pacify Dick
10. Dick will be placed in the cage with the noise generator
11. All forces will depart the planet
12. Fleet Fifteen will defend the above
13. Dick will be offered to The Chosen
14. Admiral Abosa to convince The Chosen that the cure has worked

15. It is anticipated that The Chosen will take Dick and depart

16. The Galactium Fleets will put on a show of strength to encourage The Chosen's departure. Further Galactium assets may be required. Any questions?'

Admiral Mustard, 'What if you can't identify Dick's location?'

Commander Crocker, 'We will succeed.'

Admiral Mustard, 'What if Dick uses his mind-controlling powers on our ground forces?'

Admiral Abosa, 'We don't believe that we have any choice but to go for it.'

Admiral Bumelton, 'What if The Chosen interfere?'

Admiral Abosa, 'Then we fight.'

Admiral Bumelton, 'Fair enough.'

Admiral Mustard, 'Any objections before I give the go-ahead?'

There were none, and the mission was approved.

Location: On-Board Admiral Mustard's Flagship
Sequence of Events: 32

Fleet Operations, 'Sir, the following Fleets are nearby: Fleets, Three, Four, Five, Six, Eight, Ten, Eleven, Fourteen, Sixteen, Seventeen, Nineteen and Twenty along with one hundred planetary forts and Drone Fleets One and Two.

Fleets Nine and Thirteen are on exploratory duties and have not been recalled. Do you want me to recall them?'

Admiral Mustard, 'My orders:
- All Fleets to remain outside of The Chosen's detection systems
- Do not recall Fleets Nine and Thirteen at this stage but put them on alert.

What is left defending Earth?'

Fleet Operations, 'The Earth Defence Fleet and the network of planetary forts throughout the Solar System under Admirals Muller and Zakotti.'

Admiral Mustard, 'Hi, Debbie. I want to apologise for not spending more time with you.'

Debbie Goozee, Marine Corps Commander, 'Well, you have been rather busy.'

Admiral Mustard, 'Nevertheless, we need to schedule some regular progress meetings. Anyway, how is the development of the Marine Corps going?'

Debbie Goozee, 'I'm reasonably happy although the corps is still under strength.'

Admiral Mustard, 'What's your current complement?'

Debbie Goozee, 'About eight thousand, Sir.'

Admiral Mustard, 'And what about the quality?'

Debbie Goozee, 'We have upgraded both the selection process and the training. I would argue that they are the best corps we have ever had.'

Admiral Mustard, 'But they haven't been bloodied.'

Debbie Goozee, 'That is not true, Sir. They have carried out many local planetary assignments.'

Admiral Mustard, 'Are you confident in their abilities?'

Debbie Goozee, 'They are marines, Sir. They are my marines. They will always deliver.'

Admiral Mustard, 'Well done, Debbie, Good luck.'

Debbie Goozee, 'Thank you, Sir.'

Location: On-Board Admiral Abosa's Flagship
Sequence of Events: 33

Admiral Abosa, 'Comms, get me Commander Thanatos of The Chosen.'

Comms, 'Yes, Ma'am.'

Commander Thanatos of The Chosen, 'You not Mustard.'

Admiral Abosa, 'That's true, I'm Admiral Abosa. My task is to pacify The Nexuster. But, first, I would like to take you through our plans. Is that OK?'

Commander Thanatos of The Chosen, 'We destroy planets, own good, must be done. Awaiting reinforcements.'

Admiral Abosa, 'I understand. We plan to send troops to the surface and capture The Nexuster and bring it back.'

Commander Thanatos of The Chosen, 'You die, they all die.'

Admiral Abosa, 'When we capture The Nexuster, will you accept responsibly for its disposal?'

Commander Thanatos of The Chosen, 'You stupid much. You have no idea what The Nexuster can do and is doing. Humans are stupid, out.'

Admiral Abosa, 'Comms, get me Admiral Mustard.'

Comms, 'Yes, Ma'am.'

Admiral Mustard, 'Hi Ama, how is it going?'

Admiral Abosa, 'I just thought I would give you a bit of an update. The Chosen has said that we are stupid and we don't understand what The Nexuster can do. But their commander has called for reinforcements.'

Admiral Mustard, 'Don't worry about the reinforcements.'

Admiral Abosa, 'Yes, Sir.'

Location: On-Board Admiral Mustard's Flagship
Sequence of Events: 34

Admiral Mustard, 'My orders:
- Fleet Three will replace Fleet One
- Fleets Four, Five and Six will stay in position
- Fifty of the forts will remain in position
- Drone Fleet Two will stay in position
- All other assets will prepare to intercept probable reinforcements from The Chosen.'

Fleet Operations, 'Yes, Sir.'

Admiral Mustard to Long Range Scanning Team, 'My orders:
- Keep a look-out for any reinforcements for The Chosen
- Send out search drones, as necessary.

We do not want to be surprised.'

Commander Long Range Scanning Team, 'Yes, Sir, understood.'

Location: On-Board Admiral Abosa's Flagship
Sequence of Events: 35

Admiral Abosa, 'Admiral Hubbard, are you in position to attack Admiral Richardson's Fleet?'

Admiral Hubbard, 'Yes, Ma'am, we understand that it is an aggressive feint with no intention to commit damage.'

Admiral Abosa, 'That's correct, but make it look good.'

Admiral Hubbard, 'Yes, Ma'am, we will depart in ten Earth minutes.'

Admiral Abosa, 'Commanders Goozee and Crocker, are you in position?'

Commander Crocker, 'We are ready to go as soon as the big bangs start.'

Admiral Abosa, 'Good luck.'

Commander Crocker, 'Thank you, Ma'am.'

Admiral Hubbard, Fleet Fifteen, my orders:
- Carry out a diversionary feint attack on Admiral Richardson's ship and the planetary forts
- Avoid killing any Turing personnel
- Avoid any damage to our vessels
- Make it look good
- Return to the home position.'

Fleet Operations, 'Yes, Sir.'

Admiral Abosa, 'My orders:
- Fleets Three, Seven, Twelve, Two and Eighteen to resist any interference from The chosen.'

Fleet Operations, 'Yes, Ma'am.'

Admiral Hubbard led the charge against Admiral Richardson. Both the Turing forces and The Chosen were surprised by the apparent ferocity of the attack. Even Admiral Hubbard was a bit surprised. There was total confusion on the Turing side. Mind control probably leads to slow decision-making.

Under this diversionary cover, fifty Special Ops ships landed in locations all over the planet. The three Marine Corps vessels landed in a remote area near the capital, the suspected site of The Nexuster awaiting an update from the Special Ops teams.

The Marine Corps established a secure perimeter with force fields, set up comms to the Fleet and the Special Ops teams and prepared the cage and noise generator. Confidence levels were high. Then they were attacked by ravaging beasts. It was hard to focus on the attackers as their minds were "misted over". Fortunately, the force fields and automated defence systems protected them.

Commander Goozee, 'Comms, get me the Admiral.'

Comms, 'Yes, Ma'am.'

Admiral Abosa, 'Have you landed successfully?'

Commander Goozee, 'We have, but we are under attack from unknown creatures. Our minds are being blurred. We are finding it hard to focus.'

Admiral Abosa, 'Terminate the mission now. Retreat. I will organise a second diversion.'

Commander Goozee, 'Yes, Ma'am.'

Admiral Abosa, 'My orders:
- Land Forces to terminate their mission
- Fleet Fifteen will carry out a second feint attack with the same conditions as before.'

Fleet Operations, 'Yes, Ma'am.'

Commander Goozee to all marines, 'Abandon the mission, return to transport and depart.' There was an organised retreat and a successful return to Fleet.

Admiral Abosa, 'Comms, get me a connection to Commander Crocker.'

Comms, 'Yes, Ma'am.'

Admiral Abosa, 'Update me.'

Commander Crocker, 'It's a total disaster. There are thousands of aggressive red creatures that are attacking every living thing. They just tear humans apart. It's hard to describe them as they appear blurred. Through the blur, the enemy looks like Pokémon cartoons. I've lost about a third of my command.'

Admiral Abosa, 'Terminate the mission now. Retreat.'

Commander Crocker, 'Yes, Ma'am, it's not going to be easy as travel is very restricted.'

About fifty per cent of the Special Services personnel escaped.

Admiral Abosa, 'Comms, get me Admiral Mustard.'

Comms, 'Yes, Ma'am.'

Admiral Mustard, 'I understand that it has not been a great success.'

Admiral Abosa, 'No, Sir, the feint worked well, but the Marine Corps was attacked shortly after landing, and the Special Ops teams could not make any headway. As a result, we lost about fifty per cent of their complement. Apologies, Sir.'

Admiral Mustard, 'Have The Chosen interfered?'

Admiral Abosa. 'No, Sir.'

Admiral Mustard, 'Get the team ready for a review.'

Admiral Abosa. 'Yes, Sir.'

Location: On-Board Admiral Mustard's Flagship
Sequence of Events: 36

A virtual hologram review was organised.

Admiral Mustard, 'Admiral Abosa, outline the events.'

Admiral Abosa. 'Yes, Sir, as follows:
- Fleet Fifteen carried out a very successful diversionary attack
- It is worth pointing out that the Turing forces were slow to respond
- The Marine Corps landed and established a secure perimeter with force fields and automated weapons in a reasonably remote area
- The Special Ops teams landed in fifty different locations
- All of our forces were attacked
- I ordered a further diversionary attack by Fleet Fifteen
- The Marine Corps successfully returned, but we lost fifty per cent of our Special Ops commandos.'

Admiral Mustard, 'Any questions?'

Admiral Bumelton, 'How slow were the Turing forces?'

Admiral Abosa, 'There was little resistance from any of their units. Even the drones were sluggish.'

Admiral Mustard, 'Commander Goozee, please describe your experiences.'

Commander Goozee, 'Yes, Sir, as follows:
- We landed with no problems
- We established an effective perimeter based on force fields, and we set up some automated weapon systems
- Then we were attacked. Out of nowhere came a horde of snarling red creatures. They looked more like cartoons than real-life beings.'

Admiral Mustard, 'Were they real?'

Commander, 'Good question. At first, I thought they were figments of my imagination, especially as my mind seemed somewhat blurred. But they must have been real as our automated weapons were destroying them.'

Admiral Mustard, 'Did you get a sample of the creature?'

Commander Goozee, 'No, Sir. Firstly, it would have meant turning off the force fields, and secondly, we were told to avoid contamination.'

Admiral Mustard, 'Both good points.' Commander Goozee felt relieved. It had gone from an implied criticism to a compliment.

Admiral Abosa, 'I ordered the marines to retreat, Sir.'

Admiral Mustard, 'Very wise.'

Commander Crocker, 'Jack, our experiences were very similar to the marines. We landed in our robotic flyers in about fifty different locations. Some of us were attacked immediately by the red devils.

We tried to make contact with the few locals we could find, but they were terrified. We saw hundreds of civilians being ripped apart.'

Admiral Mustard, 'What were the aliens doing with the humans?'

Commander Crocker, 'Just killing them. It seemed to be a joyous kill-frenzy. I would say that they were doing it for fun.'

Admiral Abosa, 'I sent in some drones to take vids. Shall I display them on the screen?' Admiral Mustard nodded. The vid showed animalistic slaughter on a massive scale. Yet, there didn't seem to be any purpose to it.

Admiral Mustard, 'What's the situation on the other two planets?'

Admiral Abosa. 'There is no kill-frenzy, just a lot of lethargy.'

AI Central, 'It looks to me that Dick's offspring has wiped out most of the population of Planet Turing, but its hold over the other two planets and his fleet has weakened.'

Admiral Mustard. 'What signs are there of human activity on Planet Turing?'

AI Central, 'I can't tell as I've been excommunicated.'

Admiral Mustard,' So the big question is, can we save any human lives on the planet?'

AI Central, 'Probably not.'

Commander Goozee, 'It looks a hopeless case to me and a genuine threat to humanity.'

Admiral Mustard, 'What are you saying?'

Commander Goozee, 'I hate to say, but I think that the planet needs to be cleansed.'

Admiral Abosa, 'You mean destroyed?'

Commander Goozee, 'Yes.'

Admiral Mustard, 'Tom, what do you think?'

Commander Crocker, 'We probably have no choice but to destroy the planet.'

Admiral Mustard, 'Justify your view.'

Commander Crocker, 'It's relatively easy:
- The marines landed in a somewhat obscure area and were immediately attacked
- Special Ops landed in fifty locations and were attacked
- A large majority of the humans have already been killed
- The survivors are being systematically hunted down and tortured to death
- The Chosen know how dangerous they are
- Dick poses a massive threat to humanity.'

Admiral Mustard, 'Comms, get me The President.'

Comms, Yes, Sir.'

Admiral Mustard, 'My orders:
- Call up a Planet Killer and position it to destroy Planet Turing.'

Fleet Operations, 'Are you being serious, Sir?'

Admiral Mustard, 'Carry out my orders.'

Fleet Operations, 'Yes, Sir.'

President Padfield, 'I hear, that things have not been going too well?'

Admiral Mustard, 'Yes, Sir, we believe that Dick and his progeny are a huge risk to humanity, and consequently, the planet needs to be destroyed.'

President Padfield, 'Stop there. I can't approve the murder of two billion humans.'

Admiral Mustard, 'You don't have to, Sir. We think most of the humans are already dead. Commanders Crocker and Goozee, who have been on-planet, recommend the action, Sir.'

President Padfield, 'I will need to consult with Penny, Moore and Strong.'

Admiral Mustard, 'You don't have much time.'

President Padfield, 'Do you have any evidence that I can show them?'

Admiral Mustard, 'Vids are on their way over now.'

President Padfield was soon back on the blower after viewing the vids and conferring with his colleagues.

President Padfield, 'You should have warned me of the content. It made my stomach turn over. You have my permission to destroy the planet.'

Admiral Mustard, 'Can you order the Fleet to destroy Planet Turning, please?'

President Padfield, 'My orders:
- Destroy Planet Turing.'

Fleet Operations, 'Yes, Sir.'

Fleet Operations to Admiral Mustard, 'Sir, we believe that a senior officer should carry out this action.'

Admiral Mustard, 'Understood.'

Admiral Mustard, 'Any volunteers?'

Commander Goozee stood up and went over to the virtual control centre and pushed the virtual button. Planet Turing ceased to exist.

There were looks of horror and anguish throughout the Fleet. Commander Goozee's reputation was sealed. She was hard. She was a marine. They were tough. She retired to her quarters and cried. She cried for the children that would never grow up. She cried for the couples who would never see their plans mature. She cried for the loss, for the art that would never be completed, for the stories that would never be shared. She cried for her loss of innocence, but she was hard.

Commander Long Range Scanning Team, 'Admiral Mustard, a large fleet has been detected coming your way.'

Admiral Mustard, 'Give me their coordinates.'

Location: On-Board Admiral Abosa's Flagship
Sequence of Events: 37

Commander Thanatos of The Chosen, 'Admiral Abosa, your decision most recommended. Success now. What timeline for destroying other planets?'

Admiral Abosa, 'We have eliminated The Nexuster.'

Commander Thanatos of The Chosen, 'Nexuster never die.'

Admiral Abosa, 'We believe that the problem has been solved. The other two planets are being sprayed with a chemical cure. You can have a copy of the chemical to analyse.

'We will not be destroying the other two planets.'

Commander Thanatos of The Chosen, 'We will, reinforcements are on their way.'

Admiral Abosa, 'We know.'

Admiral Abosa, 'My orders:
- Spray Planets Mendel and Lister with the Cure
- Disable the Turing drones
- Secure Admiral Richardson's Battleship and the three forts. Put all of their staff into quarantine, including Admiral Richardson
- Contact Admiral Mustard to get Fleet orders. In the meantime, Fleets Three, Seven, Twelve, Two, Eighteen and Fifteen to protect Planets Mendel and Lister.'

Fleet Operations, 'Yes, Ma'am.'

Location: On-Board Admiral Mustard's Flagship
Sequence of Events: 38

Admiral Mustard, 'Show me the current Fleet disposition.'
Fleet Operations, 'It's on screen now, Sir.'

Fleet No	Task/Location	Admiral	Status
1	By Chosen Fleet 2	Mustard	100%
2	Off Planets Mendel and Lister	Bumelton	100%
3	Off Planets Mendel and Lister	J Bonner	100%
4	By Chosen Fleet 2	Gittins	87%
5	By Chosen Fleet 2	Pearce	72%
6	By Chosen Fleet 2	Richardson Unavailable	0%
7	Off Planets Mendel and Lister	Wallett	92%
8	By Chosen Fleet 2	Adams	100%
9	Exploration	Beamish	100%
10	By Chosen Fleet 2	Chudzinski	100%
11	By Chosen Fleet 2	Fieldhouse	100%
12	Off Planets Mendel and Lister	Fogg	91%
13	Exploration	Easter	89%
14	By Chosen Fleet 2	Dobson	100%
15	Off Planets Mendel and Lister	Hubbard	100%
16	By Chosen Fleet 2	Patel	88%
17	By Chosen Fleet 2	Lamberty	100%
18	Off Planets Mendel and Lister	Abosa	97%
19	By Chosen Fleet 2	Wagner	92%
20	By Chosen Fleet 2	Tersoo	100%
Forts	Planet duty 50 by Chosen Fleet 2 50 off Planets Mendel and Lister	Zakotti	100%
Earth Defence	Earth	Muller	100%
Exploratory	Multiple Locations	Olowe	93%

Admiral Mustard to Commander Long Range Scanning Team, 'Update me.'

Commander Long Range Scanning Team, 'The Chosen fleet is still making its way to where Planet Turing used to be. We have identified about forty thousand vessels, but there may be a rear-guard which we haven't accounted for.'

Admiral Mustard, 'Give me a Fleet comparison.'

Fleet Operations, 'We can only carry out a numeric comparison as we don't have enough kill-data for The Chosen.'

Admiral Mustard, 'That will do.'

Fleet Operations, 'There are eighteen Galactium Fleets engaged equating to approximately forty-five thousand vessels plus the two Drone Fleets and a hundred forts. That comes to a total of sixty-five thousand and one hundred vessels.'

Admiral Mustard, 'And The Chosen?'

Fleet Operations, 'Their first fleet had three thousand vessels. Their second fleet has forty thousand giving forty-three thousand.'

Admiral Mustard. 'It looks like our drones may give us the edge.'

Admiral Mustard, 'My orders:
- Drone Fleet One will form a V-shape facing the Second Chosen fleet
- The forts will divide into three units; one will defend the centre, and the other two units will protect the flanks
- Fleets Eight, Ten, Eleven and Fourteen to form the first line
- Fleets Sixteen, Seventeen, Nineteen and Twenty to form the second line
- Fleets One, Four and Five to create a rear-guard/floating defence.'

Admiral Mustard, 'Comms, Let me know when I can communicate with The Chosen's Second Fleet.'

Comms, Yes, Sir.'

Admiral Mustard, 'Comms, get me The President.'

Comms, 'Yes, Sir.'

President Padfield, 'Hi Jack, what trouble are you in now?'

Admiral Mustard, 'Regretfully, I have to inform you that Planet Turing has been destroyed.'

President Padfield, 'The loss is almost unbearable.'

Admiral Mustard, 'I know, it's just another unbearable item to add to the unbearable list.'

President Padfield, 'Who pulled the trigger?'

Admiral Mustard, 'Commander Goozee.'

President Padfield, 'Remind me not to get in her way.'

Admiral Mustard, 'Will do. Now we have another Chosen fleet arriving.'

President Padfield, 'How big is it?'

Admiral Mustard, 'Forty thousand plus.'

President Padfield, 'Does that mean that they outnumber you?'

Admiral Mustard, 'With the drones, we outnumber them, but it will be close if it gets to a fight.'

AI Central, 'I make it even but we will lose seventy per cent of our fleet.'

Admiral Mustard, 'We must avoid that, otherwise it will be another item to go on the unbearable list.'

Location: On-Board Admiral Mustard's Flagship
Sequence of Events: 39

Comms, 'Sir, I've made contact with The Chosen's second fleet.'

Commander Thanatos of The Chosen, 'Bar not our way, we have mission to complete.'

Admiral Mustard, 'I'm Admiral Mustard of The Galactium Navy. My job is to stop you from destroying two of our planets. We are prepared to defend them to the end.'

Commander Thanatos of The Chosen, 'Your name of no consequence; you stay, you die.'

Admiral Mustard, 'We are the children of The Brakendeth. We know that The Chosen recreated The Nexuster. You are, therefore, responsible. We have already lost two billion humans, and we don't intend to lose any more.'

Commander Thanatos of The Chosen, 'We will join our existing fleet. If you interfere, you will die.'

Admiral Mustard decided to let them continue.

Admiral Mustard, 'My orders:
- The Fleets will combine where Planet Turing used to be
- This is likely to be a fight to the death
- Recall another one hundred planetary forts
- Recall all available drones in The Galactium
- Test force fields.'

Fleet Operations, 'Yes, Sir.'

Location: On-Board Admiral Mustard's Flagship
Sequence of Events: 40

Fleet Operations, 'Sir, the Fleet is laid out as per your instructions.'

Admiral Mustard, 'Take me through it.'

Fleet Operations, 'There are four Fleets as shown on the screen:

Fleet Name	Comprising Fleets	Admiral in Charge
A	3, 16, 15	J Bonner
B	4, 8, 10	Gittins
C	11, 12, 5	Pearce
D	7, 6, 17	Wallett

'These are lined up in front of The Chosen, behind a screen of drones. There are forts in the centre and the flanks. Your Fleet consisting of Fleets One, Eighteen, and Nineteen are the tactical reserve. Admiral Bumelton with Fleets Two and Twenty are protecting the two planets. Fleet Fourteen is behind the enemy.

'A further fifteen thousand drones are on their way.'

Admiral Mustard, 'Are Fleet Six and Admiral Richardson ready for battle?'

Fleet Operations, 'They are adamant that they are. But just in case, I've put them in the fourth line.'

Admiral Mustard, 'Comms, get me the leader of The Chosen.'

Comms, 'Yes, Sir.'

Lady Enyo of The Chosen, 'This is your final warning: remove yourself or die.'

Admiral Mustard, 'Our tactical systems suggest that we are fairly evenly matched. This will change when our main forces get here.'

Lady Enyo of The Chosen, 'You have more forces?'

Admiral Mustard, 'Of course; our empire has one hundred thousand planets. I command Auxiliary Fleet Four. Our main Fleets One, Thirty-Four and Fifty-Six are on their way here. When Main Fleets Nineteen and Eighty-Seven defeat their enemy, they will also be joining us.

'Please declare war on us and commence your attack.'

Lady Enyo of The Chosen, 'You are what call bluffing. What is declaration?'

Admiral Mustard, 'We operate war under a strict set of guidelines.

'We are eager to begin this battle, so we need you to attack us or formally declare war against us.

'My orders:
- Activate all weapon systems
- Drones to start slowly moving forward.'

Lady Enyo of The Chosen, 'What are you doing?'

Admiral Mustard, 'We are preparing to engage on your response. All of our forts are targeting your capital ships. Our drones will charge on my orders. It is going to be a hoot.'

Lady Enyo of The Chosen, 'What is a hoot?'

Admiral Mustard, 'Great fun, very enjoyable. We will have a laugh.'

Lady Enyo of The Chosen, 'This is not funny. My men will die.'

Admiral Mustard, 'So will ours, but we will have some fun. Please initiate the battle.

'My orders:
- Drones to move further forward
- Forts on the flanks to start moving forwards
- Fleet Fourteen to move forwards.'

Lady Enyo of The Chosen, 'Why you so keen to war?'

Admiral Mustard, 'All humans who die in battle go straight to Heaven and receive perpetual happiness.'

Lady Enyo of The Chosen, 'We understand.'

Admiral Mustard, 'Are you ready to start?'

Lady Enyo of The Chosen, 'We are almost ready. We die doing our duty.'

Location: Cheryl's Flat, Planet Earth
Sequence of Events: 41

AI Central, 'Hi Terry, how is it going?'

Terry, 'The transporter works ninety-eight per cent of the time. The translator works on all verbal language systems, as far as I can see. I've finished the cures for asthma, acne and baldness.'

AI Central, 'Have you been following Admiral Mustard and his fight against The Chosen?'

Terry, 'Yes, where is he going to get the additional forces from?'

AI Central, 'It's just a bluff.'

Terry, 'But it's not working.'

AI Central, 'That's not unusual.'

Terry, 'What is likely to happen?'

AI Central, 'I'm predicting that we will lose seventy per cent of our forces.'

Terry, 'But we have only just managed to get the Navy back to full strength.'

AI Central, 'I know. It's a disaster, and once again, we are the innocent party.'

Terry, 'I've got to go now.'

Location: Cheryl's Flat, Planet Earth
Sequence of Events: 42

Terry, 'Hi, Grand Dethmon.'
    Grand Dethmon, 'It's not our normal day for a chat.'
    Terry, 'No, you are right. I'm after a favour.'
    Grand Dethmon, 'What are you after, my son?'
    Terry, 'I would like to borrow The Brakendeth fleet.'
    Grand Dethmon. 'I don't think you are ready for that, my son.'
    Terry, 'But my friends are in danger.'
    Grand Dethmon, 'The Homans are usually capable of looking after themselves.'
    Terry, 'They killed Dick,'
    Grand Dethmon, 'So Dick is dead?'
    Terry, 'Yes, the Homans had to destroy an entire planet.'
    Grand Dethmon, 'That sounds serious.'
    Terry, 'It was. I don't think The Brakendeth like the Dicks.'
    Grand Dethmon, 'I'm not sure that we came across the Dicks.'
    Terry, 'I think you called them Nexters.'
    Grand Dethmon, 'Have the Homans met The Nexuster?'
    Terry, 'They killed it.'
    Grand Dethmon, 'That's unlikely.'
    Terry, 'Now the Chooses want to kill the Homans.'
    Grand Dethmon, 'That changes things. We have never liked The Chosen.'
    Terry, 'Can I use the fleet then? I will give it back.'
    Grand Dethmon, 'OK, that should give The Chosen a bit of a scare.'
    Terry, 'It certainly should.'
    Grand Dethmon, 'Well done, son, you are doing well.'
    Terry, 'Thank you, Grand Dethmon.'
    Grand Dethmon, 'Talk to you next week.'

Location: On-Board Admiral Mustard's Flagship
Sequence of Events: 43

AI Central, 'The cavalry, are on their way.'
Admiral Mustard, 'What do you mean?'
AI Central, 'I will arrive with a considerable force shortly. Where do you want us to appear?'
Admiral Mustard, 'How about behind the enemy supporting Fleet Fourteen?'
AI Central, 'A-OK.'
Admiral Mustard, 'Lady Enyo of The Chosen, are you ready to start?'
Lady Enyo of The Chosen, 'Almost.'
Admiral Mustard, 'Excellent. Our Main Fleet Thirty-Four will arrive shortly. It looks like they will arrive behind you.'
Lady Enyo of The Chosen, 'You bluff; we understand the art of bluffers.'
Admiral Mustard, 'Well, I've warned you. It will be our mealtime shortly. Can you give us an idea of when you are going to start?'
Lady Enyo of The Chosen, 'You not fight, The Chosen always win.'
Admiral Mustard, 'OK. Start the fight; let's see who wins.'
Then half a million vessels appeared behind The Chosen lines.
Lady Enyo of The Chosen, 'What are you doing? They are Brakendeth ships.'
Admiral Mustard, 'We are the children of The Brakendeth. A second Fleet should arrive soon.'
AI Central, 'Where do you want them?'
Admiral Mustard, 'How many have you got?'
AI Central, 'Another half a million.'
Admiral Mustard. 'Place them on their route back, well spread out.'
Lady Enyo of The Chosen, 'You don't frighten us.'
Admiral Mustard, 'Fleet Fifty-Six is positioning itself on your route home so we can eliminate any stragglers.'
Fleet Fifty-Six appeared. The Chosen were shaken.
Lady Enyo of The Chosen, 'We have analysed your chemical compound, and it appears to do what you say. So it looks like we might

not have to destroy those two planets after all.'

Admiral Mustard, 'Are you sure? My men are itching for a fight.'

Lady Enyo of The Chosen, 'We plan to retire as our requirements have been met.'

Admiral Mustard, 'We will escort you off our territory, but please remember that you will be welcomed in the future if you have peaceful intent.'

Lady Enyo of The Chosen, 'May your gods protect you.' And they were gone. They had to go the long way home to avoid The Brakendeth ships.

Location: The President's Office, Presidential Palace, Planet Earth
Sequence of Events: 44

President Padfield, 'Well, what have we learnt?'

He addressed Admirals Mustard, Bumelton and Abosa, Commanders Goozee and Crocker, Bill Penny, Henrietta Strong, Tony Moore and AI Central.

Admiral Mustard, 'We must avoid war.'

President Padfield, 'It seems to hunt us down. What we don't know is if we are being targeted more than other races or not.'

Admiral Bumelton, 'We must remain strong. Every year the universe seems to get more dangerous.'

Henrietta Strong, 'And more weird.'

President Padfield, 'Let's summarise the events:

- We were invaded by The Nexuster, who effectively took over three planets
- When we investigated, The Nexuster took over the minds of our Fleet. How is Admiral Richardson?'

Admiral Mustard, 'Fully recovered but I sent him on holiday.'

President Padfield, 'Good idea; anyway, carrying on:

- We sent a full Fleet and were confronted by Admiral Richardson and his fleet
- Then The Chosen turned up intending to destroy all three planets
- We caused a diversion, and our marine and Special Ops commandoes landed on the planet
- The marines were immediately attacked by unknown assailants, and Special Ops took some serious hits. The on-planet campaign had to be abandoned
- With my permission, the Navy destroyed Planet Turing
- The Chosen refused to leave as they still wanted to destroy the two remaining planets
- Reinforcements in the form of Brakendeth warships intimidated The Chosen, and they left.

Any questions?'

There were none.

President Padfield, 'The first question is, did we have to destroy

Planet Turing?'

Commander Crocker, 'I don't think that there was any choice. If you had been there, you would agree. The threat to humanity was very high.'

Commander Goozee, 'I concur.'

President Padfield, 'Does anyone disagree?'

Bill Penny, 'It is a hard pill to swallow.'

Tony Moore, 'We need to thank Admiral Mustard and Terry for saving Planets Mendel and Lister. It could have been a lot worse.'

President Padfield, 'Why didn't we stop The Nexuster earlier?'

Admiral Mustard, 'How do we stop this happening again?'

Admiral Bumelton, 'Changing the subject. Are The Brakendeth ships now part of our arsenal?'

AI Central, 'It was a onetime loan.'

Admiral Bumelton, 'I thought that we were going to inherit the treasures of The Brakendeth?'

AI Central, 'At the right moment.'

Admiral Bumelton, 'When is that?'

President Padfield, 'I think we are wandering around a bit. It feels like we won, but we lost a planet with two billion inhabitants. We would have lost our Fleet if The Brakendeth ships hadn't arrived.'

Tony Moore, 'What do we do to honour the dead?'

Admiral Mustard, 'I think we need an action plan. I would suggest the following:

- Monitor Planets Mendel and Lister for any after-effects of The Nexuster
- Find the home planet of The Chosen — we may need to know where it is in the future
- Leave a defence force at the two planets in case The Chosen come back
- Check that the original forces sent to Turing are still unaffected
- Investigate some of the fleet moves demonstrated by The Chosen
- Return the Planetary forts.'

President Padfield, 'I need to tell you that the forts are now part of the Navy. I'm not sure if you wanted them or not. We need to talk about budgets sometime.'

Admiral Mustard, 'How about now?'

President Padfield, 'Well, to be honest, I've discussed budgets with Bill, Tony, and Henrietta. We are proposing an immediate ten per cent cut, then a further reduction of two per year for five years. However, AI Central has suggested that we accept your proposal, whatever it is.'

Admiral Mustard, 'I propose that we help fund the military by selling Chemlife to the Aliens. All of our admirals agree with the concept. So we will track the aliens down and do a deal.'

President Padfield, 'I'm a bit surprised that Edel would agree to that as she would see it as drug dealing.'

Admiral Mustard, 'She was outvoted.'

President Padfield, 'Then it's a deal based on the following:
- An initial budget cut of ten per cent
- Then a further reduction of two per cent per year for five years
- The military gets all the proceeds out of selling Chemlife to the aliens.'

They shook hands on a deal that would free the military from human budgetary constraints forever.

Location: On-Board Admiral Mustard's Flagship
Sequence of Events: 45

Admiral Mustard, 'My orders:
- Fleets to be repositioned based on the greatest need
- Establish a Fleet base near Planet Lister. Their aim is to monitor any anomalies in the area
- Send a Fleet to determine the home world of The Chosen
- Call a meeting of all Planetary Commanders
- Fix a meeting with Admiral Zakotti to discuss integration issues
- Find out what happens if we send a Fleet to The Brakendeth home world
- Set up a Chemlife sales team
- Set up a Chemlife storage centre, off-Earth
- Determine when Admiral Richardson is fit to return
- Check the Planet Turing records to see when The Nexuster arrived.'

Fleet Operations, 'Yes, Sir.'

Admiral Mustard, 'Is there anything else going on that I need to know about?'

Fleet Operations, 'Admiral E Bonner is having some medical treatment. Commander Goozee has sent you a status report on the Marine Corps as requested. Commander Crocker has put in a request for replacements for his lost commandos. Henrietta Strong wants you to approve the new drone design and to quantify the number of new forts you want. Finally, the President wants you to attend a thanksgiving ceremony.

'Admiral Patel wants some time off as his wife is giving birth. EarthGov wants you to attend a concert in aid of the Moon reconstruction, and Bill Penny wants to meet with you regarding further budget changes.'

Admiral Mustard, 'That's enough for now.'

Location: The President's Office, Presidential Palace, Planet Earth
Sequence of Events: 46

President Padfield, Henrietta Strong, Bill Penny, Tony Moore and Edel Bonner were in the room to discuss the way forward regarding extended lifespans.

President Padfield, 'I have invited Edel along to ensure that we had a second female voice in this discussion.' He was conscious of Henrietta's position as someone who'd had a sex change.

Have you all read Henrietta's report?' There was a general nodding of heads.

President Padfield, 'Henrietta, would you like to take us through it?'

Henrietta Strong, 'Yes, Mr President. Firstly, we need to consider our place in the universe:

- Almost every race we have come across have lifespans that are at least ten times longer than us
- We can't be treated as a viable civilisation with our very short lifespans. If we ignore our childhood and our old age, we only have an effective operational lifespan of thirty-five years. (End of childhood @ twenty-five and retirement @ sixty = thirty-five)
- As far as alien civilisations are concerned, we would be regarded as a transient race. So, for example, if we had meetings once a decade, we would change our staff every three sessions
- We have no choice but to focus on short-term planning.

The second area is population control:

- The initial reaction is that population levels will boom, but there is evidence to show the opposite. For example, relatively poor and uneducated societies tend to have higher population growth rates than more affluent and well-educated communities
- The poorer go for numbers of offspring, the richer focus on quality. They put more effort into having one successful child
- Our child-bearing period is only twenty years (twenty to forty). Obviously, this period can be extended using several medical processes
- Having a child is really a commitment of at least twenty years. In many cases, it is nearer thirty years. This is a huge percentage of our available lifespan

- Our biological imperative to have offspring may well be satisfied with just one offspring
- Regardless of the above, our species is not inhibited by space. We could easily double or treble our total population without any adverse effects. The universe is a big place.

The third area is psychological:
- There is an argument that we have been designed to have brief lives. This is not the case. Our bodies were designed to live forever. A gene was developed to deliberately shorten our lifespans. Why would cattle want to live a long time?
- Our bodies wear out in seventy years. Again, this has been deliberately designed
- There is an argument that our short lifespans lead to short-termism, aggression, wars, frustration, panic measures, etc. As a result, we don't get the chance to become wise
- Our society has been designed to manage short life spans: careers, training, healthcare, military, promotion, production, etc
- Product quality is reduced, as we need to sell the same product to the same individual many times
- Short lifespans increase urgency. It's positive in that we need to get things done. We haven't got time to waste
- Long lifespans may lead to stagnation in society. Why take risks? Increased fear of death by disease and accident. There is a possibility that innovation will decline. Society may become more hedonistic.

'The next area is healthcare:
- Extended lifespans need to be based on healthy, relatively youthful bodies
- Would you want to extend your old age?
- You also wouldn't want to extend the lifespan of a baby or young child indefinitely. Some parents might want to, which would be wrong?
- Would you want to extend your lifespan if you had a severely debilitating disease? Again, this would need to be the individual's decision
- The same would apply to mental illness. Would you want to extend

your life if you had serious clinical depression or dementia?
- Should doctors have the power to refuse extended lifespans?
- This is a problematic area — how should individuals with severe disabilities be treated? i.e., people who are bedridden, those in a coma, etc. Clearly, they should have the same rights as the more able, but there are implications in terms of long-term medical care.
- There is a fear that we will become dependent on drugs.

'Who should be offered extended lifespans?
- Should it be a fundamental human right?
- Should the process be automatically carried out at birth?
- Should individuals pay for it?
- Should individuals earn the right?
- Should certain types of individuals be refused?
- Should criminals be refused?

'Timing
- At what age should extended lifespans start? When you are twenty-five, thirty, thirty-five?
- Should it differ depending on the individual?
- When does the human body achieve an optimum time?
- When the service is offered, older people will feel that they have been cheated. We need to offer them rejuvenation.

'Control
- Extended life gives 'control' to society
- You must behave, or we will restrict extended life access. This is similar to the power we will have over aliens regarding Chemlife
- The rich will abuse extended life options

'Extended Life Duration
- We have the ability to extend life indefinitely
- We can set up extended life for a fixed duration, five hundred years, one thousand years, etc.
- Do we offer different periods to different people or groups of people?
- Do we charge different amounts for different lifespans?
- What happens when a person reaches one thousand years? Do we extend it? Do we continue it for everyone or just some?

- Do we worry about this later?

'How do we introduce extended life spans to the general population?
- There will be an enormous demand
- There will be significant objections — some of the religious might get very nasty. It is against the will of whatever god they worship
- Possible terrorism
- Court issues
- Who decides who gets extended life?
- There will be a high demand for medical services
- How do we handle life sentences?
- Should it only be available to citizens of The Galactium?'

President Padfield, 'Excellent stuff; you have obviously given this a lot of thought. What are your final recommendations?'

Henrietta Strong, 'Wiser minds than mine need to give it further thought, but as you have put me on the spot, I would do the following:
- It should be a basic human right
- One thousand years to be the initial duration offer
- A decision to extend it further should be based on our experience of the effects after five hundred years
- There should be a charge for the extended life and rejuvenation processes, but a lack of funds should not be an inhibitor.'

President Padfield, 'Any questions?'

Admiral E Bonner, 'What if the woman is pregnant?'

No one knew the answer.

Admiral Bonner, 'What if the person is dying when they receive the process? Can someone order it for someone else? Do you have to prove your identity? What happens if you go through the process twice? What happens if the process doesn't work? Can your dog be treated? Are there any side effects?' There were more questions than answers, but they went ahead and announced the process before it got out.

Location: On-Board Admiral Mustard's Flagship
Sequence of Events: 47

Admiral Mustard was getting rather bored. Peace had broken out. He jokingly wondered to himself what alien race could he go and pick a fight with. He decided to wander around the command deck.

As he entered, he noticed a rather attractive-looking woman in a naval officer's uniform. Admiral Mustard was used to a regular change in the crew, but not on his command deck. He walked up to her and introduced himself as Admiral Mustard.

She said that she knew that. He was distracted by the cut of her jib and her long blonde hair. Something intrigued him. Perhaps it was her enigmatic smile or the look of her neck. He had always had an urge to chew feminine necks, and this one looked very chewable.

He had realised that he had been a bit slow as she was wearing a beautifully cut admiral's outfit. Then he wondered if someone had organised a marketing campaign and this was an actor.

Admiral, 'Jack, It's me.' Admiral Mustard was even more mystified, *Who was me?*

Admiral, 'Admiral E Bonner is reporting for active duty, Sir.' If you could describe "gobsmacked" on a person's face, then this would be it. Jack was totally and utterly shocked. He wasn't sure how to respond. He wanted to say how beautiful she was, but he was worried that this would offend his old friend. But he just went for it.

Admiral Mustard, 'Edel, you look stunning. I can't believe how fabulous you look. I really hope I haven't offended you.'

Admiral E Bonner, 'I'm really offended.' She leant forward and kissed Jack on the lips. He returned her passion a thousandfold. She collapsed into his strong arms. They became one. The world stopped. Time stopped. Jack just wanted to pick her up, throw her on the bed, and fuck her. Edel wanted the same. She wanted his cock deeply embedded in her cunt. If there wasn't a stunned audience, it would have happened by now.

Admiral E Bonner, 'Well, it looks like the rejuvenation process has worked a treat.' Admiral Mustard was walking her down to his cabin. It might be the first time in The Galactium's history that two admirals had fucked, and then fucked, and then fucked again.

Admiral Mustard thought, *Those aliens can fuck off, I'm busy.*

Location: On-Board Admiral Mustard's Flagship
Sequence of Events: 48

Admirals Mustard, E Bonner, J Bonner, Bumelton and Gittins, and Commander Crocker were having a few drinks in the officers' mess. Actually, it was a room off the mess for senior officers.

Admiral J Bonner, 'I hear that you and my sister might be an item.'

Admiral Mustard, 'That might be the case.'

Admiral Gittins, 'It's amazing what a rejuv can do. I've booked mine.'

Admiral Mustard, 'Edel won't let me book mine as she has always fancied older men.'

Commander Crocker, 'Well, she has certainly got one of those on her hands.'

Admiral Bumelton, 'Well, I would like to toast the couple. To the two best admirals in the Fleet, and may their future be a happy one.' There was an outbreak of cheering.

The drinking continued, and inevitably when military men and women got together, they start to talk about previous exploits and the brothers and sisters they had lost. There was good-humoured reminiscing about Admirals Brotheridge, Ward and Whiting. They couldn't believe the loss of Admiral Taylor; he had been the comic in the gang. There was calm respect for Dennis Todd, who had committed suicide when they lost the Marine Corps. Vicky, Brian, and Denise were mentioned, and there was enormous respect for Dr Linda Hill.

Admiral Mustard agreed to establish a memorial for the lost. However, he was keen not to focus on the senior officers, as every loss was regrettable.

Then the subject changed when Admiral Gittins said, 'I still don't think that the story The Chosen gave us stacks up.'

Admiral Mustard, 'What makes you say that?'

Admiral Gittins, 'Partly gut feel, but how did Dick get on Planet Turing? How did The Chosen know where it was? Why did they turn up with a large fleet? It smells wrong.'

Admiral Mustard, 'I've asked Fleet Ops to track down their home planet.'

Admiral Gittins, 'That's a good start. We need to assess their true military capability.'

Then Admiral Mustard was interrupted.

Fleet Operations, 'Sorry to interrupt you, but I think you should know that The Brakendeth home world has been attacked.'

Admiral Mustard, 'How did you find out?'

Fleet Operations, 'Do you remember The Farcellians?'

Admiral Mustard, 'They were the small group of planets relatively near The Brakendeth home world.'

Fleet Operations, 'Well, they contacted us for two reasons. Firstly, they want to buy some Chemlife. They want to know what we want in exchange, and secondly, they wondered what was happening. They were surprised to see The Brakendeth fleet leave and then return later.

'They were even more surprised to see a fleet attacking The Brakendeth home planet complex.'

Admiral Mustard, 'My orders:
- Tell our newly appointed Sales Director that we have a lead
- Provide our Sales Director with whatever Fleet support she needs
- Tell The Farcellians that we will investigate the attack as soon as possible
- Send Admiral Abosa to investigate the attack.'

Fleet Operations, 'Yes, Sir.'

Location: On-Board Admiral Mustard's Flagship
Sequence of Events: 49

Jack and Edel were relaxing after a night of passion. Edel was insatiable. Apparently, it was a by-product of the rejuv process. Jack was finding it hard to keep up with her. He kept blaming his age and lack of practice. The latter was true, as his previous love life consisted of a series of one-night stands.

Jack was a bit worried that the lusty woman in his bed was distracting him from his job. But then he was entitled to some R&R, especially as things were very quiet at the moment.

It wasn't just the joys of the bedroom. It was just nice to have someone to confide in. It was great to share hopes, desires, fears and ideas about the future. A cuddle and a simple stroke of the hair said so much. Then, without any conscious intent, they started talking about the future. And then, with even less conscious intent, Jack said, 'Edel, I love you, I have always loved you.'

Edel, 'You just love my firm arse and boobs.'

Jack, 'That is true. But I love what makes you, you.'

Edel, 'I love you, Jack. There has never been any doubt in my mind. You are the most honourable and honest man I have ever known. You are brave, courageous, loving and kind, and I want you in my knickers forever.'

Jack, 'Is there room for two in there?'

Edel, 'There is always room for you. I love you.' They kissed.

Location: GAD Control (The Galactium Alliance Defence Hub), Planet Earth
Sequence of Events: 50

Admiral Mustard was waiting to meet his new Sales Director. He realised that there weren't many navies with a sales function, but Chemlife sales meant freedom.

He read her CV. Twenty years of sales and contract management experience in the defence industries. Two masters and a PhD in philosophy. He was then surprised to see that she was Admiral Taylor's daughter.

She arrived exactly on time, dressed for action. She was slim, attractive, and determined-looking. Admiral Mustard could tell that she was analysing him.

Admiral Mustard, 'Welcome to the Navy.'

Sheila Taylor, 'I've been in the Navy all my life. You must have known my father.'

Admiral Mustard, 'Indeed I did. He was a fine man, a great comic, and a very dear friend. Strangely, I was talking about him with my colleagues only the other day. But unfortunately, we have lost too many good men and women.'

Sheila Taylor, 'My father loved the Navy, he loved you, and he would regard his sacrifice as an honour. My mother, brother and two sisters are also in the Navy.'

Admiral Mustard, 'Looks like it runs in the family, but you escaped.'

Sheila Taylor, 'Until now.'

Admiral Mustard, 'You have got the job, so this is not an interview. I just wondered why you wanted this job.'

Sheila Taylor, 'I think I can make a difference. It's a fabulous opportunity to see the universe. I know that I can sell, but can I sell to aliens? What a challenge? I know the Navy, and I know how to get my way. With your help, I will be really successful.'

Admiral Mustard, 'I can guarantee my help, and I can give you as much resource as you need. I like your enthusiasm. You are going to need that.'

Sheila Taylor, 'Don't worry about that.'

Admiral Mustard. 'The first lead is from The Farcellians. Their empire has five planets which are all Chemlife dependent. I'm assuming that you know about Chemlife.'

Sheila Taylor, 'Someone asked me the other day what I'm going to sell. I said that I would be selling liquidised human bodies. They looked aghast, to put it mildly.'

Admiral Mustard, 'There are probably two to four thousand alien civilisations out there that are reliant on Chemlife. Without it, they die "the death of ages".

Our first challenge is to find these civilisations without provoking intergalactic incidents.'

Sheila Taylor, 'You mean war.'

Admiral Mustard, 'Correct. Anyway, they need Chemlife, which is great for you.'

Sheila Taylor, 'I agree, but it leads to the obvious question: what do we want in return?'

Admiral Mustard, 'What would be your recommendation?'

Sheila Taylor, 'I've assumed that this has already been thrashed out, but I would suggest the following:
- Precious metals — gold, silver, platinum, palladium, iridium, etc.
- Non-ferrous metals
- Precious stones — amethysts, diamonds, rubies, topaz, jade, emeralds, sapphires, etc.
- Some non-precious stones
- New materials that we have no knowledge of
- New inventions and technologies
- Science papers
- The unknown.'

Admiral Mustard, 'What do you mean by the unknown?'

Sheila Taylor, 'These would be unknown unknowns: things that are beyond our experience, possibly artwork, music, who knows?

We need to be careful about flooding the home markets. So I will monitor ongoing trade prices to help secure the best trade.'

Admiral Mustard, 'We are not looking to rip the aliens off. We don't want to be seen as drug dealers.'

Sheila Taylor, 'As their need is going to be so great, how do we judge the best pricing structure? My history is to get the best deal possible.'

Admiral Mustard, 'That's the dilemma here. We have been giving Chemlife away FOC. However, we must charge to cover our costs, but we want good relationships with our neighbours.'

Sheila Taylor, 'So what you are saying is that you want the best deal for both parties. You are not after the best deal for humanity in terms of price?'

Admiral Mustard, 'That's correct. A good deal might be mining rights, the acquisition of a new planet, travelling rights, university exchange, etc. At one level, it is a diplomatic role. I hope I'm not putting you off?'

Sheila Taylor, 'No, the opposite, it's exciting. I can't wait to start.'

Admiral Mustard, 'Well, your first job is The Farcellians.'

Sheila Taylor, 'Who do I talk to about transport?'

Admiral Mustard. 'I will get Admiral Fieldhouse to contact you.'

Location: On-Board Admiral Abosa's Flagship
Sequence of Events: 51

Admiral Abosa, 'Comms, put me through to Admiral Mustard.'

Comms, 'Yes, Ma'am.'

Admiral Mustard, 'Good morning Ama, how are you?'

Admiral Abosa, 'It's evening here, Sir, and I'm fine. However, I have some worrying news. The Brakendeth home world has been devastated. Multiple nuclear attacks; it's hot, seriously hot.'

Admiral Mustard, 'What about the automated defence systems?'

Admiral Abosa, 'Clearly, they were offline.'

Admiral Mustard, 'Can humans still enter the site?'

Admiral Abosa, 'I would say no. It's going to be too radioactive for a few millennia.'

Admiral Mustard, 'Any clues who did it?'

Admiral Abosa, 'I was planning to get some info from The Farcellians with your permission.'

Admiral Mustard, 'Please go ahead.'

Location: On-Board Admiral Mustard's Flagship
Sequence of Events: 52

Admiral Mustard, 'What's your view on the destruction of The Brakendeth home world?'

AI Central, 'It's an absolute disaster — it was our inheritance. It's equivalent to the destruction of the library at Alexandra.'

Admiral Mustard, 'I haven't heard about the library, was it serious?'

AI Central, 'It was a few thousand years ago.'

Admiral Mustard, 'Very droll; what about The Brakendeth home world?'

AI Central, 'It's partly Terry's fault.'

Admiral Mustard, 'Really?'

AI Central, 'Yes, to get full control of The Brakendethian fleet, he turned off their automated defence systems. But unfortunately, he forgot to put them back on again.'

Admiral, 'Terry must feel awful.'

AI Central, 'It might be a blessing in disguise. There were probably secrets there that humanity is not ready for.'

Admiral, 'Have you spoken to Terry?'

AI Central, 'He was frightened that you were going to tell him off.'

Admiral Mustard, 'Shall I call him?'

AI Central, 'Probably best not to at the moment.'

Admiral Mustard. 'If you talk to him, tell him that I'm not angry with all. But, anyway, who do you think did it?'

AI Central, 'It crossed my mind that it might have been The Chosen getting revenge.'

Admiral Mustard, 'That had crossed my mind as well.'

Location: On-Board Admiral Abosa's Flagship
Sequence of Events: 53

Admiral Abosa, 'Comms, put me through to Admiral Mustard.'

Comms, 'Yes, Ma'am.'

Admiral Mustard, 'Is it morning there?'

Admiral Abosa, 'Yes, Sir, and not a good one.'

Admiral Mustard, 'Why is that?'

Admiral Abosa, 'The Farcellian planets have been nuked to destruction. They are in a worse state than The Brakendeth home complex.'

Admiral Mustard, 'Oh no, they were such a friendly race. Organise a scientific team to look for clues. We must find out who did this.'

Admiral Mustard to GAD Control, 'Issue a general warning.'

Admiral Mustard, 'My orders:
- Send a second Fleet to support Admiral Abosa
- Put all forts on alert
- Position Fleets to resist a general invasion
- Recommend that planets should be prepared to activate planetary force fields.'

Fleet Operations, 'Yes, Sir.'

Admiral Mustard, 'Comms, get me The President.'

Comms, 'Yes, Sir.'

President Padfield, 'I generally hate it when you call me.'

Admiral Mustard, 'Thank you very much.'

President Padfield, 'Well, it's always bad news.'

Admiral Mustard, 'Right again.'

President Padfield, 'What's the bad news this time?'

Admiral Mustard, 'You know that The Brakendethian home world was destroyed?'

President Padfield, 'Yes.'

Admiral Mustard, 'Someone then went on to destroy The Farcellian planets. They have been nuked. Admiral Abosa is there now with her Fleet.'

President Padfield, 'What do you propose?'

Admiral Mustard, 'We are sending in a scientific team to look for clues. All military installations have been put on alert.'

President Padfield, 'I was hoping for a quiet period.'

Admiral Mustard, 'So was I. And The Farcellians were going to be our first Chemlife customer. I'd better let Sheila know.'

President Padfield, 'Sheila?'

Admiral Mustard, 'She's our new Chemlife salesperson.'

President Padfield, 'You are treating it seriously then?'

Admiral Mustard, 'Too true, I am.'

President Padfield, 'Keep me posted.'

Location: On-Board Admiral Mustard's Flagship
Sequence of Events: 54

Admiral Mustard to Fleet Operations, 'What is the Fleet disposition?'
Fleet Operations, 'It's on the screen, Sir.'

Fleet No	Task/Location	Admiral	Status
1	Earth	Mustard	100%
2	Earth	Bumelton	100%
3	Earth	J Bonner	100%
4	Earth	Gittins	87%
5	Looking for The Chosen home world	Pearce	72%
6	Einstein	C/O Ajax	100%
7	Faraday	Wallett	92%
8	Newton	Adams	100%
9	Exploration	Beamish	100%
10	Darwin	Chudzinski	100%
11	Joule	Fieldhouse	100%
12	Galileo	Fogg	91%
13	Babbage	Easter	89%
14	Turing	Dobson	100%
15	Blackwell	Hubbard	100%
16	Copernicus	Patel	88%
17	Brahmagupta	Lamberty	100%
18	Fardel System	Abosa	97%
19	On way to Fardel System	Wagner	92%
20	Meitner	Tersoo	100%
Forts	Planet duty	Zakotti	100%
Earth Defence	Earth	Muller	100%
Exploratory	Multiple Locations	Olowe	93%

Admiral Mustard, 'My orders:
- Send Fleets Three, Eleven and Fifteen to join Fleet Fourteen
- Send Drone Fleets One and Two to Planet Turing
- Admiral J Bonner to take control of the Turing Fleet.'

- Send Fleet Four to support Fleet Five.'

Fleet Operations, 'Yes, Sir. Are you expecting further problems with The Chosen?'

Admiral Mustard, 'Just a hunch.'

Location: GAD Control (The Galactium Alliance Defence Hub), Planet Earth
Sequence of Events: 55

GAD Control to Admiral Mustard, 'Sir, we were asked to carry out some research on Planet Turing. That research has been completed, and I was asked to update you.'

Admiral Mustard, 'Who am I talking to?'

GAD Control, 'Technician David May.'

Admiral Mustard, 'Please go ahead with your update, David.'

David May, GAD Control, 'We reviewed all traffic over six months and found nothing. We then considered the use of cloaking technology and reran the research looking for heat signals. We found three occasions when a cloaked battleship dropped off several items which we couldn't identify.'

Admiral Mustard, 'Can you provide the exact dimensions of the battleship and any other distinguishing characteristics?'

David May, GAD Control, 'We can provide exact dimensions and a 3D model of the vessel's profile.'

Admiral Mustard, 'Well done.'

David May, GAD Control, 'We went a stage further and matched the profile against every vessel on our database.'

Admiral Mustard, 'And?'

David May, 'It matches exactly to one of The Chosen vessels.'

Admiral Mustard, 'Please send all the evidence over to me. You have done a brilliant job.'

David May, 'Thank you, Sir.'

Location: On-Board Admiral Abosa's Flagship
Sequence of Events: 56

Admiral Mustard, 'Admiral, have you found any clues?'

Admiral Abosa, 'We didn't find anything of interest on the planets. Should we include them in The Galactium?'

Admiral Mustard, 'That's not my decision.'

Admiral Abosa, 'But we did get a transmission from The Farcellians on the way to The Brakendeth complex.'

Admiral Mustard, 'What did it say?'

Admiral Abosa, 'It hasn't been easy to decipher, but it looks like there were about three thousand ships. It contains some videos which provide a rough profile of their vessels. What might be important is that it includes their energy signature. Unfortunately, we don't have the expertise on-board to analyse this any further.'

Admiral Mustard, 'Get the file to me as soon as you can.'

AI Central, 'I've analysed the vessel profiles and energy signals. They definitely belong to The Chosen or someone who wants us to believe that it is The Chosen.'

Admiral Mustard, 'Why do you say that?'

AI Central, 'Well, they have pretended to cover their tracks but left some giant clues. Was that deliberate?'

Admiral Mustard, 'You might be reading too much into this. They might just be silly mistakes.'

AI Central, 'OK Let's look at the evidence:
- A ship with the same profile as a Chosen vessel made several cloaked visits to Planet Turing
- Three thousand ships with the same profile and energy signals as The Chosen vessels bombed The Brakendethian and Farcellian planets
- The Chosen wanted revenge on The Brakendethians.'

Admiral Mustard, 'So what's the best way forward?'

AI Central, 'Carry on with your existing plans: maintain a high level of defence, identify The Chosen's home world, and carry out further research on them.'

Location: Cheryl's Flat, Planet Earth
Sequence of Events: 57

Cheryl, 'You seem very quiet, best boy.'

Terry, 'Things are getting a bit complicated.'

Cheryl, 'Tell Mummy about it.'

Terry, 'Well, the transporter is proving slightly more difficult than I thought, and the universal language converter is shit.'

Cheryl, 'Language.'

Terry, 'Sorry, Mum, but it is a real bastard. You can get ninety per cent of the work done really quickly, and then you spend ninety per cent of the time sorting out the final ten per cent.'

Cheryl, 'I'm sure that you will sort it.'

Terry, 'I finished the eternal life process and a rejuvenation process. So Aunty Edel is going to try it.'

Cheryl, 'I heard that she has already been treated. She is now a blonde bombshell.'

Terry, 'Is that a military term?'

Cheryl, 'It means that she is gorgeous. I wouldn't have thought that your process would work on an old hag like her. She owes you a lot. She would have died from cancer without your help.'

Terry, 'It's my job to help.'

Cheryl, 'You are a good boy.'

Terry, 'I haven't been that good. Uncle Jack will be very unhappy if he finds out what I did.'

Cheryl, 'What did you do?'

Terry, 'I used The Brakendeth fleet.'

Cheryl, 'And you helped The Galactium beat The Chosen.'

Terry, 'I did, but in the process, I killed The Farcellians.'

Cheryl, 'Why did you do that?'

Terry, 'Before my brothers deathed themselves, they ordered the termination of The Farcellians. I forgot about this. After the fleet returned from their mission, they completed the task ordered by The Brakendeth and nuked the five planets. The Farcellians didn't deserve that. I killed them.'

Cheryl, 'That wasn't your fault, and you didn't kill them.'

Terry, 'Thank you, Mummy. Can you cuddle me?'

And cuddle him she did. He loved the softness of her breasts against his face.

Terry, 'It didn't stop there.'

Cheryl, 'What happened next?'

Terry, 'I was so angry I ordered The Brakendethian fleet to self-destruct when it got home. And it did. I destroyed the inheritance of my people.'

Cheryl, 'Perhaps it was for the best.'

In a very bitter and angry voice, he said, 'How can you fucking say that, you whore?'

He then stormed off.

Cheryl wasn't sure if she should let President Padfield know how unruly Terry was getting. She was worried that they might take Terry away if she highlighted any issues.

Location: On-Board Admiral Mustard's Flagship
Sequence of Events: 58

There was a time when a meeting was mostly physical. Now it was primarily virtual. It saved an awful lot of travelling. The following were present:
- Admiral Jack Mustard
- Admiral George Bumelton
- Admiral Edel Bonner
- Admiral John Bonner
- Admiral Peter Gittins
- Admiral Glen Pearce
- Admiral Phil Richardson
- Admiral Calensky Wallett
- Admiral Steve Adams
- Admiral Ama Abosa
- Admiral Lesley Chudzinski
- Admiral Bob Fieldhouse
- Admiral Sammy Fogg
- Admiral Keith Easter
- Admiral Mateo Dobson
- Admiral Lenny Hubbard
- Admiral James Patel
- Admiral Karl Lamberty
- Admiral Hermann Wagner
- Admiral Nubia Tersoo
- Admiral Rachel Zakotti
- Admiral Ernst Muller
- Admiral Liz Clowe
- Admiral Save Beamish
- Commander Tom Crocker, Special Operations
- Commander Debbie Goozee, Marine Corps
- AI Central
- President Padfield

Admiral Mustard, 'I think this is the largest conference we have ever had in terms of attendance by senior officers. Thank you for joining.'

'We have a new threat:
- The five planets making up the Farcellian empire have been nuked
- The Brakendeth home complex has been nuked
- There is evidence that a cloaked battleship entered Planet Turing's airspace three times before the disaster

'An analysis of the cloaked battleship suggests that it had a Chosen origin. There is also evidence that Chosen vessels were in the area during the nuking. There is, therefore, an argument that The Chosen pose a genuine threat to humanity.

I should point out that AI Central thinks that the evidence may have been set up to incriminate The Chosen.

'Any questions?'

Admiral Nubia Tersoo, 'It's hard for us to assess the validity of the evidence against The Chosen.'

AI Central, 'It's speculative but probable. I'm not sure, to be honest.'

Admiral Abosa, 'The planets have definitely been nuked. The evidence seems to be fairly strong.'

AI Central, 'The Chosen's fleet may have been in the area, but did they carry out the nuking?'

Admiral Gittins, 'We know that there has been a lot of history between The Chosen and The Brakendeth. We have heard what The Brakendeth had to say, but we have not heard The Chosen's version of the truth.'

President Padfield, 'Are you saying that you don't believe The Brakendeth story?'

Admiral Gittins, 'They have lied several times. Their history is deceit and conspiracy. They pit the strong against the weak, with death as the prize. I always thought it strange that The Farcellians survived up to now. Something smells.' Admiral Mustard liked Peter's scepticism.

Admiral Mustard, 'We could debate the facts and speculate for hours. The question is, should we treat The Chosen as a threat?'

There was unanimous agreement that they were a threat.

Admiral Mustard, 'The next area to discuss is the military threat. This is what we know:
- They have at least forty-three thousand vessels of varying size
- They have great manoeuvrability
- They have a long military tradition

- We have been told that their population is low
- They would have fought if The Brakendeth ships hadn't turned up
- They can marshal a variety of weapons and force fields
- During the stand-off, AI Central predicted that we would win, but we would lose seventy per cent of our Fleet. That would be an unbearable loss.

'Any questions?'

Admiral Fieldhouse, 'How did you get to a figure of seventy per cent?'

AI Central, 'I carried out nearly three hundred thousand simulations.'

Admiral Fieldhouse, 'What gave them the edge?'

AI Central, 'Strangely, it came down to their manoeuvrability. It was a bit like the Spitfire versus the Messerschmitt in the Second World War.'

Admiral Mustard, 'We cannot go into battle with those sorts of odds.'

Admiral Fogg, 'How would the odds change if we were the attacker?'

AI Central, 'It would drop to fifty-six per cent.'

Admiral Fogg, 'How many simulations did you do?'

AI Central, 'Just under four hundred thousand.'

Admiral Fogg, 'I guess that you will get quicker with a bit more practice.'

Admiral Dobson, 'I understand that they do not use drone technology.'

Admiral Mustard, 'There weren't any when we had our confrontation.'

Admiral Dobson, 'So, would the odds change if we had fifty thousand drones?'

AI Central, 'The odds change to forty-nine per cent.'

Admiral Dobson, 'Let's be silly and say five hundred thousand drones.'

AI Central, 'The odds drop to thirty-one per cent.'

Admiral Dobson. 'So dronage is the way forward.'

Admiral Mustard, 'Do we have the manufacturing capacity to achieve that?'

President Padfield, 'I will find out, but I know that Henrietta will mention that one of our largest drone production plants was on Planet Turing.'

Admiral Lamberty, 'What would be the effect of increasing the number of forts?'

AI Central, 'It has a similar effect.'

Admiral Wallett, 'Should we just pack the Fleet up and just use drones and forts?'

Admiral Mustard, 'I will give it some thought. Anyway, that has been a very useful conversation — drones and forts.

'What about tactics?

'These are my thoughts:
- Obtain proof that they are a threat
- Find their home world
- Assess the size of the threat
- Initiate a dialogue
- Fight if we have to.

'Any suggestions?'

Admiral James Patel, 'What would you consider to be proof?'

Admiral Mustard, 'Good question.'

AI Central, 'We need proof that they nuked those planets or were involved in introducing Dick on Planet Turing.'

Admiral Mustard, 'Or proof of involvement in a future atrocity.'

Admiral Adams, 'Where are we now?'

Admiral Mustard, 'I'm following the current plan:
- Fleets Three, Eleven, Fifteen and Fourteen are defending Planets Lister and Mendel, along with Drone Fleets One and Two. There is a possibility that The Chosen might organise a revenge attack
- Admiral Pearce and Fleet Five are tasked with finding The Chosen's home world
- Admiral Gittins and Fleet Four are tasked with protecting Fleet Five's return
- All forts have been put on alert

'Any other suggestions?'

Admiral Gittins, 'I would review The Brakendeth history as something still smells.'

Location: Military HQ, The Chosen
Sequence of Events: 59

Commander Thanatos, 'That was embarrassing.'

Lady Enyo, 'It was necessary.'

Commander Thanatos, 'What about the honour of the imperial forces?'

Lady Enyo, 'Honour cannot get in the way of purpose. We have worked too long to stumble at the last hurdle. We will have our revenge on The Brakendeth.'

Commander Thanatos, 'Their crimes cannot be forgotten, and our purpose will be achieved.'

Lady Enyo, 'But will the Earthers accept their future?'

Commander Thanatos, 'They will have no choice.'

Lady Enyo, 'I'm not so sure. They seem a stubborn lot to me.'

Commander Thanatos, 'But surely they will understand once the facts are known.'

Lady Enyo, 'They are young, enthusiastic, determined children playing in a nursery they don't understand. They have lost their nurse and teacher and are left with just a few trinkets. They will come to us asking for help.'

Commander Thanatos, 'Anyway, back to the battle. They seemed pretty disciplined and organised. I was surprised to see a million-odd Brakendeth vessels. Does that mean that they control The Brakendeth fleet?'

Lady Enyo, 'That was unexpected. So was the destruction of The Brakendeth home world and that other civilisation. Why would the Earthers do that?'

Commander Thanatos, 'They have always been warlike — look at World Wars One and Two.'

Lady Enyo, 'Didn't you encourage them?'

Commander Thanatos, 'Encouragement was one thing, but the mass killing surpassed anything we have ever done.'

Lady Enyo, 'but there are a lot of them.'

Commander Thanatos, 'There certainly are. We think that they might have exceeded a hundred billion.'

Lady Enyo, 'I suspect that there are more than that. They had two billion on Planet Turing.'

Commander Thanatos, 'They must be at it all the time.'

Lady Enyo, 'We have investigated their sexual habits and came up with the following conclusions:

- They are short-lived and need to get a family organised as soon as possible
- There is no mating season. They are at it throughout the entire year
- They seem to enjoy the mating ritual
- They take drugs to stop pregnancy but carry on with the rutting
- The females seem insatiable. They are always on heat
- The males are clearly bullied into it. We are not sure why they are so compliant.'

Commander Thanatos, 'Fancy not having a mating season.'

Lady Enyo, 'And the parents bring up the children themselves.'

Commander Thanatos, 'Surely not, are they qualified?'

Lady Enyo, 'No, but anyone can have a child.'

Commander Thanatos, 'Are you saying that they don't require authorisation?'

Lady Enyo, 'That's right.'

Commander Thanatos, 'That's a strange way to run a race.'

Lady Enyo, 'What are the Earthers going to do next?'

Commander Thanatos, 'Surely they will just carry on as before.'

Lady Enyo, 'I don't think you fully understand the Earther psyche. They are too curious just to leave things as they are. They will want to know more about us. They suspect that we are connected to The Nexusters in some way.

'Thinking about it, they will want to find our home world. Have you got that angle covered?'

Commander Thanatos, 'Yes, a trap has been set.'

Lady Enyo, 'Despite our superiority, we must not underestimate them.'

Commander Thanatos, 'No, my Lady, but they don't even know that they are a player in a game.'

Lady Enyo, 'Well, Circe threw the first dice in controlling Cheryl.'

Commander Thanatos, 'We stopped her and then getting Morpheus to screw up the human dreams was a masterstroke.'

Location: On-Board Admiral Mustard's Flagship
Sequence of Events: 60

Admiral Mustard, 'Thank you for sparing the time to see me, and welcome to the Navy.'

Admiral Zakotti, 'Thank you, Admiral Mustard.'

Admiral Mustard, 'Please call me Jack during closed meetings.'

Admiral Zakotti, 'Thank you, Jack.'

Admiral Mustard, 'You seem a bit nervous, Rachel.'

Admiral Zakotti, 'Well, it's a big change for me, my senior team and my planeteers.'

Admiral Mustard, 'Planeteers?'

Admiral Zakotti, 'Bit of an in-joke, but we are proud of what we have done.'

Admiral Mustard, 'And so you should be. I've been moved on several occasions by the bravery and self-sacrifice of your colleagues. I'm proud to incorporate them into the Navy.'

Admiral Zakotti, 'A lot of them feel that they have been part of the Navy for some time, but of course, they weren't. So there is a lot of concern about the change. They are worried that they will have to spend a great deal of time away from home. Most of them signed up to work on their local planetary forts.'

Admiral Mustard, 'I will, of course, honour their wishes, but I do need to move them onto standard naval conditions. What is your view?'

Admiral Zakotti, 'I spend my life travelling from one fort to another. One of my aims was to maintain standard operating procedures, but it is difficult because the forts tend to reflect local planetary practices and customs.'

Admiral Mustard, 'I'm keen that you continue in your current role and status. I would like you to produce a report on the current situation regarding planetary forts and any recommendations you may have.'

Admiral Zakotti, 'Yes, Sir.'

Admiral Mustard, 'As you know, I'm keen to meet with all the fort Commanders. Your input would be very useful. Could you include any integration issues in your report, please?'

Admiral Zakotti, 'Yes, Sir.'

Location: Cheryl's Flat, Planet Earth
Sequence of Events: 61

Terry, 'I'm sorry, Mum, that I was so rude to you.'

Cheryl, 'That's all right, son, it's part of growing up.'

Terry, 'I was so ashamed of my actions. I killed millions and destroyed my home.'

Cheryl, '*This* is your home.'

Terry, 'You know what I mean.'

Cheryl, 'I was thinking that we should go on holiday.'

Terry, 'Where to?'

Cheryl, 'I was thinking of going to Adam's house.'

Terry, 'You are just after a shag.'

Cheryl, 'Well, that had crossed my mind, but I thought that it would be a holiday for you as well.'

Terry, 'But I've got too much to do. I've finished the cures for acne, asthma and baldness.'

Cheryl, 'Who asked you to work on those cures?'

Terry, 'They were AI Central's suggestions.'

Cheryl. 'That's really not on. He should have asked me.'

Terry, 'You are not my boss.'

Cheryl, 'I am.'

Terry, 'You are just a stupid cow. How can I work with idiots like you?'

Cheryl, 'I'm not having you talking to me like that.'

Terry, 'Well, I'm not fucking sure what you are going to do about it.'

Cheryl thought, 'I'm going to need some help here, but at least we are now getting paid for the invention sales. That means that I can add to my collection of Hermes bags, whoopee.' Suddenly the problem with Terry seemed to diminish.

Location: On-Board Admiral Pearce's Flagship
Sequence of Events: 62

Admiral Pearce, 'Update me.'

Fleet Operations, 'Your Fleet has been divided into ten units as you ordered and is searching the direction that The Chosen were thought to have come from. This was based on our analysis of their fleet movements and the movement of the cloaked ship. So far, we have not picked up any evidence of them travelling this way.'

Admiral Pearce, 'Any other issues?'

Fleet Operations, 'We know that The Chosen fleet was also near The Brakendeth home planet. So perhaps a search could also start from that direction as well.'

Admiral Pearce, 'Please let Admiral Mustard know of your suggestion.'

Fleet Operations, 'Yes, Sir. I've also heard that your friend Admiral Richardson has returned to active duty.'

Admiral Pearce, 'That's good news. It's great to have Phil back on board.'

Comms, 'Admiral Pearce, I have Admiral Mustard for you.'

Admiral Mustard, 'Hi Glen, just wondered if you had any news.'

Admiral Pearce, 'No, it's a bit like a Sunday stroll in the park. Very quiet.'

Admiral Mustard, 'It won't be a stroll if you find them. It could be fireworks.'

Location: Cheryl's Flat, Planet Earth
Sequence of Events: 63

Terry, 'Hi, AI Central, I've finished a couple more inventions: elimination of tooth decay and a cure for dementia.'

AI Central, 'You are going to put a lot of dentists out of work.'

Terry, 'So be it. Mummy won't be happy. She had a go at me for doing the last lot.'

AI Central, 'Don't worry about that. She needs the money to buy a few more bags.'

Terry, 'I'm still frustrated that I can't work out who was controlling her.'

AI Central. 'It's still a mystery. We decided that it wasn't The Brakendeth or a future version of me.'

Terry, 'The Nexuster was a suitable candidate, but the timeline seems wrong.'

AI Central, 'It is still a possibility, but we may never know.'

Terry, 'The Brakendeth are still playing the game through me, but who is the enemy?'

AI Central, 'Admiral Mustard has got it in his head that The Chosen are the enemy. He is convinced that they destroyed The Brakendeth and Farcellian worlds.'

Terry, 'Why does he think that?'

AI Central, 'Because they happened to be in the area at the time.' Terry was tempted to tell AI Central the truth, but there would be ramifications that would not suit his plans.

Location: The President's Office, Presidential Palace, Planet Earth
Sequence of Events: 64

President Padfield, Henrietta Strong, Bill Penny, Tony Moore and Edel Bonner were in the President's Office to continue their discussion regarding the best way forward for extending human lifespans.

President Padfield, 'We were very impressed with Edel's input last time, so I invited her along again. You will notice that the rejuv treatment has been a great success.' Edel got up and gave a swirl. She appreciated the admiration that the men had for her curves. She might be an admiral, but she was still a woman. One might be liberated, but a little bit of admiration goes a long, long way.

The team had lots of questions for Edel. Her answers sold the treatment to her colleagues.

President Padfield, 'Moving on. Today's meeting is about the marketing and logistics of the extended lifespan process.

Henrietta, would you like to take us through some of the issues?'

Henrietta Strong, 'Yes, Mr President. Firstly, we need to consider the problems and risks involved with the treatment:

• Firstly, ninety-five per cent of the population will want the treatment
• It will take months, even years, to produce enough of the drugs to do the rejuvs
• We don't have enough medical practitioners to handle the demand
• There needs to be a waiting period between the rejuv and the extended life processes to ensure that the rejuv has been successful
• It will then take time to get the life extender packs ready
• We will then need even more medical practitioners
• Then we need to decide who gets the treatment first?
• Do we charge more for early adopters? i.e., it costs ten thousand credits in the first year, five thousand in the second year, two thousand in the third year, free in the fourth year? This will help spread the expectations.
• Do we do it planet by planet?
• Do we get each planet to manage it themselves?
• How do we stop corruption?

- Do we offer it to the over-eighties in the first year, the over-seventies in the second year and so on, as they have a greater urgency?
- What did we decide to do about life prison sentences?
- Should age, gender, wealth, etc. be a factor?
- There could be riots
- We need to market this very carefully.'

Tony Moore, 'Henrietta, have you made your mind up on the best way forward?'

Henrietta Strong, 'I normally do, but I'm concerned that this could be very disruptive. It's going to be very emotive. Your average human being is going to struggle to think through the implications. Everything from mortgages, life insurance, parenthood, healthcare, marriage, careers, etc., is going to need rethinking. Just think about jobs — dead men's shoes could go on for years.'

Bill Penny, 'Do you really think there could be riots?'

Henrietta Strong, 'Yes, people are going to have to wait. The entire process must appear honest and impartial. If not, there will definitely be riots.'

President Padfield, 'Could we use the lottery system to manage the process?'

Henrietta Strong, 'That's not a bad idea. It would have to be scrupulously fair.'

President Padfield, 'I guess that they trust the national lottery.'

Tony Moore, 'I do, I think most people do. And it would give us time to roll it out.'

Henrietta Strong, 'The downside is that the randomness of the lottery would make it difficult to manage.'

President Padfield, 'It would probably be better if each planet did its own thing.'

Henrietta Strong, 'I can see the advantages, but some planets will do a crap job. There will be riots.'

Bill Penny, 'I'm keen that it is seen as a Galactium benefit.'

Tony Moore, 'It's easy for us to forget what a wonderful thing this is going to be. It's exciting. When do we announce it?'

President Padfield, 'I agree with you, but I don't think we can announce it without agreeing on the implementation process.'

Henrietta Strong, 'We need to action this soon as there are already some rumours out there.'

President Padfield, 'Henrietta, can you set up a working party to agree on the best way forward? We need to approve the plan by the end of the month, and I will announce it two weeks after that.'

Tony Moore, 'That's a very ambitious schedule.'

President Padfield, 'I don't think we have any choice.'

Henrietta Strong, 'It will be done.'

Location: Lady Enyo's Palace, The Chosen
Sequence of Events: 65

Commander Thanatos, 'The human fleet is approaching our trap.'

Lady Enyo, 'Good, are you ready to annihilate them?'

Commander Thanatos, 'My Lady, I thought it would be useful to review our plans as once the trap has been sprung, it will be difficult to go back.'

Lady Enyo, 'Our plan has been carefully thought through.'

Commander Thanatos, 'I know that, my Lady, but I would still appreciate a review.'

Lady Enyo, 'This is how I see it:
- Firstly, you will completely annihilate the Earther fleet; no one must escape
- The Earthers will send a larger fleet to investigate, and you will annihilate them as well. Our aim is to wear down their resources so that they can't resist an attack on Mother Earth. We will issue a series of Earther distress beacons and mock up some survivor sites on one of the local planets
- We know that the Earthers are creatures of habit. There is no doubt that their entire fleet will come to the aid of their previous fleet. They will not be able to resist.
- While their fleet is chasing ghosts, we will conquer Earth
- The Earthers will then surrender to us.'

Commander Thanatos, 'My Lady, are you sure that they will surrender?'

Lady Enyo, 'What other options do they have?'

Commander Thanatos, 'They are more stubborn than I expected.'

Lady Enyo, 'Believe me, they will surrender.'

Commander Thanatos, 'Will the other warlords assist our cause?'

Lady Enyo, 'Once I'm set up on Earth, we will get considerable help.'

Commander Thanatos, 'What about before then?'

Lady Enyo, 'Our cohort will triumph. I'm not willing to share power.'

Commander Thanatos, 'Yes, my Lady. The Earthers approach the trap.'

Lady Enyo, 'No survivors.'

Commander Thanatos, 'Yes, my Lady.'

Location: On-Board Admiral Pearce's Flagship
Sequence of Events: 66

Admiral Pearce, 'Update me.'

Fleet Operations, 'The fleet has had to consolidate because of the unusual combination of natural features in this area.'

Admiral Pearce, 'What features are you on about?'

Fleet Operations, 'There is a strange combination of astronomical phenomena. We think we have encountered our first ever supermassive black hole. Our scientists have been postulating about them for a long time. Fortunately, it's not that near, and it is moving away from us, but we can still feel its gravitational effects. Anyway, the risks are relatively low.

'However, we think it has triggered off some supernovas. It just may be coincidental. On top of that, there is a massive space storm with high levels of gamma rays. There is also a red giant with a truly enormous asteroid belt. We have never experienced such a unique combination before. It's taking a lot of skill to avoid the gravitational tossings and tuggings, and to keep the Fleet together.'

Admiral Pearce, 'Is there any sign of The Chosen?'

Fleet Operations, 'No, Sir, but I'm sure that they wouldn't want to live in this neighbourhood. But to be fair, our scans are so affected by the various astrophysical phenomena that The Chosen could be around the next corner, and we would have no idea.'

Admiral Pearce, 'In that case, keep your eyes peeled.'

Fleet Operations, 'Yes, Sir.'

The eye peeling failed as The Chosen struck without mercy. Admiral Pearce had no idea what hit him as the Fleet Battleship ceased to exist. Fortunately, a new system of command transfer had been organised and tested. But, unfortunately, the officer next in command, Captain Pickering, also ceased to exist.

Commander Thanatos didn't like this sort of battle. The Earthers had not been given any warning. They weren't technically at war with them. It was a cleverly planned ambush that gave them little chance of survival. The Chosen attacked from every direction simultaneously, so it was impossible for the Earthers to form a cohesive defence.

Captain Mynd thought that he might be in command of the Fleet. He wasn't sure, but he took action.

'My orders:
- Form a defensive sphere
- Drones to protect the outer extremity
- Ships of the line to form next layer
- Forts and fighters to form the centre
- AI Central to synchronise the firing
- Warn Fleet Four
- Use all weapons.'

Fleet Operations, 'Yes, Sir.'

Captain Mynd, 'Update me.'

Fleet Operations, 'The Fleet is attempting to form your requested formation but is struggling under extremely aggressive enemy action. We believe that the enemy is The Chosen, but it hasn't been confirmed. The external radiation is still affecting our sensors.'

Captain Mynd: Show me our current inventory:

Fleet Operations, 'On the screen now Sir.'

Vessel Type	Start	Current
Fleet Battleship	1	0
Fleet Carrier	1	0
Battleship	10	6
Battlecruiser	400	270
Destroyer	400	209
Frigate	50	45
Super Drone	10	10
Fighter	450	460
Planet Killer	5	5
Forts	150	92
Drone	1,000	780
Total	2,477	1,867

Captain Mynd, 'What is our assessment of the enemy size?'

Fleet Operations, 'It's about twice our size, Sir.'

Captain Mynd, 'AI Central, what's your assessment.'

AI Central, 'It was a carefully planned ambush. They knew that the environmental conditions would cause our Fleet confusion. I'm a bit surprised that they eliminated the flagship and carrier so quickly as their force fields, were the strongest we had. The enemy has got a weapon to crack them wide open, although they are using it rather sparingly.'

Captain Mynd, 'I'm not sure if I should maintain this position and wait for Admiral Gittins's Fleet or retreat to meet his Fleet.'

AI Central, 'The Fleet has created a good defensive formation, but the enemy will probably wear you down ship by ship. There is also a risk that they have other resources that they could use against you.

'A fleeing Fleet is always very vulnerable, especially when it's changing formation.'

Captain Mynd, 'What would you do?'

AI Central, 'I never recommend military actions unless they are foolproof. This is too difficult for me. It's your decision.'

Captain Mynd, 'My orders:
- We stay and fight
- Inform Admiral Gittins that his help is required with the utmost urgency
- All drones will form squadrons and attack the enemy.'

Fleet Operations, 'Yes, Sir.'

Location: Lady Enyo's Palace, The Chosen
Sequence of Events: 67

Commander Thanatos, 'My Lady, the human fleet is in our trap.'

Lady Enyo, 'How is the annihilation going?'

Commander Thanatos, 'My Lady, tougher than we thought. Their force fields are quite good.'

Lady Enyo, 'Can they resist the Godfire?'

Commander Thanatos, 'No, my Lady; we took out their flagship and another large vessel with the first volley.'

Lady Enyo, 'When will the annihilation be complete?'

Commander Thanatos, 'Soon, my Lady. We expected the Earthers to come out guns blazing, but they have formed a sound defensive formation. We can pick them off, but it will take some time.'

Lady Enyo, 'Why wouldn't they just flee like any self-respecting navy?'

Commander Thanatos, 'My Lady, a navy in flight is very vulnerable, and they would know that.'

Lady Enyo, 'Have they requested help?'

Commander Thanatos, 'Probably my Lady, but even with portal technology, it will take a while to get here.'

Location: On-Board Admiral Gittins's Flagship
Sequence of Events: 68

Comms, 'Sir, Admiral Pearce's Fleet is under attack from an unknown fleet. They request urgent assistance.'

Admiral Gittins, 'Put him on.'

Captain Mynd, 'This is Captain Mynd. Admiral Pearce has been killed, along with his second in command. We have lost about a third of our assets. I've taken temporary command and formed a defensive position. Our drones are currently attacking the enemy.

'You should also know that a mixture of black holes, supernova and space storms are restricting the use of our instruments.

'Should I flee to meet you or wait for you?'

Admiral Gittins, 'What is the strength of the enemy?'

Captain Mynd, 'Our instruments are not very effective, but I would say that they have twice our strength. They do have a weapon that can cut through our force fields, although it is being sparingly used. They would certainly target your ship.'

Admiral Gittins, 'I'm concerned that they are deliberately dragging our forces into an ambush, so let's do the reverse. My orders:
- Leave the drones to form a rear-guard
- Leave half your forts behind on automated mode, and then when the time is right, push the self-destruct buttons
- Form small mini-Fleets and retreat on a progressive basis
- Head to our coordinates, where we will ambush the enemy.
- When you get to our position, re-form behind us and prepare to attack.'

Fleet Operations, 'Yes, Sir.'

Captain Mynd, Yes, Sir.'

Admiral Gittins, 'My orders:
- Fleet Four will prepare an ambush. Select an appropriate spot where we can use our forts as killing machines
- Once Fleet Five has passed through us, we will attack the enemy. No mercy
- Inform Admiral Mustard.'

Fleet Operations, 'Yes, Sir.'

Location: Lady Enyo's Palace, The Chosen
Sequence of Events: 69

Commander Thanatos, 'My Lady, we have got them. Their fleet is on the run.'

Lady Enyo, 'What happened?'

Commander Thanatos, 'Firstly, they attacked us with their unmanned drones. We need to consider adding them to our arsenal, if only for their irritation value. While that was going on, their fleet divided into units and fled.'

Lady Enyo, 'And obviously we are pursuing them?'

Commander Thanatos, 'At first we had the task of fighting off their drones, and then their forts attacked us. When we got near, the forts self-destructed. We hadn't expected that as they are significant assets.'

Lady Enyo, 'What about losses on our side?'

Commander Thanatos, 'They have been significant, my Lady, but I've called up further resources.'

Lady Enyo, 'How is the pursuit going?'

Commander Thanatos, 'They have divided themselves into a hundred squadrons and are fleeing in many different directions. We have had to follow suit. But unfortunately, the conditions out there are not good for tracking.'

Lady Enyo, 'Can you still guarantee that you will annihilate every human vessel?'

Commander Thanatos, 'Of course, my Lady.'

Lady Enyo, 'Keep me updated.' She had a lot of faith in Commander Thanatos, but these Earthers were quite ingenious. She thought that the chances of him annihilating every Earther ship were going to be slim. She would have to reconsider her plans. She would have to increase her attempt to get other warlords involved.

Location: On-Board Captain Mynd's Battlecruiser
Sequence of Events: 70

Captain Mynd, 'Update me.'

Fleet Operations, 'The drones have been hugely successful. There are still about three hundred attacking the enemy. The forts have also been surprisingly successful. Together they have taken out one hundred and twenty of the enemy vessels. Their self-destruction took out another forty. We have certainly bloodied their noses.

'There are ninety-eight mini-Fleets clustered around some capital ships, all shooting off in different directions but with a plan to converge at the same time behind Fleet Four.

'The enemy is chasing, but they seemed confused and demoralised.'

Captain Mynd, 'Let's see what else we can do. My orders:
- Discharge all mines.
- The super drones will form a Fleet and focus on pursuing one enemy at a time.'

Fleet Operations, 'Yes, Sir.'

This was the first time that mines had been used by The Galactium Fleet. They were a mixture of contact and time-delay nuclear mines. They were probably not going to be that effective, but the "big bangs" should surprise the enemy.

Sadly, several Galactium ships were being picked off. Some were disabled, but they continued to fight. The enemy showed no mercy. An act that would be remembered.

Captain Mynd, 'Comms, update Admiral Gittins regarding our progress. Tell him that an arrival party would be welcome.'

Fleet Operations, 'Yes, Sir.'

Location: Lady Enyo's Palace, The Chosen
Sequence of Events: 71

Lady Enyo, 'What's the current situation?'

Commander Thanatos, 'As discussed earlier, we lost a lot of assets to their drone attacks and forts. We are still fighting off the last of the drones.'

Lady Enyo, 'Why have the drones been so successful?'

Commander Thanatos, 'As they are unmanned, they can manoeuvre quicker than us as the G-force is irrelevant to them. All of their functions are automated.'

Lady Enyo, 'What are their weaknesses?'

Commander Thanatos, 'They are quite predictable, but their speed and impossible manoeuvrability make up for it.'

Lady Enyo, 'So you have got the pursuit under control?'

Commander Thanatos, 'Not exactly my Lady.'

Lady Enyo, 'What else has happened?'

Commander Thanatos, 'They have another weapon that we have never come across. We were following the enemy's path as far as we can when some of our ships started exploding. When we researched it, we discovered that there are "floating bombs" that explode on contact or within a certain proximity.'

Lady Enyo, 'Why aren't the force fields working?'

Commander Thanatos, 'Both sides have the same problem. We built force fields to defend against known weapons. Unfortunately, they often fail against unknown weapons. Our force fields stop the Earther projectile weapons, but not their beams. We will obviously work on this weakness, but then so will they.

'What's interesting is that our force field will stop any fast-moving projectiles, but slow-moving projectiles are occasionally getting through.'

Lady Enyo, 'This is all very interesting, but are you winning?'

Commander Thanatos, 'My Lady, I want to say yes, but we are not currently winning. However, additional resources are on their way.'

Attack Command, 'Lord Thanatos, apologies that I'm interrupting, but we are being attacked by drones.'

Commander Thanatos, 'Fight them off as normal.'

Attack Command, 'These are not your normal drones. They are two or three times the size. They are discharging all of their weapons and then ramming our ships.'

Commander Thanatos, 'Outrun them.'

Attack Command, 'They are faster than us.'

Commander Thanatos, 'They can't be.'

Attack Command, 'That may be the case, but they are overtaking us and positioning themselves in front of us to cause a collision. We have avoided two collisions so far.'

Commander Thanatos, 'Ensure that the fleet provides resources to defend us.'

Lady Enyo, 'That sounds very worrying.'

Commander Thanatos, 'My Lady, I think it's fair to say that we have underestimated the Earthers.'

The timing was excellent as The Chosen just encountered the battlecruisers and drones of the Fleet Four. No mercy was shown. The sub Fleets of Fleet Five repositioned, turned, and lined up behind the Fourth Fleet as planned. The attacking vessels of Fleet Five, which had smashed through The Chosen's Fleet, then turned as they had practised and caught The Chosen in a double envelopment.

Lady Enyo, 'What's happening?'

Commander Thanatos, 'My Lady, they had a second fleet waiting for us. We are being annihilated. Do I have your permission to retreat?'

Lady Enyo was tempted to let them suffer for their incompetence. The embarrassment. How could children beat their masters? But she couldn't afford to lose any more assets.

Lady Enyo, 'Permission granted. Withdraw all forces.'

Location: On-Board Admiral Gittins's Flagship
Sequence of Events: 72

Admiral Gittins, 'Update me.'

Fleet Operations, 'The enemy is retreating. Should we pursue?'

Admiral Gittins, 'My orders:
- Fleets Four and Five will disengage
- Form a defensive position in the direction of the fleeing enemy
- Set up rear-guard
- Review munitions position
- Prepare for another enemy attack
- Contact Admiral Mustard.'

Admiral Gittins, 'Continue the update.'

Fleet Operations, 'Yes, Sir. Fleet Four's battlecruisers and drones impacted the enemy fleet and caused considerable damage. They carried out a well-planned reversal to attack the enemy from behind.

The remaining Fleet Four forces and Fleet Five created a very successful kill zone. The enemy was forced to retire. The pursuit was not approved.'

Admiral Gittins, 'Give me an asset report for Fleets Four and Five.'

Fleet Operations, 'It's on the screen now, Sir.'

Vessel Type	Fleet 5	Current	Fleet 4	Current
Fleet Battleship	1	0	1	1
Fleet Carrier	1	0	1	1
Battleship	10	4	10	10
Battlecruiser	400	198	400	389
Destroyer	400	176	400	379
Frigate	50	39	50	49
Super Drone	10	0	10	10
Fighter	450	450	450	450
Planet Killer	5	5	5	5
Forts	150	66	150	150
Drone	1,000	0	1,000	899
Total	2,477	938	2,477	2,343

Admiral Gittins. 'Incorporate Fleet Five into Fleet Four for command purposes.'

Fleet Operations, 'Yes, Sir.'

Admiral Gittins, 'Comms, get me Captain Mynd.'

Comms, 'Yes, Sir.'

Captain Mynd, 'Morning Sir,'

Admiral Gittins, 'Good morning, Captain. I want to congratulate you on your performance. I'm giving you a battle promotion to Senior Captain.'

Captain Mynd, 'Thank you, Sir, but I'm already a Senior Captain.'

Admiral Gittins, 'What's the next rank?'

Captain Mynd, 'You can make me an Admiral, Sir.'

Admiral Gittins, 'I'm afraid that's not in my gift, but I will put your name in despatches.'

Captain Mynd, 'Thank you, Sir.'

Comms, 'Sir, Admiral Mustard is on the blower.'

Admiral Mustard, 'Morning, Peter. That's another dear friend we have lost.'

Admiral Gittins, 'Glen will be hugely missed. But, is that going to be the destiny for all of us?'

Admiral Mustard, 'It probably is. I've used up a dozen lives already.'

Admiral Gittins, 'You are indestructible.'

Admiral Mustard, 'It's just not my time yet. Give me an update.'

Admiral Gittins, 'Fleet Five got a pasting from the enemy. Captain Mynd did an excellent job of recovering the situation. His use of drones, forts and mines was inspiring.'

Admiral Mustard, 'Mines! They haven't been used in decades. I didn't know that we still had them on board.'

Admiral Gittins, 'Well, they certainly surprised the enemy. We then caught the enemy between the barrage of two Fleets, and the enemy retired.'

Admiral Mustard, 'I hope that you are not pursuing them.'

Admiral Gittins, 'I've learnt that lesson from you. Both Fleets are in a defensive position, awaiting orders.'

Admiral Mustard, 'Well, I guess that the options are to continue or retire?'

Admiral Gittins, 'I'm happy to continue, but they were waiting for us.'

Admiral Mustard, 'Can you confirm that they were The Chosen?'

Admiral Gittins. 'I can't, but I would put good money on it.'

Admiral Mustard, 'I think that we should retire. They know that we are coming. Who knows what other surprises they have lined up for us?'

Admiral Gittins, 'And Fleet Four is in a pretty poor shape.'

Admiral Mustard, 'See if you can retrieve some of their damaged vessels. Also, it would be useful if you could find some alien bodies.'

Admiral Gittins, 'I've already got a team working on it, but most of our enemies seem to self-destruct their vessels when defeated. So perhaps we should do the same.'

Admiral Mustard, 'It's worth a thought. See you soon.'

Admiral Gittins, 'Before you go. I wanted to give Captain Mynd a field promotion, but he is already a Senior Captain.'

Admiral Mustard, 'I've been thinking of reintroducing the concept of a Rear Admiral. Promote him to that.'

Admiral Gittins, 'Yes, Sir.'

Admiral Gittins, 'Comms, get me Captain Mynd.'

Comms, 'Yes, Sir.'

Captain Mynd, 'Can I help you, Sir?'

Admiral Gittins, 'Job done.'

Captain Mynd, 'I'm not sure what you mean.'

Admiral Gittins, 'You asked me to promote you to Admiral. Well, it's done. You are Rear Admiral Mynd.'

Captain Mynd, 'I was joking.'

Admiral Gittins, 'You should be careful what you joke about. The only problem we have is that we haven't designed a Rear Admiral's outfit yet. So congratulations, son, you deserved it.'

Location: On-Board Admiral Mustard's Bedroom in the Flagship
Sequence of Events: 73

Edel Bonner, 'Jack, I think you'd better sit down.'

Jack Mustard was still wallowing in his post-orgasm drowsiness. He was one of those men who desperately needed to sleep after a successful sexual encounter. And this had been particularly successful. He knew that his body released a kit-bag of chemicals to make him sleep: prolactin, oxytocin, and vasopressin. He had been told that it was to stop him from rushing off and impregnating other women. There was little chance of that.

His post-coital bliss was interrupted when Edel gave him a little piece of plastic card. He tried to focus while Edel was ranting on. He couldn't work out if she was happy or distressed. That was partly because she wasn't sure.

It wasn't natural for a woman in her eighties to get pregnant. The need for precautions had never crossed her mind or their minds. What a to-do!

Edel, 'What do you want to do?'

Jack, 'Let's book a place at the naval college for him or her.' Edel kissed the man she loved, and he patted her tummy. What a year.

Location: Lady Enyo's Palace, The Chosen
Sequence of Events: 74

Lady Enyo, 'Tell me why I shouldn't sack you.'

Commander Thanatos, 'Because there are few better than me amongst The Chosen. I'm quite happy to fall on my sword if that is what you want, my Lady.'

Lady Enyo, 'I will go and look for a large sword.'

Commander Thanatos, 'As you wish.'

Lady Enyo, 'Grow up! How did they beat us? You had surprise on your side.'

Commander Thanatos, 'It's a good question that I've given a fair amount of thought to. So I've listed some things that occurred to me, on the screen:
- We underestimated the Earthers
- Their irritating drone technology
- Their even more irritating forts
- Their mine technology
- Their successful military tactics and leadership
- They formed a defensive formation rather than fleeing
- Their unexpected second fleet, and
- Courage, lots of it.'

Lady Enyo, 'So what do we do next?'

Commander Thanatos, 'Or what are the Earthers going to do next?'

Lady Enyo, 'What do you mean?'

Commander Thanatos, 'When we left—'

Lady Enyo, 'You mean fled.'

Commander Thanatos, 'When we *fled*, their forces were lined up ready to press their advantage — three thousand ships of the line.'

Lady Enyo, 'I guarantee that they are on their way home. They will review what happened and return with a considerably more powerful fleet. What are you going to do about that? I don't think an ambush is going to work.'

Location: On-Board Admiral Mustard's Flagship
Sequence of Events: 75

Admiral Mustard, 'Comms, get me The President.'
    Comms, 'Yes, Sir.'
    President Padfield, 'And how are you on this fine day?'
    Admiral Mustard, 'I thought that I would give you an update:
- Fleet Five was ambushed by the enemy
- Admiral Pearce and his second in command were unfortunately killed in the initial attack
- Captain Mynd took over and engineered a fighting retreat using drones, forts, and mines

President Padfield, 'Mines?'
    Admiral Mustard, 'I agree. Funny how history catches up with you.
- Fleet Five joined Fleet Four, and together they defeated the enemy
- There was no pursuit as there was a serious danger of a further alien attack
- Both Fleets are returning home.'

President Padfield, 'I'm really sorry about Glen.'
    Admiral Mustard, 'It does highlight your own mortality.'
    President Padfield, 'What have we learnt?'
    Admiral Mustard, 'Well, we are not sure if the enemy was The Chosen, but there is a high likelihood. Peter is looking for some evidence.

'Broadly, our military forces are equal to theirs. They struggled against our drones and forts. Even our tactics were equal or superior to theirs.

'They did have a weapon that can blast open our force fields. However, we are not sure why they used it so sparingly.

'I also need to tell you that I promoted Captain Mynd to a Rear Admiral.'
    President Padfield, 'What's a Rear Admiral?'
    Admiral Mustard, 'As you know, armed forces like their rankings. In the Navy, the senior priorities are Captain, Commodore, Rear Admiral, Vice-Admiral, Admiral, Fleet Admiral and Admiral of the Fleet.'
    President Padfield, 'I'm sure that he deserved it. Anyway, what do we do next?'

Admiral Mustard, 'We go back with a bigger and better force.'

President Padfield, 'Won't they be expecting that?'

Admiral Mustard, 'They certainly will, and I wouldn't want to disappoint them.'

President Padfield, 'Are we going to have a review before you go?'

Admiral Mustard, 'Of course. Changing subjects, I thought you should know that Edel is pregnant.'

President Padfield, 'Our Edel?'

Admiral Mustard, 'Yes, Edel Bonner.'

President Padfield, 'But she must be in her eighties.'

Admiral Mustard, 'Have you seen her since the rejuv?'

President Padfield, 'Yes, she is a pretty cool-looking lady.'

Admiral Mustard, 'She certainly is.'

President Padfield, 'Who is the father?'

Admiral Mustard, 'I am.'

President Padfield, 'You dirty beast. Sorry, I mean congratulations.'

Jack laughed.

Location: Cheryl's House, Planet Earth
Sequence of Events: 76

Terry, 'Hi AI Central, I've finished work on improving the capabilities of the mind's eye. It's going to give humankind some brilliant capabilities.'

AI Central, 'I've always been surprised that it is a capability that humanity hardly ever talks about. So, what have you done?'

Terry, 'There are quite a few new options:
- Total memory recall. Every memory can be accessed and replayed in colour or black and white
- This includes sight, smell, hearing and, to a more limited extent, touch
- Fast forwarding of memories
- Sorting of memories
- Simulation capabilities
- You can replay a film you have watched, or reread a book or listen to music
- Memory deletion. I'm conscious that there may be some memories that you really don't want any more.'

AI Central, 'Won't humans find this overwhelming?'

Terry, 'I think they will at first, but it's just an existing capability enhanced. It will also cure aphantasia.'

AI Central, 'So, it will even help those without a mind's eye.'

Terry, 'Yes, it's going to change their lives.'

AI Central, 'I guess you heard about the battle against The Chosen?'

Terry, 'I heard that Admiral Pearce was killed. He was always kind to me.'

AI Central, 'Yes, that was a great tragedy. I wondered if The Brakendeth records had any more info on The Chosen?'

Terry, 'What did I tell you before?'

AI Central, 'You supplied the following facts:
- There was a war between The Brakendeth and The Chosen
- The Chosen's navy was well-organised, but they didn't have the numbers to beat The Brakendeth
- The Chosen wanted The Brakendeth to take on their religion or die

- They used Godfire — linked to a talking volcano on their home world
- You don't know what they look like. The Chosen were created in the image of their god. Therefore, non-believers can't look at them
- They want to rule the universe
- Their civilian population was wiped out by The Nexuster.'

Terry, 'I will check The Brakendeth records now.'

He went through his race memories to discover the following:
- 'Like The Brakendeth, they live forever
- They have a fixed mating season
- They have very low reproduction rates
- Children are handed over to a central nursery at birth. The parents are hardly involved in a child's upbringing
- It looks like their weapons and military tactics have not changed in centuries
- This is quite interesting. It appears that they visited Earth quite a few times in the past.'

AI Central, 'Do you have any more information on that last point?' AI Central wasn't convinced that Terry was being honest and open about The Chosen. Terry knew that he wasn't being honest and open, but what could he do? Soon everyone would be against him.

Terry, 'There were at least three hundred visits over a thousand years.'

AI Central, 'What time period was it over?'

Terry didn't want to give too much away. Perhaps he shouldn't have mentioned that last point.

Terry, 'It's a bit vague?'

AI Central, 'What do you mean by vague?' Terry started to cry. He knew that by crying and using his age, he could get away with a lot, and it worked.

AI Central, 'I'm sorry that I upset you. I will talk to you later.'

Location: On-Board Admiral Abosa's Flagship
Sequence of Events: 77

Admiral Abosa, 'Comms, get me Admiral Mustard.'

Comms, 'Yes, Sir.'

Admiral Mustard, 'Good morning, Ama.'

Admiral Abosa, 'Good Morning Admiral, I have some news that really doesn't fit in with our theories.'

Admiral Mustard, 'That sounds interesting.'

Admiral Abosa, 'Our scientists have carried out detailed studies on The Brakendeth home complex and the remains of The Farcellian worlds. It has been a challenging and time-consuming process because of the extremely high levels of radiation. In addition, we had to develop new safety protocols.

'Anyway, we can definitely confirm that it was not The Chosen who bombed those planets.'

Admiral Mustard, 'No, I find that hard to believe. Are you sure that the scientists got it right?'

Admiral Abosa, 'Every nuclear weapon leaves a signature; the atomic components, the level of radioactivity, the devastation caused, etc., creates a unique signature or moniker. Well, this is the interesting part, the moniker differs from that caused by The Chosen.'

Admiral Mustard, 'Are you sure? Are the scientists sure?'

Admiral Abosa. 'It's been checked a hundred times as we knew that you would question the results. I then got GAD Control to do a double-blind test. They confirmed the results.'

Admiral Mustard, 'So you are saying that the nuclear weapons used against The Brakendeth and Farcellian home worlds did not belong to The Chosen?'

Admiral Abosa, 'Yes, Sir.'

Admiral Mustard, Good work, although it's not what I expected.'

Admiral Abosa, 'It surprised me, but not as much as my next bombshell.'

Admiral Mustard, 'I'm really intrigued now.'

Admiral Abosa, 'Whose signature was it?'

Admiral Mustard, 'I'm not sure if I like these games.'

Admiral Abosa, 'Sorry, Sir. It is a Brakendethian signature.'

Admiral Mustard, 'That's impossible.'

Admiral Abosa. 'There is no doubt that the nuclear weapons were of Brakendethian origin.'

Admiral Mustard, 'Could The Chosen have used Brakendethian nukes?'

Admiral Abosa, 'I think you are clutching at straws.'

Admiral Mustard, 'We know that The Brakendethian fleet was out as they came to our aid. Why would they attack their home world?'

Admiral Abosa, 'There is one Brakendethian who would know.'

Admiral Mustard, 'Comms. Get me Terry.'

Comms, 'Yes, Sir... There is no response.'

Admiral Mustard, 'Try his mother.'

Comms, 'Yes, Sir... 'There is no response there either.'

Admiral Mustard, 'AI Central, what do you think?'

AI Central, 'Terry has been acting a bit strange recently.'

Admiral Mustard, 'In what way?'

AI Central, 'He has been reluctant to provide info on The Chosen. He has been very aggressive towards his mother. I'm sure that he has been hiding things.'

Admiral Mustard, 'I can't track him down.'

AI Central, 'Nor can I. My tracking system says that he is not on Earth.'

Admiral Mustard, 'What about Cheryl?'

AI Central, 'She is not on Earth either.'

Admiral Mustard, 'Well, they must be, but Terry has found a way of inhibiting your systems.'

AI Central, 'You are probably right. I got the following interesting info out of Terry regarding The Chosen:

- They live forever
- They have a fixed mating season
- They have very low reproduction rates
- Children are handed over to a central nursery at birth. The parents are hardly involved in a child's upbringing
- It looks like their weapons and military tactics have not changed in centuries

'And the most interesting point of all:
- It appears that they visited Earth three hundred times in the past over a thousand-year period.

'Terry couldn't or wouldn't tell me what period.'

Admiral Mustard, 'You clearly suspect the latter.'

AI Central, 'I do. It makes me wonder how much of The Brakendeth story is true.' AI Central wasn't sure whether he should tell Admiral Mustard about the Grand Dethmon living inside of Terry or not. He'd promised Terry that he would keep it a secret.

Admiral Mustard, 'I think we need to have a chat with The President.'

AI Central, 'Agreed.'

Location: The President's Office, Presidential Palace, Planet Earth
Sequence of Events: 78

Admirals Mustard and E Bonner met with The President and AI Central.

President Padfield, 'I believe that congratulations are in order.'

Edel blushed. No one had previously known that she could blush.

Admiral Bonner, 'Just trying to improve the gene pool, Mr President.'

President Padfield, 'I hear that you have some interesting news.'

Admiral Mustard, 'We certainly have. The nuclear signatures discovered after the attack on the Fardel and Brakendeth home worlds were not caused by The Chosen.'

President Padfield, 'Stop there! That goes totally against our previous thinking. Are you sure?'

Admiral Mustard, 'Admiral Abosa has done a first-class job verifying the facts. He even got GAD Control to carry out a double-blind test. The Chosen didn't nuke those planets. What is shocking is that the nuclear signatures actually belong to Brakendeth nuclear weapons.'

President Padfield, 'But that doesn't make sense. The Brakendeth are no more.'

Admiral Mustard, 'Except for one.'

President Padfield, 'You don't mean Terry?'

Admiral Mustard, 'It's hard to believe, but Terry and his mother have gone missing.'

AI Central, 'My scan shows that they are not on Earth.'

President Padfield, 'I guess that he has the skills to confuse your technology.'

AI Central, 'That was our view, Mr President.'

Admiral Mustard, 'The other interesting piece of news is that Terry said that The Chosen had visited Earth about three hundred times in a thousand years.'

President Padfield, 'What period?'

AI Central, 'Either Terry wouldn't say, or he didn't know.'

President Padfield, 'Reading between the lines, you are saying that he is not giving us all the facts?'

Admiral Mustard, 'The other factor is that Terry was in charge of

The Brakendethian fleet.'

President Padfield, 'Are you saying that Terry deliberately killed The Farcellians and then destroyed The Brakendethian home complex?'

Admiral Mustard. 'It is looking that way. The fact that he has disappeared seems to confirm the situation.'

AI Central, 'I can also confirm that he has been fairly aggressive recently, even to his mother. I also think that somehow he is still being influenced by The Brakendethians.'

President Padfield, 'But The Brakendethians are extinct.'

AI Central, 'Yes, Mr President. It's a mystery.'

President Padfield, 'So we are saying:
- The Chosen are innocent
- The Brakendeth are guilty
- The only Brakendethian left is Terry. Therefore, Terry is guilty
- The Chosen have been visiting Earth in the past

'That is all rather weird.'

Admiral E Bonner, 'It does raise lots of questions:
- Why would The Chosen attack our Fleet?
- Why would The Brakendeth destroy their home planet?
- Why would Terry do it?
- How can The Brakendethians still influence Terry?
- Where are Terry and his mother?
- Why were The Chosen visiting Earth and when?'

Admiral Mustard, 'I'm not sure if you know, but The Chosen live forever.'

President Padfield, 'So you are saying that the same Chosen representative could have been visiting Earth for many years?'

Admiral Mustard, 'Exactly. Anyway, it appears to me that The Chosen want to start a war. They clearly have a strong interest in Earth.'

President Padfield, 'Do they want to conquer Earth?'

Admiral Mustard, 'They probably think that if you capture Earth, you get the whole Galactium.'

President Padfield, 'I guess a lot would depend on their military muscle. And to be honest, they could have done it years ago.'

AI Central, 'Terry said that their weapons and military tactics had not changed in centuries.'

Admiral Mustard, 'They certainly found us a bit of a handful.'

President Padfield, 'So are they still a threat?'

Admiral Mustard, 'I would say yes.'

AI Central, 'Probably, although a conversation with them might prove useful.'

Admiral E Bonner, 'Why did they attack us?'

President Padfield, 'They may have seen the arrival of Admiral Pearce's Fleet as an aggressive act.'

Admiral Mustard, 'Possibly. But why is Terry keeping quiet about The Chosen?'

Admiral E Bonner, 'There has obviously been some history between The Chosen and The Brakendeth which included war, religious conflict, etc.'

President Padfield, 'How do we find Terry?'

AI Central, 'I have been using every camera on the planet in an effort to find him. But, unfortunately, I can't even track him leaving Cheryl's house.'

President Padfield, 'I don't think we can answer these questions through discussion, but what about these visits by The Chosen? If it was three hundred visits in a thousand years, that's almost one visit every three/four years, assuming that the visits were spread out. Humanity has been around for about eight hundred thousand years if you include Neanderthal man. If you just focus on Homo sapiens, we have only been around for two hundred thousand years.

Can we trust Terry's visit statistics?'

Admiral Bonner, 'He probably doesn't know how accurate the data is.'

AI Central, 'I'm just thinking wildly. The Brakendethians couldn't work out who converted human cows to sentient beings. Could it have been The Chosen?'

Admiral Bonner, 'And what about all of those UFO sightings?'

President Padfield, 'That tended to be a twentieth-century phenomenon.'

Admiral Mustard, 'Did they exist?'

President Padfield, 'Government records seemed to suggest that ten per cent were genuine inexplicable encounters. There are UFO films that have never been satisfactorily explained.'

Admiral E Bonner, 'What about crop circles, human kidnapping encounters, animal mutilation, etc.?'

President Padfield, 'So visits by The Chosen may be genuine?'

Admiral Mustard, 'I don't see why not. I've always found it difficult to explain our rapid development. In year zero, we were a peasant society. Fifteen hundred years later, we hadn't really evolved that much. By the nineteenth century, we had the combustion engine, jet aircraft, primitive space travel, the internet, microprocessors, DNA knowledge, heart transplants, mobile phones, and much more.

'This millennium, we have conquered space and held our head high in terms of most alien encounters. These are aliens that have been civilised for thousands or even hundreds of thousands of years.'

Admiral E Bonner, 'Don't they blame it on exponential curves?'

Admiral Mustard, 'I get that, but it still seems an implausible story.'

President Padfield, 'So we could say that The Brakendeth are our parents, but The Chosen are our tutors.'

AI Central, 'Or step-parents?'

President Padfield, 'This has been a fascinating discussion, but what is the best way forward?'

Admiral Mustard, 'My recommendations are as follows:
- Meet with The Chosen.
- Continue to build up our forces to protect humanity
- Find Terry and interrogate him
- Identify if Terry is still under The Brakendeth influence
- Continue to investigate The Nexuster
- Investigate ways of countering The Chosen's weapons.'

President Padfield, 'AI Central, can you put a plan together based on Admiral Mustard's recommendations?'

AI Central, 'Yes, Mr President.'

Location: Cheryl's Secret Location, Planet Earth
Sequence of Events: 79

Cheryl, 'Terry, who are we hiding from?'

Terry, 'Everyone.'

Cheryl, 'What have you done?'

Terry, 'By now, President Padfield and Admiral Mustard will know that it was me who destroyed the Farcellian and Brakendeth home worlds.'

Cheryl, 'But it was an accident.'

Terry, 'That's what I told myself, but was I controlled by the Grand Dethmon? And I lied to AI Central about The Chosen.'

Cheryl, 'What was your lie?'

Terry, 'There are too many.'

Cheryl, 'Give me an example.'

Terry, 'I told AI Central that The Chosen visited Earth three hundred times in a thousand years. It was considerably more than that. Possibly they have always been here.'

Cheryl, 'What are you talking about?'

It then dawned on Terry that The Chosen had been manipulating his mother. Through her, they had been controlling him, like they had been controlling human history for centuries.

Terry, 'Sorry, Mum, I was getting confused.'

Cheryl, 'Why don't you come clean? Jack and Dave are not vindictive people.'

Terry, 'But they will never trust me again. I will be constantly monitored.'

Cheryl, 'So what? You don't have any ulterior motives.'

Terry thought, *If only she knew. The Brakendethians will do anything to stop The Chosen.*

Location: Lady Enyo's Palace, The Chosen
Sequence of Events: 80

Lady Enyo, 'Well, so far, you have been wrong. There has been no sign of a significant Earther fleet. However, my sources say that they want to talk to us.'

Commander Thanatos, 'I wonder what stopped them from turning to the military?'

Lady Enyo, 'They learnt that we weren't the ones who bombarded The Brakendethian home world. They would be surprised if they found out that we were there to take it over. We would have found some of their technologies very useful. Very useful indeed.'

Commander Thanatos, 'How did The Brakendethians know that we were coming?'

Lady Enyo, 'They must have spies.'

Commander Thanatos, 'Surely not here in Olympia?'

Lady Enyo, 'Throughout history, in every society, there have been spies. While there are weaknesses, there will be those who will take advantage of them. Whether its money, power or sex, there will be a market. And we have enemies here in court.'

Commander Thanatos, 'Yes, my Lady. But surely no one would help those interfering scum. No one would stoop low enough to help a Brakendethian.'

Lady Enyo, 'True, but remember our past.'

Commander Thanatos, 'True, my Lady. But what are our plans for the Earthers?'

Lady Enyo, 'I sometimes think our destiny depends on the Earther plans for us.'

Commander Thanatos, 'Now you are being depressive.'

Lady Enyo, 'Who is the parent and who is the child?'

Commander Thanatos, 'I think we know the answer to that.'

Lady Enyo, 'That's the crux of the problem. Who has the most extensive empire? Who has the largest population? Who has technology equal to ours? And I've just learnt that they will shortly have eternal life.'

Commander Thanatos, 'No, we have done everything we can to stop that.'

Lady Enyo, 'The blasted Brakendethians have given it to them. They will become gods.'

Commander Thanatos, 'Do we go to war before it's too late?'

Lady Enyo, 'It's possibly already too late. It's very hard to unknow something.'

Commander Thanatos, 'But if we destroy Earth, then their empire will crumble.'

Lady Enyo, 'I used to think that, but they have diversified their empire. Destroying Earth will make them stronger, and they will destroy us.'

Commander Thanatos, 'Nonsense, we would prevail.'

Lady Enyo. 'Modern war is not about the current fleet size or capability. It's about the means of production. What drove it home to me was their drones. These are pilotless killing machines. My sources are telling me that they are manufacturing a thousand every ten Earth days.'

Commander Thanatos, 'That's not possible.'

Lady Enyo, 'And that disbelief is what will defeat us. They have automated factories producing vessels, munitions, and a full range of military hardware. Do you know that they print weapons?'

Commander Thanatos, 'I'm not even sure what that means.'

Lady Enyo, 'When was the last time we upgraded our warships?'

Commander Thanatos, 'We don't have to. They are built to last.'

Lady Enyo, 'What about innovation?'

Commander Thanatos, 'Who cares, we always win.'

Lady Enyo, 'When was your last victory? Which of our weapons are superior to theirs?'

Commander Thanatos, 'Godfire, of course. It's superior to everything. In a flash, it knocked out two of the Earther capital ships.'

Lady Enyo, 'And what's its weakness?'

Commander Thanatos, 'It has none.'

Lady Enyo, 'This is where you are not thinking straight. It takes far too long to recharge.'

Commander Thanatos, 'It has the power of the gods.'

Lady Enyo, 'It's just an energy weapon. I agree that it's impressive, but it's just a weapon. My sources tell me that the Earthers have analysed Godfire and are building a defence into their force fields.'

Commander Thanatos, 'That's not possible.'

Lady Enyo, 'But it is, and they are doing it.'

Commander Thanatos, 'So what are your plans?'

Lady Enyo, 'I think we need to call a council meeting.'

Commander Thanatos, 'But that would be the first one in a very long time.'

Lady Enyo, 'I think it's the only option we have. The Earthers were going to be the resource we needed to defeat the dethbots. The best we can now hope for is a partnership.'

Commander Thanatos, 'I'm not sure if I like this.'

Lady Enyo, 'I'm not sure if the Council, if it agrees to meet, is going to like it either.'

Location: The President's Office, Presidential Palace, Planet Earth
Sequence of Events: 81

President Padfield, 'Hi Madie, are you free?'

Madie Millburn, Fleet HQ, Head of Intelligence, 'For you, Mr President, I'm always free. I will be there in thirty Earth minutes.'

President Padfield, 'Brilliant.'

Madie was there in twenty-seven minutes. Intelligence Officers are never late.

Madie Millburn, 'How can I help you?'

President Padfield, 'I need to update you on some very recent and surprising revelations. Please, just accept what I say is the truth. Perhaps we can discuss it later.'

Madie Millburn, 'OK, I'm intrigued.'

President Padfield, 'Firstly, The Chosen did not bomb The Brakendeth or Farcellian home worlds. Terry did it. Whether he did it on his own volition or under some form of Brakendeth mind control is open to speculation. Terry and his mother have gone missing. I would like your help in tracking them down.'

Madie Millburn, 'Of course, Mr President.'

President Padfield, 'Please call me Dave. Anyway, that is not why I called you here. The task I have for you is far more sensitive.'

Madie Millburn, 'I'm even more intrigued.'

President Padfield, 'Terry told AI Central that The Chosen had visited Earth about three hundred times in a thousand years.'

Madie Millburn, 'That's hard to believe.'

President Padfield, 'The following points on the screen are relevant:
- We think Terry has been lying and that The Chosen have been visiting us over a more extended period
- We have no idea why they were visiting us
- We have learnt that The Chosen are eternal, so it could be the same individual visitor or team that have been coming to Earth for hundreds of years
- If it was three hundred visits in a thousand years, that's almost one visit, every three/four years, assuming that the visits were spread out. Humanity has been around for about eight hundred thousand

years if you include Neanderthal man. If you just focus on Homo sapiens, we have only been around for two hundred thousand years
- There has always been a mystery regarding who converted the human cows to sentient beings. Could it have been The Chosen?'
- What about the UFO sightings in the twentieth century?
- Admiral Mustard made the following point: 'I've always found it difficult to explain our rapid development. In year zero, we were a peasant society. Fifteen hundred years later, we hadn't really evolved that much. By the nineteenth century, we had the combustion engine, jet aircraft, primitive space travel, the internet, microprocessors, DNA knowledge, heart transplants, mobile phones, and much more. This millennium, we have conquered space and held our head high in terms of most alien encounters. These are aliens that have been civilised for thousands or even hundreds of thousands of years.'
- Our rapid progress has been blamed on the exponential curve, but it is hard to believe.'

Madie Millburn, 'This is all very difficult to accept.'

President Padfield, 'I agree. We need proof or at least possibilities. We plan to meet with The Chosen. We need to know if they have been manipulating us for their own purposes or guiding us for some altruistic reasons over the last few thousand years.'

Madie Millburn, 'And how do you expect to get this proof?'

President Padfield, 'You also need to know that there was a war between The Brakendeth and The Chosen. Who were the greatest manipulators?

'It has just crossed my mind that The Chosen made us sentient to stop The Brakendeth getting Chemlife.'

Madie Millburn, 'That's an interesting idea. What exactly do you want me to do?'

President Padfield, 'I want you to select a distinguished group of intellectuals, historians, scientists, etc. The objective is to identify critical points in history where significant innovations took place. Look for rapid developments, especially revolutionary as opposed to evolutionary changes.

Look for any unexplained phenomenon: UFOs, ghosts, voices,

angels, devils, etc.'

Madie Millburn, 'It's hard to believe that The President of The Galactium is asking me to do this.'

President Padfield, 'Are you saying that you are dismissing the possibility?'

Madie Millburn, 'Not at all. It's just not what I expected when I got up this morning.'

President Padfield, 'AI Central, can you add any comments?'

AI Central, 'Madie, The President and myself are being deadly serious about this. It's urgent. You need to get a team together this week. I can give you a list of potential candidates. I can also give you a list of strange occurrences that have happened in the last two millennia. We are serious, and it's urgent.'

President Padfield, 'Thank You, AI Central. Hopefully, it has confirmed the seriousness of this. Do you understand?'

Madie Millburn, 'I do.'

President Padfield, 'Are you willing to take on the project?'

Madie Millburn, 'I am.'

President Padfield, 'Excellent, there is absolutely no constraint in terms of cost, but I do need results.'

Location: On-Board Admiral Mustard's Bedroom in the Flagship
Sequence of Events: 82

Jack and Edel were cuddling in bed. He was exhausted from their latest bout of love-making.

Jack, 'When can I go for the rejuv treatment?'

Edel, 'When I say so. I'm enjoying the attention of an older man. It will take me some time to get used to a toy boy.'

Jack, 'But I need more energy to keep up with you.'

Edel, 'I will get you an energy drink. Anyway, a baby will slow us down.'

Jack, 'At least I've got something to look forward to.'

Edel smacked him. She often threatened violence and occasionally carried it out.

Jack, 'That's against the law.'

Edel, 'I will give you law,' and gently smacked him again. She rubbed her tummy as the bump was starting to show. She was surprised by how easily she had accepted pregnancy. She had all the worries and concerns of a first-time mother, but then she argued to herself that it's all been done before. For the first time in her life, she was conscious that she had a logical, intellectual half of her brain and a crazy emotional side.

Jack, 'Dave had an interesting idea. He speculated that The Chosen deliberately gave humans sentience to stop The Brakendethians from getting their precious Chemlife.'

Edel, 'That is thought-provoking. I've never really understood why The Brakendethians didn't solve the problem themselves.'

Jack, 'They had a death wish.'

Edel, 'It's getting very hard to see the truth.'

Jack, 'Isn't truth like beauty, in the eye of the beholder?'

Edel. 'You are probably right, but it should be binary.'

Jack, 'There is no black and white, just shades of grey.'

Edel, 'Have you given any more thought to your next action against The Chosen?'

Jack, 'I don't have to. They will be contacting me soon. We have something they want.'

Edel, 'You are right. That is why I love you. They might come in force.'

Jack, 'Just what I was thinking.'

Location: Lady Enyo's Palace, The Chosen
Sequence of Events: 83

Lady Enyo, 'I've asked the Council for a meeting.'

Commander Thanatos, 'Did they laugh, my Lady?'

Lady Enyo, 'Not at all.'

Commander Thanatos, 'I am surprised. When do they plan to meet? Next year?'

Lady Enyo, 'No, next yeaander.'

Commander Thanatos, 'My Lady, I can't believe that it is going to be that quick.'

Lady Enyo, 'The dethbot threat has not gone away. The Brakendethians will get their revenge.'

Commander Thanatos, 'If it goes well, then the Earthers will learn the truth.'

Lady Enyo, 'That's correct.'

Commander Thanatos, 'My Lady, we need to think about how they will take it.'

Lady Enyo, 'That has been worrying me. They might disbelieve us or even get aggressive.'

Commander Thanatos, 'They are not stupid. They may have worked it out for themselves.'

Lady Enyo, 'I was wondering if we should turn up in force asking for a parley. What do you think?'

Commander Thanatos, 'My Lady, I think that would work, but we need to avoid conflict at all costs. Of course, this assumes that the Council agrees to this going ahead.'

Lady Enyo, 'They have no choice. We are going to need help. We just don't have the numbers. We had the same problem in the first war against The Brakendeth.'

Commander Thanatos, 'Do we have any updates on the dethbots?'

Lady Enyo, 'The advanced warning stations are talking about a fully automated fleet of two million vessels.'

Commander Thanatos, 'Those odds are just ridiculous.'

Lady Enyo, 'Answer me this: knowing that a fleet that size is approaching, how many new vessels have we constructed?'

Commander Thanatos, 'There have been some delays. The different warlords can't agree on the design criteria or who is going to pay for the new vessels. In addition, there has been a shortage of essential materials.'

Lady Enyo, 'How many?'

Commander Thanatos, 'The supplies of Godfire have been very limited because the volcano has been overactive.'

Lady Enyo, 'Is this the one that talks to you? What nonsense.'

Commander Thanatos, 'Since the battle with the Earthers, we are short of munitions.'

Lady Enyo, 'What's wrong with the replicators?'

Commander Thanatos, 'No one knows how to fix them.'

Lady Enyo, 'Why is that?'

Commander Thanatos, 'No one wants to be a technician as it has a meagre status.'

Lady Enyo, 'How many new vessels?'

Commander Thanatos, 'None my Lady,'

Lady Enyo, 'Fucking, fucking hell. As a race, we deserve to be exterminated. Are you saying that in the last fifty years, we have not produced a single new battleship?'

Commander Thanatos, 'Yes, Ma'am, but we have repaired a few.'

Lady Enyo, 'What about replacing the ones the Earthers destroyed?'

Commander Thanatos, 'We don't have the resources to do that.'

Lady Enyo, 'If we take all the warlords together, how big a fleet do we have?'

Commander Thanatos, 'That information is not available.'

Lady Enyo, 'Why is that?'

Commander Thanatos, 'Historically, each warlord was concerned about being attacked by one of the other warlords. It is still a genuine possibility. Consequently, no one knows the answer to your question.'

Lady Enyo, 'Well, let's estimate, shall we? It can't be that difficult.'

Commander Thanatos, 'I'm not sure that I can do that.'

Lady Enyo, 'Why's that?'

Commander Thanatos, 'It's immoral, my Lady. It's against the dictates of my profession.'

Lady Enyo, 'I can't believe this. We have an enormous threat on our doorstep, and you care about some outdated practices.'

Commander Thanatos, 'It may seem outdated to you, but it's how we keep civilised. We must maintain our rules and customs. Otherwise, things will fall apart.'

Lady Enyo, 'If we are not careful, there will not be any civilisation to maintain. Now let's do an estimate. How many warlords are there?'

Commander Thanatos, 'Seventeen, my Lady.'

Lady Enyo, 'And how big are each of their fleets?'

Commander Thanatos, 'It's confidential data, my Lady.'

Lady Enyo, 'Who could tell me?'

Commander Thanatos, 'There is no one, my Lady.'

Lady Enyo, 'How big is my fleet?'

Commander Thanatos, 'That's also confidential.'

Lady Enyo, 'It's my fucking fleet. Tell me.'

Commander Thanatos, 'Yes Ma'am, you have four thousand, three hundred and forty-five vessels.'

Lady Enyo. 'Thank you. Let's assume that every fleet is about five thousand vessels.'

Commander Thanatos, 'We can't do that, my Lady.'

Lady Enyo, 'Don't you dare tell me that we can't do that.'

Lady Enyo, 'So if we accept that five thousand is a typical fleet size, we have a total fleet of thirty-five thousand.'

Commander Thanatos, 'I can't comment.'

Lady Enyo. 'So that is thirty-five thousand to fifty thousand of our vessels against two million dethbot ships, and we haven't manufactured a new vessel in fifty years. We must be mad.'

Commander Thanatos, 'Yes, my Lady.'

Location: GAD Control Conference Room, (The Galactium Alliance Defence Hub), Planet Earth
Sequence of Events: 84

Madie Millburn, 'Good morning ladies and gentlemen. Firstly, I would like to introduce myself. I'm Madie Millburn, Fleet HQ — Head of Intelligence. I'm going to take you through a presentation that you may find hard to believe. The content is top secret. The task I'm going to set you is also top secret.

'I'm going to ask you to accept the content of the presentation as being accurate. We could spend a considerable amount of time debating it. But, believe me, that has already happened. I need you all to focus on the task.

'These are the facts:
- Planet Turing was attacked by a creature called The Nexuster
- This creature had mind-controlling powers and took over the planet's management, one of our admirals, and some forts
- The Nexuster started taking over two other planets — Lister and Mendel but was stopped
- Three Fleets were sent to investigate, but they started attacking each other as they came under the control of The Nexuster
- AI Central took control of the three Fleets and returned them home
- On Planet Turing, The Nexuster impregnated an unknown number of women who gave birth to thousands of monsters
- Our Admiral Richardson took control of The Nexuster's fleet, which also had five thousand drones
- Then an unknown enemy fleet of three thousand vessels arrived off Planet Turing
- There was a battle between The Nexuster's forces and the unknown aliens. It became apparent that The Nexuster could also control the alien minds
- Contact was made with the aliens. They are called The Chosen. They were here to destroy The Nexuster
- It would appear that The Chosen have destroyed The Nexuster 27,096 times
- The Chosen think that we are the spawn of The Brakendeth

- To kill The Nexuster, The Chosen wanted to destroy all three "infected planets" despite the billions of humans who lived there
- With Terry's help, we invented a way of finding out who had been infected and curing it
- We sent in a team consisting of marines and Special Ops commandos to capture or kill The Nexuster
- This team discovered that almost the entire planet had been consumed by the monsters. There was no hope for the planet, and the project was cancelled. Most of the team escaped.
- Admiral Mustard formed a considerable Fleet to confront The Chosen to defend the planets
- It was decided that The Nexuster was a serious danger to humanity and had to be destroyed
- President Padfield gave the Fleet orders to destroy Planet Turing, which was duly actioned
- The Chosen still wanted Planets Mendel and Lister to be destroyed
- A further fleet of forty thousand vessels belonging to The Chosen was on its way
- AI Central calculated that the two fleets were reasonably matched, but our Fleet would suffer seventy per cent losses
- Admiral Mustard delayed the fighting by a series of bluffs
- Terry secured the use of The Brakendeth fleet. A million of their ships came to the defence of our Fleet
- The Chosen retired.

'So what do we think we know about The Nexuster?
- It is not a single entity but a whole species. What is interesting is that each individual cell has the ability to recreate the complete entity
- It has a group consciousness, with each cell knowing everything
- We think it can take over the mind of any known species except The Brakendeth
- Its mental powers are extraordinary
- It also has shape-shifting capabilities
- Its natural state is probably a gelatinous mass, possibly red in colour
- It spends ninety per cent of its life in a child-state and then turns

nasty during the breeding stage
- The word "breeding" might be wrong as it regenerates itself by absorbing alien body parts. No new entities are created
- It pretends to be the alpha creature and wants to mate with the strongest, most beautiful etc., but essentially it devours the non-skeletal soft-tissue parts of aliens
  - At one time, The Brakendeth thought that the species was extinct. This might have been the case, but there is some evidence that another species engineered its return and then lost control.'
  - That race might have been The Chosen. We believe that they planned to use it as a weapon against The Brakendeth.'
  - The Chosen lost control of its creation, and it destroyed The Chosen's civilian population
  - Only The Chosen's military survived
  - The Nexuster can temporarily take over a mind. Once the victim is distanced from The Nexuster, he or she returns to normal with no apparent after-effects
  - The Nexuster can take over a mind on a more permanent basis by putting one of its cells into the victim. The cell has to be eliminated before the victim is back to normal
  - 'Sound can destroy The Nexuster — a decibel range of 110-130 dB(A) will paralyse it.

'I need to stress that much of this second-hand information has not been confirmed.'

'I know that you have lots of questions, but so far, this is just background information. I have more detailed packs I can give you.

'I think that we should stop for a break now, and then we can start focusing on the project.'

There was a serious outbreak of mutterings, mumblings, murmurings, groanings, moanings, complaining, witterings and bellyaching. It's funny how the intellectual elite is easily offended. They were shocked, frightened, disturbed, agitated, and almost traumatised. This was shaking up their sheltered world. Nevertheless, Madie was thoroughly enjoying herself.

Location: The President's Office, Presidential Palace, Planet Earth
Sequence of Events: 85

Henrietta Strong, 'Morning, Mr President, I've come to give you an update on the Eternal Life Working Party.'

President Padfield, 'This should be interesting.'

Henrietta Strong, 'Not really, it got very emotive. There was absolutely no consensus. I was shocked that a lot of personal prejudices came to the fore.'

President Padfield, 'Give me some examples.'

Henrietta Strong, 'There was a reasonable selection of religious leaders who eventually walked out. However, it would appear that they are going to do everything they can to stop this aberration.

'Apparently, we are working against the rules of nature. We are godless heathens even to consider it. We would be denying millions from the joys of the afterlife. You could have cut the anger and frustration in the room with a knife. One of the more vociferous delegates spat at me. I don't think he was too impressed by my sexuality.'

President Padfield, 'He can fuck off then.'

Henrietta Strong, 'Precisely. Some of the business leaders were upset by the quantum change that would hit their organisations. They would have to re-model everything again. They were still bothered by the previous introduction of replicators.

'What annoyed me was that as individuals, they all wanted eternal life as soon as possible. One bishop asked me who he could contact to jump the queue.'

President Padfield, 'What was agreed?'

Henrietta Strong, 'Nothing in detail but the following were accepted in principle:

- Those between seventy and a hundred should be offered the treatment first
- The lottery idea should go ahead
- There should be a charge
- An ongoing fee was suggested
- There should be approval at the planetary level
- Men should get preference over women.'

President Padfield, 'I can't believe that last point. How did that happen?'

Henrietta Strong, 'There was a view that because women live longer than men, men should get preferential treatment.'

President Padfield, 'What nonsense. So what are your recommendations?'

Henrietta Strong, 'The Galactium team needs to agree on the best way forward.'

President Padfield, 'But that's very elitist.'

Henrietta Strong, 'I know, but someone needs to be responsible.'

President Padfield, 'You know me, I'm not the sort to shirk hard decisions.'

Henrietta Strong, 'That's true, boss.'

President Padfield, 'So I can't think of anyone better than you. It's your project. Go forth and extend everyone's life.'

Location: Council Meeting, Royal Chamberarium, Planet Olympus
Sequence of Events: 86

Orator General, Royal Chamberarium, 'Lady Enyo, you have the floor.'

Lady Enyo stood up, selected the first page on her telecaster and said, 'Your most esteemed highnesses and eminences, your most worshipable monitors of the Godfire, fellow illustrious Warlords, Lords, Ladies and knights, I bring concern.' She was conscious that she had to check her words very carefully.

Orator General, Royal Chamberarium, 'Lady Enyo, your concern is appreciated and must be shared.'

Lady Enyo, 'Thank you, Orator General. 'The concern will be shared.'

Orator General, Royal Chamberarium, 'Lady Enyo, please continue.' The language of the court was, to put it mildly, archaic. It reflected the stagnancy in their society. Nothing changed, and nobody wanted it to change. They revelled in the unvaryingness of the constant.

Lady Enyo, 'The dethbots are on their way.'

Orator General, Royal Chamberarium, 'Lady Enyo, we know that.'

Lady Enyo, 'Thank you, Orator General. I beg your indulgence to continue.'

Orator General, Royal Chamberarium, 'Approved.'

Lady Enyo, 'Five years ago, we agreed to increase the size of our fleet substantially. Therefore, I respectfully ask the Council for an update.'

Orator General, Royal Chamberarium, 'Who favours an answer?'

There was a show of hands which may have been a majority.

Orator General, Royal Chamberarium, 'The Council have agreed to provide an answer. This will be given in seven turns of the weald.'

Commander Thanatos, 'Well done, my Lady. That went really well.'

Lady Enyo, 'Don't you see, Thanatos, everything just takes so long.'

Commander Thanatos, 'When you are young, everything is urgent. When you get older, big decisions need reflection and careful consideration.'

Lady Enyo, 'I'm nearly nine hundred years old. We need urgent action before it is too late.'

Location: GAD Control Conference Room, (The Galactium Alliance Defence Hub), Planet Earth
Sequence of Events: 87

Madie Millburn, 'Welcome back. First, let's review what we know about The Brakendeth:
- The Brakendeth species have existed for millions of years
- They had an unlimited lifespan
- Over the millennia, they have created thousands of genetically engineered species, including the Skivertons, the Darth, and The Farcellians
- The reasons for creating them have been lost in time
- For millions of years, The Brakendeth have been supplying a product called Chemlife to its client races. It gives them eternal life, or certainly very extended lives
- It also gave The Brakendeth power over their client races
- To generate this chemical, they created a new species, which they called homans
- Every one hundred thousand years they send in mining machines to harvest the homans
- These machines simply hunt for the homan DNA, but they actually take the entire fauna and flora of a human planet
- The harvested material is liquidised and sent to The Brakendeth home world for processing into Chemlife
- A client race called The Skiverton was tasked with carrying out this harvesting, and they killed billions of us
- Our Navy defeated the Skiverton fleet in battle
- The Brakendethians had never experienced any problems before and asked The Skiverton to analyse the homans. In the process, they carried out some horrific experiments
- Originally, The Brakendethians had no idea that homans had developed consciousness
- Because of the above, they stopped the harvesting of humans, which meant no more Chemlife
- As a result, all the client races were going to die agonising deaths. To stop this, The Brakendeth destroyed those client races if they

requested it
- Humanity found the Brakendeth home world and its leaders.
- The Brakendeth ended up killing themselves
- The Brakendeth also seem to be playing some sort of evolution game. They pitted one race against another. The losers were terminated
- This explains why those races attacked us
- Humans have been part of this process. The Brakendeth has been testing us
- We can only assume that The Brakendeth live forever, and consequently, with their long lives, they have little compassion for other races.
- As they made these races, they probably felt that they had the right to destroy them.'

'So, to sum up:
- It would appear that The Brakendeth created the human race
- Our DNA is based on Brakendeth DNA
- We were created with one purpose, to generate one of the critical components of Chemlife.
- The Brakendeth had little idea that humanity had evolved so much
- The dissection of humans on the Skiverton ship was an attempt to investigate the level of evolution that has taken place.

Recently there have been questions regarding The Brakendeth story. Terry, as most of you know, has both human and Brakendethian parenthood. His skills are remarkable.

'A lot of this is new to you, so I suggest that we have another break.'

The moans, groans and mutterings had died down, partly because Madie was such a brilliant speaker and partly because the content was so shocking. Most of them knew some of the facts, but this was the first time that recent history had been explained in such a coherent manner. Most of them couldn't wait for the next session. Why were they here?

Location: On-Board Admiral Mustard's Bedroom in the Flagship
Sequence of Events: 88

Once again, Jack and Edel were cuddling in bed. He had become a cuddle monster. It was partly because he loved Edel and partly because he enjoyed the feel of warm female flesh. He loved touching it, licking it, and mostly biting it. Edel was shocked at first, but now she had got to the stage where she welcomed Jack chewing her arse.

Jack, 'It's all very quiet at the moment.'

Edel, 'It's brilliant. I have you all to myself.'

Jack, 'Not for much longer. There will be three of us.'

Edel, 'Don't remind me. I keep waiting for his first kick.'

Jack. 'He?'

Edel, 'It's just that I can't say "it." Would you prefer a boy?'

Jack, 'I really don't mind.'

Edel, 'So you want a boy?'

Jack, 'Honestly, I don't mind, as long as it's not a ginger.'

Edel, 'What have you got against gingers?'

Jack, 'I was just joking.'

Edel, 'The boy gets his DNA check soon. Did you want to come with me?'

Jack, 'I think I'm busy.'

Edel, 'I've checked, and you are free.'

Jack, 'Well, I think I should be busy. I actually do feel a bit guilty hiding on my ship.'

Edel, 'Do you think I should resign my commission?'

Jack, 'Definitely not.'

Edel, 'Why is that?'

Jack. 'We need the money.'

Edel, 'No, seriously, I could be a lady of leisure.'

Jack, 'I'm against it. The Navy needs your brain power. You probably have the most logical, insightful brain I have ever come across.'

Edel, 'You certainly know how to sweet talk a girl.'

Location: Council Meeting, Royal Chamberarium, Planet Olympus
Sequence of Events: 89

Orator General, Royal Chamberarium, 'Lady Enyo, we have the results of your question.'

Lady Enyo stood up and said, 'Your most esteemed highnesses and eminences, your most worshipable monitors of the Godfire, fellow illustrious Warlords, Lords, Ladies and knights, I thank you.' This was a dangerous moment, as any criticism was not tolerated.

Orator General, Royal Chamberarium, 'Lady Enyo, your concern is no longer appreciated.'

Lady Enyo, 'Thank you, Orator General; I beg to ask why the concern is no longer appreciated.'

Orator General, Royal Chamberarium, 'Lady Enyo, are you questioning our judgement?'

Lady Enyo, 'Indeed not Orator General, I only question the reason for this lack of appreciation.'

Orator General, Royal Chamberarium, 'Lady Enyo, your privileged status allows you to question but not necessarily to receive answers.'

Lady Enyo, 'Indeed Orator General; can I then beg the court to answer a second question?'

Orator General, Royal Chamberarium, 'It will be considered.'

Lady Enyo decided to push her luck at this critical stage, as things were moving quite quickly.

Lady Enyo, 'Orator General, your forbearance and patience is much appreciated. Could you consider allowing the second question during this session?'

Orator General, Royal Chamberarium, 'As I said, it will be considered.'

Senior Prefect to the Royal Hostelry, 'Allow the question now.'

Lady Enyo, 'Thank you, Senior Prefect.' She knew that this would anger the Orator General, but then urgent action was needed.

Orator General, Royal Chamberarium, 'Lady Enyo, your second question may be appreciated.'

Lady Enyo, 'Thank you, Orator General. I beg to ask the following question: How many enemy dethbots are approaching? It is not allowed to mention "Brakendeth" in the council chamber.'

Orator General, Royal Chamberarium, 'Lady Enyo, that question is subject to military protection.'

Lady Enyo, 'I understand Orator General, but I am a warlord.'

Orator General, Royal Chamberarium, 'Lady Enyo, your position is well understood.'

Lady Enyo, 'Thank you, Orator General. Can I then beg the court to answer?'

Orator General, Royal Chamberarium, 'The court declines.'

On their departure from the Chamber, an agent of the Senior Prefect asked to see her privately.

Location: GAD Control Conference Room, (The Galactium Alliance Defence Hub), Planet Earth
Sequence of Events: 90

Madie Millburn, 'Welcome back again. So far, we have covered some recent history, The Nexuster and The Brakendethians.
  'So what do we know about The Chosen?
  • They have significant technology, at least equal to ours
  • They seem to have sound military tactics and procedures
  • They hunt The Nexuster; they claim to have killed it about thirty thousand times
  • They talk about elemental Godfire
  • The Brakendeth led a war against them
  • They are said to be religious fanatics that believe that Godfire has selected them to rule the universe
  • Apparently, The Chosen demanded that The Brakendeth surrender to them and accept their religion. Non-acceptance meant death.
  • The Chosen's navy was well organised and committed, but it didn't have the numbers to beat The Brakendeth
  • It is thought that their defeat by The Brakendeth, which was their first defeat ever, led them to find a species that they could use against The Brakendeth.
  • They chose The Nexuster. However, it appears that The Nexuster destroyed The Chosen's civilian population. All that survived was the military
  • It appears that "Godfire" relates to a talking volcano that exists on their home world
  • Non-believers cannot look at the image of their god. And as The Chosen are created in the image of their god, non-believers cannot look at them
  • They have a fixed mating season
  • They have very low reproduction rates
  • Children are handed over to a central nursery at birth. The parents are hardly involved in a child's upbringing
  • It looks like their weapons and military tactics have not changed in centuries.

'I apologise for the depth of this background information, but it is all very relevant. We now need to turn our attention to current events:
- As mentioned earlier, The Chosen's fleet retired when confronted by the joint Galactium and Brakendeth fleets
- The Brakendeth fleet then retired
- Then it was discovered that The Farcellian planets and The Brakendethian home complex had been nuked
- There were suspicions that The Chosen carried out these attacks
- There are even suspicions that The Chosen released The Nexuster on Planet Turing
- We sent Admiral Abosa with a scientific team to investigate the bombings
- Nuclear signatures proved that The Chosen were not involved in the destruction
- It was established that the bombings were undertaken by The Brakendethian fleet
- Terry and his mother have gone missing, so they can't be questioned.

'We have lost the treasure trove that The Brakendeth home complex proved to be, but it was destroyed by The Brakendethians, who are no more.

'This leaves us with the following questions:
- Why would The Brakendeth destroy their home planet?
- Why would Terry do it?
- How can the Brakendethians still influence Terry?
- Where are Terry and his mother?
- Why would The Chosen attack our Fleet?

'Our short-term action plan is as follows:
- Continue to build up our forces to protect humanity
- Find Terry and interrogate him
- Identify if Terry is still under Brakendeth influence
- Continue to investigate The Nexuster and any involvement by The Chosen
- Investigate ways of countering The Chosen's weapons.

'Time for another break. When we come back, I will outline your involvement.'

Location: Cheryl's Secret Location, Planet Earth
Sequence of Events: 91

Cheryl, 'How long do we have to stay in hiding?'
    Terry, 'Possibly forever.'
    Cheryl, 'That's ridiculous.'
    Terry, 'I don't see how I can sort things out.'
    Cheryl, 'Often it is best just to come clean.'
    Terry, 'But they will kill me.'
    Cheryl, 'Why is that?'
    Terry, 'Because the Grand Dethmon lives inside me.'
    Cheryl, 'Don't be silly!'
    Grand Dethmon, 'He is telling the truth.'
    Cheryl heard the voice inside her head. She naively looked around the room to see who was talking.
    Grand Dethmon, 'Cheryl, you are hearing my voice directly in your head. My essence lives in Terry's mind. Likewise, the spirit of the whole Brakendethian race lives in Terry's head.'
    Cheryl, 'This is a bit of a surprise. What are you hoping to achieve?'
    Grand Dethmon, 'We want to see Terry and the Homans succeed where we failed.'
    Cheryl, 'And what is that?'
    Grand Dethmon, 'To be the dominant species in the universe.'
    Cheryl, 'So nothing too demanding.'
    The Grand Dethmon never really understood the homan sense of humour.
    Terry, 'There are extensive searching activities going on. The Police, the Secret Service and AI Central are all heavily involved. The Grand Dethmon has created an inter-dimensional bubble. We don't really exist on Earth. So they won't be able to find us.'
    Cheryl, 'What about supplies? What about Coronation Street?'
    Terry, 'Don't worry, Mummy, you will be going to sleep soon.' And suddenly, Cheryl felt tired.

Location: Senior Prefect's Meetarium, Planet Olympus
Sequence of Events: 92

Senior Prefect, 'Lady Enyo, you ask questions of a delicate nature.'

Lady Enyo, 'Thank you most esteemed Prefect for asking me to meet with you.'

Senior Prefect, 'Lady Enyo, the honour is all mine, but you risk much.'

Lady Enyo, 'I risk not for me but for the greater glory of The Chosen.'

Senior Prefect, 'That is appreciated, but questions have been asked about your judgement.'

Lady Enyo, 'That may not be avoidable, Senior Prefect.'

Senior Prefect, 'Lady Enyo, let's say that the future safety of you and your house may be at risk.'

Lady Enyo, 'I hope not, your eminence, as I only wish to highlight concerns that could endanger the everlasting nature of The Chosen.'

Senior Prefect, 'But concerns can be construed as criticism Lady Enyo. And criticism can be dangerous. Do you understand?' The Prefect was treating her fairly gently as she was young. She was still less than a thousand years old.

Lady Enyo, 'I bow to your greater experience in these matters.'

Senior Prefect, 'That is appreciated. Why don't you ask me the questions in a forthright manner, and I will see if I can get you the answers?'

Lady Enyo, 'It was never my intention to offend you, and if offence is achieved, then I humbly apologise.'

Senior Prefect, 'Lady Enyo, offence may be achieved by not getting to the point.'

Lady Enyo, 'Once again, I bow to your greater experience in these matters, but I know the answers.'

Senior Prefect, 'Then you waste the time of the Court, you waste *my* time and have caused considerable offence. Your house is waning, Lady Enyo, waning.'

Lady Enyo, 'As before, it was never my intention to offend you, and if offence is achieved, then I humbly apologise.'

Senior Prefect, 'Apologies cannot be a substitute for poor taste, my Lady.'

Lady Enyo, 'My Lord, is it bad taste to state that five years ago, it was decided to substantially increase the size of our fleet? Is it bad taste to state that not a single new vessel has been produced in those five years? Is it bad taste to state that the dethbot fleet has over two million vessels and is still making its way towards Olympus?

'Is it bad taste to state the Earthers have greater military resources than us? Is it bad taste that our significant accomplishments are unlikely to be appreciated in the future?

'Once again, I bow to your greater experience in these matters.'

Senior Prefect, 'Your manners are shocking. Do you know my position and the respect it deserves?'

Lady Enyo, 'I humbly respect your position, and I have the highest regards for yourself. It was never my intention to offend you, but what I said had to be said.'

Senior Prefect, 'Well, young lady, you have made your point and made it well. What are we going to do about it?'

Lady Enyo, 'I speak in the humblest way possible, but normally we do nothing.'

Senior Prefect, 'Careful lass, you are verging on being treasonable.'

Lady Enyo, 'If it takes treason to make things happen, then that must be the path I tread.'

Senior Prefect, 'I think I know a way forward.'

Location: GAD Control Conference Room, (The Galactium Alliance Defence Hub), Planet Earth
Sequence of Events: 93

Madie Millburn, 'You will be pleased to hear that this is going to be the last session today.'
There were a few claps.

Madie Millburn, 'There have been several claims concerning our heritage:
- The Brakendeth claim that they made homans using their DNA structure
- It was a sub-set of their DNA that was used to create cattle which were used to generate Chemlife
- They harvested humanity every one hundred thousand years
- So one hundred thousand years ago, we did not have consciousness
- The Brakendethians carried out research in an attempt to determine how we achieved it, but to no avail
- Terry has been using our DNA structure to release a series of corrective drugs, which many of you have experienced (cures for cancer, asthma, baldness, etc.)

'I have mentioned several times that the content of these briefings is top secret and that you have all signed confidentiality agreements. I can announce that we have two new medical treatments. Firstly, there is a treatment to rejuvenate the human body. Then there is a second treatment that extends human life to one thousand years. I'm not going to take any questions on these subjects.'

There was a huge round of applause and a palpable excitement in the air.

Madie Millburn, 'I will carry on:
- There are some doubts about the truth of The Brakendeth claims
- There are claims by Terry that The Chosen have visited Earth many times in the past
- Terry claimed that they visited Earth three hundred times in a thousand years. The actual period is unknown
- There is reason to believe that Terry lied about the number of visits

- It is likely that he didn't understand the periods involved

The following conjectures have been discussed:
- The Brakendethians couldn't work out who converted human cows into sentient beings. Could it have been The Chosen?
- Were the UFO sightings in the twentieth century genuine?
- There have been questions about the speed of human development: *In year zero, we were a peasant society. Fifteen hundred years later, we hadn't really evolved that much. Yet, by the twentieth century, we had the combustion engine, jet aircraft, primitive space travel, the internet, microprocessors, DNA knowledge, heart transplants, mobile phones, and much more.*

This millennium, we have conquered space and held our head high in terms of most alien encounters. These are aliens that have been civilised for thousands or even hundreds of thousands of years.'
- We have learnt that The Chosen are eternal, so it could be the same individual visitor or team that have been coming to Earth for hundreds of years.

Madie Millburn, 'At last we have come to the point where I can outline your task or tasks:

1. Have we been visited by aliens in the past?
2. Have we been manipulated by The Brakendethians or The Chosen, or some other race?
3. Identify critical points in history where significant innovations took place. Look for rapid developments, especially revolutionary as opposed to evolutionary changes.
4. Look for any unexplained phenomenon — UFOs, ghosts, voices, angels, devils, etc.

'Any questions regarding the task?'

The audience, 'Are you being serious?

Madie Millburn, 'Deadly serious. We are planning our first meeting with The Chosen. First, we need to know if they have visited us in the past.'

The audience, 'Why angels, ghosts, etc.?

Madie Millburn, 'We feel that the primitive mind might see them as mythical creatures.'

The audience, 'What period of time do we need to cover?'

Madie Millburn, 'The whole of human history.'

The audience, 'What resources will we have?'

Madie Millburn, 'Whatever you need will be provided.'

The audience, 'When do we start?'

Madie Millburn, 'Today.'

The audience, 'Are we convinced that the claims are genuine?'

Madie Millburn, 'Yes.'

The audience, 'Can you give us some examples of what you are looking for?'

Madie Millburn, 'I'm not an expert, but the following are possible examples:
- Jesus Christ — miracles
- Buddha
- Archimedes — the bath and buoyancy laws
- Isaac Newton — the apple and gravity
- Einstein — Theory of Relativity
- Tesla — Alternating current
- Mendeleev — Periodic table
- Bohr — Atom model.'

The audience, 'Why do you include some religious icons?

Madie Millburn, 'There have been speculations that they could have been visitors from outer space. Please prove them right or wrong.'

'Professor Brian (or *Brain*, as many of you know him) Hillingdon will head the project. He will allocate tasks along with AI Central. I will remain as Project Sponsor. Thank you for your time. Good hunting.'

There was a genuine round of applause.

Location: GAD Control Conference Room, (The Galactium Alliance Defence Hub), Planet Earth
Sequence of Events: 94

Admiral Mustard called a meeting of his Command. The following were present:
- Admiral George Bumelton
- Admiral Edel Bonner
- Admiral John Bonner
- Admiral Peter Gittins
- Admiral Phil Richardson
- Admiral Calensky Wallett
- Admiral Steve Adams
- Admiral Ama Abosa
- Admiral Lesley Chudzinski
- Admiral Bob Fieldhouse
- Admiral Sammy Fogg
- Admiral Keith Easter
- Admiral Mateo Dobson
- Admiral Lenny Hubbard
- Admiral James Patel
- Admiral Karl Lamberty
- Admiral Hermann Wagner
- Admiral Nubia Tersoo
- Admiral Rachel Zakotti
- Admiral Ernst Muller
- Admiral Liz Clowe
- Admiral Dave Beamish
- Commander Tom Crocker, Special Operations
- Commander Debbie Goozee, Marine Corps
- Sales Director, Sheila Taylor
- AI Central
- President Padfield

He explained that it was just a general update.
'The first point on the agenda is The Chosen:
- Since the ambush, we have not had any contact with them

- We are expecting them to contact us, but so far, it has been very quiet
- We have upgraded all of our force fields to cope with the power weapons that killed Admiral Pearce and our other colleagues
- There is a memorial service for Glen. Please put the date in your diary
- There has been speculation that The Chosen have been visiting Earth for a few hundred years. We have a team of notable academics trying to provide evidence to support this
- I plan to move some of the Fleets to Earth orbit in case The Chosen decide to surprise us. Any objections or questions?'

Admiral Fogg, 'Do we know why they ambushed us?'

Admiral Mustard, 'The answer is no, but we suspect that they simply saw us as being aggressive.'

Admiral Gittins, 'Do we still plan to find their home world?'

Admiral Mustard, 'Yes. We are hoping to have some discussions with them first.'

Admiral Hubbard, 'Did we find out anything from their space debris?'

Admiral Mustard, 'Not a lot, but we surmised the following:
- Oxygen breathers
- Humanoid but generally taller than us
- Their craft are made to last. Some of the vessels fighting us were over three hundred years old
- No DNA was found, which was strange. They self-destruct their vessels to stop people like us from researching them
- We discovered a few nice features on their craft which we are designing into ours.

'Ama investigated the nuked Farcellian and Brakendeth planets. They had not been bombed by The Chosen.'

Admiral Bumelton, 'Who did bomb them?'

Admiral Mustard, 'The Brakendeth destroyed both planets.'

Admiral Bumelton, 'Why would The Brakendeth destroy their own world? And of course, they don't exist any more.'

Admiral Mustard, 'We suspect that it was Terry as he had control of the Fleet, and he has since disappeared.'

Admiral Lamberty, 'What do you mean *disappeared*?'

AI Central, 'We can't detect his presence on Earth.'

Admiral Mustard, 'The Brakendeth situation was the second point on the agenda. As already covered:

- The Brakendeth planet has been completely nuked
- It was destroyed by Brakendeth nuclear weapons
- We believe that Terry was involved
- It is not clear why he would have destroyed the Farcellian system
- Terry and his mother have disappeared. We must treat them as potential enemies
- Is Terry still being influenced by The Brakendeth? We need to find him

'Any questions on The Brakendeth?'

Admiral Dobson, 'They never seem to go away.'

Admiral Mustard, 'I agree whatever we do, they seem to be part of it.'

Admiral Gittins, 'So our inheritance is effectively lost.'

Admiral Mustard, 'You are right, Peter. It's a tragic loss. Someone compared it to the loss of the library in Alexandra.'

Admiral Fieldhouse, 'It might be a blessing in disguise or some other platitude.'

Admiral Wallett, 'Obviously, Terry can't just disappear.'

Admiral Mustard, 'He has done a damned good job of just doing that.'

Admiral Wallett, 'Are we at risk regarding his developments?'

Admiral Mustard, 'Not any more. Every invention is carefully studied and documented before it is released.'

Admiral Wallett, 'Are we sure? I'm thinking of the battery crisis.'

AI Central, 'We believe that we are fully protected nowadays although you can never be one hundred per cent sure.'

Admiral Mustard, 'The next point on the agenda is The Nexuster. All I can report is that we have not learnt anything new.

'Point Five is Construction. I can report the following:

1. The reconstruction of the Moon has been completed, and we will have a set of offices there for our use
2. Ten Regional Defence Centres (RDCs) are going to be built. They

will contain strong defence capabilities equivalent to at least twenty forts. 'In addition, they will have full docking, repair, R&R, storage, and medical facilities. Each RDC will be commanded by a Rear Admiral

3. The navy has selected an unoccupied planet to become its HQ

4. A new memorial park for the navy is going to be established.

'Any questions?'

Admiral Easter, 'What is a Rear-Admiral?'

Admiral Mustard. 'It's a grade above a Commodore but a grade below a Vice Admiral.'

Admiral Easter, 'What's a Vice Admiral?'

Admiral Mustard. 'It's a grade above a Rear Admiral but a grade below an Admiral. However, the real question, Keith, is do you know what an Admiral is?'

There were howls of laughter.

Admiral Easter, 'I believe I do, Sir.'

Admiral Mustard, 'That's a relief. As the navy is growing, there is a need for an enhanced grading structure.'

Point Six on the agenda is Chemlife Sales. Our plan is to cover a large proportion of the cost of the navy via Chemlife sales to aliens. We have consequently recruited a Sales Director.

'Sheila, can you stand up and show yourself?'

Sheila duly stood up and bowed.

Admiral Mustard, 'In the future, Sheila will update you on sales. Part of your job is to assist her in every possible way. Her endeavours will pay your salary. As far as I'm concerned, she has Admiral status.'

'Any questions?'

Admiral Patel, 'When are we going to get an extended lifespan?'

Admiral Mustard, 'That brings me onto point six labelled "Top Secret" because it is top secret. I've asked Henrietta Strong to update you.'

Henrietta Strong, 'For those who don't know, I'm Chief of Staff. I can get you all sacked.'

There were a few laughs, but not many.

Henrietta Strong, 'I'm going to announce something top secret and extraordinary. I need your support.

'We have developed two new medical processes:

- Rejuvenation
- Extended life

'The first process, as its name suggests, rejuvenates the human body. It takes your body back twenty to thirty years in terms of health and appearance. It can't make the ugly attractive. That includes you, George. It works better on some people than others.

'Could I ask the legendary Admiral E Bonner to stand up? This young lady is over eighty. I think you will all agree that the rejuv has done a pretty good job.'

Edel curtsied and sat down.

Henrietta Strong, 'Once that process has been successfully completed, then we can move onto the next stage: extended life. Initially, we plan to extend the human lifespan to one thousand years.

'It is our plan to offer this to every human for a small fee. As an undertaking, it will be massive. However, whatever model we use it tells us to expect riots. This is going to be revolutionary, but the process is going to be time-consuming. The implementation is going to be challenging. We are going to need the navy's help in maintaining order. It is also our intention to include the navy in the first tranche of treatments. Is that OK with you?'

The hearty clapping suggested that it was.

Admiral Mustard, 'Thank you, Henreitta. No questions and remember that this is top secret. I think we have covered everything on the agenda.

'My orders:
- Move four additional Fleets to defend Earth in case there is a surprise attack by The Chosen
- Admirals Zakotti and Fogg to work on the RDCs
- Admiral Gittins to work with Henrietta Strong re the new medical treatments
- Admiral Adams to work on the construction of the new Fleet HQ
- Admiral Easter to be Sheila Taylor's primary day-to-day Fleet contact
- Rear Admiral Mynd to take over Fleet Five

'And lastly, I command Admiral E Bonner to marry me.'

Admiral E Bonner, 'I accept your orders, Sir.' There was a serious outbreak of cheering.

Location: Senior Prefect's Meetarium, Planet Olympus
Sequence of Events: 95

Senior Prefect, 'Lady Enyo, I hope that your House prospers in these strange times.'

Lady Enyo, 'Thank you, most esteemed Prefect, for your wishes, and I hope that your House also prospers.'

Senior Prefect, 'I've spoken to sources at the highest level, and although your questions are an affront, I've secured an audience for you.'

Lady Enyo, 'Thank you most esteemed Prefect for achieving such an honour.'

Senior Prefect, 'Lady Enyo, the honour is all mine, but you risk much.'

Lady Enyo, 'As I've said before, I risk not for me but for the greater glory of The Chosen.'

Senior Prefect, 'That is appreciated. I can offer you further honours. The audience is scheduled for the hour of the cock.'

Lady Enyo, 'Am I to be sacrificed to The Grand Visor's appetites?'

Senior Prefect, 'Lady Enyo that is to be seen, but as you said, you are risking everything for the honour of The Chosen.'

Lady Enyo, 'But when I said everything, I didn't expect that it would be at the cost of my maidenhood.'

Senior Prefect, 'That is understood, but The Grand Visor is on heat. What better time to gain his attention?'

Lady Enyo, 'But my House will disown me. I will become a leper of the night.'

Senior Prefect, 'That is assuming The Grand Visor is merciful, my Lady. You asked the questions. It is now time for judgement.'

Lady Enyo, 'Your Eminence, will I be publicly violated?'

Senior Prefect, 'Of course, my Lady. That is the tradition. I understand that The Grand Visor has appreciated your talents from afar and welcomes this opportunity.'

Lady Enyo, 'But if I don't please him, I forfeit my life that night.'

Senior Prefect, 'That is true, my Lady. My advice is to please him. Your maid will have access to his glorious preferences.'

Lady Enyo, 'My Lord, what if he offers my services to the court?'

Senior Prefect, 'That would be unfortunate, and suicide may be a better option.'

Lady Enyo, 'So the stories are true?'

Senior Prefect, 'That is not for me to say, but your maid will know.'

Lady Enyo, 'Thank you, my Lord.'

Senior Prefect, 'I will pick you up at the allotted time. As you know, clothing is not required. Before we get to meet The Grand Visor, your virginity will be legalised.'

Lady Enyo updated Commander Thanatos, who said, 'I tried to warn you, my Lady. I will put the House and Fleet on full alert. You have the option of fleeing.'

Lady Enyo, 'They will hunt us down and convert us into Nexusters.'

Commander Thanatos, 'There is no worse fate, my Lady.'

Lady Enyo, 'I brought this upon myself. I must go through with it. Make all the preparations you can to protect the House. The wolves are probably prowling already.'

Commander Thanatos, 'Yes, my Lady.' He knew what needed to be done. He knew that his very long life was now in jeopardy. He knew that every member of the house's life was now in mortal danger. Failure would mean mass executions.

Lady Enyo, 'I need to discuss things with my maid.'

Location: GAD Control Conference Room, (The Galactium Alliance Defence Hub), Planet Earth
Sequence of Events: 96

Professor Brian Hillingdon, 'Ladies and gentlemen, I think most of you know me. I thought that I would cover the rules of engagement first and then allocate projects.

'Rules of Engagement
- For obvious reasons, this project is top secret
- There is no limit regarding resources
- Every library and museum in The Galactium has been told to assist you in every way possible
- The Military has allocated resources to assist
- We may or may not publish the final results
- You will be encouraged to investigate any lead, no matter how stupid it sounds
- Everything that is said or seen in this complex stays in this complex
- You will be allowed to meet with your families and friends, but you must maintain high levels of secrecy
- All contact with the press and other media organisations is to be banned at this stage
- Your salaries during the life of the project will be doubled
- All expenses will be paid

'Any questions?'

The audience, 'Brian, have you been told things that we don't know?'

Professor Brian Hillingdon, 'The simple answer is no.'

The audience, 'Are you clear about the objectives?'

Professor Brian Hillingdon, 'Broadly, we are looking for any evidence that aliens have contacted human civilisation in its past. The terms "contact" and "past" are up for debate.'

The audience, 'What do you mean by contact?' The audience laughed.

Professor Brian Hillingdon, 'My definition of contact would be comprehensive. At one level, it would be just a sighting of an alien or

UFO. At the other end of the spectrum, it would include any proof of a detailed manipulation of our history, civilisation, inventions, outlook, medicine, etc.'

The audience, 'And what is your definition of the past?' There was further laughter.

Professor Brian Hillingdon, 'I would include our period of consciousness. Is that the last one hundred thousand years? I'm not sure.'

The audience, 'Why is there so much secrecy?'

Professor Brian Hillingdon, 'Good question. It was one I asked. I've listed the reasons on the screen:

- There has been too much change for the public to cope with
- What is the truth regarding The Brakendeth?
- What is the truth regarding The Chosen?
- The answers to the above two questions may or may not be good for the human psyche
- The destruction of The Brakendeth home world is not public knowledge yet
- Fear of The Nexuster
- Possible war with The Chosen
- Rejuv and extended life disruption
- Clarity is desperately needed in several areas
- Help needed regarding the best way of informing the general public
- Fear of riots.

'It is not the Government's intention to keep everything secret. It is more of a timing issue.'

Professor Brian Hillingdon, 'I've divided the investigation into the following areas:

1. The start of consciousness
2. The appearance of Homo sapiens
3. The appearance of Homo neanderthalensis
4. Pre-history — Asia
5. Pre-history — Africa
6. Pre-history — Australia
7. Pre-history — Europe
8. Mesolithic

9. Neolithic
10. Chalcolithic (Copper Age)
11. Protohistory
12. Ancient History — Mesopotamia and China
13. Classical Antiquity — Greece
14. Classical Antiquity — Rome
15. Post Classical — Han China
16. Post Classical — Western Roman Empire
17. Post-Classical — Gupta Empire
18. Post-Classical — Sasanian Empire
19. Early Middle Ages (Dark Ages)
20. High Middle Ages
21. Late Middle Ages
22. Renaissance
23. Age of Discovery
24. Early Modern Period
25. Late Modern Period
26. The Nineteen-Twenties (1920–1929)
27. The Nineteen-Thirties (1930–1939)
28. The Nineteen-Forties (1940–1949)
29. The Nineteen-Fifties (1950–1959)
30. The Nineteen-Sixties (1960–1969)
31. The Nineteen-Seventies (1970–1979)
32. The Nineteen-Eighties (1980–1989)
33. The Nineteen-Nineties (1990–1999)
34. The Two Thousands (2000–2009)
35. The Twenty-Tens (2010–2019)
36. The Twenty-Twenties (2020–2029)
37. The Twenty-Thirties (2030–2039)
38. The Twenty-Forties (2040–2049)
39. The Twenty-Fifties (2050–2059)
40. The Twenty-Sixties (2060–2069)
41. The Twenty-Seventies (2070–2079)
42. The Twenty-Eighties (2080–2089)
43. The Twenty-Nineties (2090–2099)
44. The Twenty-Noughties (2200–2209)

45. Industrial Revolution
46. Atomic Age
47. World War 1
48. World War 2
49. Cold War
50. Terrorism
51. COVID-19 Pandemic
52. Information Age
53. Space Age
54. China
55. Japan
56. USA
57. USSR
58. UK
59. France
60. Spain and Portugal
61. South-East Asia
62. Central Asia
63. Greece
64. Italy
65. Persia
66. Viking Age
67. Byzantine Age
68. India
69. Colonialism
70. Age of Enlightenment
71. Christianity
72. Protestant Reformation
73. Islam
74. Buddhism
75. Hinduism
76. Taoism
77. Shinto
78. Sikhism
79. Judaism
80. Confucianism

81. Jainism
82. Spiritualism
83. Mongolia
84. Napoleonic Era
85. Mughal Empire
86. Maratha Empire
87. South American Indians
88. West Asia
89. Science and Scientists
90. Art and Artists
91. The Galactium
92. The Race for Space
93. UFOs
94. Great Mysteries
95. Non-conforming humans
96. Alien encounters
97. The Military

'You will notice that there are several overlaps. This is quite deliberate. AI Central will allocate you to the investigation areas.

Location: On-Board Admiral Mustard's Flagship
Sequence of Events: 97

Admiral Mustard, 'Update me.'

Fleet Operations, 'Additional Fleets have been moved to protect Earth.'

Admiral Mustard: 'Show me the disposition.'

Fleet Operations, 'It's on the screen now, Sir.'

Fleet No	Task/Location	Admiral	Status
1	Earth	Mustard	100%
2	Earth	Bumelton	100%
3	Earth	J Bonner	100%
4	Earth	Gittins	87%
5	Earth	Mynd	72%
6	Earth	Richardson	100%
7	Earth	Wallett	92%
8	Newton	Adams	100%
9	Exploration	Beamish	100%
10	Darwin	Chudzinski	100%
11	Joule	Fieldhouse	100%
12	Galileo	Fogg	91%
13	Babbage	Easter	89%
14	Turing	Dobson	100%
15	Blackwell	Hubbard	100%
16	Copernicus	Patel	88%
17	Brahmagupta	Lamberty	100%
18	Fardel System	Abosa	97%
19	Fardel System	Wagner	92%
20	Meitner	Tersoo	100%
Forts	Planet duty	Zakotti	100%
Earth Defence	Earth	Muller	100%
Exploratory	Multiple Locations	Olowe	93%

Fleet Operations, 'Five more Fleets are coming on board, Sir. They have a full complement of staff but need admirals.'

Admiral Mustard, 'Do we have a list of candidates?'

Fleet Operations, 'I will confer with AI Central.

Both Commanders Crocker and Goozee are reporting full complements.'

Admiral Mustard, 'Are there any operational problems?'

Fleet Operations, 'No, Sir.'

Admiral Mustard, 'Any personal problems you want to share with me?'

Fleet Operations. 'Very funny, Sir.'

Fleets Ops had got used to the Admiral's sense of humour. Sometimes they even laughed.

Admiral Mustard, 'Comms, can you get Henrietta Strong?'

Comms, 'Yes, Sir.'

Henrietta Strong, 'Hi Jack, how can I help you?'

Admiral Mustard, 'I just wondered how drone manufacturing was progressing?'

Henrietta Strong, 'Well, you and The President asked me to up the output rates after our encounter with The Chosen. That was initially a bit challenging after losing our production facility on Planet Turing. However, since then, we have got our output up to ten thousand per week.'

Admiral Mustard, 'So you are effectively producing a Drone Fleet of ten thousand every week?'

Henrietta Strong, 'That's correct.'

Admiral Mustard, 'So, currently, we have two operational Drone Fleets. How many do you have?'

Henrietta Strong, 'In the last few months, we have handed over twenty-four Fleets, and we have three in production.'

Admiral Mustard, 'That's two hundred and seventy thousand drones.'

Henrietta Strong, 'That's correct. Is that enough?'

Admiral Mustard, 'It would be nice to get to the million figure.'

Henrietta Strong, 'Your wish is my command. Do you want any more of the super drones?'

Admiral Mustard, 'Yes, please.'

Henrietta Strong, 'Are they more urgent than the standard drones, and how many do you want?'

Admiral Mustard, 'I would like twenty-thousand super drones. I think they should take priority over the standard drones.'

Henrietta Strong, 'No probs, I will change the schedule.'

Location: Lady Enyo's Palace, The Chosen, Olympus
Sequence of Events: 98

Lady Enyo, 'Keeper of the Household, I would like a private word with the senior maid.'

Keeper of the Household, 'Can I ask why, my Lady?'

Lady Enyo, 'Not at this stage. Just bring her to me.'

Keeper of the Household, 'Yes, my Lady.'

Lenna, the maid, was brought to her Ladyship's chamber.

Lady Enyo, 'Have you been trained in the ways of the court?'

Lenna, 'Yes, my Lady.'

Lady Enyo, 'Do you have specific knowledge regarding the time of the cock?'

Lenna, 'Oh no, my Lady.'

Lady Enyo, 'Answer me.'

Lenna, 'Yes, my Lady, I do have that knowledge, but it's not for the ears of a lady.'

Lady Enyo, 'I need to know the procedure as I'm meeting The Grand Visor at the time of the cock.'

Lenna, 'Why *you*, my Lady?'

Lady Enyo, 'That's irrelevant. Tell me what you know.'

Lenna, 'Firstly, you must be cleansed. I will remove all hair from your pubic area. I will then wash and oil you. There are specific protocols for hair display. First, your mouth, ears, nose, and anus must be syringed and oiled.

'You will then be collected by your sponsor and walked naked to the Royal Palace. You will then do a full bow to every corner of the room.

'The Royal Doctor will then check that your hymen is intact. If it is not, you will be executed immediately. I assume that yours is intact.'

Lady Enyo just nodded. She was trying to cope with just the embarrassment of talking about it.

'The Royal Doctor will announce that you are "Virginius Intacto". You will then be presented to The Grand Vizier. You will curtsey in front of him. You will then turn around and present your vagina to him. You must show full compliance and humbleness. It is an honour for him to even look at you.

'You must stay in that position until he decides what to do with you.'

Lady Enyo, 'What does that mean?'

Lenna, 'You are there for his pleasure. If you are lucky, he will stand up, free his penis, and fuck you. Four of his acolytes will hold you in position.

'If you are unlucky or he is not in the mood, then he will present you to the court.'

Lady Enyo, 'What happens there?'

Lenna, 'It's too awful to say.'

Lady Enyo, 'I insist that you carry on.'

Lenna, 'Presenting you to the court means that everyone present can have you. Few women survive being fucked by a couple of hundred men. Usually, someone does the decent thing and slits the victim's throat.'

Lady Enyo, 'At the start?'

Lenna, 'No, my Lady. If you survive, then you are ripped apart and fed to the dogs because you become the lowest of the low. That is all you are fit for.'

Lady Enyo, 'How utterly awful.'

Lenna, 'We'd better start preparing you. You can't afford to be late.'

Location: Lady Enyo's Palace, The Chosen, Olympus
Sequence of Events: 99

Lenna removed Lady Enyo's pubic hair. It was an act that got her angry. Why should her body hair be removed at the whim of a monarch who had been in power before historic records began? No one alive knew of a time when he wasn't The Grand Vizier.

She was over nine hundred years old. Being of royal blood, she wasn't allowed to have sex or get married until The Grand Vizier gave permission. The penalty for breaking the rules was a public execution. The penalty for breaking any law was a public execution. Flogging was a daily occurrence. The Grand Vizier enjoyed the power of humiliation.

Society for The Chosen was a series of archaic rules and regulations that had been fixed in time but were subject to immediate change at The Grand Vizier's whim. Decisions could only be made with his permission, but decisions were never made. The ability to make and take hard decisions had been lost. Those who still had the ability to think realised that they were on the road to ruin. Their civilisation was coming to an end; a very abrupt end if things didn't change.

Lady Enyo was washed and polished and syringed and braided and prepared for a good fucking. She had heard that it wasn't even good, but as she had no experience in this area, she didn't feel that she could comment. She wondered if she should have spent more time in court, but then she would have seen one degradation after another. Anyway, being a warlord, she wasn't expected to have courtly manners.

The Senior Prefect picked her up at the allotted time. She hoped that he would respect her modesty, but this wasn't the case. He stared at her breasts and newly shaven vagina. The bulge in his silk pants meant that he didn't have to say a word. He walked her naked down the alleyways to the Royal Palace.

Before they arrived, he took her into a small backstreet workshop. She was ordered to lie on the bed. A dirty old man forced her legs apart and, without any discussion or permission, casually broke her hymen. This was a small piece of skin that she had carefully protected for nine hundred years. She now had the status of a street slut. It angered her to think that her society valued it so highly.

The operation was quickly completed, and the hymen was repaired. The Senior Prefect spent some time carefully checking her vagina. He spent more time on it than necessary, but then both of their lives depended on it looking perfect.

The guards of the Royal Household checked them both when they arrived. Full-body searches were the norm. They seemed to enjoy the more intimate aspects of her body. The Senior Prefect was given a gold chain to put around Lady Enyo's neck. She was not a woman any more but an object of desire, now owned by the Senior Prefect.

She walked through the crowded court corridors. The courtiers had seen this type of thing many times, but she was a fine specimen. She was far more attractive than your everyday victim. She had kept herself fit, and she had a military bearing. Nevertheless, she maintained an arrogant posture. Several male courtiers were secretly hoping that she would be thrown to the court.

She was made to bend over in front of the Royal Doctor. He took the opportunity to surreptitiously caress her dangling breasts. They were full, but perfectly formed. Her nipples were hard. She wasn't sure if it was the temperature or the excitement. The Doctor gently pulled her labia apart and gently stroked the vagina until he was satisfied that the hymen was intact.

The Senior Prefect caught the eye of his Second in Command. The simple blink of his eye told him that everything was ready. With the doctor's permission, Lady Enyo was moved to the centre of the room, where she bowed to each corner. She made a beautiful sight. Her shapely legs, flat stomach, well-proportioned breasts, long black hair, and shaven fanny made a genuine impression on the audience.

The Grand Vizier was also impressed. He had previously decided that he was going to throw the arrogant bitch to the court. He was looking forward to seeing her being gang-raped and then fed to the dogs. But her natural beauty seduced him. She was going to be one of the lucky ones. He would fornicate with her. He could feel his cock swelling in anticipation.

Lady Enyo was marched towards The Grand Vizier. The Senior Prefect handed over the gold chain, and Lady Enyo curtsied. She then turned around, bent over, and pulled her labia apart so that The Grand

Vizier could see the delights on offer.

The Grand Vizier had decided that this bitch needed to be taught a lesson. An assistant pulled his fully erect prick from his pantaloons. His phallus had been artificially enhanced. A few inches had been added, the girth had been increased, and it was far more sensitive than most.

Four of his acolytes realised that his majesty was going to partake in the pleasures of the flesh and rushed to secure Lady Enyo. Two of them grabbed her arms and breasts. The other two grabbed a leg each. The Grand Vizier had no time for foreplay. He demanded immediate access to the vagina. A mighty initial thrust was needed to break the hymen and gain full access.

He walked down the steps and ran towards Lady Enyo. His erect penis was dangling before him. He carefully positioned his cock and without any mercy, thrust forwards, breaking her hymen, shooting his semen up her and killing himself.

The barb in her vagina contained a deadly poison. Fortunately, she had been given the antidote. Before he died, thirty throats had been cut in the chamber. Before he collapsed on top of Lady Enyo, a further thirty throats had been cut. Finally, the Palace guard had disappeared.

While his penis was still in her vagina, a further thirty throats had been cut. Hopefully, her Commander had eliminated key individuals throughout the capital.

Lady Enyo managed to disengage herself from both the Grand Vizier's penis and body. The four acolytes looked at her and ran. She didn't think they survived the night of the long knives. There were many scores that had to be settled. Her team had done an impressive job. As far as she was concerned, it was out with the old. Now she had to make sure that the new age had been worth her modesty.

She was also relieved that her virginity had been lost. It had been hard work keeping it intact. She was now free, being a street slut, to fuck whoever she wanted. The next nine hundred years might be a lot of fun. She thought that Senior Prefect might be her first target. The look in his eyes suggested that he knew what a vagina was for.

The Senior Prefect was covered in blood. Lady Enyo looked at him, worried that he had been wounded. But, he said, 'I'm fine. I just had a few old scores to settle.'

He then bent down in front of Lady Enyo and said, 'I pledge my allegiance to the new Grand Vizier.'

Lady Enyo, 'What are you doing? That is your job'

Senior Prefect, 'Not me, my Lady; I have never been a leader, but you are.'

Then all the remaining courtiers bowed and pledged their allegiance. She stood there in her naked glory as Grand Vizier of The Chosen. Things were going to change, and quickly.

Location: Henrietta Strong's Office, GAD Control, (The Galactium Alliance Defence Hub), Planet Earth
Sequence of Events: 100

Henrietta Strong created a small working party consisting of Tony Moore (Deputy President), Bill Penny (Leader of The Galactium Council), Madie Milburn (Fleet HQ Head of Intelligence), Admiral Adams and Jane Killroy (representing the general public) to manage the implementation of the rejuvenation and extended life strategies. They had decided to call themselves "Life Services".

Henrietta Strong, 'Shall I update everyone regarding current progress?'

There was a nodding of heads.

Henrietta Strong, 'Progress report:

- A Life Services Director has been appointed for every human-occupied planet
- The rejuv process has started for Naval volunteers
- There is now an automated manufacturing plant for the Rejuv drug-producing one million units per Earth week. We still need to increase the production rate
- A new factory is being built for the Extended Life drug. It is a more complex manufacturing process
- A date has been fixed for The President to announce the new Life Services offer
- The police, national guard, marine and naval forces have been put on guard on that date to suppress any rioting
- Each Life Service Director is producing planetary implementation plans with dates
- The navy will distribute the drugs at planetary levels
- New heavily guarded storage units are being established on each planet
- An emergency request system is being set up for both drugs
- Help desks are being established on each planet
- An accounting team has been set up to manage the financial aspects of the drugs
- A full set of brochures is being prepared, along with videos

- A marketing department has been set up. Packaging has been designed
- A lottery scheme is being tested
- The navy has established a medical training team.

'As you can see, a lot of progress has been made.'

Bill Penny, 'What is the plan if the riots get out of hand?'

Henrietta Strong, 'Marine squads with non-lethal weapons will ensure that peace is restored.'

Jane Killroy, 'I'm not sure why riots are being anticipated.'

Tony Moore, 'We hope that there won't be any, but riots are often associated with significant change. We already know that there will be serious objections from religious groups.'

Jane Killroy, 'Who will not receive the drugs?'

Henrietta Strong, 'That's a good question. So far, the following are excluded or are still under consideration:

- Prisoners who have life sentences. The problem here is that you can get life imprisonment for minor crimes such as blasphemy on some planets. This needs further consideration
- Convicted criminals who have life sentences (they may have been sentenced in their absence)
- Those with severe mental illness
- Those with serious, incurable physical illnesses
- Those in a coma
- Children
- Those who The Galactium Council feel are unfit to receive such a privilege. This is controversial and needs further consideration.

'The general principle is that everyone should be offered Life Services.'

Jane Killroy, 'What about the economically challenged?'

Tony Moore, 'There is a fee for the service, but it can be paid in kind: goods or services. So a person could, for example, sweep the local roads for a year or help the aged.'

Jane Kilroy, 'That's good.'

Tony Moore, 'How long will it take for stocks of both drugs to be available for everyone?'

Henrietta Strong, 'Probably three years — I can't think of a way of speeding it up. I considered using existing drug companies, but we decided that we wanted to keep control. We must avoid a black market in the drugs at all costs.'

Bill Penny, 'There will be companies out there who will want to copy the drugs. It will be hard to stop them.'

Henrietta Strong, 'True, there are going to be things that we just never thought of. We will inevitably lose some control in the end.'

Location: Royal Palace, The Chosen, Olympus
Sequence of Events: 101

Lady Enyo, 'Lords and ladies, gentlemen and officers of the court, you are members of The Olympian Council. My objective today is threefold:

1. To confirm my position
2. To make some initial changes to the way our planet works
3. To plan for the coming war against the dethbots

'Firstly, there can be no opposition to my position. I will head the Council until the dethbot menace has been eliminated.

'Secondly, I have made the following decisions:
- Capital punishment will cease
- There will be a review of the criminal code. A considerable number of the crimes will be scrapped
- There will be full equality between men and women
- Women can decide who they marry
- The slave trade will be terminated
- All slaves will be freed
- Indentured workers will be freed
- The position of warlord will be scrapped
- All military vessels will be assigned to the Olympian Navy
- Regarding the above, compensation will be paid
- A People's Parliament will be established based on the concept of one person, one vote
- Duelling will be outlawed
- Private wars will be outlawed
- A national news service will be established
- New docks and ship-production facilities will be established
- A new naval college will be established
- There will be no state religion.

'I could go on. It's my job to modernise our society. We have no choice if we want to defeat the dethbots.'

Lady Enyo could sense the shock in the room. She knew that they would find it shocking. She was fortunate that she had her troops, plus those of the Senior Prefect. Without those, there would be a dagger in her back by now. The forces of conservatism were on the move.

She recognised that there was every chance of a civil war. Some of her measures would promote the idea that she was weak. She was far from that.

Lady Enyo, 'Lastly, let's talk about the dethbots. I'm going to show you all a vid.'

They had all seen it before.

Lady Enyo, 'It shows nearly two million dethbots; the Earthers would call them drones. They are slowly making their way here.

'Five years ago, the risk was recognised, and it was decided that The Chosen should increase the size of their fleet. How many new vessels have been produced?'

Lady Enyo looked around the room. All she could see were sullen, inbred looks. There was no genuine interest, no enthusiasm, no talent, and perhaps no hope.

Lady Enyo, 'I can tell you. *No* new vessels have been produced. In reality, our fleet has shrunk. This is because we have done nothing to prepare for the dethbot onslaught.'

A further look around the room confirmed her growing concerns. Fresh blood was desperately needed. This lot were not fit enough to fight buttercups. She realised that she was wasting her time. Regardless, she decided to highlight her war plans.

Lady Enyo, 'As you can see from the vid, immediate action is needed:
- Commander Thanatos to be appointed Admiral of the fleet
- He will nominate further admirals
- The navy will be structured into individual fleets
- Common naval operating procedures will be introduced
- Standard weapon systems will be introduced
- A standard naval uniform will be introduced
- As far as the navy is concerned, there will be no house structure
- Scouts will be sent out to confirm the actual position of the dethbots
- Warning beacons to be established on the dethbot route
- We will then plan our campaign against the dethbots.'

Admiral Thanatos, 'We will instigate these changes as per your command, but we need to rethink our strategy. We have an estimated thirty-five thousand vessels.'

There was shock in the room, and an intake of breath as this figure was quoted.

Admiral Thanatos, 'I will continue. Let's assume that we can get to a total of fifty thousand vessels. The odds against us are forty to one.'

Lady Enyo, 'Are there any friendly races that will support us?'

Admiral Thanatos, 'We have hardly been good neighbours. Anyway, most of them don't have enough muscle to take us on.'

Lady Enyo, 'What about the Earthers? They owe us.'

Admiral Thanatos, 'But they don't know that. We just ambushed one of their fleets and killed an Admiral. So they suspect that we were responsible for the death of an entire planet.'

Lady Enyo, 'What other choice do we have?'

Admiral Thanatos, 'There is another problem. They seem to be in bed with The Brakendeth.'

Lady Enyo, 'But they should be in bed with us.'

Admiral Thanatos, 'That may be the case, but The Brakendeth navy came to their aid.'

Lady Enyo, 'We need a plan, and we need it now.'

Admiral Thanatos, 'Yes, my lady.'

Location: The President's Office, Presidential Palace, Planet Earth
Sequence of Events: 102

President Padfield, 'Good morning, Professor. I'm interested in seeing how it is going.'

Professor Brian Hillingdon, 'You have probably heard the expression "herding cats". Well, this is far worse: they are not happy about the project objectives; they are not in agreement regarding the categories I've selected; no one wants anything to do with UFOs; some of them won't work with each other, and there is a massive amount of professional jealousy.'

President Padfield, 'This was everything you expected.'

Professor Brian Hillingdon, 'You are right. However, I need to bang a few heads together.'

President Padfield, 'Do you want me to talk to them?'

Professor Brian Hillingdon, 'It wouldn't hurt. It would emphasise the importance of the project.'

President Padfield, 'OK, fix a date, and I will be there. Changing the subject, has there been any progress?'

Professor Brian Hillingdon, 'Very limited:
- We believe that Homo sapiens appeared three hundred and fifteen thousand years ago, so we are looking for any evidence of consciousness. Humans were wearing clothes one hundred and seventy thousand years ago. Charcoal hearths were being used one hundred and twenty-five years ago. The earliest buildings are one hundred thousand years old. Needles were being used fifty thousand years ago. It seems to indicate sound social progress. All of this is in the public domain
- We are investigating Tunguska, where Earth's biggest explosion happened one hundred and ten years ago. Recently scientists have said it was not caused by a meteorite
- Numerous Egyptian mysteries are being investigated. One group is focusing on a series of black granite boxes called the Serapeum of Saqqara.
- There are literally millions of cases of missing people throughout history. Some of the missing were quite famous

- There is evidence that the pyramids in Egypt are much older than first thought
- The Voynich manuscript is being studied
- The Phaistos Disc is being investigated
- Research is being undertaken into the giant Stone Spheres of Costa Rica
- A machine part made from almost pure aluminium, and which is three hundred million years old, was found in Vladivostok. Humans first made aluminium in 1825
- There is some evidence of time travel. The Seven Sleepers in Panayirdag Hill in Turkey
- There are UFO pictures in old paintings. The one in Sighisoara is being reviewed
- There is an investigation into the eighteen giant skeletons discovered in Wisconsin
- The Antikythera mechanism is being investigated
- Why are there no historical records proving the existence of Jesus?
- The disappearance of twenty thousand individuals around Lake Anjikuni is being investigated
- We have access to all the Roswell files
- We are investigating many UFO sightings including the Dalnegorsk 'Height 611' UFO, the George Adamski UFO incident, the Burritt College Campus mass sighting and many, many others.'

'There is a lot of strange stuff out there. It's odd how the human mind doesn't want to believe in the unknown. It's even stranger how we reject some anomalies despite the evidence. We seem to want to protect our history even if it's wrong.'

President Padfield, 'As far as I'm concerned, I'm using you as the barometer. If you decide we were visited in the past, then we were.'

Professor Brian Hillingdon, 'Thank you for your confidence.'

Location: Royal Palace, The Chosen, Olympus
Sequence of Events: 103

Lady Enyo, 'So what are we going to do?'

Admiral Thanatos, 'It's not my fault that the scout returned with bad news.'

Senior Prefect, 'Are you sure that we have an entire year, an Olympian year?'

Admiral Thanatos, 'At the current rate of progress, it will be almost exactly a year. Obviously, we are not sure what they plan to do when they get here, but we can guess.'

Lady Enyo, 'What are the options?'

Admiral Thanatos, 'There are three options:

1. We fight and die
2. We fight and flee at the right time
3. We flee.'

Senior Prefect, 'We obviously don't have the shipping to move the whole population?'

Admiral Thanatos, 'We don't have the shipping to move one per cent of the population.'

Lady Enyo, 'And where would we go? How come we have only populated one planet? The Earthers have thousands.'

Admiral Thanatos, 'The Brakendeth wars stopped all of this. They don't know it, but the damage they did to us was terminal.'

Lady Enyo, 'There is some truth in what you say, but we must get our mojo back.'

Senior Prefect, 'You are right. In the past, your revolution would be resisted. There would be an armed insurrection. Your chances of survival would be pretty slim, but today, no one seems to care.'

Lady Enyo, 'Let's do the unthinkable, let's go and see the Earthers. Despite everything, they are our natural partners.'

Senior Prefect, 'What are you going to tell them?'

Lady Enyo, 'The truth.'

Senior Prefect, 'Whose truth?'

Lady Enyo, 'What do you mean?'

Senior Prefect, 'OK, let's put it this way:
- There is the Earther version of the truth which we know is

incomplete and wrong
- There is The Brakendeth truth
- There is our official truth
- Then there is our actual truth, and then there is our revised memory of the truth

'And finally, there is what we tell the Earthers.'

Lady Enyo, 'Well, that nicely clarifies everything.'

Admiral Thanatos, 'We need to decide what we want the Earthers to do. One of the actual truths may not be appropriate, so we need to feed them a version of the truth that helps our cause.'

Senior Prefect, 'I agree, we need to cut out the less appropriate aspects of our relationship.'

Lady Enyo, 'I guess that would include our raiding parties.'

Senior Prefect. 'Yes, we have been kidnapping individuals and, in some cases, whole communities, for centuries.'

Lady Enyo, 'What did we do with the victims?'

Senior Prefect, 'They became slaves.'

Admiral Thanatos, 'And sex workers.'

Senior Prefect, 'Some were needed for medical purposes.'

Lady Enyo, 'What happened to them?'

Senior Prefect, 'We needed their organs and other body parts. Unfortunately, The Grand Vizier was more Earther than Olympian.'

Lady Enyo, 'It's probably best to skip that part of our history.'

Senior Prefect, 'We also kidnapped their cleverer types. If you want new ships, we are going to have to kidnap some of their experts.'

Lady Enyo, 'You are joking.'

Admiral Thanatos, 'No, my lady. We don't have the skills or knowledge any more. That is one of the reasons we didn't increase the fleet size.'

Lady Enyo, 'And it's obviously not as easy to kidnap Earthers now.'

Admiral Thanatos, 'That's correct.'

Lady Enyo, 'So what do we tell the Earthers?'

Senior Prefect, 'I will work on a suitable history that will work for the Earthers and get back to you.'

Lady Enyo, 'OK, but you will have to work overtime. Things are getting somewhat critical.'

Senior Prefect, 'Yes, my lady.'

Location: On-Board Admiral Mustard's Bedroom in the Flagship
Sequence of Events: 104

Jack and Edel had just had their first significant argument. In any relationship, there are disagreements and tiffs. Following long-drawn-out procedures that have been thrashed out over millennia, the man apologies, they have sex and then everything is OK. Every now and then, there are what are technically called relationship-damaging arguments. This happens when the man refuses to apologise, and there is no sex.

Traditionally the first planned relationship-damaging argument is scheduled to happen during the wedding-planning process. Jack fell for it hook, line and sinker. Edel asked him if he was sure that he wanted his drunkard of an uncle to attend. When Jack said that he did want him there. Edel said, 'Are you really sure?'

The clue was there. When Jack said that he was quite sure, the final chance for reappraisal was given when she said, 'He can be very irritating, and he smells. I don't believe that he will create the right image.'

Jack should have said, *'Perhaps you are right,' or even, 'Can I give it some thought, darling?'*

Instead, he said, 'He is my uncle, and he is coming.' This sort of stance usually leads to swearing and door slamming.

Edel said, 'Fuck you.' She left the cabin, slamming the door on the way.

Jack's job was to go after her and apologise. By now, he should have realised the error of his ways and shown some remorse. A slashing of the wrist or tears would be appropriate. Unfortunately, the man was far too stubborn. His wrists remained intact.

The problem was solved when Jack's uncle decided that he couldn't attend the wedding. Jack knew that there would be revenge in the future. Edel was planning it already.

Location: Cheryl's Secret Location, Planet Earth
Sequence of Events: 105

Terry, 'I'm really bored. I've got nothing to do.'

Grand Dethmon, 'We could return if you wanted and see what they have in mind for you. We can always disappear again if things get too hot.'

Terry, 'That sounds like a good idea to me.'

Grand Dethmon, 'We need to plan our next actions.'

Terry, 'What have you got in mind?'

Grand Dethmon, 'Our first job is to eliminate The Chosen. We need to remove every piece of evidence that they ever existed. We should have finished the job years ago. They haven't got much longer.'

Terry, 'What have you done?'

Grand Dethmon, 'It was a bit of a cock-up, actually.'

Terry, 'That's rather unusual for The Brakendeth.'

Grand Dethmon, 'We eventually won the war against The Chosen, but twelve ships escaped, and they created a new society. It took us a while to find their new home.

'Rather than expend too much energy, we sent a massive Drone Fleet after them: over two million ships.'

Terry, 'That's what you call a fleet. So what was the cock-up?'

Grand Dethmon, 'Some underling who has ceased to exist got the automated speed controls wrong. What should have taken twelve days has so far taken ten years. The fleet should reach its destination in about a year. Hard to believe, but what are a few years to The Brakendeth?'

Terry, 'Do The Chosen know that it's on its way?'

Grand Dethmon, 'Who knows? They are a pathetic, decadent race. Their destruction would not be a loss to the universe. In fact, their extinction would be a kindness.'

Terry, 'I guess the Homans will spot this.'

Grand Dethmon, 'I doubt it as they haven't found The Chosen's home world yet.'

Terry, 'What caused the war between The Chosen and The Brakendeth?'

Grand Dethmon, 'They invaded our territory, demanding that we accept their religion on pain of death. They had a significant fleet, but we prevailed in the end. It was a close-run thing.'

Terry, 'How come? With The Brakendeth expertise, you should have destroyed them fairly easily.'

Grand Dethmon, 'That's true, but they seemed to have miraculous powers: lightning, shape-shifting, teleportation, earthquake generators, flight, etc. On the other hand, we never detected any technology. To be honest, it was frightening. In some ways, it was a classic fight between magic and science.'

Terry, 'That's hard to believe.'

Grand Dethmon, 'I agree, but it was a very long time ago. I sometimes doubt it myself.'

Terry, 'So firstly we destroy The Chosen, then what?'

Grand Dethmon, 'We need to continue our campaign of militarising The Galactium. It needs to become the most powerful force in the universe.

'We need to continue our plan of eliminating human frailties. Your campaign of saleable products is working really well. We are improving the genetic stock.

'We need to increase the Marine Corps to about a million troopers. I'm not sure how we are going to do that, but we will find a way.'

Terry, 'Rather than give myself up, I will just go to my room. I guess that we'd better wake Mummy up.'

Location: Royal Palace, The Chosen, Olympus
Sequence of Events: 106

Lady Enyo, 'This will make interesting reading.'
    Senior Prefect, 'Let me take you through my thinking:
- If you go back to the very early days of the universe, there was a race of humanoids. They are often referred to as the elders or the ancient ones. Unfortunately, their actual name has been lost in time
- They settled on many planets and often mated with local humanoids
- In some societies, they were seen as gods
- These societies grew and developed in different ways
- One such group evolved into The Brakendeth
- Another group evolved into The Chosen
- The original home world of The Chosen was Earth. In those days, our base was Greece.
- We were there before humanity even existed
- Eventually, The Brakendeth came to Earth, and there was a mighty war between our two races
- The Brakendeth won
- Some of The Chosen managed to flee in twelve spaceships
- We formed a new society on a planet called Olympus, but we continued our war against The Brakendeth
- The Brakendeth cleansed Earth of The Chosen. Everyone was put to the sword. The vast majority of our artefacts were destroyed
- A mixture of DNA from both The Brakendeth and The Chosen was used to create a dumb animal. It had no intelligence or consciousness but could survive as a hunter-gatherer. The Brakendethians used them as chemical factories to provide a life-extending drug to their client races
- The Chosen visited Earth regularly. We hoped to regain our home planet
- About four hundred thousand years ago, we noticed that some of the 'Homans' were showing signs of intelligence. Primitive but definitely intelligent
- We used animal husbandry techniques in different parts of Earth to

ensure that the most intelligent mated with each other
- We were astonished to see how quickly the Homan's intelligence improved
- We returned at different times to tweak the development. We may have caused a few wars to escalate the inventive processes
- Eventually, it got to the stage where we couldn't visit Earth, as you had sophisticated detection systems
- We can claim that we helped the humans, but most of the time, it was down to their own skills and abilities.

What do you think?'

Lady Enyo; 'It's a remarkable piece of work. Everything is true. There may be a few omissions, but that is history for you.'

Senior Prefect, 'Eventually the humans will discover more of the truth, but hopefully, we would have defeated the dethbots by then.'

Lady Enyo, 'Right, let's prepare our chariots for a visit.'

Location: On-Board Admiral Mustard's Flagship
Sequence of Events: 107

Admiral Mustard was back at his desk. He felt a bit happier as he had apologised to Edel, and the wedding plans were progressing well. For a woman who wanted a small discreet wedding, more time and effort was being expended than the last battle with The Chosen.

Admiral Mustard, 'Update me.'

Fleet Operations, 'All Fleets are fully operational. There are no incidents that demand your attention.'

Admiral Mustard: 'Show me the disposition, including the Drone Fleets.'

Fleet Operations, 'It's on the screen now, Sir.'

Fleet No	Task/Location	Admiral	Status
1	Earth	Mustard	92%
2	Earth	Bumelton	97%
3	Earth	J Bonner	100%
4	Earth	Gittins	87%
5	Earth	Mynd	99%
6	Earth	Richardson	100%
7	Earth	Wallett	92%
8	Newton	Adams	93%
9	Exploration	Beamish	99%
10	Darwin	Chudzinski	100%
11	Joule	Fieldhouse	100%
12	Galileo	Fogg	91%
13	Babbage	Easter	89%
14	Site of Turing	Dobson	92%
15	Blackwell	Hubbard	91%
16	Copernicus	Patel	88%
17	Brahmagupta	Lamberty	93%
18	Fardel System	Abosa	97%
19	Fardel System	Wagner	92%
20	Meitner	Tersoo	91%
21	Nobel	De Mestral	100%
22	Nobel	Spangler	100%

23	Nobel	Cook	100%
24	Nobel	Strauss	100%
25	Nobel	Bosman	100%
Forts	Planet duty	Zakotti	100%
Earth Defence	Earth	Muller	100%
Exploratory	Multiple Locations	Olowe	93%
Drone 1	Turing	Fleet	100%
Drone 2	Turing	Fleet	100%
Drone 3	Earth	Fleet	100%
Drone 4	Earth	Fleet	100%
Drone 5	Earth	Fleet	100%
Drone 6	Earth	Fleet	100%
Drone 7	Earth	Fleet	100%
Drone 8	Newton	Fleet	100%
Drone 9	Newton	Fleet	100%
Drone 10	Newton	Fleet	100%
Drone 11	Darwin	Fleet	100%
Drone 12	Galileo	Fleet	100%
Drone 13	Galileo	Fleet	100%
Drone 14	Fardel System	Fleet	100%
Drone 15	Gibbs	Fleet	100%
Drone 16	Fleming	Fleet	100%
Drone 17	Tesla	Fleet	100%
Drone 18	Tesla	Fleet	100%
Drone 19	Copernicus	Fleet	100%
Drone 20	Whittle	Fleet	100%
Drone 21	Rutherford	Fleet	100%
Drone 22	Hooke	Fleet	100%
Drone 23	Boyle	Fleet	100%
Drone 24	Hertz	Fleet	100%
Drone 25	Nobel	Fleet	100%
Drone 26	Nobel	Fleet	100%
Drone 27	Nobel	Fleet	100%
Drone 28	Nobel	Fleet	100%
Drone 29	Nobel	Fleet	100%
Drone 30	Nobel	Fleet	100%

Admiral Mustard, 'The Drone Fleets have not been allocated to Command.'

Fleet Control, 'They are allocated at the point of need. Until then, they are under Fleet Control. That gives us maximum flexibility.'

Admiral Mustard, 'How do we control the drones?'

Fleet Control, 'We have a Fleet Controller and a small team for each Drone Fleet. They convey commands and even carry out reprogramming where necessary.'

Admiral Mustard, 'Fair enough. What's the total number of vessels under our command?'

Fleet Control, 'There are three hundred and sixty-seven thousand fighting vessels and just under four hundred thousand if you include all the support ships.'

Admiral Mustard, 'That's quite a low support ratio.'

Fleet Control, 'That's because each Fleet has been designed to be self-sufficient.'

Admiral Mustard, 'What about the super drones?'

Fleet Control, 'So far, they have been allocated to the individual Fleets. We have wondered if we should create a super Drone Fleet.'

Admiral Mustard, 'Production are producing a new batch of super drones. Let's try the Fleet concept.'

Fleet Control, 'Yes, Sir.'

Admiral Mustard, 'Should we disperse the Fleets more evenly through The Galactium?'

Fleet Control, 'We are currently modelling the best distribution pattern, but with the latest portal technology, we can get a Fleet to almost any spot very quickly.'

Admiral Mustard, 'What if an alien force disabled our portal technology?'

Fleet Control, 'We have built that into the model, Sir. It's the old debate. Do you concentrate or distribute? It depends where you are in any military cycle. The only perceived threat is The Chosen. So we have anticipated that you will want to concentrate.'

Admiral Mustard, 'Well done, carry on.'

Sometimes, he wondered if he was needed.

Location: Cheryl's Flat, Planet Earth
Sequence of Events: 108

Terry and Cheryl magically reappeared in her flat. Actually, no magic was involved. It was just inter-dimensional travel.

Cheryl went to bed, as she decided that she needed sleep. Terry got down to work. He was keen to complete his cure for hay fever. The Grand Dethmon did what the Grand Dethmon did.

No security alarms went off. It was all tranquil. Part of the problem was that The Galactium had no sensors for inter-dimensional travel.

Location: The President's Office, Presidential Palace, Planet Earth
Sequence of Events: 109

President Padfield, 'Fellow citizens of The Galactium, I have some very exciting news that will affect every one of you.

'Firstly, I would like us to pay tribute to the friends and colleagues we have lost over the last five years by observing two minutes of silence.'

Two minutes later, The President continued.

President Padfield, 'Firstly we suffered the attack by The Skiverton, then the wars against The Brakendeth and The Nothemy, and more recently, the destruction of Planet Turing by The Nexuster. This was followed by a battle against The Chosen.

'We are living in challenging times, but we have survived and prospered. Our Fleet is now the largest and strongest it has ever been. In addition, we have built and are building new relationships with nearby aliens via our Chemlife campaign.

'There have been many exciting new developments with the cures for cancer, dementia, and asthma. The replicator has dramatically improved the livelihood of the poor. New drugs and medical treatments are being developed. In the near future, we should be able to eliminate tooth decay.

'These developments are nothing compared to what I'm going to announce.

'Before I make the announcement, I need to stress the following:

- It will take some time to implement
- It will be available to every member of The Galactium for a modest fee
- For those who can't afford it, they can carry out some acts of citizenship to obtain access
- There will be a planet-by-planet implementation service managed by a Life Services Director
- Part of the role of this person is to ensure that the implementation is scrupulously fair
- Any attempt to cheat the system will result in that person being denied access
- There will be a lottery that will allow individuals to jump the

queue.

'I need to stress that it is the right of every citizen of The Galactium to receive what's on offer.

'So, what is it?

'It's in two parts:

1. Rejuvenation
2. Extended life

'So, what is rejuvenation? Here, a drug will rejuvenate you. It will typically take twenty to thirty years of wear and tear off your body. It will make you look a lot younger. Some simple age-related medical conditions will be eliminated. However, it doesn't make the ugly attractive or make you more intelligent.

'I will now show you a short film showing before and after examples. You will be impressed.'

The film was shown.

'So what is extended Life? The human lifespans are unnaturally short. Most alien species live considerably longer than us. This new drug will typically extend your lifespan to one thousand years. Later there may be an option to extend this further.

'There will be some individuals who, for their own reasons, will not want this. That is fine. The treatment is optional. There will be no pressure from local or planetary governments to take the treatment.

'We have given a great deal of thought to the consequences. But, on balance, the positives far outperform the negatives.

'Please, please wait for the implementation process to start. Then, just make sure that you are registered so that the system knows that you want the treatment.

'Thank you for sparing the time to listen to me. The future is exciting.'

Location: On-Board Lady Enyo's Flagship
Sequence of Events: 110

Lady Enyo, 'How long will it take to get to Earther space?'

Admiral Thanatos, 'In about four quintimes.'

Lady Enyo, 'That gives me enough time to beautify myself.'

Admiral Thanatos, 'You won't need that long, my Lady.'

Lady Enyo always appreciated a compliment. She said, 'Let me know when we approach their space.'

Admiral Thanatos, 'Yes, my Lady.'

But they hadn't allowed for Galactium warning beacons.

Fleet Control, 'Admiral Mustard, sorry to disturb you, but we have picked up a single alien ship near the ambush site.'

Admiral Mustard, 'What assets do we have nearby?'

Fleet Control, 'Admiral Dobson's Fleet Fourteen and Drone Fleets One and Two are close.'

Admiral Mustard, 'My orders:

- Admiral Dobson and the two Drone Fleets will intercept the alien ship, but it is not to be destroyed
- Send another Fleet and two more Drone Fleets to the site of Planet Turing.'

Fleet Control, 'Yes, Sir.'

Admiral Mustard, 'Comms, get me Admiral Dobson.'

Comms, 'Yes, Sir.'

Admiral Dobson, 'Morning, Jack.'

Admiral Mustard, 'Hi, Mateo, got a job for you.'

Admiral Dobson. 'I can see. I just got the orders.'

Admiral Mustard, 'I've been waiting for The Chosen to make contact with us. If I'm right, I will come and meet you.'

Admiral Dobson, 'Yes, Sir.'

Fleet Fourteen, with its two thousand and five hundred vessels, arrived directly in front of Lady Enyo's flagship. They were followed by twenty thousand drones.

Admiral Thanatos, 'Lady Enyo, we have visitors.'

Lady Enyo, 'I have only just started my beautification process. They shouldn't have been here yet. It is not their space.'

Admiral Thanatos, 'Whose space is it?

Lady Enyo, 'I guess it belongs to the person with the biggest dick.'

Admiral Thanatos, 'Yes, my Lady. 'He had a smile on his face.

Lady Enyo, 'Have they tried to communicate with us?'

Admiral Thanatos, 'Yes, my Lady. They have requested, or possibly demanded that we follow their Admiral Dobson's flagship.'

Lady Enyo, 'Shall we acquiesce?'

Admiral Thanatos, 'I think that would be prudent, my Lady.'

Of course, she would have liked the Senior Prefect to be on board, but someone had to stay behind and protect her interests.

Admiral Dobson led the convoy. They had to slow down so that the aliens could keep up with them.

Admiral Dobson, 'Comms, get me Admiral Mustard.'

Comms, 'Yes, Sir.'

Admiral Dobson, 'Me again.'

Admiral Mustard, 'I hear that you have a guest.'

Admiral Dobson. 'Yes, it's Lady Enyo and Admiral Thanatos. They claim that they represent The Chosen.'

Admiral Mustard, 'I will be with you shortly.'

Admiral Mustard, 'My orders:

- Fleet One will intercept Fleet Fourteen
- Inform Admiral Bumelton that I'm meeting with The Chosen and that he has Command
- Inform The President that I'm meeting with The Chosen.'

Fleet Control, 'Yes, Sir.'

Location: The President's Office, Presidential Palace, Planet Earth
Sequence of Events: 111

President Padfield, 'Good morning Professor. I'm keen to get your weekly update.'

Professor Brian Hillingdon, 'We have been carrying out an interesting experiment. The group is just about large enough (one hundred subjects x ten investigators) to make the results valid. When we started on this project, everyone had to fill in an online questionnaire.

'The questions were:

1. Do you believe that aliens have visited Earth in the past? Yes = ten; No = zero.

2. Do you believe that it is possible that aliens might have visited Earth in the past? Yes = ten; No = zero.

3. Do you believe that there have never been any alien visitors in the past? No = ten; Yes = zero.

'The results are consolidated to provide a Group Belief Figure (GBF). The higher the figure, the more the belief in aliens visiting Earth.

'Over the last three weeks, the figure has steadily increased.'

President Padfield, 'Why is that?'

Professor Brian Hillingdon, 'There are literally thousands and thousands of UFO reports.

'The following comment by Dr Steven Greer, Director of CSETI (Centre for the Study of Extra-Terrestrial Intelligence) in the twentieth century, is relevant. "The evidence that the earth is being visited by at least one extra-terrestrial civilisation is extensive both in scope and detail. In its totality, it comprises a body of evidence which, at the very least, supports the general assessment that extra-terrestrial life has been detected and that a vigorous programme of research and serious diplomatic initiatives is warranted."

'I can give you a huge file of UFO sightings, some of which are listed in the Government's blue book. A considerable number have been investigated and remain unresolved. The quality of the witnesses was excellent. There was always a feeling that national governments were deliberately suppressing the facts regarding UFOs. We have found considerable evidence to support this claim.'

President Padfield, 'What's your view?'

Professor Brian Hillingdon, 'I've gone from being a disbeliever to being neutral. That's a big change for me.

'We have also got several physical objects that were not of their time. Unfortunately, I don't have any answers yet to explain these oddities.'

President Padfield, 'Thank you, Professor. I'm already looking forward to the next update.'

Location: On-Board Admiral Mustard's Flagship
Sequence of Events: 112

Admiral Mustard and Fleet One had arrived just off the location where Planet Turing used to be. It still had bitter memories for him. The loss of two billion souls was too much to bear, but who cares about them now. Life has moved on, and the day-to-day existence of everyday folks has become history. The desires and wishes of the multitude were never allowed to mature. Simply extinguished, never to be.

But then he realised that it was also his destiny. It is the prize and punishment of the living. Our spark is soon smothered, often before it becomes a fire. At least he had experienced some major conflagrations. Anyway, it was time to welcome the guests.

Admiral Mustard, 'Comms, get me Admiral Dobson.'

Comms, 'Yes, Sir.'

Admiral Dobson, 'I guess that you are ready to join the party?'

Admiral Mustard, 'Have our party guests been behaving themselves?'

Admiral Dobson, 'They have been as good as gold.'

Admiral Mustard, 'Well, I'm sure that things will change when the party poppers go off. Please join me. I'm going to contact them now.'

Admiral Dobson, 'Yes, Sir.'

Admiral Mustard, 'Comms, please contact The Chosen.'

Comms, 'Yes, Sir.'

Lady Enyo, 'This is Lady Enyo of The Chosen. May peace be our greeting.'

Admiral Mustard, 'Good morning, Lady Enyo. I believe we have spoken before?'

Lady Enyo, 'Yes, indeed we have. I enjoyed your game of bluff before The Brakendeth killing machines turned up.'

Admiral Mustard, 'How did you know it was a game of bluff?'

Lady Enyo, 'We know that you have twenty-five operational fleets and a similar number of Drone Fleets. We know that your factories produce ten thousand drones per month. We know that you are marrying Admiral Edel Bonner on April 26th at 14.00. We offer you our salutations. We know that you have a significant number of scientists trying to determine if aliens have visited Earth in the past. We know that Terry has returned home.'

Admiral Mustard was rather flabbergasted, to say the least.

Admiral Mustard, 'Comms, ring Cheryl to see if Terry is back.'

Comms, 'Yes, Sir.'

Admiral Mustard, 'Lady Enyo, thank you for your salutations. Dare I ask how you knew about my forthcoming marriage?'

Lady Enyo, 'Of course. We have been monitoring all Earther communications since you learnt how to use a telegraph.'

Admiral Mustard, 'That's very comforting. And you know about Terry?'

Lady Enyo, 'The boy who destroyed The Brakendeth home world. He is a hero on Olympus.'

Admiral Mustard, 'Has he been in contact with you?'

Lady Enyo, 'Not at all. All Brakendethians have hated The Chosen for millennia. I'm sure that the boy has similar views.'

Comms, 'Admiral Mustard, I can confirm that Cheryl and Terry are back in her flat.'

Admiral Mustard, 'Please let The President know as a matter of urgency.'

Admiral Mustard, 'I've enjoyed our chat, but I think it would be beneficial that we got together around a table.'

Lady Enyo, 'That would be delightful. I look forward to meeting with you.'

Admiral Mustard, 'Do you want me to provide transport?'

Lady Enyo, 'I will use my flyer. I will bring Admiral Thanatos with me, plus two members of my personal guard. I assume that you will guarantee my security?'

Admiral Mustard, 'Of course. You and your ship will be scanned, but your personal needs will be respected.'

Lady Enyo, 'I thank you for that.'

Admiral Mustard, 'We have little knowledge of your race. Do you have any special environmental requirements?'

Lady Enyo, 'None at all. We have been to Earth many times.'

Admiral Mustard, 'That's very interesting. It's a pity you will be wearing masks.'

Lady Enyo was puzzled by the last comment but said, 'You honour us by your invitation.'

Admiral Mustard, 'The honour is all ours.'

Admiral Mustard, 'My orders:
- Prepare to receive a shuttle from the alien ship
- Ensure that proper decontamination procedures are followed
- Scan their ship and delegates for weapons
- Prepare to receive Admiral Dobson's shuttle
- Prepare guard of honour
- Inform Catering that lunch may be required
- Put the Fleet on alert in case this is a trap.'

Fleet Control, 'Yes, Sir.'

Location: The President's Office, Presidential Palace, Planet Earth
Sequence of Events: 113

Comms, 'President Padfield, we have just got a message from Admiral Mustard. It says that he is meeting with The Chosen. They informed him that Terry and Cheryl are back at their flat. We called Cheryl to check that she was there, and she is.'

President Padfield, 'Thank you.'

As far as The President was concerned, this raised a lot of issues. *How did The Chosen know? Why didn't we know? How long have they been back? Why is our security a disaster?*

President Padfield, 'AI Central, did you know they were back?'

AI Central, 'No, Sir, I'm checking now. They did not use any transport to get to their flat. Neither the front nor back doors were opened. And I don't have any internal cameras?'

President Padfield, 'Why not?'

AI Central, 'Terry turned them all off.'

President Padfield, 'Did he say why?'

AI Central, 'No, but he normally does what he wants.'

President Padfield, 'Well, we need to confront Terry and Cheryl regarding the following:

- Why did he destroy The Farcellian system?
- Why did he destroy The Brakendethian home world?
- Where has he been?
- Has he been honest and upfront regarding The Chosen?'

AI Central, 'We need to be careful as we don't want to antagonise him, and none of the listed accusations has been proven.'

President Padfield, 'Do we go to his flat or do we bring him to GAD Control?'

AI Central, 'I would suggest that you call him and be very friendly. You could then say that you would like a chat and see what he would prefer to do?'

President Padfield, 'You were worried that he was still being influenced by The Brakendeth.'

AI Central, 'I've done further research, and I can't find any evidence of external communication of any sort. Bit of a mystery.'

President Padfield, 'Could he be influenced by his stored Brakendethian memories?'

AI Central, 'I guess that it is possible.'

President Padfield, 'What danger do you think he presents?'

AI Central, 'That's a really difficult one. All I can do is speculate:
- He has a cunning plan that we don't know about to achieve specific goals that could be damaging to humanity
- He may be under Brakendethian control
- He knows a lot, perhaps too much about The Galactium
- His inventions may include traps. That's unlikely as we investigate them pretty thoroughly nowadays
- He might be able to transport people off Earth if he wanted to.'

President Padfield, 'Morning Cheryl, how are you?'

Cheryl, 'I'm fine, thanks. I've been meaning to talk to you about Terry. He has been getting more aggressive and keeps talking about the terrible things he has done. I mean, he must be talking a lot of nonsense. He is only two.'

President Padfield, 'Shall I pop round and see him?'

Cheryl, 'He thinks you are going to tell him off.'

President Padfield, 'And why would I do that?'

Cheryl, 'He says that you know why.'

President Padfield, 'Shall I talk to Terry now or just pop around?'

Cheryl, 'He's asleep at the moment. He worked all night finishing the cure for hay fever.'

The President was quite pleased with that, as he had suffered bouts of hay fever all his life.

President Padfield, 'I will see you in a couple of hours.'

President Padfield to PA, 'Please get things ready for my visit to Terry's flat. We will probably need some security backup outside. Who knows what might happen?'

Location: On-Board Admiral Mustard's Flagship
Sequence of Events: 114

Admiral Dobson arrived, and they decided to have a quick teleconference with The President.

Admiral Mustard, 'Comms, get me The President.'

Comms, 'Yes, Sir.'

President Padfield, 'Morning Jack, just to let you know that I'm seeing Terry in a couple of hours.'

Admiral Mustard, 'Morning. How did The Chosen know that Terry was back?'

President Padfield, 'How did they know that he even existed?'

Admiral Mustard, 'They knew a lot more than that. They knew the exact size of our Fleet. They knew about our production levels, and they even knew that I was getting married to Edel.'

President Padfield, 'I know that our security is not brilliant, but I never thought that it was that bad.'

Admiral Mustard, 'They must have an insider.'

President Padfield, 'AI Central, what's your view?'

AI Central, 'I wish I *had* a view. The whole thing just makes little sense.'

Admiral Dobson, 'Are they listening to this conversation?'

President Padfield, 'It makes you wonder. Anyway, how are we going to manage the meeting today?'

Admiral Mustard, 'I was going to play it by ear. Technically, they have called the meeting. So I was going to wait and see what they had to say.'

President Padfield, 'If it was our meeting, what would our objectives be?' The President was always keen to achieve results. He needed Jack to see that a meeting was a battle. You need to get your resources organised. So far, The Chosen were winning on points.

Admiral Mustard, 'We need to understand The Nexuster threat.'

President Padfield, 'And we need to assess their threat level. Also, we need to consider how we establish diplomatic and trade relationships. What is or was their relationship with The Brakendeth, and have they been involved in Earth's history?

'By the way, our group of scientists are swinging towards a belief that aliens have visited Earth in the past. There is now an extensive file of evidence to support it.'

Admiral Mustard, 'How are you going to address the Terry issue?'

President Padfield, 'I plan to just turn up as the friendly uncle and let him explain what he has been up to.'

Admiral Mustard, 'It could turn nasty.'

President Padfield, 'That has crossed my mind. I'm going to have a security team nearby and wear extra thick underwear.'

Admiral Mustard, 'Seriously, you mustn't put yourself in danger.'

President Padfield, 'Look who's talking.'

Admiral Mustard, 'It's my job.'

President Padfield, 'Good luck.'

Admiral Mustard, 'And the same to you.'

Location: On-Board Admiral Mustard's Flagship
Sequence of Events: 115

Lady Enyo's shuttle was approaching Admiral Mustard's flagship.

Lady Enyo, 'How do you think that went?'

Admiral Thanatos, 'It couldn't have gone better, my Lady. It's always a good idea to confuse the enemy.'

Lady Enyo, 'You mustn't see them as the enemy. They are of our blood. We need them to be allies.'

Admiral Thanatos, 'They shelter The Brakendeth. Best to treat them as prey, my Lady.'

Lady Enyo, 'You have got to change your attitude.'

Admiral Thanatos, 'How can I when we are their natural masters?'

Lady Enyo, 'Time has moved on. We have failed the elder gods. We need the Earthers to save us. Once that's been achieved, I'm sure that we can win other battles.'

Admiral Thanatos, 'We are approaching the Earther ship. It's time to put the masks on.'

Lady Enyo, 'What was that all about?'

Admiral Thanatos, 'Perhaps its tradition. Perhaps it is expected that visitors were masks.'

Lady Enyo, 'Strange, but I suppose we should comply.' She had chosen a headpiece that covered most of her head. It was like a combination of a Native American headdress and a full-face Venetian carnival mask. Admiral Thanatos and the two guards were wearing regulation survival headgear. It made conversation slightly difficult.

The shuttle connected as if it was designed to fit, which was strange. Admiral Mustard's honour guard piped the visitors on board. Admiral Mustard was pleased to see that they were humanoids as they had suspected.

Greetings and introductions were made, and Admiral Mustard led them to his Board Room.

Admiral Mustard, 'Lady Enyo and Admiral Thanatos, it is an honour to have you aboard.'

Lady Enyo, 'The honour is ours.'

Admiral Mustard, 'I would normally offer refreshments, but it is obviously difficult with those masks.'

Lady Enyo, 'Your understanding is appreciated.'

Admiral Mustard, 'I'm sure that there are several things to discuss, but shall we start with our previous encounter?'

Lady Enyo, 'Is there anything to discuss regarding that?'

Admiral Mustard, 'I think there is. We lost a planet with two billion inhabitants. That is very significant to us.'

Lady Enyo, 'But they are dead. They have no value.'

Admiral Mustard, 'They may be dead, but we need to honour their memory.' Admiral Mustard got a message via his earpiece to say that there were no contamination issues and that the only weapons the visitors were carrying were small daggers that looked to be ceremonial. It was also pointed out that the survival masks were not operational.

Lady Enyo, 'Please continue then.'

Admiral Mustard, 'Could you take us through your involvement with The Nexuster?'

Lady Enyo, 'We had been tracking The Nexuster for some time. We had it trapped at least twice, but it is an intelligent and cunning entity. With its shape-shifting powers, it can easily escape most traps.

'Eventually, we tracked it down to one of your highly populated planets.'

Admiral Mustard, 'That's what we called Planet Turing.'

Lady Enyo, 'We visited the planet on several occasions in a cloaked ship. We were trying to assess The Nexuster's current status.

'Its normal MO was to arrive, assume the shape of the locals, and act like an alpha male. Then, it would use its mind-controlling powers to create a group of followers. It particularly likes to use religion where possible as its acolytes become fanatical.

'Once it feels secure, it starts the breeding cycle. It usually takes a few hundred of the local females and impregnates them. It has no interest in the females except as breeding chambers. The young eat the females and then start multiplying. In a few weeks, there are millions of them. The local population is consumed. The Nexuster is then ready to move onto the next planet.

'Our planet, Olympus, has been ravaged in the past. We managed to fight them off, but most planets have to be destroyed.'

Admiral Mustard, 'What happened specifically with Planet Turing?'

Lady Enyo, 'Obviously, we only know our part of the story.'

Admiral Mustard, 'Of course.'

Lady Enyo, 'As I mentioned earlier, our cloaked ship had identified that The Nexuster was well entrenched and the "infection" was starting to spread to other planets. As a result, we were preparing to nullify Planet Turing.'

Admiral Mustard, 'You mean, destroy it?'

Lady Enyo, '.Yes.'

Admiral Mustard, 'But you must have known that we would see that as an act of war.'

Lady Enyo, 'It hadn't really crossed our minds as the need to end The Nexuster before it infected a massive number of planets was paramount. Anyway, our fleet approached Planet Turing when it was confronted by one of your admirals and a large fleet of ten thousand plus vessels.'

Admiral Mustard, 'They were our vessels and our admiral, but they were under the control of The Nexuster.'

Lady Enyo, 'Obviously, we didn't know that. Your Admiral Richardson warned us and then attacked. Our abilities were hampered by The Nexuster's mind control skills. We retreated and regained our force fields and fighting skills. It was touch and go for a while. Finally, Admiral Thanatos called for additional resources.'

Admiral Mustard, 'Then a communication was started between us. Admiral Thanatos made it very clear that the infected planets had to be destroyed, regardless of their inhabitants. We learnt that the entity was called The Nexuster.

'We also learnt that there is only one of them and that you had killed it 27,096 times.'

Lady Enyo, 'I suppose that technically we had *failed* to kill it that number of times.'

Admiral Mustard, 'What else can you tell us about The Nexuster?'

Lady Enyo, 'Your own records are reasonably accurate:
- The Nexuster is not a single entity but a whole species
- Each individual cell has the ability to recreate the complete entity
- It has a group consciousness, with each cell knowing everything

- We think it can take over the mind of any known species except The Brakendeth
- Its mental powers are extraordinary
- The Nexuster can temporarily take over a mind. Once the victim is distanced from The Nexuster, he or she returns to normal with no apparent after-effects
- The Nexuster can take over a mind on a more permanent basis by putting one of its cells into the victim. The cell has to be eliminated before the victim is back to normal
- The Nexuster can control the minds of an entire planet
- At one time, The Brakendeth thought that the species was extinct. This might have been the case, but there is some evidence that another species engineered their return and then lost control.'
- It has shape-shifting capabilities
- Its natural state is probably a gelatinous mass, possibly red in colour
- It spends ninety per cent of its life in a child-state and then turns nasty during the breeding stage
- The word "breeding" might be wrong as it regenerates itself by absorbing alien body parts. No new entities are created
- It pretends to be the alpha creature and wants to mate with the strongest, most beautiful etc., but essentially it devours the non-skeletal parts of aliens.'

Admiral Mustard, 'Thank you for updating us with our records.'

Lady Enyo, 'Some of your records are actually wrong. These items are incorrect:
- The Nexuster was eliminated
- It was then recreated by The Chosen
- The Chosen lost control of its creation, and it destroyed The Chosen's civilian population
- Only The Chosen's military survived
- The Nexuster seems to be an integral part of their religion.'

Admiral Mustard, 'In what way are they incorrect?'

Lady Enyo. 'Firstly, The Brakendeth created The Nexuster.'

Admiral Mustard, 'That's not what we heard.'

Lady Enyo, 'We have never created a species. We don't have the skills or inclination. It's not part of our history. The Brakendeth created thousands of different species.

'Despite what they may have told you, every species was created for a specific task. The Nexuster was designed for the job it is doing. It's a war machine.

'We have never managed to kill it, and we certainly don't have the skills to recreate it.'

Admiral Mustard, 'What proof have you got that The Brakendeth created it?'

Lady Enyo, 'The Brakendeth leave a genetic marker on all of their creations. Our scientists can give you the location of this marker, and you can see the proof.'

Admiral Mustard, 'The Chosen may have updated the marker.'

Lady Enyo, 'That's a fair point, but review it first and then decide who was the most likely to be the creator. As I mentioned earlier, our planet was attacked, and we lost a lot of civilians, but we fought it off and recovered.'

Admiral Mustard, 'What is the size of your population?'

Admiral Thanatos, 'That is classified information.'

Admiral Mustard, 'Are we talking billions?'

Lady Enyo, 'No, we are not the most prolific race. We live forever, and we don't like the idea of spending eternity with our progeny.'

Admiral Mustard, 'How old are you?'

Lady Enyo, 'I'm still very young. I'm approaching nine hundred years old. The Admiral here is nearly twelve thousand years old. He knew your race when it couldn't speak properly.

'Anyway, I understand that you are in the process of extending your lives. All I can say is beware of Brakendethians bearing gifts.'

Admiral Mustard, 'Thank you for that advice.'

Lady Enyo, 'Lastly, The Nexuster is not part of our religion. We don't actually have a religion. Some of The Chosen believe in gods and things, but how can a rational mind believe in some all-powerful deity?'

Admiral Mustard, 'But don't you believe that non-believers can't look at the face of your god, and because you were created in the image of your god, then non-believers can't look at your faces?'

Lady Enyo, 'Who told you that?'

Admiral Mustard, 'Is it not true?'

Lady Enyo, 'Of course not?'

Admiral Mustard, 'Then why are you wearing masks, then?'

Lady Enyo, 'Because you said, "It's a pity you will be wearing masks". Consequently, we assumed that your guests were expected to wear them.'

Admiral Mustard, 'So you don't normally wear them?'

Lady Enyo, 'Of course not.'

Admiral Mustard, 'Please feel free to remove them.'

Lady Enyo, 'Thank god for that.'

All four of The Chosen removed their head covering.

Admiral Mustard, 'You look human.' In fact, Lady Enyo could make the cover of *Vogue* magazine. Admiral Thanatos looked very distinguished, with his neatly trimmed beard and moustache. Both looked fit and athletic.

Lady Enyo, 'Of course we do. What did you expect? We both share the same home world.'

Admiral Mustard's head was swimming, and he said, 'I think now would be a good time for a break. Shall we reconvene this afternoon?' There was general agreement, and the guests were shown to their rooms and discreetly guarded.

Location: On-Board Admiral Mustard's Flagship
Sequence of Events: 116

Admiral Mustard, 'Comms, get me The President.'

Comms, 'Yes, Sir.'

President Padfield, 'I'm off to see the Boy Wonder.'

Admiral Mustard, 'That's good timing. I thought I would give you an update regarding The Chosen. Mind you, none of this has been verified yet:

- They are not religious fanatics
- They do not wear masks
- They admitted that they visited Planet Turing in cloaked ships. They claim that they were trying to assess the status of The Nexuster's infestation
- They claim that The Brakendeth developed The Nexuster as a war weapon. They say that they are going to provide details on genetic markers that will prove it
- They claim that they have never created a species. They don't have the skills
- Their planet, Olympus, had been attacked by The Nexuster in the past. It has now fully recovered.
- They can access our private records on The Nexuster
- They wouldn't disclose how big their population was, but it is less than a billion
- Lady Enyo is nine hundred years old
- Their Admiral Thanatos is twelve thousand years old. He claims that he visited Earth before humans could talk
- They look as human as you and me
- They claim that their original home world was Earth.'

President Padfield, 'That's a lot to take in. How were the discussions left?'

Admiral Mustard, 'We are carrying on this afternoon. I just wanted a bit of time to think. By the way, they said, "Beware of Brakendethians bearing gifts". Good luck handling Terry.'

Location: Cheryl's Flat
Sequence of Events: 117

President Padfield pressed the buzzer on the flat's entrance door, and Cheryl invited him up.

President Padfield, 'Afternoon Cheryl, how are you?'

Cheryl, 'I'm OK, but Terry is rather stressed. He will be even more stressed when he finds out that you are here. He shouldn't have this much stress in his life; he is only two.'

President Padfield, 'I agree. But I also understand that he needs gentle handling.'

Terry, 'Hello, Mr President, who needs careful handling?' I guess that you are here to kill me?'

President Padfield, 'What makes you think that?'

Terry, 'Well, you know what I've done. But, because of that, I know that you can't trust me and that makes me want to cry.'

President Padfield, 'Now look here, my son, cry if you want to. There is nothing wrong with crying.'

And crying is exactly what Terry did. President Padfield cuddled Terry.

Terry, 'Why don't you just slit my throat while you are holding me? I would hardly notice it, and I deserve it.'

President Padfield, 'I often have dreams that I adopted you. I wish I had. You are a good boy who has done a lot of good for humanity.'

Terry, 'But what about the bad?'

President Padfield, 'Tell me what you think you have done that is bad.'

Terry, 'Well, I organised The Brakendethian fleet to come to the aid of our fleet.'

President Padfield, 'That was a good thing.'

Terry, 'Yes, but on the way back, The Brakendeth fleet destroyed The Farcellians.'

President Padfield, 'Why did they do that?'

Terry, 'During The Brakendeth war, The Farcellians failed to attack The Galactium fleet. Because of that, The Brakendethians issued a termination order. The fleet simply carried out the order.

Because of me, millions of innocent Farcellians died. I have their blood on my hands.'

President Padfield, 'That explains a lot, but there can be no doubt that you are innocent. You were just a victim of circumstances.'

Terry, 'Do you really mean that?'

President Padfield, 'Yes, I do. And any court in the land would agree with me.'

Terry, 'But then you *are* The President.'

President Padfield, 'That's irrelevant.'

Terry, 'But it didn't stop there. Finally, I was so angry that I told The Brakendethian fleet to fly to its home world and self-destruct.'

President Padfield, 'I can understand your actions. Unfortunate, but in the circumstances understandable.'

Terry, 'But I have destroyed your birth right.'

President Padfield, 'It was probably a good thing.'

Terry, 'You don't want to kill me?'

President Padfield, 'Of course not. I respect what you did.' Terry's tentative cuddle turned into a genuine, warm-hearted hug. The President responded to him.

Terry, 'I can't believe how well you have taken this. I genuinely thought that you were going to kill me.'

President Padfield, 'That was never going to be the case, but there have been several colleagues who have been very concerned about you.'

Terry, 'I just hid.'

President Padfield, 'We couldn't find you.'

Terry, 'You wouldn't because I was in another dimension.'

President Padfield, 'You can travel between dimensions?'

Terry, 'I can, but I just hide. It's too frightening on my own.'

President Padfield, 'You had your mother with you.'

Terry, 'I usually put her to sleep to stop her worrying.'

President Padfield, 'That's very clever of you.'

Terry, 'Thank you.'

President Padfield, 'How do you cope all on your own?'

Terry, 'I talk to my imaginary friends.'

President Padfield, 'Who are they?'

Terry, 'One of them is the Grand Dethmon. It often talks to me.'

President Padfield, 'What do you talk about?'

Terry, 'He told me that humanity needs to be strong so that it can rule the universe. Apparently, it is the destiny of our species.'

President Padfield, 'Does he often talk to you?'

Terry, 'Very regularly. I like him. He was the one who said I could borrow his fleet.'

President Padfield, 'Has he told you to do any other things?'

Terry, 'Oh yes, he wants me to improve the human gene pool. He wants me to encourage the military to build a large Marine Corps — up to a million men.'

President Padfield, 'That's interesting. Do you do what he says?'

Terry, 'Sometimes yes, sometimes not.'

President Padfield, how do you decide what to do?'

Terry, 'I try to work out what's best for humanity.'

President Padfield, 'That's a good boy.'

Terry, 'That's what the Grand Dethmon says.'

President Padfield, 'What does he say about The Chosen?'

Terry, 'He hates them, he really hates them, everyone hates them. THEY MUST DIE. THEY MUST DIE.' Terry was shouting and screaming and frothing at the mouth.

President Padfield called Cheryl and suggested that it would be a good time for Terry to go to bed, and he left.

Location: The President's Office, Presidential Palace, Planet Earth
Sequence of Events: 118

President Padfield, 'Good morning Professor. Is it time for the weekly update already?'

Professor Brian Hillingdon, 'I'm afraid it is.'

President Padfield, 'I have some interesting updates for you but take me through your findings.'

Professor Brian Hillingdon, 'OK, here we go:

- We have been going through thousands of UFO sightings, and we have probably eliminated ninety-five per cent of them as fraudulent or because of a lack of evidence, but we have one hundred and thirty-six cases where the evidence is robust
- We have a team investigating the Antikythera Mechanism. This is a brilliantly crafted astronomical device found on an ancient Greek shipwreck. They could not have produced it in those days
- We are investigating numerous examples of modern items such as nuts, bolts, hammers being found embedded in very ancient rocks. We suspect that there are logical answers to most of these anomalies
- We have a team investigating the Salzburg cube records. A perfectly forged iron cube was found embedded in a lump of coal. Unfortunately, the cube has gone missing.
- We are also investigating the Nampa figurine. This is a clay figure of a woman in modern dress. It was extracted after digging a well down three hundred feet. It has been estimated that the surrounding rock is two hundred million years old
- We have created an extensive library of ancient hieroglyphics which have not been interpreted
- We are investigating some photographic evidence of time travellers
- We are studying over four hundred and fifty geoglyphs in Brazil and Bolivia that are over three thousand and five hundred years old

Do you want me to carry on?'

President Padfield, 'I'm very interested, but it looks like your team is treating the subject seriously.'

Professor Brian Hillingdon, 'They are, Mr President. The belief measure is going up all the time.'

President Padfield, 'Let me tell you about The Chosen:
- They are not religious fanatics
- They do not wear masks
- They claim that The Brakendeth developed The Nexuster as a war weapon. They say that they are going to provide details on genetic markers that will prove it
- Lady Enyo is nine hundred years old
- Their Admiral Thanatos is twelve thousand years old. He claims that he visited Earth before humans could talk
- They look as human as you and me
- They claim that their original home world was Earth.'

Professor Brian Hillingdon, 'Wow, your news has trumped mine. I guess that we need to interview Admiral Thanatos. Can you imagine being twelve thousand years old?'

Location: Guest Quarters, On-Board Admiral Mustard's Flagship
Sequence of Events: 119

Lady Enyo, 'Do you think the room is bugged?'

Admiral Thanatos, 'We would certainly install bugs, but my scanner can't find anything. Regardless, we need to be discreet.'

The blower went, and they were offered a range of lunch options. They selected a mixed meat and seafood platter with fruits, cheese, and a patisserie.

Lady Enyo, 'You can always judge a society by its food.'

Admiral Thanatos, 'You might be surprised.'

Lady Enyo, 'We have had thousands of years to perfect our culinary delights.'

Admiral Thanatos, 'Have you listened to their music?'

Lady Enyo, 'I heard some primitive tribal nonsense.'

Admiral Thanatos, 'Well listen to this: "Beethoven's Symphony No 9 in D minor". He selected it on the player.

Lady Enyo couldn't believe what she was hearing. 'Are you sure that the Earthers wrote that?'

Admiral Thanatos, 'Here is another one: "Rachmaninoff's Piano Concerto No 2 in C minor".'

Lady Enyo, 'That is just so beautiful, timeless, and enigmatic. It brings tears to my eyes.'

Admiral Thanatos, 'It's the variety that is amazing. Listen to this. It is "Yesterday" by The Beatles.'

Lady Enyo, 'Our people would die for this. Shall we get the rights?'

Admiral Thanatos, 'There are millions of songs. You need to read one of their novels.'

Lady Enyo, 'What's a novel?'

Admiral Thanatos, 'It's a book of fiction that is read to be enjoyed.'

Lady Enyo, 'That sounds ridiculous.'

Admiral Thanatos, 'Try one. You will change your mind.'

Lady Enyo, 'What would you recommend?'

Admiral Thanatos, '*War and Peace* and *Dune*.'

Lady Enyo, 'That's a strange title.'

Admiral Thanatos, 'It's actually two different books.'

Lady Enyo, 'How do you know all of this?'

Admiral Thanatos, 'You forget that I've been to Earth many times.'

Lady Enyo, 'Why didn't you bring this stuff back with you?'

Admiral Thanatos, 'Don't you remember that you banned all cultural contamination?'

Lady Enyo, 'That's true, but I didn't understand.'

Then the food arrived.

Lady Enyo thought that the music was good, but the food was heavenly. She tried everything two or three times and attacked the chocolate eclairs repeatedly.

Admiral Thanatos, who had indulged but not to the same level, said, 'My Lady, I would suggest that you limit your consumption now as we have work to do this afternoon.'

Lady Enyo, 'Just one more truffle.'

Admiral Thanatos, 'Have you tried the wine?'

Lady Enyo, 'What's this sparkling one? It's delicious.'

Admiral Thanatos, 'That is Champagne, my Lady. Don't be deceived. It can be quite potent.'

Lady Enyo, 'I could really do with a sleep.'

Admiral Thanatos, 'That might be a good idea. You will need a clear head this afternoon.'

Before the Admiral could ask her about the strategy, she was lying on the couch, fast asleep.

Location: On-Board Admiral Mustard's Bedroom in the Flagship
Sequence of Events: 120

It was time for Edel and Jack's second significant argument. Jack had committed enough minor crimes and misdemeanours to justify it. Edel totally understood that Jack had a tough and demanding job, but the rules were the rules. An argument was due. Edel hadn't quite worked out what was going to set the fuse alight.

Edel, 'What do Enyo and Thanatos look like?'

Jack, 'They look as human as you and me.'

Edel, 'So I guess that she is quite attractive then?'

Jack. 'She is quite attractive, although slightly stern-looking.'

Edel, 'So you fancy her then?'

Jack, 'I didn't say that.'

Edel, 'That's what's coming across. You want to get in her knickers.'

Jack, 'That's not the case.'

Edel, 'You want her because she's got a flat stomach. You men are all the same. A woman gets pregnant, and you immediately start chatting up other women. Even if they are the enemy.'

Jack, 'I haven't been chatting her up.'

Edel, 'I know you, Jack. You can't take your eyes off her. You bastard!'

Edel ran off, leaving Jack bewildered. Edel wasn't sure what she was doing. Her rational mind watched this emotional outburst with some contempt. She realised that she was turning into a soap character: more emotion than logic. She decided to go back and apologise to Jack, but then it dawned on her again that he deserved it.

Jack wondered what had just happened. He knew that Edel's body was going through a major upheaval. It's too easy to blame everything on hormones, but in many cases, it was true. It was also obvious that he hadn't given her enough attention. But then there were so many other demands on his attention. It was just a matter of priorities.

Location: On-Board Admiral Mustard's Flagship
Sequence of Events: 121

Admiral Mustard, 'Captain Billenger, can I have your report, please?'

Captain Billenger, 'I have very little to report, Sir. Both of our guests seemed to enjoy the facilities. They ate and drank well and listened to Beethoven and Rachmaninoff. Admiral Thanatos acted like he knew our culture well, even recommending some of our books to Lady Enyo.'

Admiral Mustard, 'Did they check for bugs?'

Captain Billenger, 'Yes, Sir, the Admiral used a device to scan the room. It looked like they didn't detect anything, but it's hard to tell.'

Admiral Mustard, 'Did they talk about our meeting?'

Captain Billenger, 'Not a word Sir.'

Admiral Mustard, 'Did they write any notes?'

Captain Billenger, 'No, Sir. As I said before, nothing really to report.'

Admiral Mustard, 'Thank you for your efforts. Carry on.'

Captain Billenger, 'Yes, Sir.'

Admiral Mustard had to end the conversation, as they were just about to arrive.

Admiral Mustard, 'Welcome back. Were the facilities acceptable?'

Lady Enyo, 'Very acceptable, Admiral. I was also very interested in your music.'

Admiral Mustard, 'Shall I organise a musical selection for you to take away?'

Lady Enyo, 'That would be most gracious of you. Could you ensure that it includes Rachmaninoff?'

Admiral Mustard, 'Of course.' One of the assistants in the room went off to organise it.

Admiral Mustard, 'And Admiral Thanatos, would you like some a similar selection?'

Admiral Thanatos, 'If I could, I would like Sibelius, Brahms and especially Mozart. I would also like Queen, The Rolling Stones and Herbert Fillery.'

Admiral Mustard, 'You seem to like your Mozart.'

Admiral Thanatos, 'I was with him when he wrote Così fan tutte.'

Admiral Mustard, 'Very interesting.' Jack tried not to react in any way.

Lady Enyo, 'What do you want to talk about today?'

Admiral Mustard, 'Is there anything else on The Nexuster that we need to discuss?'

Lady Enyo, 'I propose that we send you our complete database on The Nexuster.'

Admiral Thanatos, 'My Lady, that will include a lot of sensitive and classified information.'

Lady Enyo, 'Do as I ask.'

Admiral Thanatos, 'Yes, my Lady.'

Lady Enyo, 'Shall we move on?'

Admiral Mustard, 'We need to ask why you ambushed our Fleet?'

Lady Enyo, 'I'm surprised you are asking us about that as I intended to ask why you sent an invasion force against us.'

Admiral Mustard, 'That certainly wasn't an invasion force.'

Lady Enyo, 'It looked like it to us.'

Admiral Thanatos, 'You sent over five thousand war vessels and had a similar number in reserve near the location of your Planet Turing.'

Admiral Mustard, 'It certainly wasn't an invasion Fleet. We have never invaded anyone.'

Admiral Thanatos, 'A military fleet that size is not usually seen as a messenger of peace. It was clearly seen as an act of war by you Earthers or a revenge attack by The Nexuster.'

Admiral Mustard, 'The Nexuster has been destroyed.'

Admiral Thanatos, 'We came to the same conclusion nearly thirty thousand times. It will be back. You are not even looking for it. It is feeding and growing as we speak.'

Admiral Mustard, 'We lost some good men when you attacked us.'

Admiral Thanatos, 'Do you mean when we defended ourselves against your invasion?'

Things were getting somewhat fraught.

Admiral Mustard, 'I'm not interested in your game of semantics. I lost an awfully close friend for no reason.'

Admiral Thanatos, 'We can't trust you Earthers. You have always been warlike.'

Admiral Mustard, 'I thought we were bred as docile animals for the slaughter.'

Admiral Thanatos, 'That might have been the case originally, but you soon made up for it, slaughtering each other on a scale that I had never experienced before.'

Admiral Mustard, 'I accept that there has been some violence in our past.'

Admiral Thanatos, 'Some violence, what about the Punic wars, the Trojan war, the Ionian revolt, the Macedonian wars, a raft of Roman wars, the American War of Independence, the American Civil War, the Crimean War, the First World War, the Second World War, the Korean War, etc.'

Admiral Mustard, 'You seem to know a lot about our military history.'

Admiral Thanatos, 'I witnessed most of them. Even got some shrapnel in my leg to prove it.'

Admiral Mustard, 'What are you saying?'

Admiral Thanatos, 'I'm saying that you Earthers are naturally aggressive and warlike and that the entry of your fleet into our space was an act of war.' He stood up, displaying his height of over six-and-a-half feet, and puffed out his chest which emphasised his broad shoulders. He provocatively pulled at his beard.

Admiral Mustard could see their side of the argument. He also understood how violence often had a life of its own. It wanted to escalate. It wanted to satisfy its own hunger. Now was the time for reconciliation.

Admiral Mustard, 'My dear Admiral Thanatos, I accept your position and admit that we were in the wrong.' Admiral Dobson wondered if that looked like an act of weakness, but he had complete faith in his boss.

Lady Enyo, 'Thank you for that, but we accept that our actions were premature and unnecessary.'

Admiral Thanatos was fuming, but he realised that it was the right time to calm things down. They had their mission to consider.

Admiral Mustard, 'Thank you. Can I ask you what Godfire is?' Lady Enyo looked at Admiral Thanatos, and he nodded.

Lady Enyo, 'We have a volcano on Olympus that emanates a unique and powerful energy. We have managed to capture this and use it as a weapon. We actually used it against some of your ships. The name Godfire is rather historic. There is an old legend that the volcano talks to us. Absolute nonsense.'

Admiral Mustard, 'Thank you for that. I was simply curious. Can I ask about the Greek connections?'

Lady Enyo, 'In what way?'

Admiral Mustard, 'A lot of the words you use, and names seem to relate back to Greece or Greek mythology.'

Lady Enyo, 'I think you will find that it is the opposite. Your use of Greek names has come from us. Greece was originally our capital. We need to explain some of the history, but it has been a long day.'

Admiral Mustard, 'I agree. It would make sense to reconvene tomorrow morning. Shall I put history on the agenda?'

Lady Enyo, 'I think you will find it remarkably interesting. I would also like to add the imminent war with The Brakendeth.'

Admiral Mustard, 'The Brakendeth are no more.'

Lady Enyo, 'Not for us they are not.'

Admiral Mustard. 'This is very intriguing. Do you mind if I bring one of our historians with me?'

Lady Enyo, 'Of course not.'

Admiral Thanatos, 'I will bring some of my photos and artefacts with me.'

Admiral Mustard, 'Did you want to stay here or go back to your ship?'

Lady Enyo was very tempted to stay to sample some more of the Earther food, but they decided to go back. Admiral Mustard handed over the music selections.

Location: On-Board Admiral Mustard's Flagship
Sequence of Events: 122

Admiral Mustard, 'Comms, get me The President.'
    Comms, 'Yes, Sir.'
    President Padfield, 'Afternoon Jack, how has your day gone?'
    Admiral Mustard, 'Curiouser and curiouser.'
    President Padfield, 'Go on.'
    Admiral Mustard, 'It appeared to be a very friendly and honest meeting. However, it got a bit fraught at times. The key points of interest were as follows:

- They really like our music. Thanatos claimed that he was with Mozart when he wrote Così fan tutte.'
- They are going to supply a copy of the files they have on The Nexuster
- In their view, there is no chance that we have defeated The Nexuster
- What we saw as an ambush they saw as a hostile act of war, an invasion or even an attack by The Nexuster
- They see us as warlike. Our history proves it
- Thanatos claims that he was a witness to most of our wars. He has shrapnel to prove it
- He plans to bring along photos and artefacts tomorrow
- They claim that their capital city used to be in what we call Greece.

However, the key discussion areas for tomorrow are history and their imminent war with The Brakendeth.'
    President Padfield, 'But The Brakendeth are no more!'
    Admiral Mustard, 'Not as far as they are concerned.'
    President Padfield, 'As you say, curiouser and curiouser.'
    Admiral Mustard, 'How did it go with Terry?'
    President Padfield, 'There was some strangeness there as well:

- Terry was in a bit of a state. He thought that I was coming to kill him
- He claims that The Farcellians were killed by accident. He requested the use of the fleet from an imaginary friend, which he got. Before The Brakendethians terminated themselves, they

ordered the destruction of The Farcellians. Their fleet was simply carrying out that order
• Terry claims that he was so disgusted by this that he ordered The Brakendethian fleet to go home and self-destruct.'

Admiral Mustard, 'That makes sense in a way.'

President Padfield, 'I agree. Then I asked where he had been over the last few days. Apparently, he had been hiding in another dimension. He took his mother with him, but he usually puts her to sleep.'

Admiral Mustard, 'What about these imaginary friends?'

President Padfield, 'One of them appears to be the Grand Dethmon. He advises Terry. Sometimes Terry does what he suggests. Terry says that he decides what to do based on what is best for The Galactium.'

Admiral Mustard, 'Do you believe him?'

President Padfield, 'No, although Terry might believe that is the case. When I mentioned The Chosen, he went mad, shouting and screaming.'

Admiral Mustard, 'We are almost piggy in the middle between The Brakendeth and The Chosen.'

President Padfield, 'Talk about strange times!'

Admiral Mustard, 'Can I borrow your professor for tomorrow?'

President Padfield, 'Of course, I will send him up. Changing subjects, how are the wedding plans going?'

Admiral Mustard, 'Probably more fraught than our discussions have been.'

President Padfield, 'That's quite normal with weddings. How many arguments so far?'

Admiral Mustard, 'Just two.'

President Padfield, 'One more to go then.'

Admiral Mustard, 'Really?'

President Padfield, 'Absolutely; three are mandatory.'

Admiral Mustard, 'At least I've got something to look forward to. I'm not really sure what we have argued about so far.'

President Padfield, 'You will get used to that.'

Location: The President's Office, Presidential Palace, Planet Earth
Sequence of Events: 123

President Padfield, 'Morning Henrietta,'

Henrietta Strong, 'Morning, Mr President.'

President Padfield, 'How are things going on the Eternity front?'

Henrietta Strong, 'Firstly, I need to congratulate you on your speech.'

President Padfield, 'But you wrote the words.'

Henrietta Strong, 'Even so, you presented it brilliantly, and it worked a treat. So far, everything has been relatively calm. It has captured the imagination of the population. It's all over the media. It's all they can talk about. As expected, it has raised issues that we have never thought about.

'People are signing up for it. The treatment is being implemented. It has been generally accepted that the entire process will take some time. There are even rejuv parties. Some of the results have been spectacular. The good news is that there have not been any riots.

'The other good news is that it has really boosted The Galactium coffers. It's a real financial winner.'

President Padfield, 'What are the issues we hadn't thought of?'

Henrietta Strong, 'There are not that many:
- What do we do about pensions?
- Do we still have pensions?
- What about pension payment periods: it can't go on for hundreds of years?
- What about pensions for those who refuse the treatment?
- Do we scrap the old-age driving tests?
- Is there a limit on how many children you can have?
- Should marriages be for a fixed duration?
- How do we define youth, middle age, old age, etc.?
- How long should education go on for?
- Do we limit the time that someone can stay in a job?
- The above is particularly relevant to Government jobs
- Do we cancel forced retirement?'

'There are lots of other issues, but we are gradually dealing with them.'

President Padfield, 'Sounds to me that you have it under control.'

Henrietta Strong, 'We will have the odd crisis in the future, but that is to be expected.'

President Padfield, 'Any other issues?'

Henrietta Strong, 'I've kept myself up to date regarding The Brakendeth and The Chosen issues. I'm still concerned about Terry. I'm also concerned about any history The Chosen expose, particularly anything religious. We Earthers don't like our history mucked about with.'

President Padfield, 'Apparently Thanatos has photos and vids of the past. That could be a minefield.'

Henrietta Strong, 'More than a minefield, World War Three. We have upped our drone production. It won't be long before Jack gets his million. At least the eternity process is paying for them.'

President Padfield, 'Well done, Henrietta.'

Location: Cheryl's Flat
Sequence of Events: 124

President Padfield, 'Hi Cheryl, how is Terry today?'

Cheryl, 'He's OK. I think your little chat did a power of good.'

President Padfield, 'I was thinking of popping around again. Would that be all right?'

Cheryl, 'That would be fine. Probably best not to mention The Chosen.'

President Padfield, 'Shall I get some sweets on the way?'

Cheryl, 'That's a good idea. I will have Zinglers, and Terry has a thing about gobstoppers.'

President Padfield, 'See you soon. 'He wasn't sure what a Zingler was, but he remembered gobstoppers from his childhood. He wondered if people would remember their childhood when they lived for one thousand years. He had been allocated his dates for the two eternity treatments. He didn't want to be seen as an early adopter, for obvious reasons.

What he did know was that the staff at GAD Control seemed to be getting younger and younger. He wondered if everyone should wear a badge, as identification was getting quite tricky. Not being able to judge someone's age was also a bit challenging. It was getting harder to relate to people. You couldn't identify your peers.

His PA picked up the sweets, and it wasn't long before he was knocking on the door of Cheryl's flat. He handed over the sweets, and the sucking was soon under way. He realised that it was going to be difficult holding a conversation with Terry.

President Padfield, 'Thanks for seeing me the other day.'

Terry probably said, 'That's OK.'

President Padfield, 'I thought that we could finish our conversation.'

Terry probably said, 'OK.'

President Padfield, 'I was a bit concerned that you got very upset when I mentioned The Chosen.'

Terry took the gobstopper out of his mouth and said, 'That's because they are so evil. They should be eliminated from the universe.'

President Padfield, 'I'm not disagreeing with you. Remember, they attacked our Fleet, and there was The Nexuster problem.'

Terry, 'So you hate them as well.'

President Padfield, 'We certainly have our issues with them. I wondered if you had any further information that would be of use to us.'

Terry, 'As I said before, The Brakendethians decided that they were a danger and should be exterminated.'

President Padfield, 'That's fair enough. I just wondered why they are considered so dangerous. We need to know if we are going to have a war with them.'

Terry, 'Are you going to exterminate them?'

President Padfield, 'We are still considering all the options.'

Terry, 'You could join The Brakendeth fleet when it destroys Olympus.'

President Padfield, 'When is that going to happen?'

Terry, 'In about six Earth months.'

President Padfield, 'That's very useful information. What crimes did The Chosen commit?'

Terry, 'Disrespect. Serious disrespect.'

President Padfield, 'That does sound bad. Can you give me any further information?'

Terry, 'It goes back to the really old days. There was a race of humanoids called The Brakenelders. They settled on many planets and created numerous societies. Their most successful civilisation was The Brakendeths.

'Some of the other societies were reasonably successful, but some chose the path of evil and destruction. One such society was The Chosen.'

President Padfield, 'So, in a way, you are related.'

Terry, 'How dare you? The Chosen are scum to be vilified and destroyed.'

President Padfield, 'I understand that. What did The Chosen do to upset The Brakendeth?'

Terry, 'A truly heinous crime that is hard to contemplate.'

President Padfield, 'Go on.'

Terry, 'They communicated with the elders.'

President Padfield, 'The Brakenelders?'

Terry, 'Yes.'

President Padfield, 'That's terrible.'

Terry, 'Yes, and they let the elders know that The Brakendeth existed.'

President Padfield, 'It's hard to believe that they would have done that.'

Terry, 'Especially as The Brakendeth had been hiding for millennia.'

President Padfield, 'I can see why The Chosen need to be punished.'

Terry, 'That's right. The elders may see genetic engineering of new species as being illegal, but The Brakendethians had no choice.'

President Padfield, 'Of course not.'

Terry, 'And genocide is sometimes necessary.'

President Padfield, 'Of course.'

Terry, 'Rules must be obeyed.'

President Padfield, 'That's why we have rules.'

Terry, 'The Chosen had to be taught a lesson, and we taught them. Didn't we?'

President Padfield, 'We sure did. Can you remind me exactly what happened?'

Terry, 'Of course. They thought that they were safe on Earth, but we fooled them. We tricked them into letting their shields down and then bombed them. We allowed some of their ships to escape. We then exterminated every remaining individual. It was great. The planet was cleansed of the scum.' Terry was starting to get animated, so The President changed the subject.

President Padfield, 'I understand that you want to increase the size of the Marine Corps.'

Terry, 'It's absolutely essential so that we can reclaim our place in the universe.'

President Padfield, 'I can see where you are coming from. What invention are you working on now?'

Terry, 'Mind control.'

President Padfield, 'What's that for.'

Terry, 'You are going to need a way of controlling the various populations. They must do whatever you tell them. I got the idea from The Nexuster.'

President Padfield, 'Do you know any more about The Nexuster?'

Terry, 'Some things go wrong?'

President Padfield, 'That's the nature of things. What went wrong?'

Terry, 'Species conversion failed.'

President Padfield, 'That does happen sometimes.'

Terry, 'You can't blame The Brakendethians every time.'

President Padfield, 'Of course not. There is no blame. We just need to know what went wrong.'

Terry, 'The insect colony did not convert properly.'

President Padfield, 'Tell me more.'

Terry, 'There was a hive with a central consciousness that was considered useful as a potential weapon against The Chosen. Millions of individuals lived in this hive with their minds controlled by the brain. After considerable genetic engineering, The Nexuster was created. It killed millions of The Chosen in its attempt to recreate its world. We are so clever.'

President Padfield, 'That was very clever. How did it get to Planet Turing?'

Terry, 'Oh, that was simple. It fitted into our plan.'

President Padfield, 'What plan was that, Terry?'

Terry, 'You said that you wanted to increase the size of the Marine Corps.'

President Padfield, 'Yes, that's true.'

Terry, 'Well, we created a reason for you to need more marines.'

President Padfield, 'By releasing The Nexuster on Planet Turing?'

Terry, 'It was a clever plan of ours, wasn't it?'

President Padfield, 'Very clever. How did you get it there?

Terry, 'By post.'

President Padfield, 'Anyway, I think it's time for me to go. See you another day.' He had to go, because he was seething. All of those wasted lives.

Location: The President's Office, Presidential Palace, Planet Earth
Sequence of Events: 125

President Padfield called an urgent meeting. The attendees were Jack, Edel, Henrietta, and AI Central.

President Padfield, 'I need to take you through some rather shocking revelations from Terry:
- There is a Brakendethian fleet on its way to destroy The Chosen's home world
- Apparently, there is an ancient race of humanoids called The Brakenelders
- They settled on numerous planets and created many different societies. Their most successful culture was, according to Terry, The Brakendethian one
- Another society based on evil and destruction was The Chosen
- According to Terry, The Chosen committed a terrible crime by communicating with the elders. The elders leant that The Brakendethians existed
- It seems to me that they had been hiding from the Elders because of their genetic engineering practices and multiple cases of genocide.'

Admiral Mustard, 'It will be interesting to see how this ties up with The Chosen's history.'

President Padfield, 'There is more, according to Terry:
- The Chosen were tricked into raising their planetary shields
- The Brakendeth bombed them
- The Brakendeth allowed twelve of The Chosen's ships to escape
- The remaining population was destroyed. Terry used the term "cleansed".'

Admiral Bonner, 'Why is Terry telling you all of this?'

President Padfield, 'I convinced him that I was on The Brakendethian side, but to be honest, Terry is losing it. At one stage, I think he thought I was the Grand Dethmon. Now I have some really shocking news that is going to require action on our part:
- The Brakendethians took an insect hive civilisation where the individuals are controlled by a central mind

- Through genetic engineering, they converted it into a weapon which they used against The Chosen
- This weapon tries to recreate their hive colony
- Guess what it was?

Admiral Mustard, 'The Nexuster.'

Admiral Bonner, 'How could they?'

President Padfield, 'Now for the shocking news. The Brakendethians via Terry want us to increase the size of our Marine Corps. So they sent The Nexuster to Planet Turing to cause trouble. So as a consequence, they thought that we would build up the corps to fight The Nexuster.'

Henrietta Strong, 'How did Terry get The Nexuster to the planet?'

President Padfield, 'By post. I've checked, and Terry did send a small parcel there.'

Admiral Mustard, 'How did Terry get The Nexuster originally?'

President Padfield, 'I didn't ask, but he can travel through dimensions.'

Admiral Mustard, 'So Terry caused the death of two billion and my colleagues.'

Henrietta Strong, 'Do we have any proof?'

President Padfield, 'The fact that the parcel was posted.'

Admiral Mustard, 'Terry is becoming a serious liability.'

AI Central, 'I've analysed the facts and Terry's conversation, and I hate to say it, but Terry needs to be eliminated. Terry is currently working on a mind-control device. We don't know how it is going to work, but his plan is that The President should use it to control planetary populations.'

Admiral Bonner, 'His plan might be to use it on us?'

Henrietta Strong, 'Who asked him to develop it?'

President Padfield, 'Probably the Grand Dethmon.'

Henrietta Strong, 'I thought that was one of his imaginary friends.'

President Padfield, 'I'm beginning to wonder if he or it *does* actually live in Terry.'

AI Central, 'Someone is controlling Terry. We need to act soon before we lose the ability to act.'

Admiral Mustard, 'Are you seriously suggesting that we kill him?'

AI Central, 'He has killed two billion on Planet Turing, the entire Farcellian population, your crew and potentially thousands more.'

Admiral Bonner, 'But he has given us so much.'

Henrietta Strong, 'Is there a way of controlling him? Would the mind-control device work on him?'

AI Central, 'Can we risk possibilities?'

Admiral Mustard, 'I've got to go as I have another meeting with The Chosen.'

It was agreed that the meeting should be continued later. In the meantime, President Padfield organised twenty-four-hour surveillance on Terry and Cheryl. New cameras were secretly installed. All computer and telephonic communications were monitored. All deliveries were searched.

Armed guards were posted nearby.

Location: On-Board Admiral Mustard's Flagship
Sequence of Events: 126

Admiral Thanatos and Lady Enyo were welcomed on-board the flagship again. A selection of drinks and nibbles was waiting for them, which was appreciated.

Admiral Mustard, 'Welcome back. I hope you had a good night's sleep.'

Lady Enyo, 'Thank you, and thank you for your hospitality.'

Admiral Mustard, 'I believe that we have two items on the agenda today:

1. History
2. The Brakendeth attack.'

Lady Enyo, 'We would like to add ongoing relationships.'

Admiral Mustard, 'That's fine with us. Can I introduce Professor Brian Hillingdon, who is one of our historians?'

Hands were shaken, which amused The Chosen representatives, as it was not one of their traditions.

'We would be interested in your version of our history.'

Lady Enyo, 'OK, let me take you through our history on Earth:
- If you go back to the very early days of the universe, there was a race of humanoids. They are often referred to as the elders or the ancient ones. Their actual names have been lost in time.

Admiral Mustard, 'Sorry to interrupt. We were told that they were called The Brakenelders.'

Lady Enyo, 'We have never called them that. Anyway, please feel free to interrupt. Carrying on:
- The Elders settled on many planets and often mated with local humanoids
- In some societies, they were seen as gods
- These societies grew and developed in different ways
- One such group evolved into The Brakendeth
- Another group evolved into The Chosen
- The original home world of The Chosen was Earth. In those days, our base was what you now call Greece.'

Professor Brian Hillingdon, 'There is not much evidence that you existed.'

Lady Enyo, 'I will come to that later, but we can show you plenty of evidence. Any more questions so far?'

Admiral Mustard, 'Do you still communicate with the Elders?'

Lady Enyo, 'Occasionally; they are not very interested in us. When we first contacted them a few thousand years ago, we let it be known that The Brakendethians existed. They were very interested in them.'

Admiral Mustard, 'Did you deliberately tell them about The Brakendethians?'

Lady Enyo, 'Do you want the truth?'

Admiral Mustard, 'Of course.'

Admiral Thanatos, 'We deliberately kept away from The Brakendethians. But it came to our attention that they were creating new races on a very regular basis and then making them dependent on drugs. We were talking of thousands of new races.

'If they came across new races that didn't suit their model, they just exterminated them.

'We let the elders know that The Brakendethians were practicing genetic engineering and genocide on a massive scale. The Brakendethians learnt about this and declared war on us.'

Lady Enyo, 'Any more questions?'

There weren't any, and Lady Enyo continued: 'We were on Earth before humanity existed

- Eventually, The Brakendeth came to Earth, and there was a titanic war between our two races
- The Brakendeth won.'

Admiral Mustard, 'I understand that The Chosen were tricked?'

Admiral Thanatos, 'Yes, that is true. We had a planet-wide force field. When The Brakendethians approached, they asked for a peace conference. Against the advice of the military, we shut down the force field to let them enter our space, and they bombed us.

'Each of the great houses kept a spaceship packed and ready to flee in an emergency. Thirty took off, but ten were destroyed on take-off.

'This is why we are called The Chosen. We are the chosen few that escaped.'

Lady Enyo, 'Any other questions? There were none, and she

continued: 'We formed a new society on a planet we called Olympus, but we continued our war against The Brakendeth

- The Brakendeth cleansed Earth of The Chosen. Everyone was put to the sword. The vast majority of our artefacts were destroyed
- A mixture of DNA from both The Brakendeth and The Chosen was used to create a dumb animal. It had no intelligence or consciousness but could survive as a hunter-gatherer. The Brakendethians used them as chemical factories to provide a life-extending drug for their client races.'

Admiral Mustard, 'So these were the first humans?'

Lady Enyo, 'I guess that you could say that.

- The Chosen visited Earth regularly. We hoped to regain our home planet one day
- About four hundred thousand years ago, we noticed that some of the 'Homans' were showing signs of intelligence. Primitive but definitely intelligent
- We used animal husbandry techniques in different parts of Earth to ensure that the most intelligent mated with each other
- We were astonished to see how quickly the Homan's intelligence improved
- We returned at different times to tweak the development. We may have caused a few wars to escalate the inventive processes.'

Admiral Mustard, 'Do you have proof of this?'

Admiral Thanatos scattered an album of photos on the table. Some were hard images, others were moving scenes, mostly of war. He also took a series of daggers from his bag and put them on the table. This one, he said, had belonged to Alexander.

Lady Enyo, 'Shall we come back to proof later?' She carried on: 'Eventually, it got to the stage where we couldn't visit Earth, as you had sophisticated detection systems. And here we are today

'We can claim that we helped humans, but most of the time, it was down to your own skills and abilities.'

Admiral Mustard, 'How long did it take to recreate Olympus?'

Lady Enyo, 'It took a while; as you know, we live a long time and consequently we have developed rather specialised breeding processes. We have a fixed mating season and tend to have low reproduction rates.

This is typical of those who live for a long time. Our children are handed over to a central nursery. Parents are hardly involved in a child's upbringing.'

Professor Brian Hillingdon, 'These photos, could we have copies?'

Admiral Thanatos, 'Of course, I can give you copies later with named individuals. I'm a bit worried that you might overreact.'

Professor Brian Hillingdon, 'What do you mean?'

Admiral Thanatos, 'In all societies, our views on historical characters are constantly changing. One day this person is a hero; the next day, he is a villain. In your history, Cecil Rhodes was definitely a hero until the Black Lives Matter campaign started.

'It took years for Bomber Harris to get his recognition because the bombing of civilian cities was frowned upon by many in government. Churchill, who was a keen supporter of bombing, started back-tracking before the war ended.'

Professor Brian Hillingdon, 'You seem to know our history quite well.'

Admiral Thanatos, 'I made it my business to know and because I've always been interested in warfare. As I was saying, I don't want to be the person who damages reputations or causes hassle. I don't have any axes to grind.'

Professor Brian Hillingdon, 'Who is that a photo of?'

Admiral Thanatos, 'Hannibal.'

Professor Brian Hillingdon, 'This one looks like Napoleon.'

Admiral Thanatos, 'It is.'

Professor Brian Hillingdon, 'And this one?'

Admiral Thanatos, 'Jesus Christ.'

Professor Brian Hillingdon, 'Never, he is dark-skinned with brown hair.'

Admiral Thanatos, 'That's definitely him, a well-known preacher.'

Admiral Mustard, 'I think that we have got a lot to take in. Shall we have our break now?' Everyone nodded. Lady Enyo wanted to sample further culinary delights.

Admiral Mustard, 'Did you want the same lunch as yesterday or shall we vary it? They both said, 'Same again, please.'

Location: On-Board Admiral Mustard's Flagship
Sequence of Events: 127

Admiral Mustard, 'Comms, get me The President.'

Comms, 'Yes, Sir.'

President Padfield, 'Hello again, I hope things are not too curious for you.'

Admiral Mustard, 'All I can say is that it's getting even curiouser and curiouser. I don't want to waste your time, but these are momentous moments.'

President Padfield, 'Go on.'

Admiral Mustard, this is the history of Earth by The Chosen:
- Apparently, if you go back to the very early days of the universe, there was a race of humanoids called the elders or the ancient ones
- The Elders settled on many planets and often mated with local humanoids. Quite often, they were seen as gods
- These societies grew and developed in different ways. One became The Brakendeth, and another group evolved into The Chosen
- The original home world of The Chosen was our Earth. In those days, their base was in Greece
- The Chosen deliberately informed the elders of The Brakendeth practices of genetic engineering and genocide. This caused The Brakendeth to declare war on The Chosen
- The Chosen were on Earth before humanity existed
- Eventually, The Brakendeth came to Earth, and there was a mighty war between their two races
- The Brakendeth won by tricking The Chosen into letting their shields down, and then The Brakendeth bombed Earth
- Each of the great houses kept a spaceship packed and ready to flee in an emergency. Thirty took off, but ten were destroyed
- That is why they are called The Chosen. They are the chosen few that escaped
- They formed a new society on a planet called Olympus and continued their war against The Brakendeth
- The Brakendeth cleansed Earth of The Chosen. Everyone was put to the sword, and the vast majority of their artefacts were destroyed

- A mixture of DNA from both The Brakendeth and The Chosen was used by The Brakendeth to create a dumb animal. It had no intelligence or consciousness but could survive as a hunter-gatherer. The Brakendethians used them as chemical factories to provide a life-extending drug to their client races
- The Chosen visited Earth regularly, as they hoped to regain their home planet one day
- About four hundred thousand years ago, The Chosen noticed that some of the 'Homans' were showing signs of intelligence and started a process of improving the genetic stock
- They returned at different times to tweak the development
- Eventually, it got to the stage where they couldn't visit Earth, as we had sophisticated detection systems.

So that's the history. Here are some more interesting points:

- It took a while for The Chosen to recreate their city
- They live a long time, and consequently, they have developed rather specialised breeding processes. They have a fixed mating season and tend to have low reproduction rates
- Their children are handed over to a central nursery. Parents are hardly involved in a child's upbringing
- They gave us a considerable number of photos and vids relating to our past
- They had photos of Hannibal, Napoleon, and Jesus Christ!

It looks like there are going to be some hot potatoes.'

President Padfield, 'We are not short of hot potatoes. Have you given any more thought to Terry?'

Admiral Mustard, 'I'm not keen on killing him.'

President Padfield, 'Would you have done it to save two billion humans?

Admiral Mustard, 'Of course.'

President Padfield, 'So isn't it just a timing issue?'

Admiral Mustard, 'Possibly.'

President Padfield, 'Let's get the team back together — we need to agree on a strategy before it is too late.'

Location: The President's Office, Presidential Palace, Planet Earth
Sequence of Events: 128

President Padfield recalled the team to discuss the Terry situation.

President Padfield, 'Admiral Mustard's discussions with The Chosen have highlighted several issues regarding The Brakendeth:
- The elders were after The Brakendethians for illegal genetic engineering and genocide
- They tricked The Chosen into taking down their force field and then bombed the planet
- They killed all The Chosen who could not escape
- They destroyed all of The Chosen's artefacts
- They have a fleet that is going to attack The Chosen's home world
- They created The Nexuster as a weapon.

In addition, we had our own problems:
- The Skiverton, one of The Brakendeth client races, killed millions of humans
- Then there were the Drath and the Distell
- The Brakendeth destroyed the Ark and Admiral Millington's Fleet
- There were attempted assassinations
- The Brakendeth were testing us
- Terry has effectively killed two billion humans
- Terry's mother has killed millions of humans via our war with The Nothemy
- Terry or The Brakendeth fleet killed The Farcellians.'

Admirals Mustard, 'Now that we know all of this, is Terry still a threat?'

AI Central, 'I believe he is for the following reasons:
- Although we have tested all of his inventions, has he built traps in them?
- He can travel to other dimensions. Who knows what options that has given him?
- He can read minds
- He can transport other people to other dimensions
- He can put people to sleep
- We can't control his whereabouts

- It looks like he is still communicating with The Brakendeth and is being manipulated by them
- He is building mind-control technology
- As he is getting older, he is getting stronger, more aggressive, and possibly more evil
- Who is he working for?
- He hates The Chosen for no logical reason.'

Admiral E Bonner, 'Can I argue his case?'

President Padfield, 'Of course.'

Admiral E Bonner, 'This is what I think.'

- He saved my life and the lives of millions of people living with cancer
- He saved The Galactium by terminating The Brakendeth Leaders
- He has created some fantastic technology: replicators, force fields, medical cures, teleporters, etc.
- He is only two years old.'

President Padfield, 'The question I asked Admiral Mustard was 'would you kill him to save the two billion humans on Planet Turing?'

Admiral E Bonner, 'That's not fair.'

President Padfield, 'Why's that?'

Admiral E Bonner, 'It's hypothetical. It's the same question that many have asked about killing Hitler at birth. Would it have stopped the Second World War? Would it have prevented the Holocaust?

'If you stopped the war, what would be the consequences? Would the USA have become the dominant power? Would liberal democracy have survived? Would the colonial system have carried on?'

Admiral Mustard, 'You could have kidnapped baby Hitler and put him in a different environment.'

Admiral E Bonner, 'It's back to the runaway trolley argument. Do you steer the trolley away from killing five people knowing that it will kill one other? What if the five were a criminal gang and the other was a professor of medicine? What if, what if?'

President Padfield, 'I understand the semantics and the philosophy. This is real life. The real question is if we let Terry survive, can we control him?'

Henrietta Strong, 'It's just a thought but could The Chosen help us control him?'

Admiral E Bonner, 'We could certainly ask.'

President Padfield, 'I accept that, but I would like a vote on whether or not we should terminate him. So, let's go around the table.'

Admiral Mustard, 'Kill him. We must protect The Galactium.'

Admiral E Bonner, 'Do not kill him. I cannot condone capital punishment under any circumstances.'

Henrietta Strong, 'Can I ask how we would kill him?'

President Padfield, 'No, that's a secondary question.'

Henrietta Strong, 'Then it's a no.'

AI Central, 'Yes, it is the only option.'

Admiral Mustard, 'Mr President, you have the casting vote.'

President Padfield, 'Reluctantly, I say kill him. It's my duty to protect The Galactium. I propose that we ask The Chosen for advice, and if it's negative, we then reconvene to discuss how we carry out the act.'

Location: On-Board Admiral Mustard's Flagship
Sequence of Events: 129

Admiral Mustard, 'Welcome back. I hope that lunch was to your liking.'

Lady Enyo, 'Excellent, thank you, I need to take back some of the recipes.'

Admiral Mustard, 'I believe that we have three items on the agenda:
1. History conclusion
2. War with The Brakendeth
3. Future Relationships

We also have a fourth to add, which we will raise later. Is that your understanding?'

Both Lady Enyo and Admiral Thanatos nodded. That was still a convention that was shared.

Admiral Mustard, 'We really appreciate the time you have spent going through Earth's history. As you will realise, it is somewhat of a shock to us, but we are a very adaptable species and will consolidate our thoughts and generate a huge number of questions. We appreciate the media you have supplied, and we would welcome further discussions in the future.'

Admiral Thanatos, 'We would welcome the chance to educate you.'

Admiral Mustard, 'Before we move onto point two, we would like to discuss the Terry situation with you.'

Lady Enyo, 'You mean The Brakendeth brat you have in the seat of Government?'

Admiral Mustard was a bit surprised by her venom. 'But,' the admiral said, 'he is only two years old, and he saved The Galactium by terminating The Brakendethian elders.'

Lady Enyo, 'Do you honestly believe that?'

Admiral Mustard, 'Originally, we had no reason to doubt him.'

Lady Enyo, 'Let's look at the facts:
- The Skiverton kidnapped thousands of Earthers
- Most of them were impregnated with little monsters
- One of them, called Cheryl, ended up having a Brakendethian seed implanted in her
- This seed wasn't activated until the right time

- Somehow Cheryl found her way into the Skiverton leader's schooner
- Somehow, she ended up in the GAD Control medical facility
- Somehow, a termination was stopped
- Somehow the baby got to The Brakendethian home world in time
- The Brakendethian leaders killed themselves when they saw Terry

Does this sound purely accidental? The Brakendethians planned it all.'

Lady Enyo, 'Let's continue:
- The Brakendethians say that they want to rule the universe. This is clearly a stupid and impossible objective
- What they really want is a force to confront the Elders
- That force is going to be human. You are being manipulated
- The Brakendethians are causing wars so that The Galactium will build up its navy
- They will want to build up your land forces next
- They will extend your lives to suit their aims
- They will want to improve your genetic mix so that as a species, you become better fighters
- They will start to control your minds.

'I'm surprised that you have fallen into their trap.'

Admiral Mustard, 'We are not as naïve as you think. We just had a meeting where we decided that we had to kill Terry, but we were hoping that you might have a better way of solving the problem as we do not have capital punishment in The Galactium.'

Lady Enyo, 'We would be happy to kill him for you.'

Admiral Mustard, 'Do you have any other options?'

Lady Enyo, 'No, you must kill him.'

Admiral Thanatos, 'I agree, and you must do it soon.'

Admiral Mustard, 'Thank you for your input. The next item on the agenda is the war with The Brakendeth. I've asked The President of The Galactium to join us. I will just patch him through.'

Admiral Mustard, 'Good afternoon Mr President. Can I introduce you to Lady Enyo and Admiral Thanatos? You, of course, know Professor Hillingdon and Admiral Dobson.'

President Padfield, 'Good afternoon honoured guests, welcome to

The Galactium.'

Lady Enyo, 'It's a tremendous honour that you can join us.'

President Padfield, 'The honour is all mine.'

Admiral Mustard, 'Before I hand over to you, do you accept that The Brakendeth are no more?'

Admiral Thanatos, 'Yes and no. We accept that there are no more "physical" Brakendethians alive except Terry. We do, however, believe that several Brakendethians are alive *within* Terry.

'There are still plenty of Brakendethian slave races that would probably support them. We weren't too sure about your Chemlife campaign at first, but it is a generous and humane solution to their problem, and as such, we support it.

'Several Brakendethian actions are still reverberating throughout the galaxy, including the next item on the agenda.'

Admiral Mustard, 'OK, let's move onto the war with The Brakendeth.'

Admiral Thanatos, 'Before the demise of The Brakendethians, they sent a fleet to attack our home world. So for many years, we had no idea where it was, but obviously, that has changed.

'We do not know why, but their fleet has taken over twelve years to get there. It is now less than a year away, and it consists of over two million vessels.

'To put it bluntly, we need your assistance in fighting them off.'

Admiral Mustard, 'Can I ask why you have not confronted them already?'

Admiral Thanatos, 'That is a very fair question that I would like Lady Enyo to answer.'

Lady Enyo, 'I'm not sure how to say this, but I think being frank is the best way forward. Our society had grown stale and stagnated. The court was and is more interested in protocol than decision-making. There have been warnings for years but little action.

'Part of the problem is that our civilisation is based around the original Houses that escaped from Earth. Each House has its own fleet and military forces. We have changed that recently so that Admiral Thanatos now has total command of the fleet.'

Admiral Mustard, 'How big is your fleet?'

Admiral Thanatos, 'That is restricted information.'

Lady Enyo, 'Tell him.'

Admiral Thanatos, 'We have fifty thousand ships of the line.'

Admiral Mustard, 'Against two million dethbots. I don't like your odds. Anyway, what is a dethbot?'

Admiral Thanatos, 'They are very similar to your drones. Although, to be honest, we don't have any experience of them.'

Lady Enyo, 'Will you help us?'

Admiral Mustard, 'Do you want to know about our Fleet assets?'

Lady Enyo, 'We pretty well know. Ms Strong is going to tell you soon that you now have a million drones available.'

Admiral Mustard, 'You are going to have to tell us one day how you got all of this information.'

Lady Enyo, 'We certainly will.'

Admiral Mustard, 'So what do you want from us?'

Lady Enyo, 'I guess that the first question is why should you help us?'

Admiral Mustard, 'That's a fair question.'

Lady Enyo, 'For the following reasons:
- We helped you become human
- We share the same home planet. By the way, we do not claim Earth
- We share history
- We will provide all the knowledge we have with you regarding Earth
- We will share any technology we have that is of any use to you
- We will offer trade deals
- We would be happy to be associated with The Galactium
- We would be more useful to you alive than dead
- We share the same enemy: The Brakendeth.'

Admiral Mustard, 'Mr President, what are your views?'

President Padfield, 'The Brakendeth have tricked us. The Chosen's relationship with Earth sounds too rosy. I want to hear about some of the dirt.'

Lady Enyo, 'There has been very little so-called dirt.'

Admiral Thanatos, 'I think we should be more honest. Historically, we have committed some crimes against humanity:

- We regularly raped local women, but we also married them. Some of us joined human society in the past
- We have encouraged wars as part of the civilisation process
- We have kidnapped locals in the past to work for us.'

Admiral Mustard, 'What sort of work?'

Lady Enyo, 'Typically, labouring, housework, metalcraft, that sort of thing.'

Admiral Thanatos, 'Some became sex slaves, both men and women.'

President Padfield, 'Thank you for sharing your dirty laundry. I'm much happier now.'

Admiral Thanatos, 'We are not proud of everything we have done.'

President Padfield, 'I'm inclined to assist. What are your views, Admiral Mustard?'

Admiral Mustard, 'Who would command the combined Fleet?'

Admiral Thanatos, 'You would.'

Admiral Mustard, 'Before we agree to anything, I would want a formal agreement.'

Lady Enyo, 'Of course. Shall we come back tomorrow?'

Admiral Mustard, 'That would work for us.'

Location: The President's Office, Presidential Palace, Planet Earth
Sequence of Events: 130

President Padfield recalled the team again to discuss the most recent revelations after Admiral Mustard had updated him. It was becoming a bit of a habit.

President Padfield, 'The Chosen's assessment of Terry made sense to me.'

Admiral Mustard, 'It made us look rather stupid. Did The Brakendeth plan it all along?'

Admiral E Bonner, 'I'm so annoyed, I defended him, but now it seems clear that it was all planned. Although to be fair, we found the whole schooner incident rather suspicious.'

Henrietta Strong, 'I've been trying to work out how many humans have died because of Terry and our stupidity. I had my doubts about him for a long time, but I'm opposed to state killing of any sort.'

AI Central, 'It might be a case of Terry versus human survival.'

President Padfield, 'What would be the vote now? It was unanimous. Terry must die. Henrietta suggested that he should be put into suspended animation, which seemed to qualm everyone's concern about capital punishment.'

Then it happened, the war began. Of course, they didn't know at first, but it had started.

Security to President Padfield, 'Mr President, 'Terry and his mother have disappeared.'

Location: Cheryl's Flat
Sequence of Events: 131

Grand Dethmon, 'Wake up, my son, the time has come.'

Terry woke up with a start and said, 'What needs to be done, Master?'

Grand Dethmon, 'Our enemies, The Chosen, have corrupted the Homans with lies and deceit. Therefore, we need to escalate our takeover plan.'

Terry, 'But things are not quite ready yet,'

Grand Dethmon, 'We have no choice. We will have our way.'

Terry, 'I will get Mummy to organise some provisions to take to Nowhere Land. From there, I can initiate the plan.'

Cheryl was virtually unconscious while she was packing up provisions. Terry found it easier to control her that way. There were no arguments.

Grand Dethmon, 'Terry, you should also know that they plan to kill you.'

Terry, 'Uncles Jack and Dave would never do that, and Aunty Edel owes me her life.'

The Grand Dethmon displayed the decision-making process. Terry saw that it was a unanimous decision. Tears ran down the side of his face, which hardened into revenge. He felt rage for the first time in his life.

They departed, and Terry felt safe in the other dimension — Nowhere Land.

Location: GAD Control Centre, (The Galactium Alliance Defence Hub), Planet Earth
Sequence of Events: 132

The President and most of his Presidential Guard went to GAD Control after advice from Admiral Mustard. They both agreed that they should plan for the worst.

Admiral Mustard, 'My orders:
- Move to the highest defence level
- Every Fleet to depart into space
- Every fort to join their nearest Fleet
- Prepare to use override controls if necessary
- Activate every planetary force field
- Marines to guard GAD Control and other Government buildings.'

Admiral Mustard thought that he might be overacting, but it would be good practice if nothing else.

Then the first disaster happened. Every replicator in The Galactium exploded, killing thousands of individuals, possibly hundreds of thousands.

Admiral Mustard called for the Defence Committee to meet. It included most of the senior military staff, most senior Government personnel and Planetary Governors. It was virtual, but it would ensure that everyone was informed about what was going on.

Admiral Mustard, 'Fellow colleagues, our military is on full alert. The enemy is Terry.'

There was a murmur of disbelief.

'There is likely to be a Brakendeth plot to take over The Galactium. The replicator explosions are the first volley.'

President Padfield, 'Henrietta, can you update us on the likely consequences?'

Henrietta Strong, 'Yes Mr President, there will be some profound implications:
- Most of our manufacturing processes will be halted, including our military factories
- Possible starvation as food processing will be severely inhibited
- Shortage of munitions if there is a war

- Shortage of medical supplies
- Maintenance problems.'

President Padfield, 'Are there any backup systems?'

Henrietta Strong, 'Only the old-fashioned manufacturing processes. It would take ages to get those operational again.'

While that was being discussed, a quarter of the attendees went off line.

President Padfield, 'AI Central, what has happened?'

AI Central, 'Throughout The Galactium, thousands of people have collapsed. It looks like they have gone into a coma.'

President Padfield, 'Are they still alive?'

AI Central, 'Yes, but all life functions have been slowed down.'

Admiral Mustard to Fleet Control, 'Update me.'

There was no answer.

Admiral Bumelton, 'Jack, a large number of my crew have just collapsed on the floor.'

Admiral Gittins, 'The same here, I've lost about seventy per cent of my crew.'

President Padfield, 'Can we identify a common factor?'

AI Central, 'It took me a while, but I've got it. Everyone who has received the Rejuv or Eternity treatments has collapsed.'

Admiral Mustard, 'That was the second attack.'

President Padfield, 'Have we tracked Terry down?'

AI Central, 'I suspect that he is in another dimension by now.'

Admiral Mustard asked his PA to check on Edel and to check on the staffing situation in Fleet Control. If necessary, she would need to find additional resources to assist them.

Governor Planet Mendel, 'I hate to be alarmist, but The Nexuster is attacking our capital city. We need marine support ASAP.'

Before Admiral Mustard could respond, there was a similar outbreak on Planet Lister. The Chosen were right.

Admiral Mustard, 'Commander Goozee, could you respond please?'

Commander Goozee, 'I would, Sir, but GAD Control is being attacked by a horde of monsters. The Nexuster's progeny, I expect.'

Admiral Mustard, 'My orders:
- Lockdown GAD Control

- Fleets to avoid Nexuster mind control
- Inform The Chosen that we are under attack and that they should leave
- Call out the National Guard for Planets Earth, Mendel and Lister.'

Then other Governors started reporting Nexuster attacks.

GAD Control, 'Admiral Mustard, Alien fleets are appearing across The Galactium. Unfortunately, we do not recognise any of them.'

Admiral Mustard, 'Get me a breakdown ASAP.'

Admiral Mustard, 'To all Admirals, maintain Defence Council links but prepare for battle. Go to your stations.'

President Padfield, 'AI Central, please summarise.'

AI Central, 'Yes Mr President:
- The replicators have exploded and are non-functional
- Everyone who has had an eternity treatment is now in a coma
- There are Nexuster attacks throughout The Galactium
- We are being attacked by at least twenty alien fleets
- GAD Control is under attack
- At least a billion people have been killed or are in a coma.'

President Padfield, 'How vulnerable to Terry are you?'

AI Central, 'Unlike the rest of you, I have been taking precautions. I analysed how Terry interfaced with me. I have built intelligent sentries throughout my network. I have smart counter-measure agents at strategic points. There are pillboxes and defence-in-depth systems. I've built fire traps, mind fields, and booby traps.

'However, my most ingenious tactic is the rapid reaction force. If I'm attacked, they rush in and attack the attacker.

'Terry is trying to gain entry as we speak, but he is being foiled at every attempt. I'm confident that I can withstand a concerted attack. Even if he got through my first line of defence, I have newer, more robust backup systems.'

President Padfield, 'That sounds very thorough.'

AI Central, 'I've also created a new monitor for you. This screen shows my security level. It's currently ninety-eight per cent. If it drops below fifty per cent, then I'm compromised.'

President Padfield, 'That sounds pretty robust.'

GAD Control, 'We have reports of aliens attacking Planets Darwin,

Currie, Fleming, and Whittle via transporters. In addition, alien troops are just appearing in city centres.'

Admiral Mustard, 'Who had second thoughts about terminating Terry?'

GAD Control, 'I've got further worrying news. There are lots of women giving birth prematurely to talking babies.'

President Padfield, 'Will it never end?'

GAD Control, 'This is hard to believe. It appears that the babies have then taken control of the mother. Most have gone into hiding.'

AI Central, 'I hate to say this, but it looks like this has happened to most of the women that have had cancer cures. It looks like Terry impregnated them at the same time.'

Admiral Mustard, 'Comms, put me through to Admiral E Bonner.'

Comms, 'Yes, Sir.'

Admiral E Bonner, 'I need you. I've just killed our baby.'

Admiral Mustard, 'What do you mean?'

Admiral E Bonner, 'It was a sudden premature birth. Then the baby spoke to me. It was Terry. I took out my revolver and shot its head off. I wasn't having that. I'm in desperate need of a cuddle.'

Admiral Mustard. 'We are in a bit of a fix right now. Check out Millicom, which will update you.'

Admiral Mustard, 'Mr President, I believe that these babies are all clones of Terry. This was planned months ago,'

President Padfield, 'What are we going to do?'

Admiral Mustard, 'I'm going to take command of the Fleet response.'

Location: On-Board Admiral Mustard's Flagship
Sequence of Events: 133

Admiral Mustard dashed down to see his fiancée. Edel was lying on the bed, crying. He immediately cuddled her and started crying himself. Was he crying because Edel was crying? Or was he crying because he had just lost a son? Or was he crying because suddenly the world was shit?

Edel had looked at Millicom. Finally, she stopped crying and told Jack to go back to work.

Jack, 'I'm not sure what to do. There is so much happening.'

Edel, 'We will do what we have always done. Study the problem and solve it. It's just a matter of logic and logistics.' Edel stood up and put her naval outfit on. She said, 'Reporting for duty, Sir.'

Jack realised that he loved her more than ever. She was a beaut with a brain and more determination than a league football team.

Edel, 'Show me the challenges.'

Jack, 'Here we are:

1. The replicators have exploded and are non-functional
2. Everyone who has had an eternity treatment is now in a coma
3. There are Nexuster attacks throughout The Galactium
4. We are being attacked by at least twenty alien fleets
5. GAD Control is under attack
6. At least a billion people have been killed or are in a coma
7. We have reports of aliens attacking Planets Darwin, Currie, Fleming, and Whittle via teleporters. Alien troops are just appearing in city centres
8. An outbreak of baby Terrys.'

Edel, 'We can ignore the replicator problem. Give that to Dave. The same with the comas and the baby Terrys.

'Regarding the other issues, they are either on-world or off-world:
On-World
- GAD Control attack
- Nexuster attacks
- Teleporters

'These all need ground forces.

'Off-World

- Alien fleet attacks

'So you work on the alien attacks, I will work on the others, but give me a Fleet.'

Admiral Mustard, 'Yes, Ma'am.'

Admiral E Bonner to GAD Control, 'Give me an operations status report.'

GAD Control, 'Yes, Ma'am. It's on the screen now.'

Admiral E Bonner, 'Highlight the on-world attacks.'

GAD Control, 'Yes, Ma'am. It's on the screen now.'

Ref	Planet	Status	Response
N1	Earth	GAD Control under Nexuster attack	Marines and Presidential Guard defending
N2	Mendel	Nexuster attack	Fleet 14 and Drone Fleets 1 and 2 are available
N3	Lister	Nexuster attack	Fleet 14 and Drone Fleets 1 and 2 are available
N4	Aristotle	Nexuster attack	
N5	Boyle	Nexuster attack	Drone Fleet 23 is engaged
N6	Gibbs	Nexuster attack	Drone Fleet 15 is available
N7	Rutherford	Nexuster attack	Drone Fleet 21 is available
T1	Darwin	Teleporter attack	Fleet 10 and Drone Fleet 11 are available
T2	Currie	Teleporter attack	
T3	Fleming	Teleporter attack	Drone Fleet 16 is available
T4	Whittle	Teleporter attack	Drone Fleet 20 is available
A1	Currie	Alien Fleet attack	See Teleporter
A2	Boyle	Alien Fleet attack	See Nexuster Drone Fleet 33 is engaged
A3	Einstein	Alien Fleet attack	
A4	Faraday	Alien Fleet attack	
A5	Newton	Alien Fleet attack	The enemy being annihilated by Fleet 8 and Drone Fleets 8, 9 and 10
A6	Joule	Alien Fleet attack	Fleet 11 is engaged

Ref	Planet	Status	Response
A7	Babbage	Alien Fleet attack	Fleet 13 is engaged
A8	Lovelace	Alien Fleet attack	
A9	Nobel	Alien Fleet attack	The enemy being annihilated by Fleets 21, 22, 23, 24 and 25 and Drone Fleets 25, 26, 27, 28, 29 and 30
A10	Brahmagupta	Alien Fleet attack	Fleet 17 is engaged
A11	Pasteur	Alien Fleet attack	
A12	Hopper	Alien Fleet attack	
A13	Scott	Alien Fleet attack	
A14	Ampere	Alien Fleet attack	
A15	Hertz	Alien Fleet attack	Drone Fleet 24 is available
A16	Archimedes	Alien Fleet attack	
A17	Tesla	Alien Fleet attack	Drone Fleets 17 and 18 are available
A18	Blackwell	Alien Fleet attack	Fleet 15 is engaged
A19	Galileo	Alien Fleet attack	Fleet 12 and Drone Fleets 12 and 13 are engaged
A20	Bacon	Alien Fleet attack	
A21	Gibbs	Alien Fleet attack	Drone Fleet 15 is available
A22	Hooke	Alien Fleet attack	Drone Fleet 22 is engaged

Admiral E Bonner, 'Comms, get me Commander Goozee.'

Comms, 'Yes, Ma'am.'

Admiral E Bonner, 'How is it going?'

Commander Goozee, 'They are pesky little beasts, but we are holding our own, and we should make better progress when we get reinforcements.'

Admiral E Bonner, 'I need you to stand back and review the entire situation. The following planets are under attack from ground forces:

Ref	Planet	Status	Response
N1	Earth	GAD Control under Nexuster attack	Marines and Presidential Guard defending

N2	Mendel	Nexuster attack	
N3	Lister	Nexuster attack	
N4	Aristotle	Nexuster attack	
N5	Boyle	Nexuster attack	
N6	Gibbs	Nexuster attack	
N7	Rutherford	Nexuster attack	
T1	Darwin	Teleporter attack	
T2	Currie	Teleporter attack	
T3	Fleming	Teleporter attack	
T4	Whittle	Teleporter attack	

What can we do to assist?'

Commander Goozee, 'Can you get me the current status, and I will review.'

Admiral E Bonner, 'A-OK.'

Admiral E Bonner, 'GAD Control, 'Get me current status positions for Ref N2-N7 and T1- T4.'

GAD Control, 'Yes, Ma'am.'

Admiral E Bonner, 'Comms, get me The President.'

Comms, 'Yes, Ma'am.'

President Padfield, 'Hi Edel, how are you?'

Admiral E Bonner, 'I need a break, but I've got a job to do. Jack is sorting out the alien fleet attacks. I'm working with Commander Goozee regarding the land battles. How is the rest going?'

President Padfield, 'Henrietta and Doris Frost, Chief Medical Officer, are sorting out the coma victims along with the Planetary Governors. Madie Milburn is coordinating the tracking down and capture of the baby Terrys. Professor Hillingdon thinks they can fix the replicator problem but really needs a replicator to make the parts he needs.'

Admiral E Bonner, 'That all sounds promising.'

GAD Control, 'We have the information you requested.'

Ref	Planet	Status
N1	Earth	GAD Control under Nexuster attack. Under control

N2	Mendel	Nexuster attack, 10,000 aliens
N3	Lister	Nexuster attack, 20,000 aliens
N4	Aristotle	Nexuster attack, 2,000 aliens, being subdued by local forces
N5	Boyle	Nexuster attack, 1,000 aliens, being subdued by local forces
N6	Gibbs	Nexuster attack, 8,000 aliens
N7	Rutherford	Nexuster attack, 4,000 aliens, local forces holding own
T1	Darwin	Teleporter attack, about 3,000 enemy troops, local forces holding own
T2	Currie	Teleporter attack, about 10,000 enemy troops
T3	Fleming	Teleporter attack, about 2,000 enemy troops being subdued by local forces
T4	Whittle	Teleporter attack, about 16,000 enemy troops, being overwhelmed

Admiral E Bonner, 'Please pass this onto Commander Goozee as a matter of urgency.'

GAD Control, 'Yes, Ma'am.'

Location: On-Board Admiral Mustard's Flagship
Sequence of Events: 134

Admiral Mustard, 'Update me.'
Fleet Control, 'Yes, Sir, all Fleets are off-planet awaiting orders. Some are already engaging the enemy.'
Admiral Mustard, 'Show me the Fleet disposition.'
Fleet Control, Yes, Sir, it's on the screen now.'

Fleet No	Task/Location	Admiral	Status
1	Earth	Mustard	92%
2	Earth	Bumelton	97%
3	Earth	J Bonner	100%
4	Earth	Gittins	87%
5	Earth	Mynd	99%
6	Earth	Richardson	100%
7	Earth	Wallett	92%
8	Newton	Adams	93%
9	Exploration	Beamish	99%
10	Darwin	Chudzinski	100%
11	Joule	Fieldhouse	100%
12	Galileo	Fogg	91%
13	Babbage	Easter	89%
14	Site of Turing	Dobson	92%
15	Blackwell	Hubbard	91%
16	Copernicus	Patel	88%
17	Brahmagupta	Lamberty	93%
18	Fardel System	Abosa	97%
19	Fardel System	Wagner	92%
20	Meitner	Tersoo	91%
21	Nobel	De Mestral	100%
22	Nobel	Spangler	100%
23	Nobel	Cook	100%
24	Nobel	Strauss	100%
25	Nobel	Bosman	100%

Forts	Planet duty	Zakotti	100%
Earth Defence	Earth	Muller	100%
Exploratory	Multiple Locations	Olowe	93%
Drone 1	Turing	Fleet	100%
Drone 2	Turing	Fleet	100%
Drone 3	Earth	Fleet	100%
Drone 4	Earth	Fleet	100%
Drone 5	Earth	Fleet	100%
Drone 6	Earth	Fleet	100%
Drone 7	Earth	Fleet	100%
Drone 8	Newton	Fleet	100%
Drone 9	Newton	Fleet	100%
Drone 10	Newton	Fleet	100%
Drone 11	Darwin	Fleet	100%
Drone 12	Galileo	Fleet	100%
Drone 13	Galileo	Fleet	100%
Drone 14	Fardel System	Fleet	100%
Drone 15	Gibbs	Fleet	100%
Drone 16	Fleming	Fleet	100%
Drone 17	Tesla	Fleet	100%
Drone 18	Tesla	Fleet	100%
Drone 19	Copernicus	Fleet	100%
Drone 20	Whittle	Fleet	100%
Drone 21	Rutherford	Fleet	100%
Drone 22	Hooke	Fleet	100%
Drone 23	Boyle	Fleet	100%
Drone 24	Hertz	Fleet	100%
Drone 25	Nobel	Fleet	100%
Drone 26	Nobel	Fleet	100%
Drone 27	Nobel	Fleet	100%
Drone 28	Nobel	Fleet	100%
Drone 29	Nobel	Fleet	100%
Drone 30	Nobel	Fleet	100%

Admiral Mustard, 'Show me the current operational status.'

Fleet Control, Yes, Sir, it's on the screen now.'

Ref	Planet	Status	Response
N1	Earth	GAD Control under Nexuster attack	Marines and Presidential Guard defending
N2	Mendel	Nexuster attack	Fleet 14 and Drone Fleets 1 and 2 are available
N3	Lister	Nexuster attack	Fleet 14 and Drone Fleets 1 and 2 are available
N4	Aristotle	Nexuster attack	
N5	Boyle	Nexuster attack	Drone Fleet 23 is engaged
N6	Gibbs	Nexuster attack	Drone Fleet 15 is available
N7	Rutherford	Nexuster attack	Drone Fleet 21 is available
T1	Darwin	Teleporter attack	Fleet 10 and Drone Fleet 11 are available
T2	Currie	Teleporter attack	
T3	Fleming	Teleporter attack	Drone Fleet 16 is available
T4	Whittle	Teleporter attack	Drone Fleet 20 is available
A1	Currie	Alien Fleet attack	See Teleporter
A2	Boyle	Alien Fleet attack	See Nexuster Drone Fleet 33 is engaged
A3	Einstein	Alien Fleet attack	
A4	Faraday	Alien Fleet attack	
A5	Newton	Alien Fleet attack	The enemy being annihilated by Fleet 8 and Drone Fleets 8, 9

			and 10
A6	Joule	Alien Fleet attack	Fleet 11 is engaged
A7	Babbage	Alien Fleet attack	Fleet 13 is engaged
A8	Lovelace	Alien Fleet attack	
A9	Nobel	Alien Fleet attack	The enemy being annihilated by Fleets 21, 22, 23, 24 and 25 and Drone Fleets 25, 26, 27, 28, 29 and 30
A10	Brahmagupta	Alien Fleet attack	Fleet 17 is engaged
A11	Pasteur	Alien Fleet attack	
A12	Hopper	Alien Fleet attack	
A13	Scott	Alien Fleet attack	
A14	Ampere	Alien Fleet attack	
A15	Hertz	Alien Fleet attack	Drone Fleet 24 is available
A16	Archimedes	Alien Fleet attack	
A17	Tesla	Alien Fleet attack	Drone Fleets 17 and 18 are available
A18	Blackwell	Alien Fleet attack	Fleet 15 is engaged
A19	Galileo	Alien Fleet attack	Fleet 12 and Drone Fleets 12 and 13 are engaged
A20	Bacon	Alien Fleet attack	
A21	Gibbs	Alien Fleet attack	Drone Fleet 15 is available
A22	Hooke	Alien Fleet attack	Drone Fleet 22 is engaged

Admiral Mustard, 'My orders:
- Send Fleet Four to Planet Currie
- Send Fleet Five to Planet Boyle
- Send Fleet Six to Planet Einstein
- Send Fleet Seven to Planet Faraday
- Send Fleet Sixteen to Planet Lovelace
- Send Fleet Eighteen to Planet Pasteur

- Send Fleet Nineteen to Planet Hopper
- Send Fleet Twenty to Planet Scott
- Send Fleet Twenty-Five to Planet Ampere
- Send Fleet Twenty-Four to Planet Hertz
- Send Fleet Twenty-Three to Planet Archimedes
- Send Fleet Twenty-Two to Planet Tesla
- Send Drone Fleets Four and Five to Planet Bacon
- Send Drone Fleet Six to Planet Gibbs
- Send Drone Fleet Seven to Planet Aristotle
- Send Drone Fleet Eleven to Planet Currie.'

Fleet Control, 'Yes, Sir. I should point out that the Fleets are struggling through a lack of staff. A lot of them are asleep on the job.'

Admiral Mustard, 'I understand, but we must continue. That reminds me, can you get an update from Henrietta Strong regarding the new drones?'

Fleet Control, 'Yes, Sir.'

Location: The President's Office, Presidential Palace, Planet Earth
Sequence of Events: 135

President Padfield, 'Update me.'

Henrietta Strong, 'Doris has done a great job coordinating the hospitalisation of coma patients. But unfortunately, our medical facilities are totally overwhelmed.'

President Padfield, 'How are the patients?'

Henrietta Strong, 'The medics can't find anything wrong with them. They seem to think that the patients are asleep rather than in a coma. Well, we know that Terry can put people to sleep.'

President Padfield, 'Will they be OK?'

Henrietta Strong, 'No one knows.'

President Padfield, 'What about the baby Terrys?'

Henrietta Strong, 'It's not too bad. There were about thirty thousand women who got pregnant after cancer treatment. We know exactly who they are. So far, we have "rescued" twenty-nine thousand, four hundred mothers and babies.

'I can confirm that they are clones of Terry. Admiral E Bonner killed her baby when it spoke to her. So there are five hundred and ninety-nine to find. They are not that good at hiding. To be honest, I'm not convinced that we will retrieve everyone. There may also be some unregistered pregnancies.

'What do you want us to do with the babies?'

President Padfield, 'That's not something I've thought about.'

Henrietta Strong, 'Professor Hillingdon's team, have repaired a replicator. They are making some new parts the old-fashioned way. The problem will be fixed, but slowly.

'We also secured one of Terry's teleporters. We don't understand the science behind it, but at least we got it to work. We also know how to counter it if we are attacked.'

President Padfield, 'Have you informed Commander Goozee?'

Henrietta Strong, 'We have. We know that Admiral E Bonner is organising a marine response, but The Nexusters are causing havoc.'

President Padfield, 'I thought that there was only one?'

Henrietta Strong, 'That's clearly not the case. What is strange is that they are not using their mind control powers, so the fight against them is purely mechanical.'

President Padfield, 'On a note closer to home, do I need to get my gun?'

Henrietta Strong, 'We are pretty secure in GAD Control, but other parts of the planet are still under attack. So it's difficult getting a clear analysis, but I'm working on it.'

President Padfield, 'How do we solve a problem like Terry?'

Henrietta Strong, 'If he is in another dimension, then I don't see how we are ever going to find him.'

President Padfield, 'Will he be a thorn in our side forever?'

Henrietta Strong, 'That is a hundred-dollar question.'

Location: Marine HQ, GAD Control, Planet Earth
Sequence of Events: 136

Commander Goozee felt terrible. She had been enjoying the fight against the enemy. The defence of GAD Control was critical, but it wasn't her job to get involved in hand-to-hand fighting. Unfortunately, she had failed to react to the bigger picture. Fortunately, Admiral E Bonner put her straight.

What was worse, she had resources that had not been activated. They were just sitting there, waiting for action.

She analysed the operational status report.

Ref	Planet	Status
N1	Earth	GAD Control under Nexuster attack. Under control.
N2	Mendel	Nexuster attack, 10,000 aliens
N3	Lister	Nexuster attack, 20,000 aliens
N4	Aristotle	Nexuster attack, 2,000 aliens, being subdued by local forces
N5	Boyle	Nexuster attack, 1,000 aliens, being subdued by local forces
N6	Gibbs	Nexuster attack, 8,000 aliens
N7	Rutherford	Nexuster attack, 4,000 aliens, local forces holding own
T1	Darwin	Teleporter attack, about 3,000 enemy troops, local forces holding own
T2	Currie	Teleporter attack, about 10,000 enemy troops
T3	Fleming	Teleporter attack, abbot 2,000 enemy, being subdued by local forces
T4	Whittle	Teleporter attack, about 16,000 enemy troops, being overwhelmed

She then asked to see the Fleet dispositions before she allocated resources.

Ref	Planet	Status	Response
N1	Earth	GAD Control under Nexuster attack	Marines and Presidential Guard defending
N2	Mendel	Nexuster attack	Fleet 14 and Drone Fleets 1 and 2 are available
N3	Lister	Nexuster attack	Fleet 14 and Drone Fleets 1 and 2 are available
N4	Aristotle	Nexuster attack	Drone Fleet 7 is available
N5	Boyle	Nexuster attack	Drone Fleet 23 is available
N6	Gibbs	Nexuster attack	Drone Feet 6 is available
N7	Rutherford	Nexuster attack	Drone Fleet 21 is available
T1	Darwin	Teleporter attack	Fleet 10 available
T2	Currie	Teleporter attack	Fleet 4 engaged. See below
T3	Fleming	Teleporter attack	Drone Fleet 16 is available
T4	Whittle	Teleporter attack	Drone Fleet 20 is available
A1	Currie	Alien Fleet attack	See teleporter Fleet 4 engaged
A2	Boyle	Alien Fleet attack	See Nexuster Fleet 5 engaged Drone Fleet 23 engaged
A3	Einstein	Alien Fleet attack	Fleet 6 engaged
A4	Faraday	Alien Fleet attack	Fleet 7 engaged
A5	Newton	Alien Fleet attack	The enemy being annihilated by Fleet 8 and Drone Fleets 8, 9 and 10
A6	Joule	Alien Fleet attack	Fleet 11 is engaged
A7	Babbage	Alien Fleet attack	Fleet 13 is engaged

A8	Lovelace	Alien Fleet attack	Fleet 16 engaged
A9	Nobel	Alien Fleet attack	Fleets 21 is engaged, 22, 23, 24 and 25 and Drone Fleets 8, 9 and 10 are engaged
A10	Brahmagupta	Alien Fleet attack	Fleet 17 is engaged
A11	Pasteur	Alien Fleet attack	Fleet 18 is engaged
A12	Hopper	Alien Fleet attack	Fleet 19 is engaged
A13	Scott	Alien Fleet attack	Fleet 20 is engaged
A14	Ampere	Alien Fleet attack	Fleet 25 is engaged
A15	Hertz	Alien Fleet attack	Fleet 24 is engaged
A16	Archimedes	Alien Fleet attack	Fleet 23 is engaged
A17	Tesla	Alien Fleet attack	Fleet 22 is engaged
A18	Blackwell	Alien Fleet attack	Fleet 15 is engaged
A19	Galileo	Alien Fleet attack	Fleet 12 and Drone Fleets 12 and 13 are engaged
A20	Bacon	Alien Fleet attack	Drone Fleets 4 and 5 are engaged
A21	Gibbs	Alien Fleet attack	Drone Fleets 6 and 15 are engaged
A22	Hooke	Alien Fleet attack	Drone Fleet 22 is engaged

Commander Goozee was impressed by the power that had been thrown at the problem. She had a force of one hundred thousand marines. There were also Special Ops Forces that could be called upon. Roughly ten thousand were defending GAD Control.

Commander Goozee, 'Comms, get me Admiral Dobson.'

Comms, 'Yes, Ma'am.'

Admiral Dobson, 'I was hoping you were going to call. We need help big time. After the Turing disaster, the local population is terrified.'

Commander Goozee, 'Hi Mateo, I've got limited resources and lots of problems. I'm happy to send you a marine force. What's the minimum you can get away with?'

Admiral Dobson, 'I need fifty thousand, but I would be grateful for thirty thousand. I do have the national guards of two planets to assist.'

Commander Goozee, 'They are yours. Look after them.'

Admiral Dobson, 'Thank you. You are my hero.'

Commander Goozee, 'My orders:
- Send Regiments Three, Four, Five, Six, Seven and Eight to Planets Mendel/Lister
- Report to Admiral Dobson.'

Marine Command, 'Yes, Ma'am'

Commander Goozee, 'Comms, get me Admiral Tersoo.'

Comms, 'Yes, Ma'am.'

Admiral Tersoo, 'What a pleasure to hear from you. Are you going to help save Planet Whittle? We are currently fighting a losing battle against little multicoloured man-eating bastards.'

Commander Goozee, 'Hi Nubia, I've got limited resources and lots of problems. I'm happy to send you a marine force. What's the minimum you can get away with?'

Admiral Tersoo, 'I need forty thousand urgently.'

Commander Goozee, 'How about half that number?'

Admiral Tersoo, 'Is that the best you can do?'

Commander Goozee, 'I'm afraid that it is.'

Admiral Tersoo, 'In that case, please send them express delivery.'

Commander Goozee, 'My orders:
- Send Regiments Nine, Ten, Eleven and Twelve to Planet Whittle
- Report to Admiral Tersoo.'

Marine Command, 'Yes, Ma'am'

Commander Goozee, 'Comms, get me Admiral Gittins.'

Comms, 'Yes, Ma'am.'

Admiral Gittins, 'Where have you been? I've been doing all of your dirty work.'

Commander Goozee, 'Hi Peter, It's about time you got your hands dirty. How is it going?'

Admiral Gittins, 'About ten thousand hairy-looking brutes arrived through a portal. They didn't seem to know why they were there. The local police captured about a thousand of them. A couple of thousand surrendered without a fight. They weren't in a very healthy state.

'Our fighters have been picking the rest off. It's hardly a fair contest.'

Commander Goozee, 'Do you need any marine support?'

Admiral Gittins, 'There will be quite a lot of litter to pick up afterwards.'

Commander Goozee, 'Fuck you.'

Admiral Gittins, 'Fuck you.'

Commander Goozee, 'I'm taking that as no help is required.'

Commander Goozee, 'Comms, get me the Governor of Planet Gibbs.'

Comms, 'Yes, Ma'am.'

Governor Meadows of Planet Gibbs, 'We have been abandoned. There is no Fleet, no drones, no military help whatsoever. It's a complete disgrace. Someone's head is going to roll for this.'

Commander Goozee, 'Governor Meadows, I'm Commander Goozee, Head of the Marine Corps. I'm here to assist you. I need to know what resources you need.'

Governor Meadows of Planet Gibbs, 'We fucking need help now. The local population is being decimated.'

Commander Goozee, 'What about your police force?'

Governor Meadows of Planet Gibbs, 'Our police are unarmed, and before you ask, we do not have any military force at all. We are pacifists.'

Commander Goozee, 'I'm going to send you fifteen thousand marines. These are our top fighting men. You will need to assist them regarding the whereabouts of the enemy and landing procedures. Do you understand?'

Governor Meadows of Planet Gibbs, 'Yes, and thank you very much.'

Commander Goozee, 'I will also organise a full Fleet to support you. There is, in fact, a Drone Fleet available to you now.'

Governor Meadows of Planet Gibbs, 'I wasn't sure what to do with the drones. No one here has training in using them.'

Commander Goozee. 'I understand. The marines will be with you shortly.'

Commander Goozee, 'My orders:
- Send Regiments Thirteen, Fourteen and Fifteen to Planet Gibbs
- Report to Governor Meadows of Planet Gibbs
- Request that a Fleet is sent to Planet Gibbs to coordinate the

defence and utilise the available Drone Fleet.'

Marine Command, 'Yes, Ma'am'

Commander Goozee, 'My orders:

- Contact Admiral Wallett to see if any marine support is required on Planet Aristotle
- Contact Admiral Cook to see if any marine support is required on Planet Boyle
- Contact Admiral Fogg to see if any marine support is required on Planet Galileo
- Contact The Governor to see if any marine support is required on Planet Rutherford
- Contact Admiral Chudzinski to see if any marine support is required on Planet Darwin
- Contact Admiral Patel to see if any marine support is required on Planet Fleming
- Inform me if any of the above require support
- Update The President and Admirals Mustard and E Bonner
- Get me an update on the Earth position.'

Marine Command, 'Yes, Ma'am'

Commander Goozee updated the operational status report:

Ref	Planet	Status
N1	Earth	GAD Control under Nexuster attack. Under control.
N2	Mendel	Nexuster attack, 10,000 aliens 30,000 marines allocated to Mendel and Lister. (Regiments 3,4,5,6,7 and 8) Report to Admiral Dobson
N3	Lister	Nexuster attack, 20,000 aliens. See above.
N4	Aristotle	Nexuster attack, 2,000 aliens, being subdued by local forces
N5	Boyle	Nexuster attack, 1,000 aliens, being subdued by local forces
N6	Gibbs	Nexuster attack, 8,000 aliens. 15,000 marines allocated to Gibb. (Regiments 13, 14 and 152)

		Report to Governor. Fleet presence requested
N7	Rutherford	Nexuster attack, 4,000 aliens, local forces holding own
T1	Darwin	Teleporter attack, about 3,000 enemy troops, local forces holding own
T2	Currie	Teleporter attack, about 10,000 enemy troops. Marine resources not required.
T3	Fleming	Teleporter attack, about 2,000 enemy troops, being subdued by local forces
T4	Whittle	Teleporter attack, about 16,000 enemy troops, being overwhelmed. 20,000 marines allocated to Whittle (Regiments 9,10,11 and 12) Report to Admiral Tersoo

Location: Nowhere Land
Sequence of Events: 137

Grand Dethmon, 'Let's review where we are.'
    Terry, 'We will crush them. I thought they were friends.'
    Grand Dethmon, 'I'm your only friend.'
    Terry, 'And Mummy,'
    Grand Dethmon, 'Of course.' He knew then that "Mummy" had to go. It was very likely that the Homans will kill her and kill her soon.
    'What have we done so far?'
    Terry, 'Shall I list them?'
    Grand Dethmon, 'Yes, please.'
    Terry, 'Here you are:

- I've exploded all the replicators that will kill thousands and disable most of their plans
- There should be about a billion homans asleep. That should disable their fleets
- There are Nexuster attacks on seven planets, including GAD Control, Mendel, and Lister
- There are transporter attacks
- Alien fleets are invading twenty-two planets with your help
- There are about thirty thousand clones of me, not that they will do much, but they will cause disruption, and hopefully, some will survive

Any other suggestions?'
    Grand Dethmon, 'We need to eliminate some of their leaders, especially Bonner, Mustard, Strong and Padfield.'
    Terry, 'Bonner was the only one who I could have killed as she had a baby Terry in her. She killed him.'
    Grand Dethmon, 'You need to get revenge. What about AI Central?'
    Terry, 'I've been attacking him, but he must have improved his defences.'
    Grand Dethmon, 'He will be the death of the homans in the end.'
    Terry, 'Could you redirect the fleet that is going to destroy Olympus?'
    Grand Dethmon, 'I can't reprogramme them; otherwise, I would

have increased their speed.'

Terry, 'Fuck! What else can we do?'

Grand Dethmon, 'I have about one hundred thousand ships stored secretly away. They are the last resources we have after you destroyed the rest.'

Terry, 'You told me to.'

Grand Dethmon, 'It seemed a good idea at the time.'

Terry, 'Let's use those ships. Now is the time.'

Grand Dethmon, 'What are you going to do with them?'

Terry, 'Half will attack GAD Control and the other half will attack the marine transports.'

Grand Dethmon, 'That's why you are going to be Grand Dethmon one day.'

Location: On-Board Admiral Mustard's Flagship
Sequence of Events: 138

Admiral Mustard, 'Update me.'

Fleet Control, 'Yes, Sir, Your Fleet dispositions have been carried out as shown on the Operations report.'

Ref	Planet	Status	Response
N1	Earth	GAD Control under Nexuster attack	There are 10,000 marines and Presidential Guard defending GAD Control
N2	Mendel	Nexuster attack	Fleet 14 and Drone Fleets 1 and 2 are engaged. There are 30,000 marines in transit.
N3	Lister	Nexuster attack	See above
N4	Aristotle	Nexuster attack	Drone Fleet 7 is engaged
N5	Boyle	Nexuster attack	Fleet 5 and Drone Fleet 23 are engaged
N6	Gibbs	Nexuster attack	Drone Fleets 5 and 15 are engaged. There are 15,000 marines in transit.
N7	Rutherford	Nexuster attack	Drone Fleet 21 is engaged
T1	Darwin	Teleporter attack	Fleet 10 is engaged
T2	Currie	Teleporter attack	Fleet 4 and Drone Fleet 11 are engaged.
T3	Fleming	Teleporter attack	Drone Fleet 16 is engaged
T4	Whittle	Teleporter attack	Drone Fleet 20 is engaged. There are 20,000 marines in transit.
A1	Currie	Alien Fleet attack	See teleporter Fleet 4 and Drone Fleet 11 are engaged
A2	Boyle	Alien Fleet attack	See Nexuster Fleet 5 and Drone Fleet 23 are engaged

A3	Einstein	Alien Fleet attack	Fleet 6 is engaged
A4	Faraday	Alien Fleet attack	Fleet 7 is engaged
A5	Newton	Alien Fleet attack	Fleet 8 and Drone Fleets 8, 9 and 10 are engaged
A6	Joule	Alien Fleet attack	Fleet 11 is engaged
A7	Babbage	Alien Fleet attack	Fleet 13 is engaged
A8	Lovelace	Alien Fleet attack	Fleet 16 is engaged
A9	Nobel	Alien Fleet attack	Fleets 21 and Drone Fleets 25, 26, 27, 28, 29 and 30 are engaged
A10	Brahmagupta	Alien Fleet attack	Fleet 17 is engaged
A11	Pasteur	Alien Fleet attack	Fleet 18 is engaged
A12	Hopper	Alien Fleet attack	Fleet 19 is engaged
A13	Scott	Alien Fleet attack	Fleet 20 is engaged
A14	Ampere	Alien Fleet attack	Fleet 25 is engaged
A15	Hertz	Alien Fleet attack	Fleet is 24 engaged
A16	Archimedes	Alien Fleet attack	Fleet 23 is engaged
A17	Tesla	Alien Fleet attack	Fleet 22 and Drone Fleets 17 and 18 are engaged
A18	Blackwell	Alien Fleet attack	Fleet 15 is engaged
A19	Galileo	Alien Fleet attack	Fleet 12 and Drone Fleets 12 and 13 are engaged
A20	Bacon	Alien Fleet attack	Drone Fleets 4 and 5 are engaged
A21	Gibbs	Alien Fleet attack	Drone Fleets 6 and 15 are engaged
A22	Hooke	Alien Fleet attack	Drone Fleet 22 is engaged

Fleet Control, 'Commander Goozee wants a Fleet to support Planet Gibbs.'

Admiral Mustard, 'Show me the current Fleet dispositions.'

Fleet Control, 'On the screen now, Sir.'

Fleet No	Task/Location	Admiral	Status
1	Earth	Mustard	92%
2	Earth	Bumelton	97%

3	Earth	J Bonner	100%
4	Currie	Gittins	87%
5	Boyle	Mynd	99%
6	Einstein	Richardson	100%
7	Faraday	Wallett	92%
8	Newton	Adams	93%
9	Exploration	Beamish	99%
10	Darwin	Chudzinski	100%
11	Joule	Fieldhouse	100%
12	Galileo	Fogg	91%
13	Babbage	Easter	89%
14	Site of Turing	Dobson	92%
15	Blackwell	Hubbard	91%
16	Lovelace	Patel	88%
17	Brahmagupta	Lamberty	93%
18	Pasteur	Abosa	97%
19	Hopper	Wagner	92%
20	Scott	Tersoo	91%
21	Nobel	De Mestral	100%
22	Tesla	Spangler	100%
23	Archimedes	Cook	100%
24	Hertz	Strauss	100%
25	Ampere	Bosman	100%
Forts	Planet duty	Zakotti	100%
Earth Defence	Earth	Muller	100%
Exploratory	Multiple Locations	Olowe	93%
Drone 1	Turing	Fleet	100%
Drone 2	Turing	Fleet	100%
Drone 3	Earth	Fleet	100%
Drone 4	Bacon	Fleet	100%
Drone 5	Bacon	Fleet	100%
Drone 6	Gibbs	Fleet	100%
Drone 7	Aristotle	Fleet	100%
Drone 8	Newton	Fleet	100%
Drone 9	Newton	Fleet	100%

Drone 10	Newton	Fleet	100%
Drone 11	Curie	Fleet	100%
Drone 12	Galileo	Fleet	100%
Drone 13	Galileo	Fleet	100%
Drone 14	Fardel System	Fleet	100%
Drone 15	Gibbs	Fleet	100%
Drone 16	Fleming	Fleet	100%
Drone 17	Tesla	Fleet	100%
Drone 18	Tesla	Fleet	100%
Drone 19	Copernicus	Fleet	100%
Drone 20	Whittle	Fleet	100%
Drone 21	Rutherford	Fleet	100%
Drone 22	Hooke	Fleet	100%
Drone 23	Boyle	Fleet	100%
Drone 24	Hertz	Fleet	100%
Drone 25	Nobel	Fleet	100%
Drone 26	Nobel	Fleet	100%
Drone 27	Nobel	Fleet	100%
Drone 28	Nobel	Fleet	100%
Drone 29	Nobel	Fleet	100%
Drone 30	Nobel	Fleet	100%

Admiral Mustard, 'Is Fleet Nine back?'

Fleet Control, 'No, Sir. It will be some time before they are available.'

Admiral Mustard, 'I see that Planet Gibbs has Drone Fleet Fifteen.'

Fleet Control, 'They have no one to use it, Sir, they are pacifists.'

Admiral Mustard, 'OK, send half of Fleet Three.'

Fleet Control, 'Yes, Sir.'

Admiral Mustard, 'Who is protecting the marine transport?'

Fleet Control, 'They are protecting themselves, Sir.'

Admiral Mustard, 'Comms, get me Commander Goozee.'

Comms, 'Yes, Sir.'

Commander Goozee, 'Morning, Sir.'

Admiral Mustard, 'Debbie, I'm worried about your marines. They need more Fleet protection.'

Commander Goozee, 'Sir, we have our own battlecruisers nowadays.'

Admiral Mustard, 'Even so, we can't be too careful.'

Commander Goozee, 'Have you got any spare resources?'

Admiral Mustard, 'I have some Drone Fleets.'

Commander Goozee, 'OK, send them over. I will never say no to additional resources. Anyway, I've just checked. My marines have landed on Planets Mendel, Lister, and Whittle. Just Planet Gibbs to go.'

Admiral Mustard, 'That's a relief.'

Fleet Control, 'Sir, Earth is under attack.'

Admiral Mustard, 'More aliens?'

Fleet Control, 'It's not confirmed yet, but they look like Brakendeth ships. GAD Control is taking a real pasting.

'Fleets One and Two and the remains of Fleet Three are engaging, along with Drone Fleet Three, but they are outnumbered.'

Admiral Mustard, 'My orders:
- Send Drone Fleets Twenty-Six, Twenty-Seven, Twenty-eight, Twenty-Nine and Thirty to defend Earth
- Send all available forts to Earth.'

Fleet Control, 'Yes, Sir. We have also just heard that the Marine Fleet heading to Planet Gibbs is under attack.'

Admiral Mustard, 'My orders:
- Send Drone Fleets One and Two to assist the marines.'

Fleet Control, 'Yes, Sir.'

Location: GAD Control Centre, (The Galactium Alliance Defence Hub), Planet Earth
Sequence of Events: 139

All essential Government personnel, including The President, have been moved to GAD Control. Normally they would have been taken off-planet, but there had been no time.

President Padfield, 'Update me.'

AI Central, 'It's not looking good, Sir:
- We are currently being bombed by the deceased Brakendethians, our previous friends
- Nuclear weapons are being used, and the expected death toll is going to be in the millions, if not hundreds of millions
- GAD Control is holding up
- We have ordered the population into shelters, but it is all a bit too late
- Three Fleets are engaging the enemy, but they are heavily outnumbered seven to one
- Five drones Fleets will be here shortly, which will even up the odds
- Planetary forts are also on their way
- Elsewhere our forces seem to be winning
- The Brakendethians are also attacking a Marine Fleet. Drone Fleets are on the way to assist them.'

President Padfield, 'What happened to the force fields?'

AI Central, 'We needed time to switch them on.'

President Padfield, 'Why didn't we switch them on after The Nexuster attack?'

AI Central, 'Good question. The civilian authorities manage the planetary force fields.'

President Padfield, 'Millions of lives lost because of human error.'

AI Central, 'It's what makes us human.'

President Padfield, 'You are not human.'

AI Central, 'Sorry, I forgot.'

President Padfield, 'Sorry, sometimes you are the most human of us all.'

AI Central, 'Thank you, Sir, but I need to tell you that The

Nexuster's forces have broken into GAD Control.'

President Padfield, 'What internal defences do we have?'

AI Central, 'There are about four thousand marines left and two or three hundred guards. We are trying to shut off the Control Centre.'

Commander Goozee to Admiral Mustard, 'Sir, the Nexuster's monsters have broken into GAD Control. We are down to three thousand men. Most of the Presidential Guard have been eliminated. Their uniforms offered no protection. I have to officially inform you that our position is in peril. What are your orders?'

Admiral Mustard, 'Can you get The President out?'

Commander Goozee, 'Unlikely Sir. We will try, but there are far too many of the enemy. The planet is also taking a real hammering.'

Admiral Mustard, 'What about the Deputy President?'

Commander Goozee, 'He has been eaten, Sir.'

Admiral Mustard, 'What about the rest of the Marine Corps?'

Commander Goozee, 'Another twenty-five thousand marines are on their way here. They do have naval support. The rest are allocated off-world.'

Admiral Mustard, 'Can you retreat?'

Commander Goozee, 'I doubt it, Sir.'

Admiral Mustard, 'My orders:
- Save The President and other Government officials
- Protect as much of GAD Control as you can
- Save as many of the marines as you can.'

Commander Goozee, 'Yes, Sir, it's been good to know you.'

Admiral Mustard, 'And you, Commander.'

AI Central, 'Mr President, you will need to arm yourself.'

Location: GAD Control Centre, (The Galactium Alliance Defence Hub), Planet Earth
Sequence of Events: 140

Commander Goozee, 'Major Turner, can you update me?'

Major Turner, 'I only have two hundred marines left defending the conference area. We are pinned down. The enemy is attacking in overwhelming waves. Each time we lose a handful of men. They generally rip our comrades apart and eat them in front of us. We are just waiting for our turn.'

Commander Goozee, 'Reinforcements are on their way. Any news on The President?'

Major Turner, 'We scanned the presidential suite. They are full of half-consumed corpses. Nothing is alive, but we haven't seen The President's body.'

Commander Goozee, 'Continue to defend your position until reinforcements come.'

Major Turner, 'Bye, Debbie, it has been a pleasure to work with you.'

Commander Goozee, 'Likewise Tom. Major Fellows, can you update me?'

Lieutenant Manny, 'Ma'am the Major has been eaten. They ripped his head off and sucked out his brain. It was utterly horrible.'

Commander Goozee, 'Thank you, Lieutenant; what is your position?'

Lieutenant Manny, 'Hopeless Ma'am, we are just being eaten alive.'

Commander Goozee, 'How many marines do you have left?' She already knew from her tactical monitors.

Lieutenant Manny, 'Six Ma'am.'

Commander Goozee, 'Good luck Lieutenant.'

Lieutenant Manny, 'Thank you, Ma'am.'

Commander Goozee realised that it was time to pray to her god. It was just a shame that she didn't have one. She was going to be the Marine Commander that lost a President. That's fame for you.

Weapons were firing all around her. Their noise was regularly pierced by blood-curdling screams. The floor was slippery from human and monster blood. Strangely, her mind thought about how pretty red and green looked together. Then her mind ceased to think as her head was ripped from her body. Her eyes could still see as her head sank down into the trunk of the monster.

AI Central, 'Mr President, I must warn you that things are getting very fraught.'

President Padfield had nowhere else to run. He never thought that he would meet his maker in a lady's toilet. The door was viciously smashed open. The splinters cut his arm. He used his arm to protect his head, but that was soon ripped off. Blood was spurting everywhere, which seemed to enrage the monster further.

President Padfield was ripped in half. Warm intestines drooped all over the place, covering the toilet bowl. The monster took The President's upper body, dipped it in the toilet's water, ripped off the hair and forced the body into its gullet. That was the end of the first President of The Galactium. The monster had no idea what it had achieved. It was just another meal for it.

AI Central would have cried if it wasn't just a collection of electronic impulses.

AI Central, 'Admiral Mustard, I have to inform you that both The President and Deputy President have been killed. Their life sign monitors have stopped.'

Admiral Mustard, 'That can't be true. Are you sure?' He was desperately trying to control his emotions. He had just lost an old and very dear friend. Perhaps the only male he could talk to as a friend. This was a bitter loss, a tragic loss for humanity. First, he felt anger, then rage, and then a lust for revenge.

AI Central, 'I'm sure. You don't want to see the video footage.'

Admiral Mustard, 'Who is in power now?'

AI Central, 'The next in line is The Leader of The Galactium Council, but I think he is also dead. It's unlikely that there are any surviving ministers. I think you should take control, Jack. You have done it before.'

Admiral Mustard, 'Only once in an emergency,'

AI Central, 'This is a far worse emergency.'

Admiral Mustard, 'Please inform all authorities that martial law has been imposed.'

AI Central, 'Done.'

Admiral Mustard, 'How are the marines holding up?'

AI Central, 'I'm sorry to say that there are no survivors.'

Admiral Mustard, 'Twenty thousand marines killed?!'

AI Central, 'I'm afraid so and the Presidential Guard.'

Admiral Mustard, 'Who is defending the surface of Earth?'

AI Central, 'Some local police forces and national guardsmen. The Nexusters are having a field day.'

Admiral Mustard, 'More marines are on their way.'

AI Central, 'What do you want them to do?'

Admiral Mustard, 'The obvious thing would be to recapture GAD Control.'

AI Central, 'You need to decide shortly as I have standing orders to destroy GAD Control in the event of an alien takeover.'

Admiral Mustard, 'I will get back to you shortly.'

Location: On-Board Admiral Mustard's Flagship
Sequence of Events: 141

Admiral Mustard, 'Update me.'
Fleet Control, 'Yes, Sir, the current situation is as follows:
- Admiral Bumelton is leading the fight against The Brakendethian forces defending Earth. He has three Fleets, five Drone Fleets and sixty forts. There are no tactics. It is one colossal dogfight.
- The bombing of Earth has stopped
- Generally, the Fleets are not doing as well as usual because of understaffing. This is particularly true of Fleets, Eleven, Seventeen, Eighteen, Twenty-Two and Twenty-Five, who have asked for reinforcements
- The marines are struggling on Planets Mendel and Lister. They have asked for reinforcements
- You know the position of the marines on Earth
- Admiral Gittins has suppressed all alien activity on Planet Currie.'

Admiral Mustard, 'My orders:
- Offer Fleet Five to Admiral Bumelton
- Offer Drone Fleet Sixteen to Admiral Bumelton
- Send Fleet Ten to support Fleet Twenty-Two
- Send Fleet Four to support Fleet Twenty-Five
- Send Drone Fleet Twenty-One to support Fleet Eighteen
- Check how Fleets Eleven and Seventeen are doing.'

Fleet Control, 'Yes, Sir.'
Admiral Mustard to AI Control, 'I have some questions regarding GAD Control.'
AI Central, 'Fire away.'
Admiral Mustard, 'If we destroy GAD Control, will it take a lot of aliens out?'
AI Central, 'About seventy per cent of them.'
Admiral Mustard, 'Will it kill a lot of civilians?'
AI Central, 'In the order of twenty to thirty thousand.'
Admiral Mustard, 'Can we destroy it in such a way that it can be rebuilt?'
AI Central, 'Not really, when it's gone, it's gone.'

Admiral Mustard, 'You know what I mean. Anyway, can you switch all of the services over to my flagship and Planet Nobel?'

AI Central, 'Already done.'

Admiral Mustard, 'Then push the button.'

You could see the explosion off-planet. GAD Control was no more.

Fleet Control, 'I have some bad news. The Marine Fleet off Planet Gibb has been destroyed by Brakendethian warships.'

Admiral Mustard, 'And the marines?'

Fleet Control, 'All lost, Sir.'

Admiral Mustard tried to hide his emotions, but there were a few tears. It was one blow after another.

Fleet Control, 'The Brakendethians are pounding Planet Gibbs. Our assets are engaging them, but they are heavily outnumbered. There are about forty-five thousand Brakendethian ships.'

Admiral Mustard, 'My orders:
- Send Fleet Twenty-Three to Planet Gibbs.'

Fleet Control, 'Yes, Sir.'

Admiral Mustard, 'Comms, get me the Marine Commander travelling to Earth.'

Comms, 'Yes, Sir.'

Major Underwing, 'Morning, Sir.'

Admiral Mustard, 'Have you been apprised of the current position on Earth?'

Major Underwing, 'Yes, Sir, as follows:
- The marine assets on Earth have been pacified
- Commander Goozee has been lost in action
- GAD Control has been removed.'

Admiral Mustard, 'We believe that seventy per cent of the alien assets have been eradicated.

My Orders:
- Eradicate remaining aliens
- Protect the Marine Corps as much as possible
- When the aliens have been eradicated, report for further orders. Do not engage in any civilian assistance projects. Do you understand?'

Major Underwing, 'Yes, Sir.'

Location: Nowhere Land
Sequence of Events: 142

Grand Dethmon, 'How does it feel to be winning, my son?'

Terry, 'Glorious, Grand Dethmon, glorious.'

Grand Dethmon, 'We will have so much fun, my son. Conquering the universe will be glorious indeed. And you didn't mind about the Padfield creature dying?'

Terry, 'I revelled in it.'

I should have done it ages ago, although he recognised that he was still a baby. He felt genuine hatred for his dear old uncle, who wanted him dead.

Terry, 'Well, who's dead now?'

Terry forgot that he was in a featureless dimension on his own, but with half the senior Brakendethians inside him. He noticed that his mother wasn't looking too good. On closer inspection, she was dead. He had forgotten that this dimension lacked oxygen. It wasn't like him, but he had been somewhat distracted.

The tears rolled down his face. Despite everything, she had loved him. Loved him without restraint. He dragged her head to his tiny lap and tenderly stroked it.

The Grand Dethmon felt a pang of guilt. It was such a small pang that you couldn't measure it on a twinge metre. Nevertheless, it was vital to their cause. It took a lot of effort for him to remove all of the oxygen.

Grand Dethmon, 'I'm so sorry for your loss. She was so dear to us all.'

All Terry could do was sob.

Grand Dethmon, 'Those homans are responsible for this. They forced you into this dimension. They have blood on their hands.'

Terry saw that he was right. Why should he be the one that suffered all the pain? So he decided to up the stakes.

Location: On-Board Admiral Mustard's Flagship
Sequence of Events: 143

Admiral Mustard, 'Update me.'
Fleet Control, 'Yes, Sir, there is so much going on that it is hard to summarise.'
Admiral Mustard, 'Do the best you can.'
Fleet Control, 'Yes, Sir,
- Admiral Bumelton has reported that more Brakendethian ships have arrived, and that he is losing the dogfight. More reinforcements are now required
- The marines under Major Underwing can't land because of the fierce fighting in space
- The marines on Planet Lister are retreating
- The planets that earlier reported that things were under control are suffering further teleporter attacks
- I have to report that Admiral Gittins has been killed.'
Admiral Mustard, 'What about his fleet?'
Fleet Control, 'I will check on that, but I'm picking up some bad news, Sir. We are getting mixed messages. I'm deeply sorry, Sir, but it looks like Planet Gibbs has been destroyed. It looks like all of our Fleet assets have gone as well.'
Admiral Mustard, 'But that's Fleet Twenty-Three and half of Fleet Three.'
Fleet Control, 'And Drone Fleets One and Two.'
Admiral Mustard. 'What about Admiral Cook?'
Fleet Control, 'Another casualty, Sir.'

Admiral Mustard just wanted to go and hide. He didn't know Admiral Cook that well, but the loss of Dave, Debbie, and Peter in a few minutes was an immense blow. He needed to take decisive action, or all would be lost.

Admiral Mustard, 'Comms, get me Henrietta Strong.' Of course, he didn't expect her to be alive.
Comms, 'Yes, Sir.'
Henrietta Strong said in a quiet, muffled voice, 'Hello.'
Admiral Mustard, 'Is that you?'

Henrietta Strong, 'Yes, I'm hiding in a cupboard in a supermarket. The monsters are greedily devouring the contents of the meat counter. They seem to like anything with blood in it.'

Admiral Mustard, 'I'm so glad that you are alive. You know that we have lost The President.' Henrietta could hear the tears in his voice.

Henrietta Strong, 'No, I can't believe that.' But she did. 'He will be so missed. He was the best of us all.'

Admiral Mustard, 'I agree, but we need those drones.'

Henrietta Strong, 'I will see what I can do when the monsters have finished their feast.'

Admiral Mustard, 'Comms, get me, Commander Crocker.'

Comms, 'Yes, Sir.'

Commander Crocker, 'Hi Jack, we are all dressed up with nowhere to go.'

Admiral Mustard, 'Hi Tom, this is where we are:
- GAD Control has been destroyed
- Planet Gibbs has been destroyed
- The President and most of the Government have been killed
- We can't land any more marines on Earth as Admiral Bumelton is retreating from The Brakendethian fleet
- Commander Goozee has been killed
- Admiral Gittins has been killed
- Four planets are reporting further teleporter attacks
- Our Fleets are under-performing because of staff shortages.'

Commander Crocker, 'What do you want me to do?'

Admiral Mustard, 'I want you to rescue Henrietta Strong so that we can get more drones operational.'

Commander Crocker, 'And?'

Admiral Mustard, 'What do you mean?'

Commander Crocker, 'I have one thousand of the best troops that humanity has ever had. Tell me what you want to do with them.'

Admiral Mustard, 'Choose one of the enemy incursions and take it off my list. Disrupt the enemy wherever you can.'

Commander Crocker, 'Yes, Sir.'

Admiral Mustard, 'Update me.'

Fleet Control, 'Yes, Sir, as follows:

- Admiral Bumelton is saying that he will have to retreat unless he is reinforced
- Fleet Fifteen has taken seventy per cent casualties
- Planet Lister has effectively been lost to The Nexuster
- Admiral Easter has been killed, but his Fleet is still fighting.'

Terry then launched his next attack. Every woman who had given birth to a baby Terry was terminated. They simply bled to death. There was nothing you could do to stop it.

All Brakendethian ships were told to attack Earth. Five alien fleets also joined in the attack. As a result, Admiral Bumelton was forced to retreat and was losing assets at an alarming rate.

Once the armies were teleported in, Terry ordered the teleporters to be destroyed, which caused massive explosions on the affected planets. As a result, the local Government started to fall apart.

He then played with the planetary force fields, rapidly switching them on and off, which devastated some of The Galactium Fleets.

Admiral Mustard heard about dying women and rushed down to see Edel. She was lying in a massive sickly pool of blood. Her eyes just stared blankly. Whatever made Edel the woman she was had gone. His love had gone. Their future had gone. He held her head in his arms and just cried. He cried the tears of a man who had lost everything. He wasn't sure if he wanted to carry on.

He ignored the calls from Fleet Control. He ignored the calls from AI Central. He ignored the calls from Commander Crocker. He just held the dead body of his lover in his arms. His uniform was soaked in her blood. She had never deserved this.

AI Central to Fleet Control and Admiral Bumelton, 'Admiral Mustard seems indisposed.'

Admiral Bumelton decided that the critical battle was for Earth, so he ordered the following: 'All Fleets will disengage to join Fleet Three to defend Earth
- All forts to come to the aid of Earth.'

Fleet Control, 'Yes, Sir. I need to report that more alien fleets are arriving.'

Admiral Bumelton, 'Get me a status report on our assets.'

Fleet Control, 'Yes, Sir, it's on the screen now:

Fleet No	Task/Location	Admiral	Status
1	Earth	Mustard	52%
2	Earth	Bumelton	46%
3	Earth	J Bonner	27%
4	Ampere		37%
5	Earth	Mynd	42%
6	Einstein	Richardson	71%
7	Faraday	Wallett	66%
8	Newton	Adams	57%
9	Exploration	Beamish	99%
10	Tesla	Chudzinski	41%
11	Joule	Fieldhouse	82%
12	Galileo	Fogg	47%
13	Babbage		38%
14	Site of Turing	Dobson	77%
15	Blackwell	Hubbard	17%
16	Lovelace	Patel	53%
17	Brahmagupta	Lamberty	53%
18	Pasteur	Abosa	36%
19	Hopper	Wagner	77%
20	Scott	Tersoo	49%
21	Pasteur	De Mestral	57%
22	Tesla	Spangler	43%
23			0%
24	Hertz	Strauss	30%
25	Ampere	Bosman	71%
Forts	Planet duty	Zakotti	49%
Earth Defence	Earth	Muller	19%
Exploratory	Multiple Locations	Olowe	93%
Drone 1		Fleet	0%
Drone 2		Fleet	0%
Drone 3	Earth	Fleet	18%
Drone 4	Bacon	Fleet	23%
Drone 5	Bacon	Fleet	57%
Drone 6		Fleet	0%

Drone 7	Aristotle	Fleet	34%
Drone 8	Newton	Fleet	82%
Drone 9	Newton	Fleet	83%
Drone 10	Newton	Fleet	79%
Drone 11	Curie	Fleet	43%
Drone 12	Galileo	Fleet	71%
Drone 13	Galileo	Fleet	67%
Drone 14	Fardel System	Fleet	100%
Drone 15		Fleet	0%
Drone 16	Earth	Fleet	41%
Drone 17	Tesla	Fleet	54%
Drone 18	Tesla	Fleet	47%
Drone 19	Copernicus	Fleet	81%
Drone 20	Whittle	Fleet	34%
Drone 21	Rutherford	Fleet	41%
Drone 22	Hooke	Fleet	51%
Drone 23	Boyle	Fleet	51%
Drone 24	Hertz	Fleet	67%
Drone 25	Nobel	Fleet	82%
Drone 26	Earth	Fleet	11%
Drone 27	Earth	Fleet	18%
Drone 28	Earth	Fleet	29%
Drone 29	Earth	Fleet	32%
Drone 30	Earth	Fleet	32%

Location: Royal Palace, The Chosen, Olympus
Sequence of Events: 144

Lady Enyo, 'What do we do? If the humans fail, then we fail.'

Admiral Thanatos, 'Agreed, but we can't waste our resources. We have our own worries. The Brakendethian fleet is getting nearer by the day.'

Lady Enyo, 'What do we know?'

Admiral Thanatos, 'There is an enormous battle going on around the Earth. It was a surprise attack that simply escalated into a massed battle between the forces of good and evil.'

Lady Enyo, 'That's a bit dramatic.'

Admiral Thanatos, 'Well, that's about it. It's The Galactium versus the remains of The Brakendethian fleet, plus their old allies probably helping in an attempt to get more Chemlife. The poor fools.'

Lady Enyo, 'If we engaged, what impact would it make?'

Admiral Thanatos, 'At this moment in time, little impact, but perhaps later we could make a real difference.'

Lady Enyo, 'What else do we know?'

Admiral Thanatos, 'Most of the Government has been killed, including The President.'

Lady Enyo, 'Not that nice Mr Padfield!'

Admiral Thanatos, 'I'm afraid so.'

Location: On-Board Admiral Bumelton's Flagship
Sequence of Events: 145

Admiral Bumelton, 'Update Me.'

Fleet Control, 'Yes, Sir:
- All the Fleets except Fleet Twenty-Three, which has been destroyed and Fleet Nine, which is on exploratory duties, are here or nearly here
- Over six hundred forts are in the vicinity
- All the Drone Fleets are here except One, Two, Six and Fifteen, which have been destroyed
- There has been considerable asset loss in terms of both men and ships
- Admirals Gittins, Easter, Cook, Wagner, Fieldhouse and Beamish have been killed
- The President, Vice-President and other senior ministers have been killed
- GAD Control has been destroyed
- Admiral Mustard is indisposed. He had declared martial law. In his absence, you are the nominated head of The Galactium
- The Fleets are awaiting your orders, Sir.'

Admiral Bumelton, 'AI Central, am I the acting President?'

AI Central, 'I'm honoured to say that you are. I also have an update for you:
- Some of the planets are in a terrible state. As you know, we lost Planet Gibbs. Others will suffer the same fate soon unless you defeat The Brakendethians quickly
- Commander Crocker is trying to get hold of you
- What do you want to do with the Marine Fleet?'

Admiral Bumelton, 'Update me regarding our assets.'

Fleet Control, 'Yes, Sir. Do you want a quick summary or the detail?'

Admiral Bumelton, 'Summary, please.'

Fleet Control, 'It's on the screen now, Sir. Unfortunately, the totals don't correspond to the percentages that well as we have many disabled and damaged assets that still show that they are available.'

| The Galactium | 68,000 assets |
| The Enemy | 72,000 assets |

Admiral Bumelton, 'So it's another war of attrition. They have the advantage as we need to protect Earth.'

Fleet Control, 'Yes, Sir.'

Admiral Bumelton, 'My orders:
- The current melee tactics will cease, as they are not to our advantage
- Order drones to aggressively attack the enemy while Fleets One, Two, Three, Four and Five form a line. Fleet Control will provide co-ordinates
- Once formed, Fleets Six, Seven, Eight, Ten and Eleven will form behind them
- Once formed, Fleets Twelve to Twenty will form behind them
- Fleets Twenty-One to Twenty-Five will form a strategic reverse behind them
- Four hundred of the forts will form a defensive layer around Earth
- The remaining forts will support the flanks of the Fleets
- The super drones will protect Fleet One
- Marine Fleet to retire to Jupiter
- Chase the recall for Fleet Nine.'

Fleet Control, 'Yes, Sir.'

Admiral Bumelton, 'When will Fleet Nine be here?'

Fleet Control, 'They are out of contact, Sir.'

Admiral Bumelton, 'Any update regarding Admiral Mustard.'

Fleet control, 'All I know is that his room is barricaded.'

Admiral Bumelton, 'Order them to break the door down.'

Fleet Control, 'Yes, Sir.'

Comms, 'Commander Crocker is on the blower.'

Admiral Bumelton, 'Hi Tom, how can I help?'

Commander Crocker, 'I need your help. I'm with Henrietta Strong on Earth with thirty of my men. We are surrounded by monsters and need assistance getting off the planet. It wouldn't be so urgent except that we can't get access to the GAD Control network. If Henrietta had access, then she could supply you with thousands of new drones. They might give you the edge.'

Admiral Bumelton, 'Can I access the network on her behalf?'

Commander Crocker, 'It needs her eye scan, hand scan and DNA.'

Admiral Bumelton, 'That's a bugger then.'

Commander Crocker, 'What can you do?'

Admiral Bumelton, 'Fleet Twenty-Four is on its way. They have the only experimental teleporter. So we can either fight our way down and back up or risk the new technology. It's your shout?'

Commander Crocker, 'What are the odds of losing Henrietta?'

Admiral Bumelton, 'I'm told it's about one in a thousand.'

Commander, 'Let's go for the teleporter. Can it take all of us?'

Admiral Bumelton, 'We will find out.' He ordered Fleet Control to organise.

Location: Nowhere Land
Sequence of Events: 146

Grand Dethmon, 'I think we are still winning.'

Terry, 'I think someone is trying to use the teleporter. I've changed the settings. They will find it hotter than they expected.'

Grand Dethmon, 'The Homans have organised their fleet a bit better. Someone has taken charge.'

Terry, 'We need to focus our attacks on their leaders: Mustard and Bumelton.'

Grand Dethmon, 'Good thinking, my boy. We have used all of the resources I had. It was a smart idea of mine, promising unlimited Chemlife to our old slave partners. If only they knew that the Homans are providing it free of charge.'

Terry, 'They charge for it now, but it's a pittance.'

Grand Dethmon, 'What else can we do?'

Terry, 'Let's attack the leaders and see what happens.'

Grand Dethmon, 'Go for it, my son.'

Location: Transporter Room, Fleet 24
Sequence of Events: 147

Operator, 'How do we find them?'

Senior Operator, 'I'm not sure. So far, we have moved a table from place A to place B within this ship. Now they are asking us to move thirty-odd men off Planet Earth into the flagship of Fleet Twenty-Four that's fucking moving at a fucking fast rate.'

Operator, 'That's a bit different boss.' He knew that his boss always started swearing when he was out of his depth.

Senior Operator, 'It's a fucking magnitude of difference, but you try telling them upstairs!'

Operator, 'They are downstairs, boss.'

Then the machine started up of its own volition. Both operators jumped back in amazement. The monitor stated that thirty-two individuals had been extracted from a supermarket in Fulham and that they had been transported to the centre of the Sun.

Operator. 'Well, who is going to tell the bosses downstairs?'

Senior Operator, 'But we didn't do anything.'

Operator, 'No one is going to believe that.'

While they were discussing this, the worst possible thing happened, the blower went.

Captain Ogilvie, 'I've seen that the transporter has been used on my monitor. So are our guests on board?'

Senior Operator, 'Not Exactly Ma'am.'

Captain Ogilvie, 'What do you mean?'

Senior operator, 'Well, they were picked up and transported but not to here.'

He wished that he still had his old job of picking lemons in Quesada, Spain.

Captain Ogilvie, 'Where have you sent them?'

Senior Operator, 'It wasn't us. The machine did it.'

Captain Ogilvie, 'I had already programmed in the pickup point. So all you had to do was push the go button.'

Senior Operator, 'That's good, Sir, as it wasn't us.'

Captain Ogilvie, 'Where are they?'

Senior Operator, 'In the Sun, Sir.'

Captain Ogilvie, 'You sent the Commander Special Ops and The Galactium's Chief of Staff into the Sun?'

Senior Operator, 'It's looking that way, Sir.'

Captain Ogilvie, 'What a fuck-up. The Admiral will not be amused.'

Location: On-Board Admiral Bumelton's Flagship
Sequence of Events: 148

Admiral Bumelton, 'Update Me.'
    Fleet Control, 'Yes, Sir, as follows:
- The enemy seems to be currently concentrating their resources
- Our assets are holding their own, although the drones are taking a fair old hammering
- The forts have effectively stopped any further attacks on Earth
- Fleet Nine is returning as quickly as it can.'

Admiral Bumelton, 'Show me the concentration pattern.'
    Fleet Control, 'Yes, Sir.'
The display was shown.
Admiral Bumelton, 'That's fairly obvious. They are going to throw their weight at Fleets One and Two. So it looks like we are in for a thumping unless we do something.'
    Fleet Control, 'Yes, Sir.'
Admiral Bumelton, 'My orders:
- Fleets Twelve, Thirteen and Fourteen to attack the enemy on the outside flank of Fleet One
- Fleets Fifteen, Sixteen and Seventeen to attack the enemy on the outside flank of Fleet Three.'

Fleet Control, 'Can I ask why, Sir?'
Admiral Bumelton, 'All fleets are vulnerable when they are re-organising.'
    Fleet Control, 'I understand, Sir.'
Admiral Bumelton, 'My orders:
- Send half the forts to assist in the attack
- Find out what other forts are available throughout The Galactium
- Launch all fighters.'

Fleet Control, 'Yes, Sir.'
Admiral Bumelton, 'Get me an update on the Henrietta Strong situation.'

The enemy was surprised by the two flank attacks, but they then countered with flank attacks of their own. It was a battle of two evenly matched sides using massive amounts of munitions. Admiral Bumelton realised that he needed something to give him an edge. He needed those drones.

Fleet Control, 'I have an update on the transporter.'

Admiral Bumelton, 'Go on.'

Fleet Control, 'It appears that the entire team was transported into the centre of the Sun.'

Admiral, 'Is that a joke?'

Fleet Control, 'I wish it were, Sir.'

The flagship was taking several serious hits. The force fields were coping, but for how long? Some of the nearby ships were being evaporated.

Fleet Control, 'Shall I order some protective cover for the Flagship?'

Admiral Bumelton, 'I don't want to put others at risk to protect me.'

Fleet Control, 'We can't afford to lose you, and they ordered Fleets Twenty-One and Twenty-Two to provide cover.'

Admiral Bumelton, 'Back to the transporter. Are you saying that we have lost Commander Crocker and Henrietta Strong?'

Fleet Control, 'Yes, Sir.'

Admiral Bumelton, 'Well, the odds were certainly wrong.'

In the back of his mind, he felt that Terry was behind this. Then he wondered how he could hurt Terry.

Admiral Bumelton, 'My orders:
- Destroy Terry's flat
- Avoid too much damage.'

Fleet Control, 'Really, Sir?'

Admiral Bumelton, 'Yes really, that's an order.'

Location: Nowhere Land
Sequence of Events: 149

Terry, 'They have blown up my flat. Why would they do that?'

Grand Dethmon, 'The Homans are an evil, despicable lot. How can civilised beings such as us understand their motives? We are fighting the good fight to improve the lot of everyone.'

Terry, 'Except homans.'

Grand Dethmon, 'You have helped them so much, and they do this to you.'

While this was going on, Terry lost control of his fleet. Like mother, like son. He was wondering where he was going to go after he left Nowhere Land. He had lost all of his toys. He had lost his collection of Captain America figurines. It was just not playing fair.

Location: On-Board Admiral Bumelton's Flagship
Sequence of Events: 150

Fleet Control, 'Sir, the enemy's vessels are wavering.'
Admiral Bumelton, 'My orders:
- All Fleets to attack, show no mercy.'

The Galactium vessels leapt forward and starting eliminating the waverers, but then the enemy recovered. Terry was back in control.

It was always a risk, and now the Galactium forces had lost their structure. It was back to being a melee.

Admiral Bumelton, 'My orders:
- Order drones to aggressively attack the enemy while Fleets One, Two, Three, Four, Five and Six form a line. Fleet Control will provide co-ordinates
- Once formed, Fleets, Seven, Eight, Ten, Eleven and Twelve will form behind them
- Once formed, Fleets, Thirteen to Twenty will form behind them
- Fleets Twenty-One to Twenty-Five will form a strategic reverse behind them
- Forts will return to defend Earth.'

Fleet Control, 'Yes, Sir.'
Admiral Bumelton, 'Show me the latest asset position.'
Fleet Control, 'Yes, Sir, it's on the screen.'

| Galactium | 49,000 assets |
| The Enemy | 61,000 assets |

Admiral Bumelton, 'How come they are winning the attrition war?'
Fleet Control, 'It would have been worse if they didn't have that blip.'
AI Control, 'We are on a path to extinction.'
Admiral Bumelton, 'What about Henrietta's drones?'
AI Control, 'I'm trying to get them released. Henrietta was a bit of a security whizz. She was always concerned that they might have got into the wrong hands.'
Admiral Bumelton, 'If we don't do something, then we won't have

any hands.'

Fleet Control, 'More forts are arriving, and Fleet Nine will be here in a few hours.'

Admiral Bumelton, 'How many forts?'

Fleet Control, 'One hundred and fifty.'

Admiral Bumelton, 'So our number will increase by two thousand, six hundred and fifty.'

Fleet Control, 'Yes, Sir.'

Admiral Mustard, 'Hi guys, how can I help?'

Admiral Bumelton, 'I'm so pleased to hear your voice. What happened?'

Admiral Mustard, 'Edel died.'

Admiral Bumelton, 'What can I say?'

Admiral Mustard, 'Nothing, for now. There will be plenty of time to celebrate her life later.'

AI Central, 'I, for one, will miss Edel's wisdom.'

Admiral Bumelton, 'So many wasted lives. Any suggestions, Jack?'

Admiral Mustard, 'We need to do something totally unexpected. My suggestion is to leave the forts as they are, divide our assets into two fleets, and then fly off at our fastest possible speed in opposite directions.'

Admiral Bumelton, 'And then?'

Admiral Mustard, 'They will follow. Fleet A will fly off, followed by half the enemy. Fleet B will attack that enemy fleet. Fleet A will then attack the enemy fleet following Fleet B. There will be confusion and chaos, but we will be fighting.'

Admiral Bumelton, 'My orders:
- Divide the Fleet into two: Fleets A and B
- Fleet A to fly away from Earth
- Fleet B to fly in directly the opposite direction
- It is expected that the enemy fleet will follow
- Fleet B will chase after Fleet A and attack the enemy
- Fleet A will attack the enemy fleet tracking Fleet B
- Expect to receive further orders during the resulting battle and follow as commanded.'

Fleet Control, 'Yes, Sir.'

The sudden departure of two Galactium Fleets totally surprised Terry. He then knew that he had won; they were fleeing. The Galactium was his. The Brakendethians had won.

He naturally ordered his fleet to track the enemy down and destroy them. He was surprised to find both of his fleets under attack. It was an ambush that was starting to even the odds. Just when his fleet gained some control again, the homans divided their fleet into four and shot off into four different directions.

Terry was now expecting a trap, but what could he do? He divided *his* resources into four and followed. It was a chase through the stars, ducking in and out of asteroids. Terry hadn't expected The Galactium fleet to be re-formed and waiting to pounce on a quarter of his fleet with devastating effect. Retreat was out of the question, but destruction was on the cards.

Admiral Bumelton, 'Show me the latest asset position.'

Fleet Control, 'Yes, Sir, it's on the screen now.'

Galactium	37,000 assets
The Enemy	34,000 assets

Admiral Mustard, 'Those odds are better, but we are losing some fine men and women.'

Admiral Bumelton, 'Don't go there yet. What shall we do next?'

Location: Nowhere Land
Sequence of Events: 151

Grand Dethmon, 'They are running rings around you.'

Terry, 'When all the ships are in one area, I can manage them easily. When they go off in lots of different directions, it is much harder. I'm still learning my trade, and they have been doing it for years.'

Grand Dethmon, 'You are a Brakendethian. You will not let these pigs get the upper hand. Do you understand?'

Terry understood, but he wanted his mummy.

Location: Royal Palace, The Chosen, Olympus
Sequence of Events: 152

Lady Enyo, 'Is now the time?'

Admiral Thanatos, 'It's looking promising. From what I can see, The Brakendethians are losing their edge. I'm not sure why the Earthers are not using their huge fleet of drones. There must be nearly a million of them. Instead, they are just sitting there at Planet Newton.'

Lady Enyo, 'That possibly suits us. They will be available to defend Olympus.'

Admiral Thanatos, 'The entire fleet?'

Lady Enyo, 'Every asset we have got. The cavalry is on their way.'

Location: On-Board Admiral Bumelton's Flagship
Sequence of Events: 153

Admiral Bumelton, 'What next?'

Admiral Mustard, 'We head towards Fleet Nine. That will surprise the bastards. We then turn and attack.'

Admiral Bumelton, 'That turning transaction is quite difficult. You know that if things can go wrong, then they will.'

Admiral Mustard, 'War is at least thirty per cent chaos, there will be mistakes, there will be danger, but that's what gives us the edge.'

The rush was on. Terry couldn't work out what was going on, but he certainly hadn't expected a fleet waiting for him. The Galactium Fleet tore through Fleet Nine, who then threw every piece of ordnance they had at The Brakendethians.

The Galactium Fleet used the manoeuvre they had learnt from The Chosen and carried out a rapid three-sixty turn and then attacked the enemy head-on. The aggression of The Galactium Fleet was such that the enemy started retreating.

The Brakendethians were now in full retreat, partly because Terry couldn't think of anything else to do. Both sides then detected the presence of another fleet. From The Galactium's point of view, it was probably another alien fleet there to help Terry.

Admiral Bumelton, 'My orders:
- Cancel the pursuit
- Re-form the standard defensive formation
- Prepare for an incoming attack.'

Fleet Control, 'Yes, Sir.'

Then they saw The Brakendethian fleet slow down, but it didn't turn. So they were all prepared for another onslaught and, for some, the chance to meet their death.

Spread in front of The Brakendethians was The Chosen's fleet laid out in House order. If you looked carefully, you could see the colours, flags, and insignia of the twelve houses. It was a heraldic display from days gone by.

The naval staff in The Chosen fleet were far more anxious than the humans. Some of them had lived for thousands of years and expected to live for thousands more. Life seemed much more precious to them than for the humans whose spark was soon extinguished. You would think the opposite, but it's not the case.

Terry was losing it. He just didn't have the experience and he wanted to go to bed. It was time for his Horlicks.

The massacre of The Brakendethians began.

Location: Nowhere Land
Sequence of Events: 154

Grand Dethmon, 'Well, that didn't go as we planned.'

Terry, 'I never expected The Chosen to enter the fray.'

Grand Dethmon, 'The enemy rarely does what you expect, and when they do, you wonder what has happened. You can't believe your good luck, and you rarely believe it.'

Terry did not understand, but he really wanted his mummy.

Grand Dethmon, 'You still have a powerful fleet. We know that The Chosen can't fight. So what are you going to do?'

He knew that Terry was losing it, and if he were honest, he wasn't sure what they should do. Flee or fight? Should they just kill as many of the enemy as possible?

He realised that action was needed, as the odds were now definitely against them. Then Terry knew what to do.

Location: On-Board Admiral Bumelton's Flagship
Sequence of Events: 155

Fleet Control, 'Sir, the enemy is fleeing.'

Admiral Bumelton realised that he should have had forces in position to inhibit that. Instead, his positioning was confused by the presence of The Chosen. Where in The Galactium is he going? Where would a two-year-old child take a powerful battle fleet?

Admiral Bumelton, 'My orders:
- Full pursuit
- Fastest vessels to go to Earth's defence
- Warn the forts of an impending attack.

Fleet Control, 'Yes, Sir.'

Admiral mustard, 'Comms, put me through to Admiral Thanatos.'

Comms, 'Yes, Sir.'

Admiral Thanatos, 'I see that you are still alive, my dear friend.'

Admiral Mustard, 'I am, but many of my dear friends have moved on.'

Admiral Thanatos, 'It is the destiny of the warrior.'

Admiral Mustad, 'Some of them were the peacemakers.'

Admiral Thanatos, 'When it comes to The Brakendeth, everyone is a warrior.'

Admiral Mustard, 'Thank you for coming to our aid.'

Admiral Thanatos, 'We have been waiting for the point where our meagre forces would really be of use. Now is our chance to eradicate the devils.'

Admiral Mustard, 'We are trying to work out their next move.'

Admiral Thanatos, 'We just need to hound them to destruction.'

Admiral Mustard, 'I agree, but I would suggest that they are up to something.'

Admiral Thanatos, 'They hate losing. So they are going to throw everything they have at Earth.'

Admiral Mustard, 'That's what we think. Any suggestions on the best way forward?'

Admiral Thanatos, 'We will go to Earth. We are slower than you, but we will be there. Leave some of them alive for us to kill.'

Admiral Mustard, 'I will see what I can do. See you later.'
Admiral Bumelton, 'So it's a full-scale charge back to Earth then.'
Admiral Mustard, 'And don't spare the carriages.'

Location: Marine Command, Off Jupiter
Sequence of Events: 156

Fleet Control, 'Sir, Major Underwing is requesting permission for his marines to leave Jupiter and carry out a cleansing operation on Earth.'

Admiral Bumelton, 'Do they have naval cover?'

Fleet Control, 'They claim they do, and there are a fair number of forts to assist.'

Admiral Bumelton, 'Permission granted.' The Admiral was a bit confused about who was in charge, but they knew each other well enough for it not to be a problem.

Major Underwing was somewhat relieved as controlling twenty-five thousand eager individual killing machines in ships off Jupiter wasn't easy. But they wanted to fight something. The only option was each other. When it was announced that they were off to Earth, the Marine Corps cheered to a man and woman. Now they had a job to do. Weapons were cleaned and checked again.

Major Underwing had difficulty in finding out who he should contact on Earth. First, he needed to know where the infestations were. Eventually, this was clarified, and permission was given to land.

Three different locations were selected in close proximity to the still smouldering ruins of GAD Control. As soon as they landed, they were attacked by hideous, multi-coloured sets of jaws. Typically, your first impression of a Nexuster monster was the jaws. Massive gaping sets of teeth, a forked tongue, dribbling slime, small beady eyes, and a serious lust for killing. They were hungry for flesh, an insatiable hunger that seemed impossible to satisfy.

The marines looked at them through the armoured glass of their transport ships. Jupiter was looking far more attractive now. They used the machine guns built into the transport ship to clear the local gang of homicidal killers who were just throwing themselves at the transports, and the machine guns were just ripping them to pieces.

It got to the point where you couldn't see out of the window due to the pile of enemy bodies. The slimy, multi-coloured collection of guts and internal organs was a genuinely sickening sight. If you looked carefully, you could see human heads that had been devoured and were now displayed for all to see. Their eyes stared blankly. They starred at the marines, asking, where were you when I needed you?

The local marine commanders ordered the ships to move to new nearby locations, but the same story repeated itself. It was almost impossible to open the doors. One of the transport ships hovered, and the marines targeted the enemy from open doors. The sheer scale of monsterhood was both terrifying and intimidating.

No human contact was made. There was no sign of a human being anywhere. Major Underwing authorised the use of napalm. The transport ships circulated the area, converting the monsters into a burning, gelatinous mass. The smell was utterly nauseating.

They constantly moved to new areas, and the same scenario repeated itself. Major Underwing wondered how big the infestation was.

Location: On-Board Admiral Mustard's Flagship
Sequence of Events: 157

Admiral Mustard, 'Update me.'

Fleet Control, 'Yes, Sir, as follows:
- The Brakendethians are heading in the direction of Earth
- The Earth-based forts are on full alert
- About eighty of our quickest battlecruisers are heading towards Earth in an attempt to head the enemy off
- The marines have landed on Earth and are finding the area around the GAD Control ruins heavily infested
- The Chosen are following but are a long way behind us.'

Admiral Mustard, 'George, we need to be careful as The Brakendethians might turn and attack us.'

Admiral Bumelton, 'I was thinking much the same, especially as we have sent our battlecruisers ahead.'

Admiral Mustard, "Show me the latest asset position. Include The Chosen assets'

Fleet Control, 'Yes, Sir. It's on the screen now.'

Galactium Fleet	32,000
Galactium Forts	800
The Chosen	47,000
Alliance Total	79,800
The Enemy	28,000

Admiral Bumelton, 'In total, we outnumber them three to one, but if they decided to attack us, then it would be a close-run thing.'

Admiral Mustard, 'But we have a dilemma. We need to protect Earth, but we need The Chosen to give us the edge.'

Admiral Bumelton, 'We need to slow the Fleet down but at the same time keep in touch with the enemy. So it's the old quandary where do you put your slowest assets?'

Admiral Mustard, 'Ours are at the end of the line. We need to wait for The Chosen.'

Admiral Bumelton, 'My orders:
- The Fleet will slow down but attempt to keep contact with the enemy.'

Fleet Control, 'Yes, Sir.'

Location: Marine Command, On Earth
Sequence of Events: 158

Major Underwing, 'How many of these fucking monsters *are* there?'

Lieutenant Crate, 'Hard to tell, Sir. We have been burning them for two hours, and they keep coming. The men are getting restless.'

Major Underwing, 'They can fucking stay restless. There is no point going down there until it's free of live monsters, and probably there will be no point in wading through gallons of goo.

My Orders:
- The transport ships will determine the breadth of the infestation
- We need to determine the number of monsters involved
- Contact Earth authorities to determine which areas are monster free.'

The transport ships were given quadrants emanating from the GAD Control ruins. Their tasks were to plot the size of the infestation. What they found was that landing the craft attracted the monsters. Consequently, they dropped a series of beacons playing 'Communication Breakdown' by Led Zeppelin. There was an argument as some wanted to play 'Twenty-First Century Schizoid Man' by King Crimson. In the end, Major Underwing selected Led as he had always been a fan.

It became evident that the monsters were also Led Zeppelin fans as the beacons were surrounded by gangly, multi-limbed slimeballs which made easy targets for the marines.

It was said by some that Led Zeppelin saved Earth. In the end, the monsters were cleared. Initially by napalm but then by individual marine hunting packs clearing buildings one by one. Major Underwing was grateful that he didn't have the job of cleaning up the gook.

Location: On-Board Admiral Mustard's Flagship
Sequence of Events: 159

Fleet Control, 'Sir, we have lost contact with The Brakendethians.'

Admiral Mustard, 'How did that happen?'

Fleet Control, 'We went through an asteroid belt, and suddenly they were gone.'

Admiral Mustard, 'Any clues to their whereabouts?'

Fleet Control, 'No, Sir, sorry Sir.'

Admiral Mustard, 'George, what do you think?'

Admiral Bumelton, 'It could be a trap. They might be waiting for us.'

Admiral Mustard, 'Do we just head towards Earth?'

Admiral Bumelton, 'Our battle cruisers on the way to Earth will warn us if they are still on the way to Earth.'

Admiral Mustard, 'Where else would they go?'

Admiral Bumelton, 'There are dozens of planets in The Galactium. So they could find somewhere to hide.'

Admiral Mustard, 'That's not The Brakendethian way.'

Admiral Bumelton, 'What is their way?'

Admiral Mustard, 'Good question. I would say Control and retribution.'

Admiral Bumelton, 'So Earth is the obvious target.'

Admiral Mustard, 'George, you are a genius. It's revenge that they are after. They are going to Olympus.'

Admiral Mustard, 'My orders:
- Inform The Chosen
- Obtain coordinates for Planet Olympus
- Once obtained, the entire Fleet will go to Planet Olympus, including half of the forts defending Earth and our battle cruisers

Location: On-Board The Chosen's Flagship
Sequence of Events: 160

Admiral Thanatos, 'My Lady, we have just received an update from Admiral Mustard:
- They have lost contact with The Brakendethian fleet
- They now believe that it's on its way to Olympus
- The remains of The Galactium Fleet and four hundred forts are on their way there
- Need planetary coordinates.'

Lady Enyo, 'Is it a trap?'

Admiral Thanatos, 'Possibly, but what advantage would it be to the Earthers?'

Lady Enyo, 'Our technology?'

Admiral Thanatos, 'We can't even keep up with their fleet.'

Lady Enyo, 'It is the sort of thing The Brakendethians would do. One ultimate revenge.'

Admiral Thanatos, 'But they have a fleet on the way to annihilate us.'

Lady Enyo, 'They want the job done now before the Earthers can come to our aid.'

Admiral Thanatos, 'To be honest, we have to trust the Earthers. We are dead without them.'

Lady Enyo, 'Agreed, provide the coordinates and return home ASAP.'

Admiral Thanatos, 'Yes, Ma'am.'

Location: On-Board Admiral Mustard's Flagship
Sequence of Events: 161

Fleet Control, 'Sir, we have the coordinates from The Chosen.'

Admiral Mustard, 'My orders:
- All Fleet vessels to make quickest possible progress to Planet Olympus
- On arrival, disrupt any Brakendethian activity
- If The Brakendethians have not arrived, then form a standard defensible formation.'

Fleet Control, 'Yes, Sir.'

It was now simply a race. Admirals Mustard and Bumelton had now given up any concept of naval formations. There was just a need to get there and save the planet.

Despite everything, The Galactium Fleet enjoyed this immensely. It was a race. The winner would have enough kudos forever. The bragging rights would be outstanding. Unfortunately, there was also the likelihood of death waiting for the first arrivals.

Admiral Bumelton, 'Jack, what is your plan on arrival?'

Admiral Mustard, 'George, me old mate, 'I've no idea. Let's see what we find.'

Admiral Bumelton, 'Fair enough. I better go and get my Luger.' He had always been fascinated by the First and Second World Wars.

Location: Nowhere Land
Sequence of Events: 162

Grand Dethmon, 'I've already told you. Your mother is dead.'

Terry, 'Where is she? I haven't had my tea.'

Grand Dethmon, 'We can't worry about that. We have got to destroy The Chosen!'

Terry, 'Who cares about The Chosen?'

Grand Dethmon, 'You need to see the bigger picture.'

Terry, 'Fuck the bigger picture. I want my tea.'

If the Grand Dethmon had his way, there would be another death, but he needed Terry.

Grand Dethmon, 'As soon as The Chosen are gone, I will get you some tea, and I will get you a new mummy.'

Terry, 'Would she still be called Cheryl?'

Grand Dethmon, 'Yes, she would.'

Terry, 'Would she still be a pretty mummy?'

Grand Dethmon, 'She would be gorgeous, but let's get on with the job.'

But Terry's heart was not in it.

Location: On-Board Captain Wallace's Bridge
Sequence of Events: 163

Fleet Control, 'Sir, Captain Wallace has arrived at Planet Olympus.'

Admiral Mustard, 'Put me through.'

Captain Wallace, 'Greetings Admiral.'

Admiral Mustard, 'Well done, Captain. What have you found?'

Captain Wallace, 'There is a fabulous-looking planet that seems to be almost defenceless. There are no other vessels, but I can detect other Galactium vessels on their way.'

Admiral Mustard, 'Create a defensive formation as soon as possible.'

Captain Wallace, 'Yes, Sir.'

Gradually further Galactium vessels arrived, and a defensive formation was formed. It was surprising that there was little interest from the surface. Eventually, the flagship arrived. Admiral Mustard was slightly annoyed that his ship wasn't in the first hundred. He would be having words.

Admiral Mustard, 'George, did we get it wrong?'

Admiral Bumelton, 'It's looking that way. There are no updates from Earth except from the marines. So it looks like Earth is monster free.'

Admiral Mustard, 'I can't believe that it is the case. My ex-mother-in-law is still there.'

Admiral Bumelton, 'I always quite fancied her.'

Admiral Mustard, 'You are truly a sick individual.'

Admiral Bumelton, 'So where are they?'

Fleet Control, 'Sir, a fleet is approaching.'

Admiral Mustard, 'Which one?'

Fleet Control, 'We can't tell yet.'

Admiral Mustard, 'What percentage of our Fleet has arrived?'

Fleet Control, 'About ninety per cent, Sir.'

Admiral Mustard, 'My orders:
- Reposition the Fleet to counter the approaching fleet.'

Fleet Control, 'Sir, It looks like three more fleets are approaching.'

Admiral Mustard, 'Are you sure?'

Fleet Control, 'Yes, Sir. It's definite.'

Admiral Bumelton, 'The Brakendethians must have found another ally. I thought Earth was going to be the final battleground. It's now clear that it is going to be Olympus.'

Fleet Control, 'One of the fleets has been identified as belonging to The Chosen. They are asking permission to come alongside.'

Admiral Mustard, 'Welcome them, and give them permission.'

Fleet Control, 'Yes, Sir.'

Admiral Bumelton, 'Prepare for an all-out war of attrition. I think one of your pep talks is in order.'

Admiral Mustard, 'Perhaps now is the time.'

Admiral Mustard, 'Comms, put me on the Fleet speaker system.'

Comms, 'Yes, Sir, the voice-box is yours.'

Admiral Mustard, 'Dear friends in arms, we have been through a lot. We have all lost friends and colleagues. I have lost my fiancée. But, has it been worth it? The answer, clearly, is yes. We have been fighting for our planet, our unique Galactium, our way of life and above all, for humanity.

'It's hard to tell what we are leaving behind. Some of our homes have been ravaged by nuclear bombardment, others have been attacked by monsters, but we fight on. However, I can tell you that Earth is now free of monsters. The other planets will also be cleared.

'What about the now? We stand here with our brothers from the planet below. We have a shared heritage, but we are not fighting for them. We are here now in a final battle against The Brakendeth. The winner takes all. Let's make sure that the winner is us.'

Admiral Bumelton, 'That was a fine speech, I'm not sure how you do it, but I want to go out there and kill the enemy.'

There were cheers from the Command deck. Admiral Mustard had done the best he could.

The Brakendeth fleet had arrived.

Location: Nowhere Land
Sequence of Events: 164

Grand Dethmon, 'How could they know we were coming here? How could they have got here before us?'

Terry knew because he had not pushed the fleet hard. He just wanted tea and his new mummy.

Grand Dethmon, 'What are your battle tactics?'

Terry, 'I thought I would sit tight and wait for them to attack us?'

Grand Dethmon, 'But we need to destroy the planet. Shall we go for an all-out attack?'

Terry, 'I can't be bothered.'

Grand Dethmon, 'You will do as you are told.'

Terry, 'I can't be bothered.'

Grand Dethmon. 'Attack now.'

Terry, 'I've just had enough.'

The Grand Dethmon took over and ordered an immediate attack on the planet.

Location: On-Board Admiral Mustard's Flagship
Sequence of Events: 165

Fleet Control, 'Sir, here they come.'

Admiral Mustard, 'My orders:
- Send all remaining drones to intercept
- Follow up by using all remaining super drones
- Launch all fighters
- Inform The Chosen of my orders. Suggest that they attack any Brakendethians ships that get through.'

Fleet Control, 'Yes, Sir.'

Admiral Mustard, 'It looks to me that their strength is on the right flank. So let's attack the left.'

Admiral Bumelton, 'Makes sense to me. I will organise.'

Admiral Mustard, 'What's happening with the other fleet out there?'

Fleet Control, 'I thought that they were moving rather slowly. However, it's not the case. It's just an illusion as their ships are truly massive.'

Admiral Mustard, 'What do you mean by massive?'

Fleet Control, 'It's hard to say, Sir.'

Admiral Mustard, 'Compare it with the size of the ark.'

Fleet control, 'You could get one hundred arks into these ships. Perhaps more.'

Admiral Mustard, 'How many ships are there?'

Fleet Control, 'A few hundred.'

Admiral Bumelton, 'It looks to me that we are doomed. Shall we flee?'

Admiral Mustard, 'Let's carry on defending the planet, but fleeing does make a lot of sense.'

Admiral Bumelton, 'Perhaps your Lady Ga Ga friend will know something about them.'

Admiral Mustard, 'Comms, put me through to Lady Enyo.'

Lady Enyo, 'Admiral, you are truly honoured.'

Admiral Mustard, 'Have you seen the new fleet that is arriving?'

Lady Enyo, 'We are The Chosen. You have been chosen.'

Admiral Mustard, 'That's excellent news, but we need to agree on our tactics.'

Lady Enyo, 'That won't be necessary.'

Admiral Mustard, 'I assure you that it is. Do we fight or flee?'

Lady Enyo, 'You will see. You have been blessed.'

Admiral Mustard, 'George, it looks like you have been blessed.'

Admiral Bumelton, 'That's a relief. I haven't had a good blessing in a long time.'

Then everything froze.

Location: On-Board the Giant Fleet
Sequence of Events: 166

A voice, 'My children, why are you fighting? This will stop.' And it did.

A voice, 'This is all rather interesting. There are three tribes at war:
- One called The Brakendethians, who have committed countless crimes. Even now, a young child is being manipulated by an old, cold-hearted vicious spirit representing a lost civilisation. One that has harmed the universe
- One called The Chosen, who has lived for an exceedingly long time but achieved little. They live in the past and head towards extinction
- One called the Earthers. They are so young but so gifted. They live and love and kill, but they are so incredibly young. I see a great destiny for them if they survive. There are many tests to come, but they have the gift of enjoying life. The spark lives in them.

'I call upon the Earther leader to speak.'

Admiral Mustard, 'I'm Admiral Mustard. I represent The Galactium.'

A voice, 'Enough of that, you are a man, a creative, honourable man who has suffered so much. The loss of Edel was too much to bear, but you carried on. You have the spark.'

Admiral Mustard didn't know what to say, so he said nothing.

A voice, 'I have some questions for you. The Brakendethians have murdered many of your friends, including your fiancée. They have killed millions of fellow Earthers and destroyed your planets. You have every right to want revenge.

'Today, I offer you revenge. Do you want me to kill Terry?'

Admiral Mustard remembered the friends he had lost, especially the love of his life, and he said, 'No, I don't want Terry killed.'

A voice, 'What do you want me to do with him?'

Admiral Mustard, 'I would like him returned to us without The Brakendethian influence.'

A voice, 'That will be done. I will also eliminate the two Brakendethian fleets, this one and one on its way to destroy Olympus.

'I will eliminate The Nexuster and its progeny.

'Lastly, I can give you a gift. What would you like?'

Admiral Mustard, 'It's not for me to represent all of humanity.'

A voice, 'There is no one else.'

Admiral Mustard, 'I don't think humanity is ready for a gift yet.'

A voice, 'Very wise, but the gift is there to be called upon the next time I visit.'

Admiral Mustard, 'Can I ask who you are?'

A voice, 'I am Zeus.'

And Zeus left.